Everybody Pays

A "Cadillac" Holland Mystery

H. Max Hiller

INDIES UNITED PUBLISHING HOUSE, LLC
P.O. BOX 3071
QUINCY, IL 62305-3071

www.indiesunited.net

Dedication

In remembrance of Clarence Greco and Mister Civella.

You let me get my foot in the door of the French Quarter.

Everything after that was my own damn fault.

For Karen

My deepest appreciation and gratitude
for once again finding the forest for
the trees.

Hopefully your love for all things Italian
is not diminished after your hours spent
editing this tale.

One

Hew Orleans has always been comfortable with sin and corruption. It could even be said that New Orleans epitomizes sin and corruption. Nobody sees the contradiction in being comfortable with sin and corruption while deploring the city's crime rate.

Locals seldom express shock when our elected officials are indicted or mentioned in connection with some shady business transaction. One governor even ran for re-election against a world-class scumbag while under indictment, with bumper stickers imploring voters to "Vote for the Crook. It's Important." He won by a landslide.

Crime is woven into our city's fabric. One of the city's heroes is a pirate with a bar named after him. Some of its first settlers were hauled out of prisons in France and shipped to New Orleans to boost the fledgling colony's population. Their ancestors are now venerated for being the original families to settle here.

The resilience of New Orleans' underworld was made clear to me when the local FBI Special Agent in Charge informed me that surviving members of Carlos Marcello's crime family were staking a claim to one of the tables outside of the pizzeria my business partner and I recently purchased across the street from the Creole-Italian bistro we co-own and live above.

I was deeply chagrined to be pulled away from lunch with my girlfriend so SAC Michael Conroy could point this out to me because I should have already been aware of their unwelcome presence. My relationship with the Special Agent in Charge is not cordial, and I could see the delight he took in passing along this information. I viewed the table across the street through the spotting scope I set up in my living room while he named off the men drinking Chianti in the shade of its red-and-blue-striped Cinzano umbrella. I had grown up hearing most of their names, but I never paid much attention to them at the time. I was going to need to start paying a lot more attention going forward.

Pietro 'Pete' Matranga was the largest figure sitting at the round metal table. He was just over six feet tall and was little diminished by age. The man had a barrel chest and strong-looking hands, one of which he kept busy with a constant supply of lit cigarettes. Matranga was a former capo, and one of the few ranking members in local organized crime to have avoided prosecution when the indictments that took down Carlos Marcello and a few of Matranga's fellow capos were unsealed. There was much to be read into the fact that Matranga left town until the statute of limitations for his own crimes ran out. The much shorter and gaunt looking one to Matranga's left was 'Frankie' Russo, Matranga's long-time bodyguard. Conroy said the pair had only caught his attention in the past month, adding that they had lived in Miami for the past year after returning from Matranga's self-imposed exile in Sicily.

The third man was Enzo 'Hammer' Cammarato. He was built like a fire plug compared to his companions. Cammarato had served nearly twenty years for racketeering. He looked like he could still administer the beatings he had doled out as a loan shark and Mob enforcer gave him his nickname.

I recognized the fourth man at the table. His scrawny figure could not fill the cheap cotton blazer he wore to try and fit in with his far better dressed peers. Lenny Bonetti was a long-time character in the French Quarter. He was the face of the Mob on Bourbon Street when I was just a teenager. Lenny was the guy to talk to if you needed to borrow money from Cammarato, to buy dope, or to hook up with a working girl the Mob controlled. Hurricane Katrina blew away the last of the organized crime figures Lenny knew in the Quarter. He was reduced to selling stories about his criminal past to writers looking for material or character ideas.

"How long have they been meeting there?" I asked Conroy as I stepped away from the scope. I had been out of town for over a month on what began as a missing person investigation. This was not the sort of homecoming I had anticipated.

"They showed up three weeks ago. Matranga came in from Miami and rented a couple of properties out by the lakefront. Cammarato showed up last weekend. He has been living in Houston since he got out of prison, but he must have gotten homesick when he found out his old capo was back in New Orleans," Conroy informed me. "They always sit at the same table. They always come right before noon and leave just before the French Market flea market closes. Matranga pays cash for three bottles of Chianti and two antipasto plates, and he tips very well." I heard this as a veiled advisory that the local FBI office had our pizzeria under surveillance. "Any idea why they chose your place?"

"Maybe it's out of habit. The Mob used to run this corner of the Quarter. Matranga's ancestors extorted the businesses in these same buildings a hundred and fifty years ago. Sicilian immigrants started the American Mafia in the French Market. They don't teach you this stuff at the Academy?" I schooled Conroy. My father had used the entrenched nature and operations of the city's organized crime figures to justify not deluding himself into believing NOPD was going to clean up the streets under his watch. He took me on long walks through the Quarter to tell me the history of its landmarks in the Mob's history.

"Have they approached you at all?" SAC Conroy ignored my explanation to question my business partner, who was sitting on a stool at my kitchen counter. Tony turned from petting Roux, who was seated on the stool to Tony's right, to respond to the question. Sitting on chairs and stools is a habit I have found too endearing to discourage the pit bull from doing despite the wear and tear on the furniture.

"The tall one told me he knows people I know," Tony allowed. I tend to forget that Chef Tony's cooking apprenticeship began in a trattoria owned by one of Sicily's major crime families. His mother's family was already living in Messina when my own mother's family arrived in this country, and the Devereaux name was already influential in Louisiana before the Civil War.

"What did you tell him when he said that?" Conroy and I both felt confident that a capo like Matranga anticipated immediate genuflection on Tony's part.

"That I have not been home in many years and no longer speak with the men he knows." It was clear what Tony meant to convey by this response.

"Do you think he was trying to get a taste of the business beyond the meat and cheese platters?" Conroy pressed.

"That would not be smart," Tony sighed with obvious

3

annoyance.

"Really? Why is that, pray tell?" Conroy unwisely chose to mock the chef's resolve.

"I own a freezer and a chain saw," Tony responded without inflection, humor, or any consideration of his audience. I knew he would handle any attempt to strong arm him with a response certain to make Matranga reconsider the cost-to-benefit ratio of pursuing the matter. The pit bull sitting beside Tony once mauled a man to death, but I still believe Tony to be the more violent of the two.

"Yes, I suppose we do," I faked a chuckle to try to make light of his statement.

Conroy blanched and dropped the subject. He flashed me a look that betrayed how uncertain he was about how to continue with the other questions he wanted Tony to answer. My head shake recommended that he drop the subject entirely.

My phone rang and broke the silence this last exchange brought to the room.

"What's up?" I asked. The phone's caller ID showed it was Chief of Detectives Bill Avery. The ID on my phone identifies him as Big Chief. I should show him more respect, but we have known one another since he was my father's partner as a rookie detective and he is more like an uncle than a boss to me. Our connection led to the State Police assigning me to his service the day I received my detective's badge.

"I need you on a case," Avery said. "And don't give me any excuses."

Avery was aware I was on desk duty for another five days because I had shot the suspect in my last investigation. I was happy to get back to work.

"Okay, tell me where to meet you. I'm in a meeting I would like to leave." It would take ten minutes of brisk walking to get to my car.

"Glad to be of service," he laughed before he gave me an address at the lower end of the Quarter on Dauphine Street between Barracks and Esplanade.

"Well, I have to go," I informed the FBI's top agent in the city.

"I need to go cook," Tony declared and stood up.

Special Agent in Charge Conroy could take a hint and

followed us to the elevator.

two

The mansard-roofed building at the address on Dauphine Street dated to the late eighteen-hundreds. Its gingerbread trim was painted in four colors of peeling paint. The homes to either side were one-story shotguns which likely once belonged to shopkeepers or tradesmen. The multiple mailboxes at the top of the steps at the address Avery gave me suggested the home was being used as an apartment building. I noticed there were no marked patrol units or crime lab vehicles parked out front as Roux and I entered the house and I identified myself to the lone uniformed officer in the entryway. The Chief of Detectives apparently wanted to avoid attracting attention to whatever he had called me there to investigate.

"Maybe you can make sense of this," Avery said by way of greeting as Roux and I entered the large home. The foyer was tall ceilinged with an antique, but not original, chandelier and a well-worn original marble floor. The stairs and railing were rock-hard oiled cypress. New walls filled in what had once been pocket doors on either side of the foyer. The new doors had transoms, so I estimated that the conversion into rental units was made prior to the introduction of air conditioning.

"I called Captain Hammond before I called you. The State Police have cleared you to return to active duty at my request. I guess their shrink remains satisfied that you don't enjoy killing suspects," Avery informed me.

"We don't want to discuss Doctor Jorgens." Avery knows my history with the state's psychologist. Doctor Jorgens tried to derail my application to the State Police because she was uncomfortable with what she referred to as my 'peculiar' ability to compartmentalize killing other human beings. Describing it as a mental survival tool the Special Forces taught me did little to assuage her concerns.

"Indeed," he said and flashed a brief smirk before nodding his head towards the young detective standing beside him. The short, thin white guy was in his mid-thirties. He wore a suit that fit better than most NOPD detectives bother, or can afford, to wear. The average police detective wears a sport coat because their job will destroy multiple pairs of slacks long before the detective ruins the sport coat while apprehending a suspect. "This is Romulus Bassett. He is new to detective work, and I've already told him to ask me and not you if he needs any advice about being a detective. All I want you to do is to figure out what happened here."

"What do you know so far?" I saw nothing out of order. The absence of crime scene technicians under foot indicated there was nothing much to pursue.

"Come on up and I'll show you," Avery frowned and started up the stairs. Part of his displeasure likely had to do with climbing three flights of stairs more than once in the same day.

Numbers were nailed to each door, and I counted a dozen apartments on the first and second floors. A heavy cypress door opened to the staircase to the third-floor attic. This staircase was built from rough pine because only the original homeowner's servants were ever meant to see it. The ceiling height was sufficient to give Chief Avery, who stands well over six feet tall, plenty of room to walk around without conking his head. Plaster and drywall covered the walls and ceiling and someone in the distant past had installed tongue-and-groove heart-pine flooring over the original floor planks. The bathroom and bedroom were the only spaces divided off, leaving the galley kitchen, dining room, and living room open to one another. The furniture strongly suggested the landlord rented furnished apartments. The small air conditioner mounted below the window overlooking the patio would have handled the late spring heat had anyone thought to turn it on. The garret apartment was nearly a sauna without it.

"We got a call about vandalism," Avery explained as he led the way to the rear of the apartment and opened the bathroom door. "Someone pulled the sinks out of a half dozen of the bathrooms, but they chose to rip this one completely apart. It doesn't smack of being a prank or someone having a beef with the owner. I think they were looking for something, and either found what they came looking for or got spooked before they could do any more damage. Romulus is going to pursue whatever leads the crime scene provides. I need you to put your ear to the ground and let me know if anyone knows what this is all about."

"Alright," I said and nodded my head.

"There is one other thing I need to discuss with you," Avery said directly to me and motioned for Detective Bassett to leave the room. He waited until we heard the rookie detective close the door at the bottom of the stairs before speaking again.

"I hope it proves to be nothing, but there is some history with this place you need to be aware of," Avery informed me. He rarely starts things with any sort of preamble so I assumed he was having trouble deciding how to say it. "This place used to be a whorehouse run by a guy named 'Sunset' Puglisi. Puglisi was also a button man for the local Mob. The line was that you would not see sunrise if your name made his list. We are standing in what used to be his apartment. Michael Conroy and I were both rookie detectives when we worked on a murder case involving an FBI informant Puglisi killed. We found the murder weapon under the seat cushion of that chair, and Conroy and I have spent the last twenty years thinking each other planted the gun. There is also a rumor that Puglisi kept a daily journal and stashed the diaries somewhere in this house before he went to prison."

"Do you think that may be what the burglar was looking for?" I asked.

"Lord, I hope not. The rumor has been going around for twenty years, so I cannot imagine someone went to this much trouble to check it out," Avery said and shook his head.

"Alright, I'll see what the word on the street is," I said and swiveled my head to look at the tattered recliner Avery pointed to in describing where the murder weapon was located. I saw no connection between what he had just told me and what he called me there to investigate.

three

"You first," I said as soon as Chief Avery left Bassett and me alone in the house.

"Whoever did this was looking for something specific," Detective Bassett said. At least the obvious was now out in the open for us to discuss.

"Why focus on the bathroom?" I tested him.

"Come on. I'll show you the other bathrooms and you can tell me what you think," Bassett said, tabling my question for the moment.

We followed a single set of boot prints made in the plaster that had clung to the soles of the vandal's boots down to the second floor. I stepped next to one and estimated the boots were at least one size smaller than my own. I stand just over six feet tall and wear a size twelve shoe. My guess was that we were looking for someone an inch or so shorter. The single set of footprints also clued us in to the number of people who had inflicted the damage to the property.

There were six furnished studio apartments on the home's second floor. Each room had a kitchenette and its own small, but full, bathroom. Judging by the fixtures and tile choices, the bathrooms had likely been installed in the 1960s. The posters and wall art in the apartments dated the last sustained occupancy of the property to the 1980s. One of the second-floor apartments seemed to be a shrine to a musician named Prince. The comforter on the bed was a shade of deep purple and every poster hanging on the walls in the room was of the musician or one of the acts he either produced or otherwise supported.

Small piles of rubble marked where someone had knocked a hole in the wall behind each of the sinks. The vandal had taken the time to disconnect the water lines before they pulled the cabinets off the wall. Every hole measured two feet square. I let Roux sniff around in each bathroom on the remote chance there were traces of drugs or something else that might explain why anyone had gone to so much trouble. He found nothing.

"My initial thought is that someone came for the copper pipes." I was now the one stating the obvious. It just seemed to be the best plausible explanation for the identical messes in so many rooms. "It must have taken a while to realize this place still has galvanized plumbing. There are mailboxes in the alleyway, but I don't see any sign of anyone living here, do you?"

"No. That is probably why whoever did this thought they could get away with it," Bassett suggested. "They took the time to make careful holes in the bathrooms on the second floor, and they had enough privacy to make a lot of noise ripping the bathroom apart on the third floor, but it should have only taken one or two tries before they figured out there was no copper plumbing anywhere."

"Maybe someone came looking for something they hid here but forgot where they put it. Who called this in?" I asked him without sharing what Avery mentioned might be hidden in the walls. Knocking half a dozen holes in plaster and lath walls should have made enough noise to disturb the neighbors on either side. Ripping the attic apart like a madman would have made enough noise to raise the dead. Even so, there was a good chance that the immediate neighbors were not who called NOPD, because a lot of properties in that corner of the Quarter are owned by people who only use their place on weekends or during events like Mardi Gras and Jazz Fest.

"Chief Avery didn't say. I'll check it out," Bassett said and wrote himself a note in the small notebook he pulled out of his jacket pocket. "Do you really think your informants might know anything about this?"

"Calling the sort of Quarter Rats I talk to informants is a stretch," I said to disabuse him of the notion that I was running a sophisticated intelligence operation on the side. "I just hope one of them might be able to explain why the place is sitting empty."

"Maybe one of us should track down the owner to find out," Bassett suggested. My facial expression showed I didn't consider this to be the best use of my own time. He took the hint. "Yeah. I'll get on that."

"Good idea," I smiled and tried not to shame him too much. I had the good fortune to have worked alone most of my career as a detective, so I was usually the only one to hear myself say such silly things. "Call me when you have anything to chase down. I'll let you know if I hear anything that might help find your vandal."

four

Detective Bassett was too inexperienced to know there are multiple ways to learn who owns a building in the French Quarter. The obvious one is to go to City Hall and go through their property records, but that requires playing nice with city employees who delight in being of as little help as possible. Also, the name in their records is often nothing more than a holding company, which leaves you no better informed for having made the effort.

I have found the best way to learn such things is to speak with the neighbors. You'll learn a brief history of the property and some information about any previous owners. You also get their personal opinion of the current owner.

I had another means of finding the owner which was not available to Detective Bassett. I could ask one of the Vieux Carré Commissioners. The politically appointed members of the Vieux Carré Commission are tasked with preserving the historical district's architectural integrity, right down to having final approval of the color of every home's front door. Their standards are exasperating, and their actual authority has proven to be much less than everyone imagines it to be. In at least one case, a developer who could not get the Commission's approval to convert four row buildings into time-share condominiums hired a crew to level everything behind the façade of all four buildings over the course of a single weekend. The fine the outraged VCC imposed was a fraction of the attorney fees and design changes the developer faced trying to clear the Commission's hurdles. The Commission wound up approving the developer's original design because there was literally nothing left to preserve.

VCC Commissioner Ronald Jackson had patiently marshalled Tony and me through the process of opening Strada Ammazarre. The former furniture store was fortuitously a building code disaster when we took possession, so Tony had considerable support and latitude in designing the restaurant. It didn't hurt that Jackson also knew both of my parents, or that he owed his appointment to his position to my Uncle Felix's shady maneuverings in Baton Rouge. Mister

Jackson has become one of the regulars at the bistro's after-work cocktail hour, and I knew how freely his tongue could flow after only a drink or two.

"Mister Jackson," I made sure to show proper respect when I shook his hand. Ronald Jackson is still an imposing figure despite being in his late sixties, and his tight handshake was meant to convey he still meant business. "It's always a pleasure to have you with us. Might I have a moment of your time about a business matter?"

"Well, it is after five o'clock," he was quick to point out. I wondered but what I ought to have waited until he had finished at least one more complimentary martini before approaching him. "What is it that cannot wait until tomorrow?"

"Just a minor question about who owns a property. It can wait if need be," I offered him the chance to put me off, but also gave him a look that implied doing so might mean he would pay for his drinks in the future.

"Something that minor?" he waved a hand to dismiss any impression he gave of hesitation. "Ask away."

I gave him the address on Dauphine Street and a description of the building in case he did not have a photographic memory of the entire French Quarter.

"Oh, that place," he said and frowned. He took a sip of his martini. "That house has been a thorn in our side since the day the Commission was created. It was a notorious speakeasy during Prohibition and the place was handed down from mobster to mobster for years. The last one was Sunset Puglisi. He ran girls out of the place. That is why every room has its own bathroom. He was allegedly also a button man for the Mob. He went to prison for murder!"

"Who owns it now?" I was not at all encouraged that the history of the place brought me full circle to the sort of men SAC Conroy had drawn my attention to earlier.

"Some holding company. The DOJ took it from Puglisi and then held onto it for a few years. I heard rumors that a couple of agencies used the place as a safe house for informants before the government put it up for public auction right after Katrina," Jackson elaborated even further. "My guess is the government decided to cash out while the city was struggling to get back on its feet. We allowed the new owner to rent rooms to FEMA for a year or so after Katrina because of the lack of hotel rooms. It has been tied up in litigation for the last couple of years because we could not agree on how many apartments he could have."

"I don't suppose off the top of your head you know who runs the holding company?" I asked.

"It's the same guy who tried to rig the city council race. You know who I mean, don't you?"

I didn't care if my expression showed how much I didn't want this to be true. I was the detective who had uncovered the Dixie Mafia's plot to use a prolific house flipper to take control of a seat on the New Orleans City Council barely four months earlier.

"Alex Boudreaux," I sighed. I believed I had made a solid case for his prosecution and the seizure of his assets, but the case had not yet gone to trial.

"Yeah, that's the name I was looking for," Jackson beamed as though he were the one who had said it. I rolled all of this around in my head for a moment before I formed my final question.

"What's the official status of the property today?"

"Mister Boudreaux submitted plans to turn the property into a licensed short-term rental property after the FEMA tenants moved out. He was delayed in doing so because we wanted him to keep it as an apartment building. We would love to see the home go back to being a single-family residence, but it is grandfathered as an apartment building. We wanted to keep him from adding to the glut of unoccupied residences in the Quarter, but Judge Fouche says he is free to do whatever he wants with the place as the city's codes see no difference between long-term and short-term rentals. He handed down his ruling last Wednesday. I am glad that Mister Boudreaux only owns this one piece of property in the Quarter. He is more difficult to deal with than some of our larger property owners."

"So he was given the green light to proceed last Wednesday, but as of today there is no building permit and he doesn't have your permission to be working on the property?" I needed to be certain about this. It would be more than merely embarrassing to treat Alex Boudreaux as a suspect if a licensed contractor with a permit was responsible for the damage to those bathrooms. It would give the local king of gentrification grounds for a harassment lawsuit that he might well win.

"He doesn't have our permission to be working on the place. You might check with the city to see if they gave him a permit, but they have always worked closely with us," Jackson seemed to be very certain of his facts.

five

I asked my sister Tulip when she stopped by for a cocktail about an hour later to find a copy of the purchase contract Alex Boudreaux had signed for the Dauphine Street property. She called me the next afternoon and invited me to her office to discuss the contract between Alex Boudreaux and the Government Accounting Office, who owned the house after the Justice Department seized it from Sunset Puglisi following his arrest. The agreement contained an absurdly detailed inventory of the contents of each room in the house, including a count of the flatware in each kitchen. This may have been a means of padding the perceived value of the property, the physical condition of which must have been a serious downside. All I needed was confirmation that nothing in its wording implied ownership of anything hidden within the walls of the former brothel.

"What is this all about?" Tulip asked after walking me through the details.

"Avery has me working on a burglary case. Someone broke into a place that Alex Boudreaux owns on Dauphine Street. It was owned by a mobster Avery helped the FBI put away for murder. There are rumors that the guy stashed his diaries in the place before he went to prison. Avery is worried that whoever broke in was looking for them. I need to find a way to confound whoever broke in and I thought it would be interesting to see what happens if Alex acts as though he knows why someone would burglarize his vacant building," I partially explained.

"What do you have in mind?" she asked. I could tell she was intrigued by the idea of weaponizing a lawsuit.

"Would it be out of line for Alex to file some sort of petition or whatever in court to establish ownership of everything in that place, whether it is on that list or not?"

"It is out of line because it is entirely unnecessary. He legally owns everything on the property even if it is not listed. Such a motion would raise red flags," Tulip explained.

"Red flags get people's attention, and that is what I want to do. I want people to think Alex is sending a message that he knows what the burglar was after," I said.

"You are more likely to get Alex Boudreaux killed doing this than to find who or what you are after. Dan Logan is Alex's attorney and he ought not trust him," Tulip said. "Logan is always going to do what is best for himself and not for any client. Dan Logan can just as easily file the sort of motion you are suggesting on behalf of Alex's estate as for a live client. He would find a way to be the one who winds up with whatever Avery believes is hidden in those walls."

"I am not uncomfortable with Alex taking a bullet," I assured her. I knew she was equally comfortable with the idea of a dead Alex Boudreaux.

"My point is that it is a waste of energy putting his life at risk when you don't even know what you expect him to claim to be protecting with such a court filing," Tulip said and gave me her best expression of dissuasion. "I know you love to disrupt things, but I see no advantage to pursuing this exercise until you figure out who would get Alex's message or what Alex needs to protect."

"Okay, I'll hold onto this idea," I sighed. "Maybe I can put a wedge between Alex and Logan. Logan is probably curious about why Alex has done practically nothing with Puglisi's brothel in the last four years. His average flip takes about ninety days."

"Now I am curious," Tulip laughed, but I noticed she was writing something on her pad as she did so.

I explained the thorny history between Alex Boudreaux and myself to Detective Bassett and let it be his idea to not tag along while I questioned Alex that afternoon.

Boudreaux and his former attorney, a guy named 'Bear' Brovartey, managed to evade justice by confounding the FBI with their conflicting versions of events. They were both intent upon making the other guy the mastermind behind a failed attempt to control the Ninth Ward's seat on the City Council and were shielding the role played by the Dixie Mafia as much as possible. With his high-priced attorney in as much trouble as he himself was, Alex Boudreaux retained the services of the biggest scoundrel attorney in Orleans Parish: a carpetbagger from Brooklyn named Dan Logan.

I left a message with Logan's secretary that I was on my way to interview his client about a crime unrelated to the charges Alex already faced. I also left a message that I was en route with Boudreaux's secretary. I intentionally did not speak with either man directly so that neither of them could tell me whether Boudreaux wanted his attorney present. I knew from experience that Boudreaux would talk to me rather than let a room sit silent. I did not expect cooperation, but I was interested to see if the break-in would be news to him.

The DOJ had been quick to take control of Boudreaux's personal and business accounts after the FBI reviewed my evidence of the election scam. His bank accounts were seized and forensic accountants began digging into the slew of foreign-registered companies they suspected Boudreaux laundered money for through his short-term rental property scheme. This oversight placed Alex in the position of managing his business under the unforgiving supervision of a court-appointed property manager and honest accountants.

Boudreaux had abandoned his devious expansion plans in New Orleans East and began converting distressed properties in the Seventh Ward into high-end condos. The Seventh Ward encompasses parts of the Treme, the city's oldest Black neighborhood, and portions of the already heavily gentrified Marigny neighborhood. It runs from the corners of Esplanade and Rampart Street in the French Quarter all the way to the Fairgrounds above Broad Street in the back of town. This was a largely owner-occupied lower income working-class neighborhood before Hurricane Katrina forced its evacuation. Its proximity to the office towers in the CBD and the party atmosphere of the French Quarter made it a popular place to live for those who moved to town after the storm, and property values had skyrocketed in the five years since the city reopened.

The storm and gentrification drove most of the pre-storm residents out and the price Boudreaux could expect to get for a remodeled property was roughly four times what it might have sold for as a private residence before Katrina. Many of the properties he sold were owned by out-of-town investors who rented the units to short-term occupants convinced the locals would greet them with open arms. Quite the opposite was happening, but the cash-strapped city council was accepting the alarming economic gap among its citizens for the windfall of substantially higher property tax revenues.

The first thing Boudreaux's crew does to every property is strip any original cypress or heart-pine floors and millwork for resale to offset the remodeling costs. I arrived to find Boudreaux supervising the installation of new headers that would open this shotgun house's front rooms into an open living space resembling the lofts home buyers moving to New Orleans would pay top dollar for to replicate their condos in places like New York, San Francisco, or Seattle. I must constantly remind myself that gentrification does not violate any legal statutes, but it hurts as much to bite my tongue as it does to see it happening.

"I heard you were coming," Alex said as he engaged me at the door to block any further entry. "I want my lawyer present if you are here to question me."

"I have some questions, but I wouldn't call this questioning you," I shrugged and let the silence drive him crazy. I took a moment to assess the changes in Boudreaux's appearance since his arrest. He had considerably less swagger, and his thick black hair was flecked with strands of gray. He was still in very good shape, but that was because he was having to do a lot of carpentry work he used to pay people to do for him. His crew was less than half the size it was when we first met, and the parolees he used to surround himself with had been replaced by Hispanic carpenters. These undocumented workers stopped working when Alex opened the door and they saw my badge.

The silence finally drove him to cooperate. "What sort of questions?"

"Were you aware someone opened walls in your property on Dauphine Street?" I didn't want to give him any more details than necessary. The one thing none of his attorneys have made him understand is that 'Do you know the time?' should be answered only with Yes or No. Boudreaux will always tell the time on his watch.

"I received a call from my property manager that the police were investigating a break-in," he calmly responded. What he called a property manager was actually his court-appointed trustee, but I wasn't here to rub his nose in that. "What makes this a case for you? Are you still looking for something else to pin on me?"

"Alex, I would never have taken the case if I knew it involved you. I still hope someone was just trying to steal some copper pipes," I said in almost complete honesty.

"Well, what do you think I had to do with what happened?" His defensive tone and posture were disproportionate to anything I had implied to that point.

"More than you're telling me, as usual," I sighed. I glanced over my shoulder at the sound of a car door slamming behind me. Dan Logan was on the scene.

"I am sure my client told you he is not to talk to you without my being present," Logan said by way of a hello.

"He tried," I admitted. "But then he couldn't stop talking."

"What's your interest in my client today, Detective?" Logan demanded. He likes to enunciate each syllable in the word detective, apparently because he believes doing so is a way to make it sound derogatory.

"Well, Daniel, I just wanted to confirm that he was aware of vandalism in one of his properties, and to ask if he had any idea who might have done it, or why it might have happened," I explained. I made sure to break his name into enough syllables that it sounded more like Danielle.

"And has he answered the question?"

"Probably as far as he intends to," I conceded.

"Do you believe my client is lying to you?" Logan challenged.

"His lips moved," I said and focused my attention upon the attorney. "I have a dozen or so questions I would love to ask Mister Boudreaux, but you aren't going to let him, and he still thinks he's the smartest guy in the room. I suppose I will have to find the answers some other way."

The prospect of me digging into Alex Boudreaux's business and personal life once again put both men on edge. "I cannot imagine that you believe Alex damaged his own property. He is the victim here. His building has been vandalized and you stand here accusing him of being party to that."

"I didn't believe he played any part in the damage until both of you denied it," I replied. "I was prepared to accept he had no knowledge of the vandalism or who was responsible. I leave here much less prepared to do so."

I had no new evidence, and took some small pleasure in the distress my visit caused both men. I knew Dan Logan well enough to be certain that he didn't trust his client any more than I did, but I also knew Logan would defend Boudreaux's denials in court, for a large fee, if need be.

"Call me when you find anything you can prove against my client and we will all sit down again. In the meantime, kindly keep your distance," Logan barked at me with the false bravado of a chained hound. I noticed the two of them were arguing in the doorway just before I lost sight of them in my rear-view mirror.

seven

I walked the short distance from the garage on Chartres Street where I park my car to the Eighth District substation on Royal Street in the Quarter. Detective Bassett's desk gave him an enviable view down Royal Street, past the State Supreme Court building located across Conti Street. I also noted he was isolated from the other detectives who positioned their desks at a quarter turn to his own. A row of tall filing cabinets and a massive printer squeezed Bassett's desk further into the corner.

"You seem to be the odd man out around here," I couldn't help commenting. Most of the district's detectives were out, but the remaining trio gave us the cold shoulder.

"You could say that," was the most Bassett chose to elaborate. "How did it go with Alex Boudreaux?"

"I don't know that he was the one who ordered the place to be ransacked, but he knew about the vandalism before I told him about the damage," I said and sat down in a wooden chair beside the desk. I didn't want to seem to be physically talking down to the rookie detective.

"He told you all of this?" Bassett was understandably hesitant to accept my statements.

"I have learned how to parse his words. He said he was informed of the break-in, but not that he personally assessed the damage. Why wouldn't he want to check out the damage to one of his properties? If someone called you and said someone broke in and ripped out your bathroom sink, wouldn't you rush home to see what happened?"

"Okay, that's strange, but why do you think his reaction means he is lying to you about knowing anything about the break-in?" Bassett continued to argue.

"You're going to learn that Boudreaux is one of those ducks who looks like he is calmly floating along while his legs are paddling like mad where you can't see them. He likely has some new scam going or is caught up in something that he would rather we not know about."

"So, do you consider him to be a suspect?" the detective pressed.

"Yes, but not in what you are investigating. I don't think he was responsible for the damage, but he knows what whoever ripped his place apart was after," I said without suggesting what that might be. I was sure that Chief Avery was not going to like hearing about Alex Boudreaux's link to his rookie detective's case.

"Damn it," Chief Avery said right on cue when I laid out what I had turned up in the first full day of the joint investigation. "You put me right off my breakfast!"

That was a challenge. The Chief and I meet in the kitchen of Strada Ammazarre just about every weekday. This morning's breakfast for the former LSU linebacker and current heart disease candidate was a four-egg omelet stuffed with andouille sausage and pulled fried chicken with minced bell pepper, red onion, and jalapenos. The other half of his plate was filled with a half-pound or so of shredded hash browns smothered in red gravy and fried calas pastries filled with spicy boudin instead of plain rice. The three slices of melon wrapped in prosciutto he had devoured before this hardly qualified as healthy eating. I nibbled on a hot calas and sipped my coffee before I shared my assessment of the evidence.

"I cannot prove Alex Boudreaux's involvement means Junior Hauser is involved, as well. What I do know is that Junior still wants to find a foothold here."

"What could Junior gain from the break-in?" Avery wondered aloud.

Junior Hauser was barely out of high school when Marion Puglisi went to prison. Junior's father had the good sense to stay in his own lane and be the Gulf Coast's minor Mob boss while better connected mobsters like Carlos Marcello controlled New Orleans. Hurricane Katrina affected the criminal underworld in ways law enforcement was desperate to understand, and discovering Junior Hauser was moving into New Orleans by way of the city's hardest hit neighborhood had come as a complete surprise to the NOPD, State Police and the FBI. My investigation cost Junior Hauser millions of dollars in laundered money held in the accounts the government had seized. It also cost him his best attorney after Brovartey perjured himself trying to cast Alex as being solely responsible for Junior's criminal misadventure. Whether any of this taught Junior Hauser any useable lessons remained an open question.

"I have no idea, but I would not rule out his involvement. Alex's attorney used to represent Junior's big shot lawyer, so maybe there is a connection there." I was confident Junior knew as much about the burglary as Alex did. "As for whatever the burglar was looking for, Puglisi is still in prison and is likely to die there. What is the point in provoking him and what would be the point in doing so right now?"

"Oh, you want mobsters to make sense," Avery finally had a good laugh. "All I know is that the Feds always follow the money when it comes to these guys. Why don't you see if there is any sort of financial trail?"

"There must be one because the address on Dauphine Street is the only property Alex Boudreaux owns in the French Quarter. He likes to turn properties over and that isn't really an easy thing to do there. Everything costs too much to buy and the Vieux Carré Commission has already slowed his ass down for almost four years." My mind began picking at this odd singularity in Alex Boudreaux's real estate portfolio as soon as I heard Ronald Jackson's story of how he acquired the building.

"It ain't much to go on," Avery sighed. What he was really saying was that he was braced for some very messing digging on my part. I can be like a dog who has taken hold of a bone sticking out of the ground. I will dig until I know whether it is a piece of trash or a buried body.

"It's what I have," I shrugged and took another bite of the still warm savory pastry. "Well, that and one more question for you."

"Which is?" Avery asked as he stuffed his mouth with enough food to afford himself a moment or two to formulate an answer.

"I can't help noticing that your rookie detective has rubbed everyone in the office the wrong way. Anything I should know?" I, in turn, filled my own mouth for the exact same reason.

Avery frowned and chewed more slowly. He even took the time to wash the bite down with café au lait before offering what I believed was only a small part of the story.

"One of the DEA's informants was murdered and they accused Bassett of tipping off the crack dealer he was going to testify against," Avery explained.

"Could they prove that?" I asked.

"No, but Bassett did not mention he and the dealer grew up together in the Irish Channel until the DEA made the connection," Avery pointed out his personal issue with Bassett's integrity.

"That has to happen quite a bit in New Orleans," I pointed out.

"The DEA also claimed the dealer's ledger showed he made payments to Bassett. He denied having taken any cash from the dealer, but neither Internal Affairs nor the prosecutor ever learned exactly how close he and the crack dealer were." The uneasiness the Chief of Detectives had with discussing this was evident.

"So, it is possible your new detective was dirty, but he squirted free and NOPD saw fit to promote him rather than risk admitting they had another dirty cop." I thought this might sum up the situation.

"It means that any case where he is called upon to testify will open the door to his being questioned about all of this by the defense, which will destroy his credibility to any jury in New Orleans. I need to put him on cases that are more likely to be plea bargained than to go to trial." Avery obviously didn't like either the situation he was in or his new detective very much. I would need to decide how much of this to let affect my own working relationship with Bassett, but for now he and I shared the contempt of NOPD's detectives. Most of the detectives under Avery's wing envy the family connection I have with our mutual boss, but they are also resentful of how many high-profile cases I have uncovered in investigations they initially scorned.

"Duly noted," I said and joined him in filling my mouth to end the conversation.

nine

I decided to share my information, and conundrum, with the FBI. SAC Conroy was not in his office when I arrived on his doorstep unannounced. I have learned never to call first because he invariably tries to avoid me. I was not going to be able to pick the brains of his Criminal Enterprise agents over the phone, and I was unlikely to get into their inner sanctum without his permission.

"I don't know when he will return, Detective Holland," Conroy's long-time secretary apologized and gave me a brilliantly sincere smile.

"You know when he goes to the bathroom. I don't mind waiting," I chided her. The SAC keeps a schedule that is timed almost to the minute every day but Sunday.

"As you wish. You know where the cafeteria is," she smiled no less cheerfully. She was not about to offer me anything to eat or drink herself. I pulled the latest edition of The Economist from my messenger-style bag and buried my thoughts in things only a little less complicated than what I was there to discuss.

"Detective Holland," SAC Conroy sighed as he returned to his office nearly an hour later. I didn't bother speculating on how much of that time was spent trying to wait me out. "What brings you by this morning?"

"I need to speak with your agents watching the mobsters hanging out at the pizza place," I informed him. He gave me a sideways glance before he opened the office door and motioned for me to follow him. I was quick to notice that he closed the door behind us.

"Do you have something to share about what those men are up to?" he offered as he settled into his chair.

"I am hoping your own agents have an answer to that very question," I shrugged and gave him a small grin.

"You came here hoping we would share details from our investigation with you?" he laughed. I laughed as well, because that absurd idea was exactly why I was there. He had also let slip that there was an active investigation under way.

"Maybe just fill in a couple of blank spaces for me. Perhaps what I have will help them in turn," I offered. I never want to appear in his office without an offering of my own. My tips on things beyond my own ability to pursue have put enough feathers in Conroy's hat that he will take these meetings, but he always listens like a robin sizing up a worm.

"Run it by me," he said and leaned back with his hands behind his head. He was acting so casually that I knew something was happening that he didn't want me to know about.

"NOPD investigated a break-in on Dauphine Street that happened over the weekend. I was asked to back-stop the rookie detective. A half dozen bathroom sinks were pulled off the wall and one bathroom was demolished. I figured they were after the copper, but most of this was galvanized pipe," I began. He started nodding, which is his tell that he already knows everything I am sharing with him.

"Organized crime is not really the guys you talk to about stolen pipes," he pointed out. He wasn't hurrying me along, just idly throwing cold water in my direction.

"I guess you'd know more about that than I do. Didn't you get your start in the Criminal Enterprise Branch?" I discovered this about the SAC when I researched his career the first time we crossed paths. Knowing just one more thing about an opponent than they do about you can make all the difference.

"That's right. It seems like a long time ago," Conroy half-grinned.

"Well drag up those memories and consider this. The house they broke into is the only property owned by Alex Boudreaux in the entire French Quarter. He bought it using a loan from Junior Hauser's credit union. The previous owner was Marion Puglisi, and that is what brings me to your door."

"Why's that?" he asked and moved his hands forward and onto his desk. I wondered but what he was bracing himself for an accusation that he planted the gun that sent the mobster to prison.

"I could use your help to understand why Junior Hauser's point guy bought Puglisi's house but hasn't done a thing with it in five years. Or maybe you can explain why somebody broke in to open some bathroom walls. Call me crazy, but I think there might be some connection to be made. I just don't see it."

This was all I had to offer.

"That's all pretty circumstantial," the veteran FBI agent pointed out. "But I agree with you that Alex Boudreaux is still the Dixie Mafia's point guy against the New Orleans Mob. The locals aren't likely to forget or forgive the flanking move he helped Bear Brovartey try to make in the Ninth Ward. I am also sure they have been keeping an eye on Puglisi's place ever since it fell into Alex Boudreaux's hands."

"I am still trying to understand why he bought the place. He flips properties for a living but has been alright with sitting on this one for years," I tried to tempt the SAC into sharing his thoughts on the rumor about 'Sunset' Puglisi's alleged diaries.

"That's a place you might start," was all Conroy would offer.

"You were my starting point. What about talking to your guys?" I pressed.

"I don't see much point in your doing so right now," he demurred. I heard the refusal, but believed I also heard a willingness to reconsider the request if I returned with something more to share. I knew he would grab the investigation out from under me if I gave him anything worth prosecuting. He knew I was prepared to let his agents do the paperwork and spend the hours in court that came with taking away my cases.

"Alrighty, then," I sighed, slapped my hands on my knees and began to stand up. I wanted to give him enough time to change his mind about helping me.

"There is one more thing you should add to the equation," SAC Conroy finally offered. I was already opening his door when he spoke up. I turned to listen. "Puglisi is being released from prison on Friday. I find it interesting that Puglisi plans to die at home when he no longer has a place to call home."

I didn't mind that he saw me blink.

"No, that he does not," I noted and left his door open behind me.

ten

I spent so many years in the Army's Special Operations and doing contract work for various intelligence agencies that I can no longer accept anything as being a coincidence. The men sitting at the pizzeria were there for a reason and I needed to figure out what it was in order to pre-empt anything involving Tony or me. The way the timing of their appearance coincided with the burglary at one of their former partners-in-crime's home was impossible to consider unrelated. I made a beeline for the pizzeria as Roux and I began our usual lunchtime patrol. We approached the table full of aging mobsters despite the certainty of being reported by Conroy's surveillance team.

"Lenny, are you going to introduce me to your friends?" Lenny did not seem pleased to have me greet him with such familiarity.

"Oh, these are just some guys I used to work with years ago," he tried to dismiss the need for any introductions.

"You were a criminal years ago. That's why we don't let you drink at the bar across the street," I reminded him. I cared very little if this conversation embarrassed him. I extended my hand towards Pete Matranga. "This one I recognize. Time has been generous with you, Mister Matranga."

"I beg to differ," he politely retorted. "And you are?"

"State Police Investigator Cooter Holland. My partner and I own this place, and Strada Ammazarre across the street. I trust you are being well taken care of?" I wanted to get everything out in the open between us. I knew who they were, now they knew who I was, and that my partner and I were intolerant of their company at Strada. Identifying myself as a detective added to the discomfort the men had towards Roux sniffing them.

"You're Ralph's kid?" Matranga asked after a moment. There was no way Lenny had not already explained this to him. The man was looking for my reaction.

"Not exactly filling the old man's shoes, but still trying to make the city a safe place to live in," I shrugged and gently tugged on Roux's leash. He had recorded each man's unique scent in his internal registry, be it their cologne or the cigar they smoked.

"Well, it was a pleasure to meet you," Matranga said and then hid his expression behind the large wine glass in his hand. The others remained mute, and unintroduced.

Roux and I resumed our mid-day patrol of the Quarter. Walking him is my way to discreetly interact with the dozens of long-term occupants of the French Quarter that my father taught me to refer to as Quarter Rats. They are reliable sources for what is happening beneath the surface of the neighborhood. It was going to be interesting to see which ones mentioned the arrival of the old school mobsters. I skirted the riverside edge of the French Market until I led Roux through a doorway in the tall concrete floodwall across the street from the gilded statue of Joan of Arc. The boarded-up restaurant on the ground floor of the red brick building we passed once housed a restaurant my parents used to frequent despite its being owned by a former partner of Carlos Marcello's son. It is impossible to walk in the Quarter without encountering such landmarks, but I doubted whether I could convince SAC Conroy of this fact.

The route Roux and I normally follow gives me access to the French Quarter's largest gathering of homeless people. They occupy the Moonwalk and Jackson Square late at night but move to the riverfront after sunrise because the city council and NOPD don't want them to panhandle the "good people" in Jackson Square during the day.

Darnell and Boomer would have been retired with paid-off mortgages had they chosen to find steady jobs and a roof over their heads when they arrived in the 1970s instead of using the city's slim pickings of shelters and food banks to survive. They both wear scraggly beards and ponytails of gray hair that show their age. Their wardrobes would benefit more from being replaced than laundered. Neither of them discusses their tours as Marines in Vietnam, and neither of them asks about my own military service in Afghanistan or the intelligence work which nearly got me killed in Iraq.

"How are things?" I asked Boomer. A blonde-haired teenaged girl standing beside Darnell leaned over to pet Roux. I estimated she was fifteen-years old but she kept her back to me so I could not get a good look at her face.

31

"Just the usual rigmarole." Boomer's definition of rigmarole covers everything from harassment from NOPD to being rolled by teenagers from the nearby projects. Boomer was eighteen years old when he served as an artilleryman at Khe Sanh. He chooses to live under the open sky because two separate hooches he bunked in received direct hits from Viet Cong artillery and he cannot endure being indoors for very long.

"You know you can call me if you need my help," I needlessly reminded him. I nodded my head as I stepped away and Darnell followed me as I led Roux to the stairs leading up to the Moonwalk. "I see you have a new friend."

"Her name is Rebecca. She's from Denver. She says her folks took to fighting all the time and her Mom up and left. Daddy went looking for someone to take Mom's place at bedtime and she chose not to be that person." Darnell didn't need to elaborate. "You going to send someone after her?"

"Are you good with watching her for a while?" Doing nothing was not supposed to be an option but doing my job properly would only get her sent back to Denver.

"Yeah, we'll keep her close," he assured me. I pulled roughly sixty bucks in folded bills from my pocket and handed him half of it without counting. He would not accept all of it, at least not all at once, but he was willing to take 'a little' at a time to keep her fed and out of trouble.

I led Roux through Jackson Square and down the Pirate's Alley side of St. Louis Cathedral towards Royal Street. We passed by the Faulkner Bookstore, and the corner bar I use for meetings when I don't want anyone to pay attention to my presence. The block of Royal Street we entered is famous for its art galleries and antique shops selling items from European estates as old as the Quarter. A handful of blocks are barricaded every afternoon to allow only foot traffic, and each block is occupied by street musicians talented enough to headline in concert halls anywhere else on the planet. The mixture of music and voices creates a cacophony different from what the rest of the French Quarter generates on any given afternoon. The post-Katrina occupants of the apartments and homes along this stretch of Royal complain to the cops about anyone still playing music after dark. Most of them are also quick to tell their out-of-town friends how much they appreciate the local culture.

I tossed twenty bucks into Bobby Jefferson's guitar case as he began strumming Mister Bojangles for the ten thousandth time. The rail-thin Black musician is scruffy enough to make the song sound autobiographical. I steered Roux to the left and headed to Napoleon House for a muffaletta sandwich, which would be so large I would split it with him.

We settled in at a two-top table beside the French doors opening onto St. Louis Street and the back of the state Supreme Court building. The Eighth District police station was located diagonally through the block from where we sat, but I had no intention of engaging Detective Bassett in another fruitless discussion of the case.

I spotted a familiar face standing at the corner and motioned for him to join us. George Williams and I share a connection between his family and my mother's family, but he makes better use of being old-money New Orleans than I ever will. He gives tours of the cemetery Uptown where his family has kept a crypt for nearly three centuries. Tony and I worked out a deal with George to recommend one another to our respective clients when we first opened and were trying to get people through the door. The sort of people who can afford George's guided walking tours are the sort of people who can afford to tip very well. The arrangement has benefited both of us over the years. I barely caught myself before I blurted out his real name when I called to him. The Quarter is where you come to reinvent yourself, and the people who know me as 'Cadillac' all refer to George as 'Loki.'

"Hey, what's up?" Loki asked. He gave Roux a pat on the head and adjusted his hair under the rolled brim hat he wore against the nearly summer-strength sun. Roux was seated on the floor beside me. He began eyeing the remainder of my sandwich when I began to speak to Loki and the daytime bartender did his best to shoo him away while I was distracted.

"Just the usual. I'm still fighting crime one meal at a time," I laughed, but then had a thought that was job related. "You're still doing the night tours, right?"

"Yes. Are you really that bored?" he joked.

"No. It just occurred to me that you walk down Dauphine

Street, am I right?"

"On the voodoo tours, yes," he confirmed.

"I don't suppose you saw anything or anyone out of place over the weekend?" I didn't want to tell him what I was specifically curious about. Anything at all might be the key, and limiting him to a specific time or detail might work against me.

"I was wondering if anyone was going to ask about it," he said as he pulled out his cellphone. "There was a work truck blocking the sidewalk in front of a place on Dauphine for a couple of hours on Saturday. It was that big green three-story place that's been vacant for a while."

Bingo.

"Work truck?"

"That was the weird thing. It was an electrician's truck from over in Biloxi. I couldn't figure out why anyone called an out of state electrician on a weekend night. You may as well just start burning hundred-dollar bills while you wait for them to arrive," Loki said and laughed. His expression showed that he knew there was something wrong with the scene at the time. He looked hopeful that I might share some details that he could spread around the Quarter in turn.

"What made you curious?" I asked. An out-of-state work truck in front of any given residence on a weekend night is a curiosity, but it is also not something most people give a second thought.

"Everybody I know in the Quarter has been waiting for those apartments to go up for rent since Katrina. It's getting harder and harder to live within walking distance of your job anymore."

"True dat." I agreed. Loki and I have had many long discussions about the lack of affordable housing in the Quarter for the very people who make it a place others want to visit. "I don't suppose you wrote down the name of the company?"

"Better." He scrolled through the pictures on his phone and showed me one he took of the truck's door.

"Can you send that to my phone?" I asked and waited for the relayed message to ping on my phone before I let him move on to his paying client. "Thanks for keeping an eye out, as usual."

34

"No problem," he said and gave Roux a final pat. I was going to need to speak with Chief Avery about this development.

eleven

"Well, that's interesting," Avery declared after he joined the rookie detective and me at Bassett's desk and looked at the picture I had printed from my phone.

"It gets more interesting, but in all the bad ways," I warned him.

Bassett was seated and picked up the picture after Avery tossed it atop the detective's otherwise empty desktop. I made sure I remained standing so our boss could sit in the chair beside the desk while I spun the rest of the story for him.

I had spent two hours on the telephone before I contacted Bassett about the photograph. I played a hunch, and I was not at all pleased to learn that the work truck from Mississippi introduced the worst possible scenario.

"First off, the place on Dauphine was broken into at the end of Jazz Fest. There had to be hundreds more people in the Quarter that night than usual. Whoever broke in may have been counting on the police being too busy to investigate suspicious activity at an empty residence. The second thing that caught my attention was that the truck was reported stolen on Sunday morning," I began. "What makes that significant is that the company doesn't normally work on the weekend. I wonder how they noticed one of their trucks was missing if nobody was in the office until Monday."

"Maybe someone drives by to check on things over the weekend," Avery shrugged off my first question. I was inclined to agree with that, but equally inclined not to when I put the next piece into the puzzle.

"You remember that Alex Boudreaux got his financing after Katrina from that credit union Junior Hauser controls, right?" I asked Avery. Detective Bassett was going to have to sit on the sidelines for a while as the Chief and I went down memory lane.

"Go on," Avery mumbled uncomfortably.

"And you remember Councilwoman Adams' brothers were set to use a bunch of contractors who were in Hauser's pocket for their scheme?"

"Yes," Avery sighed and prepared himself for where he

sensed this was headed.

"According to building permit records, this company was set to do the electrical work for the brothers in Biloxi. They also did the electrical work for the first few projects Boudreaux did in New Orleans that Hauser financed." I said and paused to let the facts find a place to settle for each of the other detectives.

"You're saying a contractor from Mississippi with links to Junior Hauser did the damage on Dauphine Street?" Detective Bassett was quick to voice his skepticism.

"I'm saying a truck from that company was spotted in front of the house last Saturday night," I clarified. "I cannot put an employee of the company in the truck. I cannot prove Junior Hauser played any role in what happened, and I cannot prove Alex Boudreaux knew anything about the break-in. I can, however, say that the front door was not kicked in, so whoever made entry may have had a key."

"That's all pretty thin," Avery was intent upon keeping me from charging towards Hauser or Boudreaux with nothing more definitive than this against them.

"It's also only been a couple of days since you brought me in on this," I pointed out. "Give me a while. All I know for sure right now is that this was no simple break in, and that it has nothing to do with stealing copper pipes."

"I think we can all agree on that," Detective Bassett chimed in. This was supposed to be his investigation, after all, and he needed to at least appear engaged because I had just presented more evidence to NOPD's Chief of Detectives than he had come up with in the same amount of time.

"What have you got so far?" Avery now turned to his rookie detective to make that very point, and to hopefully spark something in Bassett to find evidence to counter my bad news.

"There are no operable NOPD crime cameras in that block, so I cannot verify what Detective Holland is telling us. I don't doubt the validity of his source or the photograph, though," he tried to bluff Avery into thinking he had done a lot of leg work and analysis, but wisely backed down in mid-stride. "There is also nothing in the crime lab's report to refute the idea that whoever opened the front door used a key. The only other thing the report really had to say was that the suspect wore a size ten and a half running shoe made by New Balance. That's what size I wear. How big is this Spenser Duncan character?"

"Your height but about sixty pounds heavier," I responded without meaning to demean his stature or physique. "We seem to all agree this was not a random act. What role Junior Hauser and Alex Boudreaux played in the break-in is a tempting matter to pursue, but the question that begs to be answered is not who broke in but what he was looking for."

"One thing at a time," Avery was quick to admonish both of us. "Narrow your focus. You can ask the burglar what he was after once you have him in custody."

"Let's assume the two of them are in this up to their necks," Detective Bassett spoke up all the same. "What purpose is there in knocking holes in the walls of a house once owned by a member of the New Orleans Mafia?"

"Maybe we can ask the man," I eased into the next thing I needed to share. "Conroy told me Marion Puglisi is being released from prison tomorrow, and a couple of his buddies have made themselves at home at Tony's pizzeria."

"What are their names?" Avery made no attempt to hide his anger about my having approached the FBI directly rather than routing my questions through his office as he expected. There was every reason to suspect the FBI never planned to tell him about Puglisi's release.

"Their last names are Matranga and Cammarato," I said.

"Matranga was Puglisi and Cammarato's capo. The guy Puglisi went to prison for killing owed Cammarato about fifty grand. That's why the informant was cooperating with the FBI," Avery told me. It was enough to further decrease the odds of the break-in being any sort of coincidence.

"When were you going to tell me about them?" Avery demanded.

"Maybe never. They aren't going to strong arm Tony into paying protection, and the FBI has them under surveillance. I intended to keep my distance from them to avoid getting drawn into their nonsense," I tried to explain away my failure to inform him of their presence.

"You didn't think it was worth mentioning that mobsters are frequenting a place of business you own?" Avery pressed me harder than I expected on the matter.

"Being able to feed you breakfast for free at Strada does not mean I am an equal partner in the place," I gently pushed back. "And Tony is charging the Mob guys for what they eat and drink."

"Very funny," Avery wasn't done complaining, but this development brought a long moment of uncomfortable silence. Avery seemed conflicted about what to say. "I guess I should stop hiding things of my own. The reason I called Cooter in on this is that I hoped his sources could say whether the break-in has anything to do with the old rumor that Sunset Puglisi hid either a fortune in cash or the diaries he supposedly kept for thirty years somewhere in the house before he went to prison. I have never believed the rumors, but the timing of the break-in and the return of these players is unlikely to be a coincidence."

"At least now I know what you want me to find," I said and bit my tongue rather than comment about how much time he let me waste by not pointing me in this direction from the start.

"Now that you know, what do you two intend to do?" Avery demanded.

"I'll drive over to Mississippi and talk to the locals about the supposed truck theft. As you said, finding the burglar is going to be the best way to find out what they were after," I spoke up. Avery's expression was probably meant to dissuade me from doing anything else while I was out of my jurisdiction.

"I could interview this Puglisi guy when he gets in town. Maybe he has some idea what they were looking for in his old place," Detective Bassett suggested. I was better at stifling a laugh than Avery at this idea.

"Yeah, you do that," Avery chuckled and saved the lecture on the reasons this was both a waste of time and a bad idea. Puglisi was never going to tell a rookie detective anything besides the time of day, and even that only with his attorney present. Bassett risked telling Puglisi more than he would realize he had shared until it was far too late. At least the rookie didn't know much of anything.

"Just don't mention the truck when you talk to him," I firmly warned him.

"Okay, I won't," Bassett agreed, but in a tone that told me he had no idea why you wouldn't tell a former Mob enforcer that a rival gangster had ransacked his former home less than a week before he was released from prison.

twelve

I am no more popular in Mississippi law enforcement circles than I am with the New Orleans Police Department or the FBI. Captain Nick Williams, my contact with the Highway Patrol's investigators in Mississippi, was still upset with me over shenanigans he suspected I pulled on the Duncan brothers to get them to flip on Bear Brovartey, who kept them on a retainer to do Junior Hauser's dirty deeds. The smart thing to do was to speak with the local police and get in and out of the state before anyone at the Highway Patrol learned I was there. The palpable ambivalence the local police showed about finding the car thief in the report they emailed me forced me to approach the captain in his office north of Biloxi.

"To what do I owe today's displeasure?" Captain Williams snarled when I knocked on his open door.

"Purely informational. I am not even staying for lunch," I tried to thaw the chill coming across his desk.

"You get one minute," he said and looked at his wristwatch instead of at me.

"A truck used in a break-in in the French Quarter last Saturday night was reported stolen by Everett Electric bright and early Sunday morning. Personally, I think it was reported stolen just in case it was spotted," I managed to say in barely twenty seconds. "One has to wonder why anyone would steal an electrician's truck to vandalize the plumbing in a place in another state."

"One doesn't have to wonder about that at all if one chooses not to," Williams said and leaned back in his chair before he swung both feet up on his desk to further illustrate his indifference. "What happens in New Orleans should stay there as far as I am concerned."

"Can you confirm whether or not Everett Electric is still under Junior's thumb?" I had to start somewhere, and the basics are always a good place.

"They do what he tells them to do, yes," Williams confirmed. "Burglaries like you described are not their usual thing. They muscle in on projects and then overcharge the client. Breaking and entering is not their style."

"Well, they may have had a key," I offered.

"Even so. What you are describing is still a break-in and that isn't something they have done in the past," Williams dug in. "Especially not so brazenly. You're talking out of state, in a high traffic part of New Orleans, on a busy night. I won't tell you it wasn't their truck, but I will argue with you about it having been any of their employees."

"Okay, then why would they loan one of Junior's thugs a truck? Surely there are stolen cars or vans the guy we are looking for could have used to get to and from New Orleans without making such a splash." Splash was the best word I could find to describe their being spotted. "It strikes me funny that they had to hotwire the truck they used to burglarize a house they probably used a key to enter. Maybe they were just covering their tracks by hotwiring the truck before they dumped it. I suspect that someone did all of this to try and tie Junior to the break-in."

"I have no idea if that was the plan, but the truck definitely creates a tenuous link to Junior," Williams concurred and waited for me to tell him what I knew. I intentionally paused to make him show an interest. "So, tell me, what happened in New Orleans?"

"Someone knocked a half dozen bathroom sinks off the wall of a vacant apartment building owned by Alex Boudreaux. The place was previously owned by Sunset Puglisi. He was a button guy for the Mob when we were still kids." It was all Captain Williams needed to know if he was serious about staying away from the investigation.

"Pulling sinks is something you call a plumber for, not an electrician, wouldn't you agree?" Williams asked, less to state the obvious than to admit his own confusion.

"What's the name of the plumbing company Junior has in his pocket?" I asked.

"Cassidy Plumbing Contractors, out of Long Beach," Williams answered.

"And do they have work trucks?"

"More than likely," Williams shrugged.

We sat back in our respective chairs and stared at one another for a long moment, until we both began silently looking around the office as though the answer to the still unasked question was sitting on a shelf.

"So, why not steal a plumbing truck to at least look like you are doing plumbing work?" he finally broke the silence. "Do you really think Junior had a hand in this?"

"I don't know. The electrical company Junior controls did Boudreaux's early work, so maybe Cassidy did some of the plumbing." It wasn't that much of a reach. It would be easy enough to check those records. I should have already done so. "I suspect someone is hiding their own tracks by implicating Boudreaux and Hauser."

"I can see you have a mess on your hands," Williams sighed. "Can you keep this one on your side of the border?"

"I'll try," I lied. It was way too early to know where the answers behind the burglary might lie. The break-in on Dauphine Street was more than petty vandalism if it involved stealing a work truck from another state. "I drove here to ask for a little help sorting this out, and I thought asking in person was a better way of getting your help than a phone call."

"What sort of help?" His tone was not one that gave me much hope of success.

"The truck was recovered with half a tank of gas in it. Whoever stole it must have filled the tank before they left here. Can I beg you for some manpower to canvas the filling stations for their surveillance footage from that night?"

"You want my officers to do this?" Williams sounded very unwilling to help.

"Maybe they could get the footage and then pass it off to the local cops handling the stolen vehicle case so they can watch it. I don't think the locals considered looking into the case very hard," I suggested.

"No, they probably didn't. The vehicle was recovered undamaged, other than the ignition being hotwired, so the company isn't pressing them to find the guy who took the truck. I'm sure the locals lost what interest they had in this the minute you told them what you told me about why the truck was stolen. You're opening a nasty can of worms pursuing this," Williams advised me.

"That's probably true," I admitted. "But, does that mean you will or won't do this?"

"I may need a favor from you sometime, so sure, we'll

get right on it," Williams said. "Anything else we can do for you?"

"It would be nice if you could identify the guy and tell me how he connects to Junior," I continued to press my luck. There was no value in knowing the name and not knowing the connection. I already knew I was going to have a very hard time getting an interview with the suspect if they even bothered to round him up. This was not a fight Captain Williams or the locals would have picked with Junior on their own. "Maybe this time I could ask Junior about his lackey directly."

That got Captain Williams' attention. He dropped the pen he was rolling between his fingertips and glared at me across his desk.

"Don't even think about it," he warned me.

"I think about a lot of things I shouldn't," I warned him. My closest friends know never to ask me what I am thinking because I might share some of the darkness that rolls around in my head on a daily basis.

"You can't anyway," he shrugged and sort of smiled. "He's on a cruise. He flies to Miami every couple of months and takes his sixty-foot yacht out in the Gulf for a week or so. Sort of makes you wish you could do the same thing, don't it?"

"Hookers on a yacht would get me cut in my sleep," I laughed.

"Oh, that's right. How is your lovely prosecutor these days?" Captain Williams asked, obviously glad for a safer topic to discuss.

"As beautiful and as patient with me as ever," I replied.

"Which is to say that she remains beautiful and is very unhappy with you most of the time," he chuckled and stood up. It was a less than subtle way to let me know our conference was over. I shook his hand before heading towards the door.

"Oh, one more thing. When did Junior leave port this time?" the question popped into my head at the last minute. This is the sort of question that percolates through all of the other things I have considered because it seems to have no place to fit. That seldom proves to be why it came to me when all is said and done.

"Last Thursday I believe," Williams said.

"Isn't that convenient?" I asked and left his office without waiting for a response. The captain sounded sure of his facts, and even if Junior left on Friday or Saturday, it was obvious he didn't want to be in town while the break-in occurred. To me that meant Junior knew he would need an alibi. It also meant he wasn't interested in anything the burglars brought back from New Orleans. He may have either known what they were after or that they weren't going to be bringing anything back. I was also more than a little curious about how well informed the State Police Captain was about Junior's movements.

I left the Highway Patrol headquarters and headed back to New Orleans. I respectfully waited until I was on the Louisiana side of the border before I leaned my foot on my turbocharged Cadillac coupe's gas pedal and watched the speedometer needle find its happy place in the triple digits.

thirteen

I was still in Mississippi when Detective Bassett sat down to interview Marion 'Sunset' Puglisi at the Federal Detention Center on Poydras Street. I had concerns about that, but also believed making it clear to the old-school gangster that a fresh generation of detectives in town was a good thing. Any ideas he may have had about picking up where he left off were sure to be rattled by the changes on the playing field, though likely only a little, and only for a while.

"Shouldn't I have a lawyer here?" Puglisi asked before Detective Bassett had even introduced himself.

"Are we here to discuss a crime you have committed?" The rookie tried to act as cool and tough as he could.

"I don't know why you had me hauled in here. You cost me my lunch reservation at Galatoire's," Puglisi complained, but was obviously feigning both innocence and outrage. The Federal Marshals had escorted the seventy-three-year-old parolee from signing his release paperwork to this windowless room without an explanation. Nobody bothered to inform Puglisi that he was free to walk out of the building at any time, but the rookie detective was too inexperienced to realize that this was something Puglisi knew when he sat down. Puglisi was hoping to do exactly what I feared, which was to let the inexperienced detective reveal more to him than he told the detective.

"My name is Romulus Bassett, and I am an investigator with the New Orleans Police Department. I had you brought here because I need your help on one of my cases," Bassett explained. I had to smile when Chief Avery and I reviewed the videotape of the interview. The kid was doing his best to make himself look like a veteran detective. He went out of his way to make Puglisi believe that he was working more than just this one case. Even Avery was impressed with his choice of words.

"I don't know what I can do to help you, seeing as how I only got back in town today," Puglisi continued to toy with him.

"I'm aware of your situation," Bassett said and waved his left hand dismissively. "What I need your help with probably dates back to the last time you were in town."

"You think you've got something new to hang on me, do ya?" Puglisi asked. His defenses began to rise.

"No, no, nothing like that, Marion," Bassett assured him. I liked the way Puglisi's face twitched when the NOPD detective referred to him by his first name rather than show him the respect he believed he was due by calling him Mister Puglisi.

"Then why am I here?" Puglisi demanded.

"Can you think of any reason someone would have stolen a vehicle to drive all the way from Mississippi to rip up the bathrooms in your home on Dauphine Street?" Bassett fed him a little more information than I would have, but a big fish needs a lot of bait to take even a small hook. Bassett wanted to see Puglisi's reaction, not to hear whatever spiel he came up with to hide what he knew.

"I don't own no property on Dauphine Street," Puglisi half-shrugged and half-spat. "Maybe you should be asking the Justice Department about what happened to their place. They took it from me, so anything that happens to it is their problem, not mine."

"So, you didn't leave anything behind when you moved out?" Bassett pressed. He saw the sore spot.

"I didn't move out, dammit! I was thrown in prison because the FBI back then were out to get anyone they suspected was part of what they called organized crime. Trust me, we weren't that organized. Anyway, they got people to start turning on each other to save their own asses and that's how they got me."

"You're saying you weren't selling girls for sex in the place on Dauphine Street?" Bassett challenged Puglisi's version of why he was sent to prison. He didn't bother to mention the multiple homicides attributed to the old man across from him.

"I ran a boarding house. How was I to know what my tenants was doing? They never produced a witness that said they handed me the money, and not one of the girls ever said I made them have sex with nobody. Not one," Puglisi dusted off the flimsy excuse he had used in court. Maybe he was hoping for a more sympathetic listener this time around.

"The rent you were charging those girls must have been mighty steep. You were living better than any other landlord in town when they busted you," Bassett said as flat and cool as he could without breaking into laughter.

"We done here, Detective? I answered your question, and I didn't bust your jaw when you tried to make fun of the time I spent in prison. I got nothing more to say to you than I hope I never see your face again."

"Take a good look at this face, Marion," Bassett snarled. Letting his anger get the better of him was only going to play into Puglisi's hands. Using the old man's first name again was the only way he knew he could anger his opponent. "You'll be seeing a lot more of it if you stay in town."

"Take a look at mine, kid," Puglisi snarled right back. He was on his feet and his leathery knuckles rested on the metal table as he stretched to place his face inches from the detective's face. "Don't think your badge makes you safe if I don't like you."

"Noted." Bassett did not need an explanation for what the old man just said. Neither man said a word for a long moment, and both Avery and I noted that Puglisi did not take this opportunity to leave. Bassett was the one who finally broke the stalemate. He pulled a business card from inside his blazer jacket and laid it on the table. He then used his right index finger to move it across the varnished tabletop until it was within Puglisi's reach. "Things changed while you were gone. Some things, like lunch at Galatoire's, are still possible. Running whores again is not in your future. I'll be watching you."

Puglisi glanced at the card, then briefly glanced at the back of the card before he dropped it into his pocket. I replayed the transaction a dozen times before I convinced myself I was reading something into it that was not there. I wished I was certain that the back of the card was blank, but I wasn't. I worried about seeing things because I didn't trust Bassett.

"Don't waste your time sitting by the phone," Puglisi dismissed Bassett and walked out of the room and back into the temporary custody of the Marshals outside the door. The look on the detective's face was not one of confidence as he faced the lens to turn off the camera.

"Well, that was entertaining," I said to lessen the tension Chief Avery and I both felt after watching the brief exchange. "I must say, Puglisi looks pretty good for a guy who just got out of prison."

The aging mobster was interviewed in the same clothes he wore when he went into prison, where the combination of a lousy diet and lack of exercise can leave a freed man's clothes looking like borrowed clothes. He looked no less stocky than the day he went in, and a week of eating in the Quarter ought to restore his lost weight.

"The kid did alright, though." Avery offered no opinion on the mobster's appearance.

We were sitting in my living room, analyzing the video recording on my large flat screen television. Watching the interview play out as though we were in the room with the two men had been an unexpectedly fraught experience.

"Yes, he did better than I think either of us expected. But do you think he learned more than he gave away? Puglisi didn't act surprised about the break-in, so someone had likely passed word to him when he was still in prison. His spiel about being unjustly convicted was nothing but smoke."

"Sure, it was. Did you see how tight he went when Romulus gave him the details about the break-in? There was something about the Mississippi connection that got to him. He may not have known about that until right then." Avery poured himself a second bourbon as he spoke. He usually swears off hard liquor in favor of beer because he has proven more than once to be a mean drunk, but he was going to be heading home in a few minutes and can't afford the quality of the liquor in my cabinet. I can barely justify the expense myself on some of the bottles, even using the discount I get by ordering through the bar downstairs.

"That's a good thing. Word about the break-in is all over the Quarter, but we are probably the only ones who know about the Mississippi connection. I want to see it as a sign that whoever tipped him off isn't getting their information out of NOPD. We both know that used to be the situation," I said and hid my face behind my own tumbler of Blanton's bourbon. I wasn't looking to start a fight or to open old wounds with the Chief of Detectives.

"True enough," Avery conceded. "All the same, we need to keep a tight lid on what the two of you find. I am more interested in what left that house than I am in who broke into it. The timing is making the rumors sound a lot more credible."

"Hopefully I will hear something good back from Mississippi. I asked them to round up the surveillance footage from any gas stations where the guy who took the truck may have filled up before heading this way. I imagine they have a short list of suspects for such things to work from once they get a good image," I said to let him know what came of my own day's work.

"You think they will actually invest the man hours into doing that for you?" Avery was justifiably hesitant about believing in my powers of persuasion.

"Well, they either do that or I keep nosing around in their back yard on my own," I said.

"Yeah, I'd be looking for those films if I were them. You made a big enough mess over there to last for quite a while." Avery chuckled at the memory of my last foray into the neighboring jurisdiction and then finished his drink. He set the crystal tumbler on the coaster atop the coffee table and stood up. "I'm going home to my loving wife and a nice meal. You keep me posted, and please don't let Puglisi kill my detective."

"I'll do my best. Have a nice weekend," I said and stood up to show him out. I was already a little late to the beginning of the bistro's weekend happy hour, so we took the elevator down and I walked him to the door before changing hats to become the amiable host and co-owner of Strada Ammazarre.

fourteen

Katie and my sister Tulip were standing at the restaurant end of the bar with Chef Tony when we stepped off the elevator. They exchanged brief greetings with Chief Avery as he passed by, but he didn't stop for a beer and none of us suggested that he do so. The expression on his face was still as serious as it had been when we were upstairs.

"What's that all about?" Tulip asked as soon as Avery had left the building.

"I just filled him in on a case he asked me to help out with. He gave a simple case to one of his new detectives only to have it take an unexpected turn or two," I said. I went so far as to shrug my shoulders to appear dismissive of the situation.

"Such as?" Katie immediately pounced. I don't have the ability to shrug off anything, so my charade set off her alarms.

"Someone punched holes in the walls of a house on Dauphine to get at the plumbing. Most of it was so old it was still galvanized, but the burglar didn't rip out what copper there was. We're trying to decide whether they were after the copper or something else," I tried to steer the discussion towards a new topic.

"Who owns the house?" Tony asked, quite unhelpfully.

"Alex Boudreaux," I admitted. My companions' faces contorted in unison at the very sound of the name.

"And we're off," Tulip laughed.

"There are a lot of missing pieces in the puzzle. The building was previously owned by a guy named Sunset Puglisi. He ran a brothel as an apartment building to show he had a visible means of support. He also did contract killings for the local Mob. A work truck from a company in Junior Hauser's pocket over in Mississippi was parked in front of the house when the damage was done, and Puglisi was just released from prison this morning." I limited myself to the high points of what was wrong with the vandalism theory.

"What's the NOPD detective's name?" Katie wondered. Whatever came of the case was likely to land in her office.

"Romulus Bassett," I replied. I said it as casually as I could, but I knew she kept a mental Rolodex of names and how

51

individual detectives and officers fared in court.

"You're in trouble," she assured me in no uncertain terms. "I understand why he was assigned to the case when it was something we could plea bargain. I do not see why Bassett is still on the case now that it is something this big. He is shark chum for any defense attorney who questions him about his last partner in court, and he lacks the experience it is going to take to handle these suspects."

"Agreed on all points," I said and held up my hands to show I was not going to argue. I also did not want to tell her about the video of Puglisi being questioned. That would only reinforce her opinion.

"And you can't tell me those wiseguys showing up across the street isn't connected," Katie rolled on.

"I am assuming the same thing," I agreed once again. Tulip and Tony were enjoying the show, but I knew they were no less concerned about our businesses being drawn into the investigation.

Tony's seemed almost embarrassed when he finally spoke up.

"I should have spoken with you first before taking their reservation."

"What reservation?" I demanded but showed more concern than anger in my tone of voice. I had left the meeting we had with SAC Conroy feeling confident that Tony saw the wisdom, perhaps even the necessity, of distancing ourselves from the aging mobsters. It appeared that he suffered some sort of change of heart.

"Lenny asked if he and his friends could have dinner at the table in the kitchen this evening. It was open, so I said yes," Tony explained. This was not going to be an occasion when I let him get away with his innocent immigrant businessman act.

"You knew better. We don't even let Lenny drink at the bar, and you are letting him bring the guys the FBI told us to avoid here for dinner!" I heard my own voice and held up a finger to take a pause while I swallowed about half of the chilled Manhattan the bartender had just set in front of me. My father made a point to tell me to avoid Lenny when I was just a teenager hanging out in the French Quarter with my school friends. I banned him from Strada to avoid having any association with him in the eyes of the state liquor board or my law enforcement superiors.

"They will pay," he said in his defense. "That is how we make money."

"My fear is that we will all end up paying for this," I sighed. We exchanged an expression we had not shared since debriefings on missions that went awry in Iraq. I hoped he had not opened a door there was no way to close, and that whatever was discussed over dinner that evening did not involve finding a way to drag the two of us into anything the aged criminals were plotting.

"He said a friend of theirs was coming home and they wanted to celebrate," Tony went on defending his decision.

"Well, that friend is named Marion Puglisi. He used to kill people for some of the other men who will be seated at the table," I informed him. Tony himself had spent a few years as an assassin for Saddam Hussein. It was impolite to mention that he and the evening's guest of honor had such things in common. There was also a large difference between the two. Puglisi enjoyed his wet work, by all accounts, while Tony had been forced into the service of Iraq's secret police for fear of them harming his family. We had never discussed his history with the Sicilian Mob beyond learning his cooking skills by working in one of their trattorias. I began to wonder if cooking was the only thing the Mafia taught the man my sister seemed intent upon marrying.

"Do you wish that I cancel their reservation?" Tony asked. He sounded as though he was prepared to do so if I said he should. The expression on his face, however, begged me to allow his lapse in judgement to proceed as planned. Neither of us knew what consequences there might be in backing out at this point.

"I just hope a meteorite hits their car on the way here," I answered far more honestly than my response sounded. Everyone laughed, but Tony excused himself to head back to the kitchen and I offered to buy the two women dinner anywhere else. I felt a sudden need to build an alibi.

fifteen

Katie and I sent Tulip home in a taxi after a leisurely four course meal at Muriel's on Jackson Square and walked back to Strada Ammazarre arm in arm. We tried to allow enough time for what should have been a dinner among old friends who are used to hours-long meals, but we still arrived in time for more drama than I wanted to have to deal with.

In retrospect, I should have never left Tony to handle the chef's table reservation by himself, nor placed our manager, Juaquin, in the position of arbitrator in a fight between two clearly immovable forces.

The guest list was everyone we had seen at the table across the street; Lenny Bonetti, Hammer Cammarato, Pete Matranga, Frankie Russo, plus Sunset Puglisi and a stranger in his early thirties who, in addition to being stockier and younger than the rest, was also better dressed than Matranga.

Matranga's guests drank three rounds of top shelf liquor and enjoyed multiple appetizers at the bar before moving to the table in the kitchen, where they consumed four bottles of wine from Tony's personal wine cellar at the cost of hundreds of dollars apiece. The men began their meal with a soup course and Matranga asked Tony to prepare some Sicilian dishes he could never sell on our menu to people who grew up on canned Spaghetti-Os. The party cleansed their palates with a salad, and then ordered dessert and espresso before retiring to a table on the patio for a final round of expensive cognac and cigars. Tony and Juaquin made sure to clear the patio before allowing this final indulgence in violation of the state's newly imposed health codes.

The dinner tab was comfortably into the four-figure range on the alcohol alone. This would have normally called for a discreet meeting between Juaquin and the host to be sure payment for both the tab and the gratuity was assured by one or multiple credit cards. Matranga was not the sort of man to be questioned about such things in the middle of a meal. Questioning the man's ability to pay was tantamount to insulting the man.

The question to have asked before the guests were seated

was the willingness of any one of them, or the group collectively, to pay for their meal. Tony learned the cooking part of his resume in bistros and trattorias in Sicily, Naples, and Rome where gangsters were afforded free meals without a word being said. The price of feeding them was built into the price of being able to do business at all. I let myself believe Tony trusted them to pay for this meal because they paid their far smaller tab every afternoon at the pizza place. The scene which erupted when Juaquin personally hand delivered the meal's tab to the table was ugly from the beginning, and my arrival was like tossing gasoline on a wildfire.

"Oh, so you called the police," Matranga snorted as soon as I closed the patio door and stepped towards them. Katie backed away and closed the door behind her on her way to the safety of the bar.

"I'm not here in any police capacity," I assured both sides and briefly held my hands up to show I was not armed, though I was, or waving my badge.

"The gentlemen have chosen not to pay," Juaquin informed me and handed me the hot potato of a tab, which was still tucked into the black faux leather holder. "Not the restaurant, and not their server."

I glanced up at the knot of angry men across from us at the mention of the latter transgression. Some things simply cannot be allowed to happen. The gratuity was close to half a month's rent for most of our service staff, and tabs this large usually invite a tip on top of the one imposed by the house.

"Show some class, fellas," I suggested as much as implored. I was willing to absorb the cost of the meal as a lesson for Tony and Juaquin, but I was not going to allow the server to be punished for doing her job, nor reward this bunch for their intransigence.

"Your chef should be honored that we chose your restaurant to welcome our friend home. In the old country this would not be a question," the stranger tried to school us on Mob etiquette.

"This is not the old country. This is the French Quarter. You aren't even in Louisiana right now," I gently schooled him in Louisiana's geography and politics. "We expect our guests to act like guests and to treat our employees with respect. Telling me you will not tip your server is not just an act of disrespect. It is cheap. Are you cheap men?"

"What did you call me?" Matranga had no trouble translating plain English into Mob-speak. Lenny began to shake his head in barely perceptible degrees.

"I called you nothing," I said and tossed the tab back onto the glass-topped metal table between us. "I only asked you a question, which your response has answered."

Tony and Juaquin remained noticeably mute while I dug my own hole in this conversation. Their silence left me uncertain of what had already been said, implied, or suggested as a solution before I stepped into this buzz saw.

"She works for you. You pay her if it is so important," Puglisi spoke up.

"That is certainly an option," I conceded, but not pleasantly. "As is banning the lot of you from any of our properties and reporting this incident to your parole officer. We live in a world full of options and possibilities, gentlemen."

That brought a pause to the debate. Sunset Puglisi being in the company of Lenny and Hammer Cammarato was already a clear violation of his parole stipulations against associating with known felons. Being in the presence of Matranga was enough to glue the FBI's surveillance teams to him for the short remainder of his life. Having these gangsters, old or not, at the same table was a sign of some sort of trouble on the horizon. Tony would later tell me Italian had been the only language spoken at the table, as he had personally handled taking and preparing their order and left the waitress and back-waiter to refill wine glasses and clear dishes.

"We do not carry this much money with us," Matranga finally started to budge on their position. "This is a bad neighborhood after dark."

"It's getting that way," Juaquin couldn't resist saying.

"Perhaps we could hold something of value until tomorrow," I suggested as helpfully as possible.

"That could work," Matranga gave another inch of ground.

"We would charge only a little interest to carry this overnight," Tony interjected. The look I gave him let him know I believed he and Matranga deserved one another right then.

Matranga and the one guest I did not recognize exchanged

56

a look that I did not like, but it was not something to comment upon or question. I knew that any resolution other than allowing these men to leave here with our sincerest apologies and an invitation to return was likely to bring unimaginable consequences.

"What do you have in mind? A driver's license?" The stranger abruptly took up the negotiations.

"That would put a name to your face," I said.

"My name is Vincent," the man shared.

"Do you have a last name?" I inquired.

"You wanna be pen pals?" Vincent Whoever sneered. He also neatly side-stepped any questions about his lineage and connection to the older men. "I was hoping we would have been allowed to enjoy a much more pleasant meal."

"Oh, I'm sure the meal was entirely pleasant," I said and smiled. "But, like so much else in life, it's the cost of such indulgences that pinch you in the end."

"Yes," Vincent gave a thin smile and nodded slightly. We were making headway, but the tension in the room remained high and we were no longer discussing the meal.

"Here is my watch. How is that?" Matranga suggested and removed the watch he was wearing. I recognized the watch as a Patek Philippe but did not recognize the model. Any Patek Philippe would easily pay for a year's worth of such meals.

"No," Tony said and waved the watch away.

"I don't understand," Matranga complained before I could.

"We do not want your watch. We want his watch," Tony said and pointed to Sunset Puglisi. "His watch you will come back for."

He had a point. It was unlikely that Matranga paid anywhere close to the value of the watch he was wearing. For all we knew it came from an unfortunate individual who crossed him in the past and had no need of a wristwatch to measure eternity.

"I'm not giving you my watch," Puglisi declared. He went so far as to place his hand over the wrist it was on.

"Give the man your watch, Marion," Matranga ordered him.

"They can go to hell. I'm not giving nobody my watch," Puglisi surprisingly refused his former boss.

"You'll get it back tomorrow," Vincent reassured him. He reached out and touched Puglisi's wrist and the two men exchanged a look that was not the least bit pleasant, but neither of them said another word before Puglisi frowned and surrendered his watch. The disgruntled mobster seemed to place a higher value on the sleek Citizen watch than the amount of the disputed bill.

Tony casually dropped the watch into the pocket of his soiled apron and stepped aside. Juaquin and I also cleared a path for the seething gangsters to leave the patio. I expected at least one of them to break something or overturn a bus tub of dishes on their way out the door, but they slithered silently into the night and stood on the curb as the valet retrieved a Lincoln Town Car. Frankie Russo had enough class to palm a ten-dollar bill to the valet who brought the car around before he slid behind the wheel himself.

"That went well," I hissed at my partners as soon as we were alone. "You didn't see that coming?"

"I have told them that I am not part of their thing, no matter who we both know in Sicily." Tony was unrepentant for his part in this debacle, and I took him at his word that he had tried to make it clear to them that he and our business were not in play. There had to be a reason they chose our places of business to gather and cause problems, and I was certain that Tony was still a large part of their nefarious plans.

"I think they have that message," Juaquin tried to reassure all of us.

"Sure, they do," I grumbled again. "And what did we get? A wristwatch?"

"No," Tony said and half-grinned as he pulled the watch from his apron and strapped it to his wrist. "We have taken another man's honor."

Taking Puglisi's watch apparently made the disputed dinner tab into a debt that would need to be paid in full for Matranga to make his guest whole again. I still had a lot to learn about honor among thieves.

"I can't wait to see what that's worth," I sighed and left the two of them to sort out paying the waitress what she was due. She was unlikely to need a good time piece.

I had barely stepped up to the bar beside Katie before SAC

Conroy stormed through the door and motioned for me to step aside. I excused myself yet again and went to speak with the clearly agitated FBI agent.

"Isn't it past your bedtime?" I asked and looked at my own wristwatch.

"What just happened in here?" he demanded.

"How so?" I wasn't going to touch such an open-ended question from the FBI.

"There was a big scene out on the patio. I want to see the restaurant's video footage from tonight," he finally specified his interest and began making demands.

"Hand me a warrant and you can watch any film you want," I offered. "You better hurry because our cameras are on a four-hour loop. By tomorrow morning you will be looking at an empty restaurant."

"You can stop recording. I order you to stop recording," Conroy nearly shouted in my face.

"Is that how things work now? You get to go around telling private businessmen what to do? I missed that Constitutional amendment," I resisted.

"What's your problem?"

"I choose not to live on a one-way street," I snapped right back at him. "I came to your office in good faith to speak with your organized crime agents and you said you saw no reason to allow that. Now you expect me to do whatever you say. You are the one who chose to make up the rules to whatever game we are playing. I am simply guaranteeing the co-owners of this business that you honor the letter of the laws you swore to uphold. We are not filing any criminal complaints, so you have no probable cause." I was on the verge of dragging Katie into the argument. She would reluctantly back my position, but also spend the rest of the night reminding me how stupid it is to rile SAC Conroy.

"Fine," Conroy gave up. I don't think either one of us expected him to do so. "Can you at least tell me what was going on? My agents could not get close enough to overhear the conversation. They just said it seemed to get very heated."

"There was a problem with the meal tab. It was substantially larger than they were prepared to pay, and an accommodation had to be made," I shared.

"How much larger?" Conroy asked. He was now relaxed enough to ask with a small grin on his face, as though he knew the answer.

"It was the difference between nothing and whatever we could get."

"What did you get?" Conroy pressed on.

"Something to hold until someone pays the tab in the morning. Tony took Sunset's watch as collateral."

"Pretty ballsy," Conroy almost whistled as he considered this. "So, do you really think they will pay up to get the watch back?"

"Doing so is the only way Matranga can keep Puglisi happy. I just worry about who is going to get rolled for the money," I admitted. "This is far from over."

"I'm glad you see that," Conroy said, with obvious relief in his tone.

"I guess I could show you a piece of tape. There was a new face with them tonight. A younger guy, but obviously a member of their club. He said his name was Vincent."

"Tall guy, about your build?" Conroy described the stranger exactly.

"You know him."

"His name is Vincent Contaldo. I also know his reputation," Conroy allowed, but without sharing specific details. "He is an independent contractor who has done a lot of work for the Outfit in Chicago. You do not want him for an enemy."

"What do you think he's here to do?" I was more curious than concerned. We had crossed swords, but I didn't believe either of us was looking for a real fight.

"My guess would be that it has to do with Puglisi. Whoever broke into his place was looking for something the old man left there."

"What do you think could be important enough to send someone like Contaldo?"

"I can't say," Conroy tried to deflect. "It must still be worth a lot even after this much time."

"Money?" I imagined a nice stash of bundled bills wedged into a wall for future use. The only problem with that was that they were at least two series of bills old and would stand out like Monopoly money when Puglisi went to spend any of it.

"That is as good of a guess as any. A guy like Puglisi surely put something back for his retirement." Conroy was done answering any more of my questions if he wasn't getting his own answered. He turned around and walked out the way he came in but paused to say something to Katie.

"What was that about?" she asked when I finally settled onto a bar stool beside her. Jason poured me a snifter of Armagnac for a night cap.

"His surveillance team came up empty in here tonight. I filled him in." I kept my explanation brief because I didn't want to discuss the matter with her at all. "What did he say to you on his way out?"

"He described you in a most unkind way, and I told him it was your best feature," she then kissed my cheek to silently say she didn't want to talk about it, either.

sixteen

Brunch service at Strada Ammazarre begins at ten o'clock every Saturday and Sunday morning, so Tony is in the kitchen by six o'clock. He normally does not set foot in there before noon on weekdays. He leaves opening and prep during the week in Miss J's capable hands. She helps on Saturday, but Sunday is her day to go to church and Tony would rather close the restaurant than ask her to work that one day. He turned things over to Miss J and joined Katie and me when we came down for breakfast just past eight o'clock. The cooks set platters of the things Katie normally enjoys on the buffet on the chef's table and brought a pitcher of mimosas with the carafe of coffee. To say they know our tastes is an understatement.

"Do you two have a bet on whether or not last night's bill gets paid?" Katie gently taunted the two of us. Tony found this more humorous than I expected.

"It is a small price for a nice watch and a good story," he shrugged off the idea that we were going to suffer were the tab to go unpaid.

"It's become an honor thing. They'll pay," I said with more confidence than I felt. "And then we will see what it costs us going forward."

"There is that," Katie sighed and filled her empty champagne flute with the first of many glasses of mimosas her day held in store.

"I have been thinking about this whole thing and the two questions that keep coming back to me are why us and why now," I said. "Granted, the pizzeria had only been open for a couple of weeks before Matranga and Russo came back to New Orleans, and Puglisi only just now got back in town. That explains the timing of when they appeared at the pizzeria, but it does not explain why they chose the place for their new clubhouse. Maybe they just wanted to keep to their old neighborhood. They hung out at the Italian grocery up the street back in their glory days."

"It might have to do with you," Katie was staring at Tony, and she expected either a counterargument or an explanation having more to do with his history than his cooking.

"I agree," he mumbled and leaned back in his seat. I recognized this as one of his defensive positions. Katie was inviting herself into a conversation he would have rather kept between the two of us.

"Who do you both know, and why do they think that makes you their bitch?" Katie pressed even harder. She was falling into her prosecutor mode and that was not the best approach with Tony. It was less that he won't be questioned by a woman than a matter of not wanting to be questioned about some things at all.

"I'm sort of curious about that myself," I said to encourage him to open up.

"One of Matranga's uncles worked for the man who owned the kitchen where I had my first job. My mother hoped that cooking for these men would be a way to keep me from having to do other things for them. Better a life on the stove than one on the street," Tony began explaining.

"That probably sounds really impressive in Italian," I said to try to lighten the mood that was beginning to temper the conversation.

"They noticed that I was very good with a knife, and that I am not made sick by blood. They had me do things for them that these were good things to have." Tony was not going to admit to anything specific to either of us. "I was a cook in the day and worked for them at night. I moved up in the kitchen because of what I did at night."

"And you were a chef when the Iraqis cornered you," I moved the story ahead. There was an implicit connection between his having been elevated to such a trusted status and what it must have taken, besides great cooking skills, to achieve the position of chef in a trattoria owned by Sicilian Mafiosi.

"Yes. I do not know what was said or agreed to between them and the men I worked for from Iraq, but my boss ordered me to move to Naples to work for the Iraqis," Tony had advanced his life story to that point in time during which Katie had already decided she knew all she cared to know.

"How much danger is your family in if you keep butting heads here?" I wondered.

"My mother is old. Older than your mother. There is not much they can do to her that she will not greet," Tony said. Threatening to kill old people is not an effective negotiating tool. "I send her money, but I do not use a way that they can stop me from doing so. My cousins and uncles are not so close to me that threatening them or hurting them will make me do what they want. That will just make trouble for themselves in Sicily."

"Then what can they do to you here?" Katie asked. I had to wonder if this was the only question she really wanted to have answered. I have seen her walk a witness down a path in court and know that she is smarter than to start at her destination and try to lead a witness to the same point.

"They can kill me. They can burn this place. They can hurt the two of you or your sister. They know doing any of those things will mean I will do things as well." Tony had clearly considered the consequences of taking Sunset Puglisi's wristwatch. It still seemed like a very trivial thing to have done, but this was exactly how duels used to get started.

"This is where I have to stop asking questions," Katie announced and tossed up her hands. "You two are going to do what you do; the legal system be damned."

"Legally, I can arrest Matranga for theft of services, or we can sue him over the bill. Neither of those are any guarantee that we would see a dime, and both take time we may not have. They would also make us look weak enough to embolden Matranga even further," I tried to explain the real-world problems with her way of doing things. "Trust Tony to use the system gangsters have used for centuries to settle such matters."

"Even if it means someone hurts your sister?"

"I don't think this is the sort of thing that will ever get that far," I tried to reassure all three of us.

"Fine. What are you two going to do next?" she relented, and then demanded an answer to what I now saw as being the question which had kept her awake all night.

"First, we are going to let Matranga make the next move on the bill. Then I am going to try to figure out if there is anything else going on while those guys sit at the pizzeria every day," I said. It sounded like I had some sort of plan all along, but this was simply what stumbled out of my mouth in the moment.

"How do you propose to do that?" Katie asked. Her tone had changed to the excited one she gets when I include her in my strategy planning.

"I would love to get access to the FBI surveillance, but that is not likely to happen. I guess I will just have to do my own and see what I can figure out. I will bounce any ideas I come up with off Tony. He can tell me how far off base I am and help me figure out what these guys are focused on when they sit down." The plan, such as it was, began sounding reasonable to me.

"Let me know what I can do to help," Katie offered. She seemed to accept that my plan might work without my breaking any laws. Katie's appetite returned and she began filling her plate from the platters on the table before us.

"Don't watch," Tony offered his own suggestion as he stood up. It was his garbled English way of asking her to mind her own business. Yet again, however, he summed up what we needed her to do better than the correct phrase ever would.

seventeen

Katie and I walked Roux after finishing our meal. We both made a point of finding topics as far from the previous evening's incident and the presence of men with very bad histories in our lives once again as we could.

We sat down at the sidewalk table which Matranga and his companions used at the pizzeria. It was going to be interesting to see what the altercation at the restaurant did to their routine. I sat down with the notion that I might be able to figure out what the men were looking at, or watching, each day.

"Can I bring you anything?" Richie Franklin asked shortly after we sat down. Richie and I first crossed paths when he ran a Sixth District drug gang. Tony and I offered to give Richie and his friends a chance to put their entrepreneurial skills to better use and bought the pizzeria as an experiment.

"Maybe a couple of bottles of water, and a bowl for Roux," I suggested. Richie came back with a metal bowl of water for Roux, who immediately began lapping from it, and two bottles of San Pellegrino for us. He also brought glasses with ice and lemon and set them on the glass topped table beside the tall bottles of sparkling mineral water. "Do you have a minute?"

"Always for you," Richie wisely answered. I grinned and waved a hand to dismiss the idea that he needed to drop everything for us as he does for Tony.

"What can you tell me about the guys sitting here every afternoon?" I inquired. I did not use any other identifiers because I had no idea how much Tony had shared with them about these particular regulars.

"They're really old white guys. They wear suits and ties, but I don't think any of them have real jobs. They come right after we open at eleven and always leave at five, during crew change. They order the same things every day. They get two of the meat and cheese trays and usually drink a couple of bottles of Chianti. The big guy always pays in cash, and he tips about thirty percent," Richie walked me through their typical visit.

"Do they ask for the same server?" I was trying to consider every variable.

"No, but it's usually Kenny or Darlene," Richie answered. Darlene was the sister of one of the former gang members and working here was hopefully going to help her keep her own life straight.

"Are either of them here?" The pizzeria had been open for about an hour so the day shift were all present.

"Darlene is. I'll send her out," Richie said and walked back inside the pizzeria.

One of the things that nagged at me was why the men were sitting in direct sunlight for three hours a day, the shade from the table's thin nylon umbrella not being enough to do more than reduce the sun's glare, rather than in the cool of the pizzeria itself. I was sure that privacy played a role in their reasoning, but they were not so concerned about it that they didn't broadcast their presence by sitting at a table where anyone driving past could see them.

Darlene came out and I introduced her to Katie. The waitress was barely twenty and had dropped out of high school as a sophomore, but was working on her GED along with about half the crew running the place. Her hair was twisted into a dozen tight braids she held in place with a tie at the base of her neck. She was barely five and a half feet tall and wore just enough makeup to highlight her high cheekbones and caramel skin tone.

"Yes, Mister Cadillac?" she asked after presenting herself to us. She had an order pad and a row of multi-colored ink pens in the black waist-apron she wore. The pizzeria's casual uniform was jeans and a black polo shirt with a logo over the left breast.

"Is there anything that has caught your attention about the men who sit here every afternoon?" She knew who I meant without any elaboration. She gave the question thorough consideration before she replied.

"They change the subject whenever I bring them anything, and sometimes it is kind of funny. There was a new guy with them yesterday who was really angry with one of the other guys, but they all smiled when I got to the table with their wine. I looked back outside a few minutes later and they were all arguing again."

"You don't stand in your station?" Katie had learned a few

67

things about the business by osmosis. Juaquin is always after the bistro servers about staying in sight of the people they are waiting on in case they need anything.

"We don't have stations out here right now. We take turns picking up any tables that sit out here and run back and forth," Darlene explained. Perhaps the lack of constant attention was actually one of the attractions the table had for the men in question.

"Anything else?" I was somewhat surprised she had noticed as much as she did if this table was not part of her primary focus.

"They like to watch the delivery trucks. Our deliveries, and the ones across the street, always come after lunch. They seem to be real interested in what we get," she said. I could tell she realized there was some sort of significance in this.

"That's a big help. Thank you," I said and let her get back to her station inside. We waited to be alone before either of us began sharing our impressions.

"That's one piece of the puzzle," I noted. I spotted something else as Darlene went back inside.

The door to the pizzeria was propped open to allow guests the freedom to come and go as they wished, but mostly because it released the enticing odor of the oven-fired pizzas to lure in hungry tourists. I could see the cash register from where I was seated, which I remembered was where Cammarato normally sat. It was not a reach to imagine a former racketeer keeping a running total of the sales he saw on our cash register. Things were beginning to make a lot more sense.

I doubted that the FBI realized the criminals they had under surveillance were openly building a blueprint of our operations. Matranga had a good idea of what the pizzeria was taking in by now, and he had likely worked out a formula for the sales at Strada Ammazarre, as well. He had also compiled a list of our vendors. He knew how much we could lose to any protection or skim operation he and his cronies planned to hit us with, and he knew the exact companies to lean on to interfere with our ability to do business until we bent to his will. Matranga had not yet sprung his trap, but I surmised that refusing to pay the previous evening's bill was his means of testing our resolve to fight back.

"You're onto something," Katie said to shake me out of my thoughts.

"Yeah, I am," I said and frowned. "I think these guys have been sizing us up. I won't be surprised if they try to twist our arm a bit to get some money out of us to make them go away. I don't know what their plans are for Tony, but at least he doesn't seem inclined to work for them."

"Not inclined, but how adamant against?" Katie wondered.

"I want to believe entirely." I have believed a lot of things that proved to be wrong.

"Well, I believe you two are in for a rough ride," she responded. She did not sound confident that either of us was going to be able to keep our distance from Matranga and his reunited crew.

"What do you think, Roux?" I jokingly asked our four-legged tie breaker.

His growl was an unexpected response.

"As usual, Roux is the one with the better judgement," Katie scoffed. We finished our water and headed off to the French Market.

Matranga, Russo, Cammarato, and Lenny were seated at the table when we headed back to my apartment. I was not sure what to read into the absence of Puglisi and Vincent Contaldo. I hoped at least one of them was at the bistro paying Matranga's tab, or perhaps Puglisi had decided to no longer publicly associate with anyone who might get the attention of his parole officer.

Tony was focused on one of the tables at the far end of the dining room when we returned to the bistro. He was standing at the bar and not smiling in a way that I knew meant nothing but trouble. His face was hardened into the same expression it took on just before we broke down a door in Baghdad. It was a look that let anyone on the other side of a door know we carried malice in our hearts. I was afraid he was about to storm across the dining room and do something at least one of us would later regret.

"Tony," I said to get his attention. I also spoke his name in a descending tone to remind him to breathe. I knew not to touch him until he acknowledged me. He shook his head slightly and turned to face us. "What's up?"

"Puglisi showed me his new watch. I think Matranga gave him his watch rather than pay us what we are owed," he said. It only partially explained his mood. This was an unexpected development, but it seemed to indicate they considered our attitude towards their unpaid tab to be an annoyance rather than a problem.

"Well then, Puglisi is the all-around winner. He got a free meal and a substantial watch upgrade. Matranga gave up a watch he probably didn't pay for in the first place, and the lot of them get to thumb their nose at us over the bill. What are you staring at?" He had not turned to face me in this entire conversation.

"Table Fifteen," Tony replied without any further elaboration.

"Aha," I declared once I remembered how the tables were numbered and focused my own attention where Tony's remained. Sunset Puglisi was having brunch with one of the last people I imagined he might know: Gavin Hendricks, my father's former literary agent. The pairing of these two men was an unlikely coincidence, and I took a seat at the bar to be positioned to intercept Gavin before he left the restaurant. Katie took the seat next to me and motioned for a round of drinks from Hannah, the daytime bartender. Roux hopped up on the seat to Katie's right and Hannah gave him a pat on the head in lieu of a beer.

"What did you find across the street?" Tony asked. He was able to turn his attention to other things now that I was equally bothered by whatever might be happening at Table Fifteen.

"I think they have been calculating our sales and watching our vendors. The next thing they may do is try to get you to pay them for protection or offer them a piece of the business. Is there anyone you need to warn or worry about?"

Tony listened to my analysis and then gave a brief nod of agreement about my concerns.

"There are a couple of people I should call," was all Tony said. I knew that most of our goods came from companies too large for Matranga to interfere with, but I also knew there were a couple of small seafood vendors who could be leaned on that Tony liked to use for things like our oysters and some of the local fish.

"Let's circle the wagons. I'll push Bassett and maybe we can put them all away before this escalates much further," I said and patted him on the shoulder before he headed back to the orderly world of his kitchen. Katie and I sipped our drinks, hers a glass of champagne and mine a Manhattan, while I waited for my chance to interrogate Gavin Hendricks.

eighteen

Puglisi ignored me, if he even noticed me, sitting at the bar as he made his way to the front door a step ahead of Gavin Hendricks. I had no idea how long they had been sitting at the table before Katie and I arrived, but it had been long enough to have finished part of their mimosas and to have dirty dishes on their table. They sat for another hour after we arrived. Their body language told me at least as much as overhearing their conversation might have. What likely began as an amiable meeting turned acrimonious before the two men parted company. Sunset ignored Gavin falling behind as they approached the door. Sunset's attention was on the table at the pizzeria, and he marched directly there while Gavin took a seat beside me at the bar.

"Imagine seeing you here," he tried to joke before he asked Hannah for a glass of soda water with a squeeze of lime. He must have reached the limit of his capacity for day drinking.

"I believe that's my line," I said a little too curtly. Gavin and Katie exchanged hellos before he braced himself to debrief me on his meeting. He would have gone elsewhere to have breakfast if he didn't want me to know he was working on something with Sunset Puglisi.

"I guess you what you want to know what that was all about," he continued to play. He had never been this flippant with me in the past. I chalked it up to his mimosa intake. Gavin is in his sixties, generally fit but beginning to go soft at his beltline, with a receding hairline of silver-gray hair and a close-cropped beard. He isn't near the drinking man he was when my father was still his best-selling client.

"Start with everything and we can go from there." I hoped my serious tone of voice might convince him he was the only one having fun playing his game.

"I just lost a book deal I have been working on for years," he explained. "And I could not be happier."

"That's hardly an explanation. It is more like a blurb for one of your books," I said with as little humor as I found in his still making me work for the information I wanted.

"This all began with a newspaper article I read about how

72

Meyer Lansky kept diaries," he began.

"You're saying Meyer Lansky kept records of what he did?" I interrupted.

"That was what the article claimed," Gavin repeated the distinction and then continued. "Anyway, I asked around. The Feds never thought to ask Lansky if he kept any, so they never subpoenaed them. They would still be interesting reading, don't you think?"

"Absolutely," Katie agreed. "Did you try to publish them?"

"Somebody else approached his daughter ahead of me," Gavin said and shook his head. "But it got me thinking about whether any other mobsters kept a diary."

"Because theirs might still be available?" I suggested. I could see this conversation led straight to the table of local living legends across the street.

"That's right," Gavin said. "So, I did a Freedom of Information filing with the Department of Justice for the names of any Mafia figures still doing time. The next thing I know I get a cold call from some attorney who says he has a client who had just what I was looking for. I found a publisher willing to offer six figures if the diaries named at least a couple of well-known mobsters who were still alive or that helped the FBI solve some cold cases."

"And that is how you wound up with Sunset Puglisi as a client?" I saw no reason to hide my skepticism. For one thing, Sunset was hardly a major player, even at the height of his being a scumbag.

"Marion began working for Carlos Marcello in the nineteen fifties. His rap sheet was thirty years long by the time he went to prison, and only he knows the number of men he killed or where most of them are buried. He is too long in the tooth to bother trying for any more crimes he might divulge. The sentence he was serving when we first met was meant to be a de facto life sentence, anyway," Gavin further elaborated on the logic that pointed him towards the aging mobster. "He was already doing hits for Carlos Marcello's capos when President Kennedy was assassinated. Think of the possibilities there."

"Oh, I can," I sighed and took a sip of my drink before looking him in the eye. "I can also imagine he made his pitch as tempting as he could when he saw that look in your eyes."

73

"You don't believe the stories about Marcello killing Kennedy?" Gavin challenged me. This allegation was part of the bedrock of New Orleans folk lore by the time I was born, five years after the assassination. Simply being a suspect in the murder of a president made Marcello as powerful of an underworld figure as he would have been if convicted for it. Denying any involvement was overwhelming proof of his guilt to most members of law enforcement and present-day conspiracy theorists.

"I cannot believe anyone had the poor judgement or guts to write down that they played any part in doing that, nor to implicate Carlos Marcello in print," I clarified my skepticism.

"They turned out to be the ultimate Get Out of Jail Free card," Gavin countered. "I believe Marion Puglisi's diaries detail everything he did for Carlos Marcello personally and for his former capo, a guy named Pietro Matranga. Puglisi claims he also handled contract killings for the crime families in Chicago and New York."

"Then why didn't he use this card when he could have twenty years ago?" I challenged him. Marion Puglisi did not strike me as a man who enjoyed a single moment of his incarceration.

"Marion claims a million dollars a year was deposited in an offshore bank account to keep him quiet. I think I could do a decade or two in prison for that kind of payday." Gavin finally divulged the reason he believed a guy who spent his entire career lying to anyone not part of his circle of criminals. Sunset may have lied to them as well.

"Why didn't the Justice Department object to his getting out of prison? You don't have the kind of pull it takes to get them to allow something like that if they don't want to let it happen."

"Heck no I don't," he laughed out loud. "Marion's attorney is the one who leveraged the book deal to get his client an early release in exchange for the FBI having access to the journals before they were published. It took a couple of years to make happen, but here we are today, and Puglisi just walked out your door a free man. I will be honest; I have been looking for a way out of this almost from the beginning. I never trusted his attorney."

"Okay, let me see if I have this all straight," I said and began unraveling the details as I understood them. "You were approached out of the blue about a mobster who kept a diary like Meyer Lansky supposedly did and wound up being the literary agent for an eighty-year-old low-level pimp and contract killer from New Orleans who led you to believe he knows whether Carlos Marcello killed John F. Kennedy. He claims he was paid a million bucks a year to keep quiet, when in fact Marcello could have just had a shiv put in his heart in a prison shower for the price of a carton of Marlboros. And you're telling me you played no part in his release from prison?"

"I didn't do a single thing to get him paroled. Our deal was only for the publication rights to his journals after the FBI reviewed them," Gavin repeated with a bit more insistence of how small his part in this was.

"Do you remember the lawyer's name?" I inquired.

"Marvin something or other. I have his card somewhere. I began to smell a rat after the attorney cut off all contact with Marion once the ink was dry on the publishing deal. The publisher has been after me to move forward with this but today was the first time I have spoken with Marion in two years. Frankly, I am glad to be clear of both men," Gavin told me. "I think Puglisi is out for revenge now that he is free to do so."

"What sort of revenge does Puglisi have in mind?" Katie piped up. She undoubtedly had a list of questions of her own.

"Marion told me he knows who planted the evidence used to convict him. To say the man is unhappy is a gross understatement. Now that he is out, I think he plans to get even, if you catch my drift," Gavin warned me.

"That won't do," I had to say.

Gavin frowned deeply before he explained what else transpired over brunch. "He says he is short of cash. He offered to sell me his watch."

"Did you see the watch?" I asked. I had a dreadful feeling that I had already seen the watch.

"It is a Patek Philippe. He wanted more than I could afford to spend on such things." There was something to read into Puglisi offering to sell Matranga's watch, but I was more concerned with the reason Puglisi wanted the money.

"You don't seem especially upset by the loss of the project," Katie pointed out.

"I'm not at all," he said with a throaty laugh. "He may never have kept any diaries. I may have just avoided representing the next Clifford Irving."

"Who?" Katie had to admit the limits of her knowledge of literary villains.

"He forged some diaries that he claimed belonged to Howard Hughes. It ruined a lot of careers," Gavin explained. The sound of relief in his voice made clear how happy he was to have caught himself before he made a similar mistake.

"Now he just needs to figure out how to do whatever it is he has planned and get out of town before the FBI calls his bluff," I rounded out the story. I was already considering Puglisi's options for doing so. If he could not have dinner with friends on our patio without the FBI watching every bite of food he ate, he was unlikely to be traveling anytime soon.

"Have you talked to the FBI about cancelling the book deal yet?" Katie asked.

"I spoke to Michael Conroy yesterday. He claims Puglisi has not yet handed over his journals and that he made being released a pre-condition for doing so. I guess he did not trust the government to keep its side of the bargain," Gavin told her. "He called me at Le Pavilion and asked if we could talk privately. He came to my room, and I told him I was going to let Marion back out of his book deal because I lost faith in his willingness to deal with me honestly."

"What did Conroy say to that?" My mind was filled with a variety of scenarios. Most involved Conroy being profoundly relieved.

"He sort of laughed. He never once asked if Marion told me what was in the diaries or if I had even seen them. I find that particularly odd, don't you?" Gavin asked.

"I find most things about the local FBI to be a little strange," I shared.

"Maybe Conroy knew the story about the journals was a hoax," Katie spoke up.

"What if the FBI already has them?" I asked them both.

"I'll sign you to a book deal if you can prove that is the

case," Gavin offered. He gave me the laugh I recognized as being a cover for how serious he was. It would be more than just a best seller if I proved the FBI recovered Sunset Puglisi's written confessions to decades of misdeeds that implicated dead and living New Orleans mobsters, cops, and politicians. The story everyone would want to read would be what SAC Conroy did, or did not do, with the information contained in those journals.

"I think I'll pass on that offer," I said and patted his shoulder. I was relieved that Katie began to engage him with her own questions, because my mind was focused on learning Sunset's plans for the revenge and escape I needed to thwart.

nineteen

My cellphone rang at just after three o'clock on Monday afternoon. It was hard to gauge Captain Williams' mood by his tone of voice. There was a faint manic quality to it as he tried to describe the events of his morning to me. He was still juggling anger and confusion along with relief that he was no longer part of what I was investigating.

"I have good news, and I have weird news for you this afternoon," Williams said to open the conversation. "The best news is that neither one involves me any longer."

"Then I guess it doesn't much matter which one you start with," I tried to inject my own humor into a conversation that I had no way of knowing which way was about to go. I assumed it had to do with identifying the suspect in the break-in.

"We sent a couple of video captures to Quantico for enhancement. I got them back and we put out an APB on Spenser Duncan."

"Spenser Duncan of Bear Brovartey fame?" I could not believe there were two men with the same name and criminal record running around coastal Mississippi. Spenser Duncan and his younger brother had made a plea deal to serve life in prison for two homicides in the state of Mississippi rather than serve less than a decade in Angola for their part in Junior Hauser's plot to put his own candidate on the New Orleans City Council. "I thought he and his brother were already in prison."

"As did I," Captain Williams assured me. "It turns out Spenser made a deal with the DOJ. He gets to stay out of prison while he cooperates with the FBI. I think they would like us to believe that arrangement is entirely about prosecuting Junior's dirty lawyer."

"But it may include other things," I finished the thought. "What are the odds of Spenser trying to renegotiate the sentences by ratting out Junior Hauser, as well?"

"I would have said poor until just now," Captain Williams said to lead into the second thing he had to share. "Two agents from the Marshals Service walked into my office half an hour ago and collected every tape and photo we used to identify

Spenser. They told me to close our investigation into the vehicle theft and to stop cooperating with you. I am supposed to tell you to have your boss speak directly with their office if you have any questions."

Learning why the marshals found it necessary to collect the evidence was going to create an entirely new wrinkle in my investigation. There was every reason to believe the marshals issued a similar edict to the local police detectives. The locals would roll over without a fight and never inform me of the marshals' interference.

This redoubled my interest in Spenser Duncan. I wondered whether the purpose of the unexpected intervention was to keep me from being able to prove Spenser took the truck, or if it was to keep Bassett from learning why Spenser broke into Puglisi's former home. There was absolutely no way to know the purpose behind the break-in and vandalism without questioning Spenser, whom the entirety of Federal law enforcement seemed curiously intent upon protecting.

"Interesting." I was mentally planting the question tree I needed to have Spenser climb, and how to locate him despite the further hurdles certain to rise in my path.

"To you, but not to me any longer," Williams firmly informed me. Neither his curiosity nor his keen sense of jurisdictional boundaries was conflicted by these instructions. He had wanted no part of what I had been looking into from the beginning.

"I don't suppose you kept anything back, perhaps because you knew I wasn't going to drop this?" I inquired.

There was a pause before he answered. I may have insulted him by suggesting he was giving up rather than just following orders.

"Of course I did. I still have a copy of the image the FBI sent back to us. I will email it to you and save you a trip across the border," he finally said. This was his polite way of saying stay out of his state.

"Could I trouble you to scribble Spenser's address on the back?" I suggested. That brought a hearty laugh from the other end of the line.

"We have no idea where the Duncan brothers are these days. I assumed they were being held in a jail over there, but maybe it is just protective custody, with an occasional field trip." This was something I would have to find out without his help.

"Do you want to know what this was all about when I figure it out?"

"Not particularly," he assured me. "We're satisfied to collect a favor we can use later. Be sure to call someone, make that anyone, else if you need any further assistance."

We both knew I would not hesitate to involve him the next time Junior Hauser ventured into New Orleans.

twenty

"You're saying the FBI might be behind the break-in?" Avery was incredulous at the very notion. Detective Bassett had done nothing but spin his wheels since last we spoke. Our boss's reaction to my theory about the break-in seemed to give the rookie some respite from beating himself up about his own lack of a theory to share.

"It's not like they don't have a past history of such things," I reminded him. Avery was old enough to remember the Congressional hearings into COINTELPRO in 1975. The CIA, IRS, and NSA each endured a humiliating moment in front of the television cameras during the congressional hearings which made everyone agree to change their operations. Old habits may have proved too hard to break.

"Still," Avery complained. "It's a big stretch to suggest the FBI used an informant in one of their investigations to commit a burglary. Why not do it themselves? They have people trained to do this without making a production out of it."

"Aside from not wanting to wind up in front of Congress, again? Consider, for just a moment, that creating what you call a production was the real purpose." The two NOPD officers obviously did not see what I envisioned. "Spenser Duncan is synonymous with Junior Hauser. What if implicating one of Junior's lackeys in the break-in was meant to point a finger at Junior and cause a problem with the locals?"

"Why bother doing that?" Bassett spoke up.

"Because NOPD's walls have always had too many ears. It is only a matter of time before rumors spread that Junior ordered the break-in once Spenser is identified as the suspect. Whoever they meant to convince Junior is making another move might believe the story if they heard it from a source they trusted," I tried to get them to start seeing things for themselves, but they needed more to work with to get them on board. "Word about the break-in was also meant to get back to Puglisi, because he is the one with the most personal interest in whatever they found. Puglisi probably took more of an interest in the burglary than in the perpetrator."

"Because he thinks they were after his diaries?" Avery

leaned back in his chair as much to consider what I was suggesting as it was to distance himself from the possibility that the rumors about the journals were true. Bassett let me do the talking in the obvious hope that my opinion of the case would help him avoid having to voice a foolish theory of his own.

"Puglisi just asked to be released from a book deal he made in prison for diaries he supposedly kept all the way back to the nineteen fifties. The story is that he used them to extort a million dollars a year out of the local Mob while he was in prison. He made the book deal when it looked like he might die in prison and then cancelled it after he was paroled." Dragging Gavin Hendricks into this conversation by name was not going to convince either of them to believe what I was saying, so I chose to leave him out of it.

"It makes sense that whoever broke into Puglisi's last address was looking for those diaries, whether or not it was Spenser Duncan," Avery reached my own conclusion.

"The burglary happened a week before the Feds released Puglisi from prison. The only other person I know of in New Orleans who was aware of Puglisi's release before it happened is Bill Conroy. Do you think Conroy wanted to convince Puglisi that Junior Hauser is after his diaries?" Bassett finally spoke up.

"Using Spenser means Conroy left tracks back to himself," Avery pointed out.

"And that is why Conroy was probably who asked the marshals to sweep up anything linking Spenser to the break-in. A pair of marshals went to Biloxi this morning to shut down the help I was getting from the State Police in Mississippi. I am supposed to have you call them if I want any more information. We all know that will consist of you being told to forget about Spenser as well," I belatedly informed Chief Avery.

"I'll go talk to them, anyway," Avery offered.

"The question isn't whether Spenser broke into the house, but if he found the diaries," Bassett finally joined the conversation.

"That is the question," I concurred. "But it is not the problem."

"What's the problem, then?" Bassett wondered.

"The problem is Sunset Puglisi may believe Junior Hauser did steal his diaries. Puglisi is going to want them back and to punish anyone who has them."

"Surely Conroy is not trying to start a gang war," Avery cringed at the thought. An old-fashioned gang war between old-school New Orleans gangsters backed by their counterparts in Chicago and Los Angeles against Junior Hauser and his violence-prone syndicate would put control of organized crime in the southern quarter of the country up for grabs. Chicago and Los Angles could swoop into any operations they vacated by decimating the Dixie Mafia, but Junior's criminal good-old-boys would lay rightful claim to New Orleans if they prevailed.

"I would like to think not," I tried to reassure him that the local FBI office was not run by a complete lunatic. "Conroy got his start at the FBI working organized crime cases in Florida. That means he is already familiar with the players in both camps and what it would take to spark a wildfire. Maybe he thinks he can contain this in Biloxi and hopes Puglisi will kill Junior without too much fuss. Or maybe the SAC wants to get the good-old-boys from Dixie to stretch their necks out far enough that he can chop them off."

"We are looking at a bad situation no matter what the motivation behind this proves to be," Avery surmised. "I will go speak with Conroy and see if I can get a feel for what he is up to. Maybe I can reason with him."

"Again, I would say not to bother," I continued to dissuade him.

"Well then, what do you suggest we do?" Avery asked in frustration and slammed both hands on the desk.

"We need to find Spenser Duncan," It was the only answer I saw. Spenser was the key to exposing any nefarious plot by the FBI, if there really was one, and to either absolve or prove Junior's involvement in the break-in.

"Then you two go and do that." Avery sighed and waved us out of his office.

twenty-one

"Any idea where to start looking for this Spenser Duncan character?" Bassett asked as we walked towards the elevators.

"One," I said. I could tell this was both an insufficient answer and an aggravation to my rookie partner. "The first thing we need to establish is where he was supposed to be when the break-in occurred. I'll have a better idea about where we need to look when we know the answer to that question."

"Where do you think he should have been?" Bassett pressed for answers that were going to elicit purely hypothetical responses. We were the only ones to enter the elevator, so I pulled the stop button before I began.

"Spenser is supposedly a cooperating witness. He should be under the wing of the Federal Marshals, as he is helping on a Federal case. That usually means he has a room to himself in a prison. Sometimes they will keep a witness in a safe house, and sometimes they allow the witness to remain under loose supervision in their own place. I know Spenser is not living at home, so they might have him in a safe house somewhere in New Orleans to keep him available on short notice."

"Okay. How do we find where he is?" Bassett rephrased his original question.

"I have someone we can ask to find out for us," I told him and pressed the button to get the elevator back in motion. A security guard greeted us at the ground floor, no doubt in response to the elevator's delay. He may have expected to find an amorous couple hastily rearranging their clothes, but all he found was the two of us in a hurry to be somewhere else.

The New Orleans District Attorney's office had been forced to make use of temporary quarters, including a former nightclub, while looking for a permanent place to call home after Hurricane Katrina destroyed their office. It took a few years, but they finally settled into office space across from the Orleans Parish courthouse and police headquarters on Tulane Avenue. The newly elected DA had upgraded Katie to an office of her own as a reward for forcing Bear Brovartey to confess his considerable misdeeds and handing the DA the sort of high-profile case that springboards political careers. She and her boss were both upset when the FBI grabbed the case out from under them in Judge Rogers' courtroom, but the District Attorney remained impressed enough with her to make her his deputy. The new position gave her the authority to decide which cases went to the grand jury and which received plea deals to secure some sort of justice for the victims.

"I need a professional favor," I told her after closing her office door and introducing Detective Bassett. Katie took the opportunity to judge for herself whether he looked like a crooked cop. I would have to wait for her assessment as I could not tell a thing from her expression.

"I'm intrigued by this new approach. Normally you ask for forgiveness rather than permission," she said with a smile that did not entirely conceal her concern that this was my new approach to seek forgiveness for something I was about to do.

"Who is representing Spenser Duncan? It cannot be Dan Logan because he has Bear Brovartey as his client, and he cannot represent the guy who is helping to convict his other client. Or can he?" I would not put anything past Daniel Logan.

"No, it is still Logan. Brovartey is presently being defended by an attorney that Logan recommended to him. The guy worked on John Gotti's defense team, if that gives you some measure of the trouble Brovartey is in." She was quick with her answers, but she did not bother to conceal her concern about my interest. "What's up?"

"The state police in Mississippi positively identified Spenser Duncan as being who stole the truck spotted in front of Puglisi's old place on Dauphine. I am making the short leap that he also broke into the house. He should have been monitored closely enough that he couldn't have done either thing, and this morning a pair of Federal Marshals scooped up what the state police used to identify him and told them to tell me to forget the whole thing," I filled her in on my day.

"They are covering their own asses," she wisely deduced. Bassett's head swiveled like he was watching a tennis match.

"So, I need to know for sure who should have been watching him," I elaborated. "I am not sure if I am hoping he was being held here or over in Mississippi. Either place offers its own world of possibilities."

"Are you suggesting the Feds used him to do their dirty

work, maybe for a reduced sentence?" I could tell she was angling for anything she could use to her own advantage in the future. Having proof that the marshals loaned their prisoners to other agencies to commit felonies, or that the FBI used a cooperating witness as a burglar, would be something to trade upon for years to come.

"I am only saying I need to find Spenser Duncan and convince him to tell me his end of the deal. This case is turning into a reunion of all the people I hoped I was done with. So far, I have connected Alex Boudreaux, Spenser Duncan, and Dan Logan to the crime scene. I don't want to add Junior or the FBI if I don't have to."

"Do you suppose Bill goes out of his way to assign you cases you cannot help but make a mess of?" Katie half-argued as she came around the desk and gave me a hug. I would have kissed her but for the audience in the room.

"It certainly didn't seem this complicated when we started," I tried to defend the Chief of Detectives' decision to involve me in Bassett's routine investigation.

"It never does, my love," she reminded me and sat down behind her desk. "Let me make some calls. I'll try to have an answer when I see you this evening."

"Thank you. That's all I can ask for," I said and smiled. "At least professionally."

I nudged Bassett out of her office before this word play became any more lurid and unprofessional than it already was. He held his own list of questions until we were standing outside the building.

"What did you mean by reunion?"

"Alex Boudreaux and Spenser Duncan were part of Junior Hauser's attempt to control a seat on the City Council. They had a candidate of their own and got rid of the incumbent by rolling her up in a real estate deal her brothers had going with the head of the Dixie Mafia. The Duncan brothers killed a pair of bikers and wore their colors when they planted drugs on the long-shot candidate who won the election. I believe Alex was Junior's point guy for the operation until Brovartey poked his nose into it and blew the whole thing up. Now Alex and Brovartey are spinning the Feds in circles by blaming one another for everything that happened. Spenser has avoided going to prison by agreeing to link Bear Brovartey to those biker murders. You should know the name Dan Logan from the number of criminals he has put back on the street. His being involved in this will only make things murkier." I hoped Bassett would be satisfied with this explanation of the interconnections running in the background of our investigation.

"How so?" Bassett was a slow learner.

"Consider what Katie just told us. Logan arranged for an attorney with a record of defending mobsters to represent Junior Hauser's crooked lawyer while he continues to represent the man informing on his former client. Logan moved here from Brooklyn after the storm for reasons nobody has ever been able to pin down. Now he is offering personal recommendations for Mob lawyers. Forgive me if I read something into the fact that a pair of lawyer pals are representing both sides of a Federal case," I told him a bit sharply.

"And now we're dealing with known Mob figures from here," Bassett finally began to grasp my sense of dread of what might lay on the horizon.

"Tell me which of these two things is worse," I offered. "The FBI using one of its cooperating witnesses to gather evidence against criminals and former politicians and police officers, or that same cooperating witnesses slipping his leash to hand that same information to Junior Hauser in hopes of some sort of redemption."

"That's like asking if you want to get hit by the northbound or southbound train. Neither one is good but neither one is all that much better or worse than the other," he decided after a long moment of silent consideration. The detective had a point.

twenty-two

Chief Avery arrived at Strada just as happy hour was beginning. There were only a couple of regulars present at the bar, so standing in my usual spot near the open double doors gave us more than enough privacy for our conversation. I could tell by the tension in his jawline that there was a fresh wrinkle in the case.

"What happened now?" I asked.

"Hammer Cammarato was found in the trunk of a stolen car an hour ago. He took two small caliber rounds behind his left ear," he informed me and studied my expression, which was unchanged by the news, before he continued. "Someone put the car into Bayou St. John, but it didn't sink all the way. A kid on a bicycle spotted the rear bumper near the surface."

Bayou St. John has been a convenient dumping ground for stolen cars and other inconvenient evidence for so many years that NOPD's divers routinely scour sections of it as a training exercise. The streets running alongside the bayou are low-curbed and lack guard-rails, so it is not at all uncommon for a driver to slide into the narrow canal's deceptively deep waters after an accident or during a heavy rain shower. People have also been known to drive into the bayou intentionally to drown themselves, resulting in missing person cases that go unsolved until months or even years later.

"Where was the car stolen?" It seemed like the best place to start. I was assuming the aging mobster did not die of natural causes. I also could not envision any scenario where he went into the trunk voluntarily.

"About a mile from where we found it. The owner claims she found her car was missing about four o'clock this morning when she got back from drinking with friends in the Quarter. Her parents back up her story."

"That makes for a memorable evening," I mused. "I don't suppose they are the sort of people to have a surveillance camera?"

"I don't think anyone thought to ask, but I would say not," Avery admitted.

There was little reason to hope for anything useful even if

they did. Most people mount their surveillance cameras as deterrents, so they install them to scare criminals away rather than where they have the best chance of recording criminals in action.

"The car is not the most interesting thing." There was a faint hitch in his voice as he approached the topic. "Care to guess who recently rented the house next door to where the car went missing?"

"Puglisi." It was the only name that came to mind when he said 'recently.'

"Close. According to the FBI, Pietro Matranga rented the furnished bungalow a week before Puglisi was released from prison and handed him the keys the day he got to town." Avery's elaboration indicated that he and Conroy had spoken.

"Puglisi couldn't very well come home to die if he didn't have a roof over his head," I pointed out. "That means Matranga was aware of Puglisi's being released even before we learned about it."

"It gets even stranger," Avery continued. "Guess who owns the house."

"Let's see, what could make this mess even more complicated?" I mused for only a moment. "Alex Boudreaux?"

"His holding company, anyway. Management of his properties is no longer in his hands, but he would theoretically still get to approve any new tenants." Avery was frowning.

"Did this little tidbit come from the FBI as well?" I wondered. "I am assuming you had a conversation with somebody over there today."

Jason brought me a fresh cocktail and I took a sip of the chilled Manhattan while I waited for Avery to decide how to answer the question. Avery's beefy hand was wrapped around the bottle of Abita Turbodog that Jason had placed before him when he arrived.

"The FBI took over the crime scene after I notified Conroy who was in the trunk of the car. We compared notes, and he had more to share than I did. He told me that the house in question used to be Alex Boudreaux's residence. Alex worked some sort of accounting magic and sold the house to his own holding company for more than it is worth to pay his legal fees." Avery explained. "Conroy suspects Boudreaux plans to buy it back for next to nothing if he beats the charges and can begin running his company again."

"Did you tell Conroy we know about Spenser Duncan's involvement in the break-in?"

"Yes," Avery nodded his head and finally smiled. "He did not seem at all surprised, and he asked me to keep him informed of anything else we learn about that."

"And have you talked to the Marshal's Service about how they lost him?" I prodded.

"They were only willing to confirm that they were holding Spenser in a safe house so he would be available for questioning. They are being especially tight-lipped about how he slipped away from them," Avery shared what he knew. "Dan Logan talked a judge into having Spenser's ankle monitor removed last month because he was in the constant company of the Marshals. They weren't about to confirm it to me, but it sounds like Spenser slipped out at least a day before he broke into the house on Dauphine Street."

"A day is a long time to spend on the run," I pointed out. "It is telling that Spenser chose to spend the time planning a burglary rather than getting out of the country."

"Sort of what I was thinking," Avery chuckled. He finally picked up his beer bottle and took a long drink.

"Two scenarios come to mind," I offered. "First is that his escape is just a way to cover that he was loaned out to the FBI to do the break-in on their behalf. Conroy is understandably worried we are going to link him to the crime if we find Spenser first. Second is that Spenser slipped his leash and did the break-in all on his own to try to find the diaries and make himself a new deal."

"Maybe it was half and half," Avery suggested. "Someone had to tell him about the diaries for him to know where to find them. Maybe he won't hand them over until he gets a better deal. He is in a strong bargaining position if he found them."

The part of my brain that used to imagine and dissect every possibility while I did intelligence work kicked in, and I began looking for ways to arrange the few available facts. "What are the odds he traded them to Junior for absolution? Junior must still be livid about Spenser testifying against Brovartey, and not just because it cost him his best attorney. Junior probably used Spenser and his brother for things that he never told Brovartey about. You know he must be worried about Spenser turning on him, as well."

"The truck the burglar used was too easy to tie back to Junior. The FBI would have provided Spenser with some vehicle from an impound lot if they ran things." Avery seemed to like the idea of Spenser trying to placate Junior more than the suggestion that the FBI was involved in shenanigans they could not easily explain if discovered. I liked his idea the least, because it made things the hardest to solve and meant making at least one or two more trips to Mississippi. I could not imagine Captain Williams being at all excited at that prospect.

"Well, look who's here," Katie exclaimed as she and my sister came through the doors. Both women still wore business attire from their respective days in court. Katie had, though, released her long auburn hair from the braided war-bonnet she wears in her Deputy State's Attorney mode. It made the snugness of her skirt across her hips just a little sexier. I suspected Tulip dressed as much to please Tony as she did to influence any of the civil court judges she had encountered earlier in the day.

"Katie," Avery smiled as he greeted her and accepted a kiss to the beard shadow on his square jaw. He also took a hug and similar smooch from my younger sister.

"We have a couple of things that might help you," Katie said to me as she waited for Jason to serve her the first of what was sure to be multiple glasses of Marquis de Perlade champagne. We stock the sparkling wine for one of our regulars, Ryan Fitzgerald, who introduced Katie and my sister to its drinkability. One of these days I was going to have to smack him for that.

Katie took a small sip and savored the tart bubbles on her tongue before she shared what she had learned. "Spenser was being held in a safe house in Holy Cross. There was a traffic accident out front of the place and he slipped through a back window when the marshals went to investigate the commotion. The Marshal's Service has been trying to find him without letting on that he got loose in the first place."

"Who told you that?" Avery asked. It was far more information than they had shared with him.

"Really?" Katie scoffed at the very idea of divulging her source. Avery frowned at the rebuke for only an instant before he began to laugh with the rest of us. "They gave me the address, and I had Tulip run it down for me. Guess who owns the place?"

"Alex Boudreax," Avery and I declared almost simultaneously. Tulip seemed surprised that this was the answer on the tip of our tongues.

I explained my own rationale. "He has all sorts of rental properties on that side of town. Alex Boudreaux owning the houses where Sunset Puglisi and Spenser Duncan both hang their hats is a little too coincidental, even for New Orleans."

"He might not know that's happening," Katie argued. "Management of his properties is in the hands of the court-appointed administrator until his trial is over. I think red flags would go up if he approached the rental agent about renting to either of them."

"I accept that he did not invite either of them to be his tenants. I just don't believe he doesn't know they are his tenants. I imagine someone lets him know who wants to rent any of his properties, or at least lets him know who is renting them if he asks. He may even have someone steering clients like this to his properties," I continued to defend my certainty that Alex Boudreaux was already looking for a way to spin things to his advantage. Having the diaries one of his tenants wrote and another tenant stole would give him the bargaining chips Puglisi and Spenser both needed.

"I'll have him rounded up for questioning," Avery offered. He was already reaching for his phone when I grabbed his wrist.

"I have learned that Alex is not someone you assault frontally. Logan will refuse to allow him to answer any questions if we try to interrogate him. We need to spook him and follow him when he jumps. Getting him to make mistakes was how I found most of the evidence the FBI has against him," I reminded Avery. He grudgingly conceded the point.

"I think my brother is right on this one. He needs to finesse whatever he needs to know out of Alex," Tulip took my side. "And he can beat it out of him better than you if it comes to that."

Avery was momentarily shocked by this last thought, and it took him a long moment to realize she was joking. Katie laughed it off faster than anyone else did, but she also flashed me a look to let me know she would not be in my corner if I did so.

twenty-three

Alex Boudreaux was not who I chose to speak with the next morning. He was not going anywhere, and his tongue was only going to soften more and more the longer I left him to worry about what to say when questioned about his role in recent events.

The man I did want to sit down and speak with was Marion Puglisi. I was certain he was not responsible for Enzo 'Hammer' Cammarato's death, but it was time to get a clearer picture of precisely what game he was playing.

The two-story Contemporary-style house Matranga rented for Puglisi backed up to the formidable levee on Oriole Street. The tall earthen barrier was meant to keep Lake Ponchartrain out of the expensive home's backyard. This neighborhood flooded following Hurricane Katrina because the flimsy floodwall along Bayou St. John collapsed, and the levee only served to keep the floodwaters in place. I imagined most of the people who bought any of the rebuilt homes here after Katrina took the same false comfort in the levees as the previous owners did until the storm. History only repeats itself because humans are lousy at learning from experience.

I approached the pair of FBI agents parked across the street from the house and showed them my badge and told them about my intention to interview Puglisi. They were stoic in their reactions to my presence and purpose, but they were also quick to call their boss as I turned to walk away. I estimated I would have half an hour before Conroy decided whether to interrupt our conversation. The paroled felon had no reason to cooperate, and I had no leverage if he refused to speak with me.

I knocked rather than use the doorbell. A pair of strong silent types opened the tall wooden door and stared me down. Both were wearing suits that did nothing to hide the bulges under their armpits caused by the holsters for their sidearms. They looked Italian enough that I did not mistake them for private security guys. These were men with a professional connection to the local crime syndicate and were there to keep out anyone Puglisi chose to ignore. Only an arrest warrant or

Puglisi's curiosity were going to get me past this pair.

"Good morning. I am with the State Police and I would like a moment of Mister Puglisi's time," I informed them and handed one of them my detective business card. They closed the door, and I heard the unmistakable sound of the latch being secured. I began counting and was surprised to have only reached twenty before the door opened and Marion Puglisi personally invited me into his home.

"If you're here about Hammer," he said and held up his right hand, "I swear that I had nothing to do with that."

"I couldn't imagine you did," I agreed. "I don't see where you two would have a beef, and you don't need to do something like that to get a message to your old boss."

"What sort of message do you think I'd want to send?" he asked. His tone was one of mild interest and amusement, without a bit of concern that this was a roundabout way of questioning him.

"That he needs to pay his tab so you can get your watch back," I said and laughed to emphasize it was a joke and not just a sharp reminder about that situation.

"I do miss that watch." He cracked a slight grin and showed me the Patek Philippe his former capo had given him as a consolation prize, or perhaps as collateral.

"Well, we'd appreciate it if someone would pay the tab. Tony is growing partial to your watch and he takes too much pleasure in telling people how he got it."

"That chef guy, he's wearing my watch?" Puglisi did not sound happy about this.

"It's in good hands. He keeps it in the safe when he is working," I reassured him. I couldn't miss how sensitive Puglisi was about the watch.

"I am having my breakfast. Can I get them to bring you something?" Puglisi abruptly changed the topic as he steered me towards the sunroom. There was a metal table and wire-backed chairs on the glass-enclosed porch. A forest of potted plants nearly obscured our view of the levee and backyard. His partially consumed omelet and coffee had both gone cold in his absence. He made a small hand gesture and the man standing beside the table hastily whisked the dishes away and returned a moment later with a pot of hot coffee and a second coffee cup on a saucer. We waited silently for our coffee to be poured and his manservant to close the doors behind him.

"Okay, Detective Holland, to what do I owe this visit?" Puglisi demanded.

"It is somewhere between social and business," I began. "One cop part of me is here to remind you to keep your nose clean. The other cop part of me wants to get a few answers to questions you probably don't want to answer."

"Try me, you never know," he said and picked up his coffee. It allowed him to shield his reaction to the first question I asked.

"Did you really keep diaries, or was that just some smoke you blew up Gavin's skirt because you knew the Justice Department would hear about it?"

His hand trembled just a bit and he took longer to sip his coffee than necessary. His eyes narrowed for just an instant and then he plastered on a big smile and set his coffee cup in its saucer before responding.

"You're a well-informed detective," he sighed. "Do you know that agent guy?"

"He was my father's literary agent for a couple of decades," I informed him.

Puglisi stared at me for an uncomfortably long moment. "That's right, you are Ralph Holland's kid."

"Yes," I confirmed.

"There is no resemblance there at all," he finally mused.

"There's an interesting reason why, but that's not what I came here to discuss." The facial reconstructive surgery I needed after literally having my head caved in during the ambush in Iraq cost me far more than any resemblance to either of my parents. I have a lot of titanium where there used to be skull on my left side and my sister chose my new face from a photo in an Italian version of People magazine.

"Well, you sure as hell ain't here to discuss your old man," he chuckled mostly to himself. "You don't want to hear any of them stories."

"Oh, I don't know," I said indifferently. I never imagined my father was a saint.

"Your daddy never took a bribe to look the other way, at least not from me," he needlessly reassured me. "But he got to know a couple of the girls working in my place on Dauphine Street really well before they shut me down."

"I'm sure he raided your place more than once," I deflected the insinuation.

"Yeah, that's how he knew them," Puglisi laughed sarcastically. He could tell that I understood his implication. "He was really pissed at me back in nineteen eighty-eight. He thought I gave your mom some pictures of him and one of the girls in my place."

"I'm sure that went over well. He used to tell me he left you guys alone because he knew he couldn't get a case against any of you to stick. I think he doubted he could trust the cops around him enough to even start an investigation," I shared. It took a lot of effort to keep a neutral expression about his memories of attempting to break up my parents' marriage.

"He'd try to keep us in line," Puglisi said but offered me no examples or instances. "I guess that was more than he could do with you. Didn't he pack you off to military school back in nineteen eighty-three?"

The man was notably well informed about the private life of a man who should have been his sworn enemy.

"Yeah, something like that," I admitted. My father did, in fact, pull me out of a bar on Bourbon Street when I was sixteen and sent me to the military school his own father and grandfather graduated from in Lexington, Missouri. It proved to be the first step on my path to a long military and intelligence career.

"I heard he died in Katrina. That was no way for a man like him to go out," he tried to press another button.

"It wasn't a proper way for anyone to die, but we are all past that now."

"So, Camille is still around?" Puglisi sounded both surprised and pleased to know my mother was still alive.

"I doubt she is receiving company with your...affiliations," I wanted to dissuade him of any ideas he may have had about paying her a social visit.

He howled in laughter at that response. "No, I am sure she still hates my guts. Pete and I were having our usual Wednesday lunch in the back of La Louisiane when she stormed in and threw them pictures back at me. She said she didn't care and that your daddy needed the practice. Wouldn't you know it, your daddy's former partner and the guy running the FBI here now found a gun in my place that tied me to a murder right after that happened. What were the odds?"

"Like everything else, fifty-fifty," I shrugged indifferently, but took note.

What my mother said to my father about the pictures was probably something far less flippant. They were well on their way to an estranged relationship before I went away to school. My father was living in our weekend camp in the Rigolets when Katrina came, while my mother evacuated from our home just a few blocks from the Seventeenth Street Canal in the West End. Remodeling and occupying the house in the low-lying Rigolets after the storm strikes me as being my mother's way to cast a mentally therapeutic middle finger towards both my father and Mother Nature.

"All of which brings us back around to the question of the diaries. I imagine you have a lot of things written down about people way more influential than my father. That's assuming they really do exist." I needed to refocus the conversation.

"And you can imagine what they would be worth to some of them people," Puglisi said before once again hiding behind his coffee cup.

"I imagine some people would consider killing you to keep your diaries from being shared with the world."

"You might be right," he said and set his cup down. "Then again, maybe they are the only thing keeping me alive."

He looked old, but not all that unhealthy. "I could see where promising someone your diaries might be healthier for you than handing them over."

"It also gives me time to handle some other things I want to do," Puglisi offered without any further elaboration.

"If you are talking revenge, keep in mind that it costs as much to get as it does to give." I warned him. I could not remember the exact quote about digging two graves.

"Anything else I can help you with, detective?" he asked as he began to stand up. I took this to mean the interview was over.

"I'd be interested in anything you can tell me about the attorney who arranged your book deal to get you out of prison." I wanted him to know I knew what happened but did not expect much help with identifying the attorney.

"He's a busy guy," Puglisi sported a wide grin but offered no names. "He got me out of prison and now he's here trying to keep some guy named Bear, of all things, out of jail. He sure gets around."

"I can't say I am quite as much of a fan of his work as you seem to be." I tried to sound casual about my opinion.

twenty-four

I was beginning to understand the potential dangers a daily journal of a mobster like Sunset Puglisi held for himself and anyone he wrote about. The details about my father's affair with one of Puglisi's hookers was a colorful story which could do my dead father no harm. Dragging my mother, who is very much alive, down that same memory lane would be unnecessarily cruel. I understood that my two choices in the matter were to leave her out of it, and then suffer her wrath for not warning her in advance when Puglisi's secrets went public, or to tell her what was happening and take an immediate beating for ruining her day with news about the possible existence of the journals.

Roger, my mother's still unacknowledged romantic companion, was conducting a dog obedience class at the Humane Society in Algiers, so I had her to myself, other than the housekeeper who cleans the place to my mother's standards. These exacting standards have risen in direct proportion to my mother's decreasing participation in everything that comes with owning such a large home.

I found my mother wrapped in a knitted throw on one of the mahogany recliners beside the salt-water pool overlooking the distant remains of Fort Pike. The early spring air was still too cool to spend extended periods of time outdoors without moving about. Roux approached her before I did, and she motioned for him to lie down beside her rather than scamper about in his usual excitement at being here. I have had no luck whatsoever in repeating the exact same hand gesture.

"What brings you all the way out here?" she demanded as soon as I stepped into view and waited for my own cue that I was allowed an audience.

"A little bit of everything," I eased into the conversation. "I wanted to check on you and Roger. I also have a few questions I am hoping that you might be able to answer about a case Bill has me working on."

"Roger and I are fine," she snapped to close that topic. "What sort of questions?"

"Marion Puglisi was released from prison last week." I

inched forward. Her neck stiffened and her eyes locked onto mine as she awaited the harder questions. "The story is that he kept diaries all the way back to when he started working for Marcello in the fifties. Gavin had a book deal worked out for Puglisi that just fell apart, and now there is some question as to whether Puglisi is cooperating with the FBI as part of his parole agreement."

"That horrible man," she mumbled and reached for the cocktail that should have been on the table beside her but wasn't. Roger was her bartender, but he would not be back for a couple of hours. I should have prepared a pitcher of martinis before I opened my mouth despite the hour of the morning.

"Horrible is being generous," I said to show my agreement with her assessment. "He seems to have a detailed memory about his life before he went to prison. He can name dates and precise details of things he did, or what other people did that he knows about, whether or not he ever wrote anything down. He mentioned sending you pictures of my father with a hooker and recalled that your response was direct and immediate."

I tried to make the disclosure as casual and harmless as I could. She would not have been at all happy to learn I was trying to measure Puglisi's memory against hers.

"Your father claimed he slept with the young girl to make Puglisi mad enough to come after him. I believed him, but it did not explain any of his other women," my mother sighed. I was ripping the scab off a far larger wound than I expected.

"Do you remember when this happened?" I felt like I was twisting a knife by staying on the subject.

"It was while you were still in the Army. I don't think Tulip had started junior-high school yet." It was interesting that she could recall general points in her children's lives when this occurred but not the exact year. Puglisi had almost perfect recall about the incident despite his whole world falling apart just a few weeks later. The details of a petty feud with my father were surely not worth locking into his memory as he began losing the battle for his freedom.

"He said it was in nineteen eighty-eight," I said. I needed to let the subject drop.

"It could have been. Nothing much surprised me about your father by then," my mother sighed again.

"Would you like me to get your cigarettes or something?" I offered. Smoking is her second-favorite past time and serves as a ready excuse to step away from boring or argumentative people at parties.

"Please. They are in the kitchen," she said and gave me a weak smile. I offered to bring her cigarettes only because it was more polite than asking if she needed a drink.

I left Roux with her and went to the kitchen for her cigarette case and lighter. I also stopped at the bar long enough to make a vodka martini for my mother and a highball for myself. I was trying to be a good son by not making her drink alone. She accepted the cocktail and cigarettes without a word of thanks or comment on the martini, which she took to her lips before she lit a cigarette.

"How much damage do you think Puglisi could do to our family if he kept diaries?" I pressed forward. I took a seat on the teak lounge opposite hers and Roux came over to curl behind me. He focused his attention on the movements of the house cleaner through the sliding glass doors to the living room.

"A lot, but not to me or you," she readily admitted. "Felix got his start delivering cash envelopes in Baton Rouge for Carlos Marcello when votes needed to be bought or bills that might hurt the Mob needed to die. Your uncle used that foothold in Baton Rouge to start his consulting business after Marcello went to prison. He knew all the crooked politicians, and all the crooks in town knew he could keep a secret."

"Why does that not surprise me?" I said and caught myself before I laughed aloud.

"A lot of famous people's legacies will be trashed if those diaries are released," she said in a tone that quashed any humor or irony I was finding in the matter. "And you are not above any of it either, young man."

"How so?" I challenged her.

"Didn't your father ever tell you who owned that nasty bar he hauled you out of before we sent you to Missouri?" My parents never fully explained their rationale for sending me away. What little discussion there was focused on needing to save our family's reputation from my reckless behavior.

"I always assumed it was a Mob-owned place, but that was

true of a lot of bars back then."

"Your father was sure they were planning to use you to get at him. A couple of other detectives were being blackmailed to keep bad things someone in their family had done a secret. He was worried they might get you into drugs or something worse." I kept my mouth shut as she explained this to me. Nothing good was going to come from telling her I would have been more careful had they simply explained this to me at the time. Instead, I felt banished for nearly thirty years and only welcomed home because I agreed to find an answer to my father's disappearance.

"No, he never mentioned that was the reason," I sighed and finished my own drink in two gulps. I set my glass down and reached over to scratch Roux behind his ear.

"That story is probably in the man's diaries, if he really kept them," my mother warned me. Her purpose in bringing up my own past was no more to hurt me than I meant to hurt her in warning her there might be possible disclosures about my father. She wanted me to understand the sort of accusations that were likely to be made against other people we both knew, such as Chief of Detectives William Avery. Many powerful people would face negative retrospective judgement, and the court of public opinion always rules more harshly than a court of law.

"What a mess," I declared for lack of anything else to say. I nudged Roux and stood up to leave. He padded over to get a last ear scratch from my mother, who had obviously forgotten she spent my entire childhood advocating against our having a family pet.

"Hold on just a minute." My mother held up her right hand as she set the coverlet aside and stood up. "You may as well have this now that you know about it."

"What's that?" I was at something of a loss as to what she could be talking about.

"I kept a souvenir," she nearly growled. "I figured it would be useful if your father and I ever got a divorce."

I had an inkling now of what she was talking about. I was, though, still unprepared for the photograph she pulled from beneath the larger of the three jewelry cases in her bedroom's massive closet. She had expanded her closet and updated the master bath during the post-storm renovations. I quietly assumed Roger's clothes were in a guest room closet, if only to support my mother's failed subterfuge about their romance.

The five by seven-inch photograph was not of professional quality, but my father was instantly recognizable. Anyone who knew the woman would have had no trouble putting a name to her profile on my father's lower abdomen. She looked like she was barely of legal age, which surprised me when I remembered how old the women he was accused of having slept with later had been. I studied the photo and guessed it was taken through a false mirror in the room. It suggested Puglisi extorted other influential men for similar indiscretions. The way my father faced almost directly into the camera suggested he was aware the photograph was being taken, as though he wanted the picture to be seen. He miscalculated if he believed the images would only get as far as Puglisi, or that he was never going to pay for the indiscretion.

"There were a dozen photographs. That horrible creature mailed them to our house," she recalled and shuddered at the recollection. Making sure my father was aware that Puglisi knew where our family lived was likely meant as its own threat.

"I don't suppose he mentioned the woman's name," I gingerly inquired. My mother gave me one of her most steely-eyed stares.

"No, that was certainly never part of the discussion," she responded. "Take this with you. Maybe your father told Bill what her name was. There isn't going to be any divorce, so I no longer need to hold onto this sort of garbage."

"Alright," I said and hastily placed the photograph into the messenger bag full of things like a first aid trauma kit and spare ammunition. I would have thanked her for the photograph, but that seemed like the wrong thing to say in the moment.

"I'll call Felix and let him know what you're working on," my mother offered. I never intended to involve my shady uncle in any of this, but I was not going to tell her not to warn her brother that his nefarious past might finally see the light of day.

"That's fine, just be sure to tell him to keep his distance," I pleaded with her. The last thing I needed was to need to clean up any mess Uncle Felix created by trying to reach a deal of his own with Marion Puglisi for his silence.

twenty-five

The photograph was painful to look at. I sat in the windowless office I keep in my apartment and studied it for any sort of detail that might help me understand either my father's motivation in using the woman to provoke Puglisi or the logic he applied to forgive himself for cheating on my mother. He apparently had no trouble applying that same logic in the years to come, but I wanted to believe that his moral flexibility was not fully developed at the time this particular photograph was taken.

Looking into my father's eyes reinforced my certainty that he was aware he was being photographed. He wanted whoever saw the photos of his tryst to know it was him. It was not hard to imagine what the next image in the series entailed judging by the position of the two bodies, and a tiny piece of my curiosity wondered how much his expression changed in those moments.

I estimated the woman to be in her late teens at best. It was impossible to be certain about her skin tone in the black-and-white image, but she seemed to have the classic features and skin tone of a local Creole. Her hair was loose, but it looked thick and had the sort of fine wiriness African American women retain even as their hair grows longer. Hers was pulled to her right, intentionally exposing her face to the camera she surely knew was recording their tryst. Her hair appeared to have been at least shoulder length when she was standing upright. The placement of her left hand saved me from making an uncomfortable anatomical comparison of father and son.

Three of my office walls are nearly floor to ceiling whiteboards. The fourth wall is filled with the door, a locked file cabinet, and a heavy gun safe. I diagram my cases so I can visualize both what is known and remains unknown.

The board to my left contains the photos and scribbled biographies of the running cast of characters I need to keep straight, with any interpersonal connections noted. The right hand one holds photos and diagrams of the crime scenes.

The largest of the three boards covers the back wall. I use it for building a timeline. I add any related incidents I learn about which transpired before or after the crime. I find it handy to know if I am looking at an isolated incident or a pattern of similar crimes. You are far more likely to get away with your first crime, no matter how sloppy, if you make it your only crime. Multiple events indicate I am after a far more determined and experienced criminal than the mere opportunist. Professional criminals expect me to catch them eventually and do their best to make sure any evidence I collect is hard to connect to them.

The timeline remained my best hope for making sense of this case. The line on the board in front of me was interrupted by hash marks denoting criminal acts as they occurred over time. The first surprise that came to me in reviewing the board was that Sunset Puglisi had not replaced the burglary as the center of my attention. All roads seemed to lead to him, but somewhere inside my head was the sense that the burglary held more answers than did Puglisi or his diaries.

The missing diaries would lose their validity if Puglisi were not alive to corroborate their contents. Puglisi seemed to be racing a pair of clocks. There was no telling how long he could stall the FBI or how long it would take his former capo to decide what to do about his offering a written record of his misdeeds to the FBI. Any opportunities for the retaliation Puglisi sought thanks to his early release would end with his death. Anything I hoped or needed to learn from him was on this same crowded and uncertain timeline.

It was the photograph that forced me to reconsider the entire timeline. I realized my original chronology began at the wrong point. I was confronted with the repercussions of something which may have begun twenty or thirty years before the burglary on Dauphine Street. Cammarato's murder might have settled an old score and have had nothing to do with Puglisi's journals. I had no interest in trying to find a hitman plus a separate burglar, and I instinctively knew they were not the same person. I doubted whether they even had the same motivation.

I walked out of the office and poured myself a couple of fingers of Elijah Craig bourbon and sank onto the sofa next to where Roux was napping. His paws were twitching as though he might be giving chase in his dreams. I knew not to pet him in those moments. Neither of us are creatures to startle while sleeping. Our survival instincts awaken ahead of our newly learned inhibitions.

I took a deep pull on the booze and let its warmth soothe the tension that was beginning to form over the prospect of interrogating my boss about his years as my father's partner, the time of the photograph, and the search that sent Puglisi to prison. I was sure Chief Avery never anticipated the case reaching this level of complexity when he assigned me to help Detective Bassett. Then again, maybe he did and wanted me to be the one to question him when the time came.

twenty-six

"I heard you spoke with Puglisi this morning," Chief Avery said to open the conversation over our luncheon pastas at the chef's table in the kitchen of Strada Ammazarre. Barely three hours had passed since I had walked out of the house on Oriole Street and Avery already knew I had been there. Conroy and Avery seemed to be sharing a lot more information than either of them was providing me.

"He took me on a sentimental journey through his memories of trying to wreck my parents' marriage," I offered up as a beginning topic. Chief Avery couldn't catch himself before his left eyebrow arched for just an instant. "My mother gave me the last of the photographs Puglisi mailed to our house."

"That was ugly. I found out after the fact. There was never much I could have done anyway. Your father had been promoted by then and I was just another one of the detectives working under him." Avery picked a couple of pieces of shrimp out of the angel hair pasta and its lemon-butter sauce before he said anything else. I intentionally kept my silence lest he change the subject. "He wound up sleeping in his office for a week after your mother got sight of those pictures."

"Puglisi claims the girl and my father stirred up a hornet's nest," I offered.

"To say the least," Avery sighed. It was obvious he wanted to change the subject as soon as possible. "Your father claimed he slept with her to provoke Puglisi into coming after him. Neither of us thought we could prove Puglisi murdered the informant, so your father decided that claiming self-defense would allow him to kill Puglisi legally. Then we got a tip about the gun out of the blue. Your father called the FBI and Conroy and I executed the search warrant together. The bust was good for both of our careers."

"What were the odds of Puglisi keeping the gun he used to kill someone, especially after he realized he was suspect?" It seemed beyond unlikely.

"We weren't going to look a gift horse in the mouth. The jury didn't either." Avery decided to change the subject. "What else did you learn from him? Maybe something we could take to court?"

"Not to court, but I have a better understanding of the real danger he poses in running loose. He has a mind like a steel trap whether he wrote anything down or not. He remembered the year the picture was taken, my mother's name, and what she told him after she saw the pictures like it was yesterday. If he starts to talk to the Feds, a lot of well-known people are going to see their names in the news." I said and set my fork down on my plate. I could feel my mouth getting dry, so I took a sip of iced tea before I broached the next topic. "Is there anything in your own past that we need to worry about?"

"That's a helluva question to ask," he snapped and tossed his napkin down in the middle of his food. I could tell that his anger was genuine, because there was a bite of pasta twirled on his fork and he never leaves a bite of food uneaten.

"It sure is, but I need to know about the skeletons in everyone else's closet so I don't get blindsided again. Sooner or later, I may need to count on someone that won't be able to have my back because of something they did thirty years ago." This was not the first time I found myself questioning the loyalty of those around me. An act of treachery by the handler of my intelligence mission in Iraq nearly cost me my life.

"Fair enough," Avery grumbled. "Your dad and I were never on a pad, but every cop knew where to get a free meal or a good deal on a new television. Being a cop has never paid enough, and NOPD ignored a lot of gray areas back then. There were criminals we couldn't arrest, but that didn't mean we couldn't shake them down. We'd take our wives for a meal at certain places we couldn't afford and there would be no bill. Favors like that were common for detectives and the brass. They may still be for all I know, but I don't play that game anymore, and I don't let any of my detectives think they can get away with it either."

"Our own arrangement notwithstanding." I delicately pointed out his ability to eat for free at Strada and grinned to ease the mood. He had a point about the difference in the eras. Puglisi could decimate NOPD's senior ranks by sharing just a few carefully chosen recollections of those old ways of doing things with the press or the Feds. "You and most of the brass could all be hung out to dry if Puglisi starts talking."

"Why do you think Conroy is so interested in what he has to say? NOPD isn't the only one hiding skeletons in their closet. The organized crime guys at DOJ and the FBI were cozy with the local mobsters back then as well. Puglisi is a walking time bomb," Avery assured me. The extent of the rot reached beyond New Orleans if the stories about Puglisi killing people for other Mob families was true. It was hard to tell if it was worse that Puglisi kept the missing diaries or that Puglisi was out on parole with a head full of potentially weaponized memories.

"So, everyone has a reason to worry about the man," I finally realized. "All the same, none of this explains what part dumping Cammarato's body in Bayou Saint John plays into any of this."

"Maybe it isn't related at all," Avery suggested. "Something is happening, for sure, but I am afraid none of us see what it is because we are focused on the wrong things."

"Being right about a theory like that has probably never felt this unsatisfactory," I commiserated.

"You need to find those diaries," Avery snapped me out of my thought bubble. "The FBI will use them to force NOPD into a consent decree, and to save themselves from a similar purge. Puglisi's partners don't want him sharing what he knows with anyone, and they are more likely to kill him because they have reason to believe he is talking to us after your visit this morning."

"Then here," I said and pushed the photograph towards him, face down. He glanced at it before hastily tucking it into his jacket pocket. "Find her name and I'll do my best to find her. I think the answers to what is happening right now are buried somewhere back then, and she must have been a bigger part of it than you knew."

There was no way to verbally respond to Avery's insistence that I accomplish the impossible. I had no idea where to look for what might not exist, and having him scour records to put a name with a face from nearly thirty years ago was mostly a delaying tactic on my part.

twenty-seven

Roux was still asleep on the sofa when I returned to my apartment after lunch. I lifted his leash from its hook by the front door and rattled the door handle a couple of times to wake him. It took him only a moment to realize I was offering an opportunity to get out of the confines of the apartment and not an opportunity to defend our home. He sprang upright and launched himself from the sofa to land facing me and broke into a slobbering grin as I led him to the elevator.

"Something up?" Tony challenged us as we passed the bistro's small glassed-in office next to the elevators at the rear of the building. He was organizing the day's invoices for Juaquin during the lull between lunch and the beginning of dinner prep.

"It's time to take Roux for a patrol," I unnecessarily explained myself. I always walk Roux after lunch.

"Be careful," Tony said and went back to the paperwork.

I led Roux silently through the kitchen to the delivery door opening to Decatur Street rather than through the restaurant. I paused for a moment in order to be sure we were seen by anyone monitoring my coming and goings from the bistro. I glanced across the street and noticed Matranga's table full of trouble was empty. It was still a little before their usual time to arrive, but I wondered if Cammarato's murder made his capo leery about making any more public appearances. Their continued absence could be a sign that Matranga took the homicide as a warning to himself and not as a threat against Puglisi. I began to process the possibilities as Roux and I turned the corner at Esplanade and onto North Peters.

I don't normally walk Roux through the crowded confines of the French Market's open air flea market, but the foot traffic was lighter than usual. The New Orleans Jazz and Heritage Festival is the starter's gun for the summer festivals and these same stalls had been packed with tourists from around the world for the past two weekends. The number of festivals in New Orleans had expanded in the years I was away. As a child, it used to be that there was just the unmerciful heat of summer to look forward to between Jazz Fest and Halloween. There were now one or two small festivals happening every week of the year. Some were narrowly focused, but the city has always been a place where you can find someone with your own peculiar interests in common to pass a good time.

"Hey, I need to talk to you," Darnell shouted as we approached the Moonwalk. He hurried to close the distance as Roux and I took a seat on the concrete steps leading up to the observation deck overlooking Algiers Point and Jackson Square.

"What's the problem?" I asked and waited for him to catch his breath. Roux sniffed the air and wrinkled his nose at the particularly fragrant clothes Darnell was wearing. He must not have been to one of the shelters where he could do his laundry in a while.

"There are two problems. Which do you want to hear first?" he asked. The expression on his face was not playful. I sat up straighter and focused on what he had to say. Things must have taken a bad turn if Darnell was being this serious.

"Start with the one I can solve," I suggested. I can handle most things he brings me with a couple of phone calls.

"I don't know how you are going to solve either one." He paused to consider which to hit me with first. "Someone put out a bounty on the watch Tony is wearing. There is no money offered for roughing up Tony, just for taking the watch he is wearing. Does that make any sense at all? Why would someone want his watch?"

"Because it belongs to someone else," I gave him the short version. Puglisi must have wasted very little time placing the offer for the watch on the criminal grapevine after I left his house. "What's the bounty?"

"A grand," Darnell said. That was a lot of money to the sort of thieves who might think rolling Tony would be easy. It would still be tempting even to those who knew Tony would resist rather than hand it over.

"Figures. The guy who wants it is trying to shave off most of what he owes us," I said and couldn't help but laugh at Puglisi's way of handling things. I was tempted to get the word out that we would pay a handsome reward for something of Puglisi's but nothing he owned or wore came to mind. I certainly wasn't about to spread the word that we were looking for the man's diaries. "Okay, not much I can do about that one. What is the other problem?"

"That girl from Denver, you remember her, right?" A knot formed in my gut from the range of bad things that immediately came to mind.

"I do," I said and let him continue.

"Well, she is working over at the Night Owl," he said this and drew in his breath in anticipation of a fiery reaction. This exact scenario was what I dreaded when I first spotted her, and this was why I gave him the money to keep her fed and warm. The only surprise was how fast it happened.

The Night Owl was on the lowest tier of strip joints in the Quarter. It was, in fact, such a dive that it was not located on a street many tourists walked, day or night. The place was so notoriously bad when I was a teenager that not even pubescent boys could be lured to drink there underage to ogle the burnt-out strippers the place employed. This was the club where strippers who were too old, too strung out, or clearly underage came to begin or end their careers. "She met a couple of strippers who were eating at Café du Monde and they offered her a place to stay. You know the rest."

"Is she actually stripping?" This was the worst-case scenario in my mind. Stripping at the Night Owl would eventually involve crack or meth and a manager who planned on pimping her out once her drug habit was bad enough.

"No, she is just serving drinks. For now," he stammered a bit. He obviously took her departure from beneath his protective wing as a personal failure.

"When did she leave?"

"Not long after you saw her. It's been a couple of days now since we have seen her," Darnell said. I imagined she spent the tips from her first night or two on booze and hot meals for her homeless buddies. Nobody worried about her until the gravy train ended.

"Okay, I'll look into it," I sighed. Looking into it meant pulling her out of the place by her hair if need be and sending her back to a slightly lesser hell in Colorado.

"Thank you." Darnell gave me a relieved smile. There was a time when he and Boomer would have waded through the Night Owl's bouncers and regulars to take the young girl out of harm's way themselves. Those days were long past.

A frontal assault was not going to be my tactic, either. The statistical odds were that I would get her out of the place only for her to turn around and go right back. Whatever small measure of personal integrity or pride she ever had was crushed the minute she took the job. She was counting on the manager who hired her to keep her safe from harm, but the extent of the man's concern was to minimize any damage which could diminish her potential profit. She had thrown herself into the stream of misfortune that came with living on the streets and was counting on her lousy survival instincts to stay afloat. Lecherous men were nothing new to her, but now she had the false comfort of a dry roof over her head and a wad of dollar bills in her pocket every day. Another month on this path and she would have a drug habit to feed and plenty of bad advice about how to support it.

I called Captain Hammond at the state police as Roux and I passed St. Louis Cathedral and started down Pirate's Alley. It was considerably quieter in the narrow passage than on the plaza in front of the landmark cathedral, where tourists and locals crammed together to window shop among the artists whose wares adorned the high metal fence around Jackson Square.

"I need a small favor," I said and waited for some sort of negative retort.

"You do realize that the things we do around here that are related to real police work are not called favors, don't you detective?" Captain Hammond snarked on cue.

"Okay, then I need someone from the liquor control office to roust the Night Owl. I know of at least one underage girl working there as a cocktail waitress." I reported.

"Rousting is not something they do," he reminded me. "Would you like to file a formal complaint and have me forward it to them?"

"That sounds like a lot of paperwork for a few minutes of someone's time," I told him. I was not playing around, despite the tone of our conversation. The procedure he suggested would take weeks to yield results.

There was a long moment of silence from the other end of the line.

"What's the girl to you?" Hammond asked, and rather pointedly at that.

"She's a runaway from Colorado. Her stepfather was making the moves on her, so she took off. She's sixteen and wound up at the Night Owl before I could get Family Services involved. They aren't going to go in there after her," I explained, while fibbing about ever having considered involving the state's child-care services.

"You want us to pull her out and send her home so you aren't the bad guy? Does that about sum up what you are asking me to do?" Hammond sounded even less inclined to lend a hand than when I began the conversation.

"I'll be the bad guy who sends her home," I lied. "I just don't want to play Walking Tall in a dump like that if I can avoid it. Liquor Control has a subtler hand than I do."

"I'll get back to you," he said and hung up without further comment. Threatening to break a place up on my own had hopefully spurred him to find a quick and tidy solution.

Two more people I met on our patrol informed me of Puglisi's interest in getting his watch back. It was obvious that this was the sort of opportunity the Quarter's pettiest of petty thieves must dream about. Armed robbery is safer for the guy holding the gun than the victim on the wrong end of the barrel. There were plenty of fences willing to pay for quality jewelry they could send to Atlanta or Houston and launder through a pawn shop, or to hold for a few months and then dump on eBay. None of them were offering any thief a grand for a watch, not even a Rolex.

Roux and I returned to the restaurant and Tony could tell that the walk had benefitted my dog more than it had me. I was getting a headache from the tension rising from my jaw and neck as I thought about the variety of situations I needed to resolve. Figuring out who broke into Boudreaux's property competed for my attention with deciding what to tell my sister about Puglisi and the pictures of our father, locating Spenser Duncan, and determining the validity of the story about the diaries, and then getting my hands on them if they really did exist. At least I had no reason to suspect the girl from Colorado in the vandalism to the house on Dauphine Street or what became of Spenser Duncan, or of knowing the whereabouts of

Sunset's diaries.

"Who told you?" Tony demanded as I stood waiting for the elevator.

"Told me what?"

"That there is a price for the watch," he said in his usual malapropist fashion.

"Better question is who told you?" I countered. "Richie and the guys at the pizzeria still have their ears to the ground?"

"I count on it," Tony affirmed. We both were relying on the reformed street dealers remaining tuned to the underworld they had supposedly left behind. They never tell me much of anything, but they have displayed a collective willingness to give Tony details they know full well he will repeat to me.

"Just lock it in the safe and keep your eyes open," I beseeched him. He nodded as though he agreed to do so, but I knew he was looking forward to having a chance to defend himself.

twenty-eight

"How was your day?" Katie asked when she arrived at Strada after court. The judge in her trial had allowed testimony by the defense to run an hour longer than usual because he wanted to avoid giving the attorneys for the serial rapist Katie meant to see publicly castrated any grounds for a retrial.

"Not uneventful, but not as productive as your own," I tried to deflect. Tulip would be joining us in a few minutes and the last thing I wanted to be discussing was the clear evidence of our father's infidelity and poor professional conduct.

"Right," she snapped at me for my evasiveness. Jason brought her first glass of champagne and she took a moment to enjoy its effervescence upon the tongue she intended to lash me with once this moment of Zen was complete. "So, tell me the things you can discuss standing at a bar."

"I spoke with Sunset Puglisi this morning. We discussed my father, and I will repeat that conversation in private. It led to driving out to see my mother, who was surprisingly well prepared for what I had to tell her, and that conversation we will also have in private," I danced around the issues. I certainly wasn't going to share lurid details about my father and a teenaged hooker with an entire bar full of regulars.

"What else?" she pressed. "Surely there has been some sort of development that you can tell me about. My cases are so terribly straightforward. I need you to liven up my day with the messes you make of your own."

"I figured out that the attorney who got Puglisi out of prison is the same one trying to keep Bear Brovartey out of one. I don't know what he has to do with anything else, but it is interesting that one man is doing so much for so few," I offered to discuss.

"Don't get me started on defense attorneys," Katie hissed. "What else?"

"Puglisi apparently put out a bounty on his wristwatch after we spoke. He must really hate that Tony is wearing it," I finally mentioned, and began playing down the threat when I saw her reaction. "He isn't after Tony, just the watch. I am sure he has absolutely no idea the problems he is about to cause himself."

"No, I'm sure he does not," Katie finally found something that could make her smile. "Someone is going to get hurt trying to collect that bounty and it won't be Tony."

"I will have to back Tony when it's time to let Puglisi know he isn't getting the watch back that way." I needed to test the waters for how the State's Attorney's office was going to view the matter.

"The law allows Tony to defend himself," she allowed. "But he is not an American citizen so he can't legally carry a gun and you can't legally use him as bait to set a trap. Go talk to the Mob guy again and let him know he can be sent back to prison for soliciting a crime."

"I'm sure telling him that will fix everything," I responded a bit too dryly.

"Fine, I'll have him in my office tomorrow to tell him myself. Should I mention our friend's history to let him consider the sort of retribution Tony will exact if anyone attacks him?" Katie was not in a playful mood at all. Katie knows a few things about Tony's time as an assassin for Saddam Hussein's intelligence service, and as much as she cares to know about the violent things the chef and I did during our disavowed operation in Baghdad.

"Drag him in and warn him how medieval a guy raised in medieval places can be," I suggested. The thought of her stomping on Puglisi certainly had a certain appeal.

"Or maybe we should let them find out for themselves," she suggested and focused on her drink. I sensed a trap and did not respond to her apparent permission for Tony to unleash unholy hell on whomever accosted him for Puglisi's watch.

twenty-nine

The chef's table was reserved for a group of tourists wealthy enough to stay in town for the entire week of Jazz Fest, so Juaquin seated us at one of the booths lining the far wall of the main dining room once Tulip arrived.

One of the bistro's newest hires was assigned to serve us. The petite brunette was a UNO student named Shannon. Her jitters at being our server showed. Katie assured her that the stories she had heard about how vicious she and Tulip could be involved work-related episodes and should not be taken as any indication they might bite her head off. I reminded her that my signature was not on her paycheck and told her to relax because we were the one table that she could not run off with bad service. None of this did much to calm her down, but the glass of wine Tulip offered went a long way.

"I got a very strange call from Mother today," Tulip said during our salad course. "She said I should ask you about father's infidelities. She seemed to have a particular one in mind."

"Did she now?" I asked, to stall the inevitable. I could see Katie instantly deduced that this was one of the things I had chosen not to discuss earlier. "What else did she say to ask?"

"Mother said that people might start talking about our father again because of a case you are working. I take it she is worried that people are going to say some pretty nasty things," Tulip prodded. I was going to need to remind my mother that delivering bad news of this sort is a mother's job and not the responsibility of an older brother.

"I don't know how many people would be talking, but the subject of our father's well- known philandering might crop up again. He slept with a mobster's girlfriend to punish him for killing an informant. Mother kept one of the photographs the mobster took of them together, possibly as blackmail." I did my best to close as many avenues for discussion as I could. "It was years ago and there is no reason to believe anyone is going to care."

"She kept a picture?" This was all that my younger sister noted in what I told her.

"Not a particularly good one, but both faces are very clear. I need to identify the woman in the picture and try to track her down to see if she remembers this."

"I can help with that," Tulip offered.

"Bill is working on it." I held up a hand to end discussion on the matter. I knew from experience that she would depose the witness if she found her first.

"You may as well tell her the rest," Katie said and kicked me under the table.

"The same mobster owes us for a meal. Tony is holding his watch as collateral, and the guy is offering to pay anyone who can get his watch back from Tony," I said with what I hoped was the proper air of dismissal.

"Well, that was a stupid thing to do," Tulip snorted into her napkin. It is one of her most embarrassing habits, but her highest level of a laugh comes out as a snort.

"That's what we all think. The boys over at the pizzeria told Tony about it and I heard about the bounty from Darnell. So the word is out. Hopefully so is the word that it is a suicide mission to try to take the watch," I tried to reassure my sister.

"What are you two going to do?" Tulip pressed me.

I gave her a blank stare for an instant. "Tony and me or Katie and me?"

"Either or both."

"Tony is going to stop wearing the watch around town and Katie will drag Puglisi in if anyone makes a move on Tony. I am going to do everything I can to make sure Tony doesn't get himself in any trouble defending himself. For one thing, he can't carry a gun." I was less than confident that I had made this clear to my partner when we discussed his self-defense options earlier. The truth is a gun would involve less of a mess and painful injuries for his attacker than his likely manner of defending himself without one.

"Who is this mobster, anyway?" Tulip returned to my initial explanation.

"Marion Puglisi. His street name was Sunset. He began killing people for Carlos Marcello and Chicago's Outfit back in the late Fifties. He ran a brothel on Dauphine Street just off Esplanade back in the Seventies and Eighties. That was when he and our father crossed swords over the girl, as it were," I tried to joke.

"Funny," Tulip scowled at my attempt at humor with the double entendre. Katie nudged me sharply with her elbow as well.

"Anyway, the story is that the guy killed an informant over a shylock's debt and our father's response was to try to provoke Puglisi into trying to kill him so he could justify killing Puglisi," I continued.

"That's where you get it," Katie chuckled mostly to herself. I didn't bother telling her that I had come to the same conclusion earlier when Puglisi told me the story.

"Puglisi was indicted and sent to prison before anything happened," I finished.

Shannon swapped our plates during this conversation and Tulip chewed a bite of broiled redfish crusted with breadcrumbs and soaked with Sambuca while she decided what to pursue next. The colorful maque choux mix of fried corn and bell peppers the fish filet rested upon looked delicious. Her level of distraction over the notion of a mobster threatening two generations of her family meant I could finally eat my veal piccata without her usual recriminations about animal cruelty. Katie frowned slightly when she saw my selection before focusing her attention on the massive lumps of blue crab in her serving of crab au gratin.

"But now this Puglisi guy is just walking around threatening people?" Tulip resumed the conversation.

"The story I have pieced together is that Puglisi was sentenced to twenty-five years to life for killing the informant, though he supposedly killed a lot more people than that. I found out Puglisi had a book deal with Gavin to publish the journals he supposedly wrote before he was sent to prison. You can imagine what a mobster's diary would contain. There might be something to the story about the diaries, because the Mob has been paying him a million dollars a year to keep his mouth shut and someone ripped holes in the walls of his old house days before he came back to town," I tried to get everything into one long explanation rather than have her drag me through a full deposition over dinner. I did not bother specifying which parts were conjecture and which I stood any chance of proving.

"What part of all that are you working on?" Tulip wondered.

"Bill called me in to help a rookie detective investigate the burglary. That was when he explained the connection between the house and Puglisi." I intentionally left out any mention of Alex Boudreaux's subsequent ownership. "Anything else?"

I wanted to get back to my meal. I planned to enjoy a square of tiramisu and a snifter of Armagnac, for Katie and me to walk Roux, and then to lock him out of the bedroom which Katie shares with me most weekends. Her home had become something of a child of divorce for the two of us, except we needed to spend time with it rather than for it spend time with us. Katie was entirely opposed to selling it to move in with me and I was not inclined to leave the French Quarter. So, for now, we spend every other weekend at one another's place and an occasional evening during the week. She tends to spend more time at my apartment because she needs to cook and clean far less than when I am at' her house. Also, my bar is about fifty feet longer than her bar cart, and has a bartender.

"Yeah, one question comes to mind," Tulip said after a pause long enough to make me believe she might be ready to change the subject. "Why pay him a million dollars?"

"What do you mean?" Katie asked before I could.

"You said they were paying Puglisi a million dollars a year to keep his mouth shut," Tulip reminded me. "What's a guy serving life in prison going to do with a million dollars a year? It's not like it went into his canteen fund for toothpaste."

"That's a lot of toothpaste," I reflexively agreed. I was stumped. This had not even crossed my mind as being an issue. Paying Puglisi for his silence made so much sense I was overlooking his inability to spend the money.

"Imagine his reaction if you found those millions and took them from him," Tulip grinned. Finding and freezing hidden assets amounts to a hobby for my sister. She has been known to base her choice of clients solely on the opportunity to financially punish bad people. Her reputation and track record have reached the point that simply retaining her tempts even the toughest defense counsel to settle out of court.

"It would likely be taken as the sort of provocation your father gave by sleeping with the man's girl," Katie suggested.

thirty

I decided to spend the next afternoon retracing the few steps Bassett and I had made in the case. The house on Dauphine Street was still considered to be a crime scene because the burglary remained unsolved. I wished that this were more of an inconvenience to Alex Boudreaux than it was, but I took some satisfaction in knowing he was going to feel like a suspect until Bassett or I proved his innocence.

Bassett had given me a copy of the key to the property the same day Avery assigned me to the case, so I decided to search the premises one more time as Roux and I passed by during our after-lunch patrol. I had not been back since learning the identity of two of its owners in its storied history.

The former mansion smelled musty, as unoccupied properties inevitably will, and its brick walls blocked what small amount of traffic and pedestrian noise there was nearby. The silence took some getting used to, as did the clicking of Roux's claws on the floating staircase and the wide plank heart-pine flooring in the second-floor hallway. I was able to locate the room where my father committed his dirty deed by the wallpaper and posters on the wall, though the wall décor had been moved about at some point. Puglisi's working girls were booted out the day the Justice Department impounded the property and none of the caretakers had bothered to update a single thing. That made sense to me, as the only tenants since Puglisi's girls moved out were either in witness protection or living here for free while working for FEMA during the initial response to Hurricane Katrina five years ago. Neither type of occupant was inclined to want to make it feel like home.

I used the photograph as a reference to look for the location of the camera. I found a smooth rectangle in the texture of a painted-over patch behind a poster of one of Prince's busty protégés hanging over the dresser. Any two-way mirror would have had to be mounted flush to the wall and then framed to look like a mirror, so this was the exact anomaly I sought. The poster was hanging over the head of the bed in the photograph but someone had moved it to conceal the patch where the built-in mirror hung. A regular hanging mirror was strategically angled where the poster once hung above the bed. At least this was a more honest use of a mirror.

I led Roux to the adjoining room and found that room's built-in closet bore a smooth patch which lined up to the spot in the opposite wall. It didn't really matter whether the closet was built before or after the false mirror was installed to blackmail far more prominent men than my father. The photographer would have had this room to himself to record the trysts. I could not envision Puglisi personally doing this sort of work, and I was not inclined to try to track down his camera operator. I had nowhere to begin in such a pursuit, and it was likely the guy had died in some nursing home by now. Time had covered a lot of the paths I would have pursued were this my case twenty years sooner. I was limited now to anything or anyone I stood a decent chance of finding.

Roux wandered off while I rehung the poster in the first apartment. I spotted him sniffing at the bathroom door in an apartment directly across the hall.

"We good?" I asked him from the doorway of the apartment I was standing in.

Roux glanced at me and then sat down facing the door. This is never a good sign.

"Hier," I said in a loud whisper. Roger had patiently trained Roux to respond to a dozen or so specific commands in Dutch so he would understand that what I said in that language were work instructions. We didn't want him to attack anyone by misinterpreting something I said in normal conversation.

I slid my ten-millimeter Glock sidearm from its shoulder holster and raised the pistol to a firing position. I levelled the red dot of its laser sight on the center of the door and began to inch across the room, placing each foot ahead of the other as quietly as I could.

Roux stretched flat on the bare wooden floor and began inching backwards to my position. I waited until he was behind me before taking the last two steps and placing my right hand on the door handle to the bathroom. I glanced down and made sure Roux would be out of the line of fire when I opened the door and then gently twisted the knob until the slack was out

125

of the mechanism. I eased the latch open, and then released my breath as I swung the heavy pistol through the doorway and swept the close space for any threats. I only exposed my right hand, which held the pistol, and one eye in the open doorway in case anyone opened fire. I heard no motion and took a deep breath before I stepped into the room. I remained prepared to drop flat at the first hint of danger. Roux would remain in the doorway until I ordered him to follow me or someone tried to run past me without my permission. He would waste no time in taking down a suspect with all the force and joy of a lion tackling a gazelle.

The bathroom was empty, but someone had returned to rip out the sink since my initial visit. I did a quick search of the other rooms on the second floor and found that every bathroom was now damaged. The odds of this being the work of a second vandal struck me as remote. I noticed a new footprint in the plaster dust near the door to the third floor. I distinctly remembered there being five sets when Bassett and I were there last: the burglar's, the responding officer's, Avery's, Bassett's and mine. This new set matched the size, but not the shoe, of the burglar. Whether this intruder was Spenser Duncan or not, the offender had serious cajones to return to finish the job. I thought they had done a thorough job the first time, but someone clearly believed there was something here, or perhaps they were given new information that brought them back. The footprints exposed the latest attempt.

"Hier," I repeated the command to Roux. I waited until he was beside me before I placed my hand on the doorknob to the attic apartment. I released the door handle and pressed myself to the adjacent wall after I heard something moving in the apartment. I counted to three and then opened the door with my left hand, pushing it away from where I stood and then waited another second for whoever was upstairs to say something or fire a weapon in response to my presence.

I unsnapped the heavy leash from Roux's collar and pointed to the stairwell. This was all he needed for permission to sprint to the top of the stairs. He would detain any living thing he found and failing that would begin sniffing for dangers or things like explosives or drugs that he was trained to believe I would reward him for finding.

I waited for the thudding sound of Roux's impact with a human body. All I heard was a single sharp bark so I began making my way up the narrow stairwell. I paused at a point on the stairs where I could survey the room without fully exposing myself. I swept the room with my eyes focused only on my handgun's laser sight. I then reversed the scan to take a wider view to find what had caught Roux's interest.

I gave him a slightly annoyed expression when I found no menace. I cocked my head and waved one arm around the room to order him to show me what caught his attention. I waited to move until Roux sat down beside the unmade bed at the rear of the apartment. This end of the apartment was still coated with a fine layer of dust from the destruction of the plaster and lath walls, and the drywall demolished by taking apart the bathroom. Someone had shaken the dust from the covers and slept in the bed since the last time I was in the apartment. There were footprints in the dust which did not match the shoes Avery, Bassett, or I wore when we met here. I followed the footprints and discovered that whoever was crashing in the apartment used the fire escape in the back of the house to get in and out of the apartment. There was a temptation to set up surveillance to see who was living there, but my search of the bedroom downstairs was sure to alert them to the continued interest of the police in the property.

I didn't need to ponder very hard on who was sleeping here. There was only one person who was aware the bedroom was available with the strength to climb the metal ladder leading from the apartment's rear window to the main fire escape one floor below. This near encounter convinced me that Spenser Duncan was still in town. The only curious thing was that Spenser supposedly had a key to the front door. His presence was more likely to be noted as suspicious while crossing the rear neighbor's patio than he was using the front door.

I called Detective Bassett and Chief Avery to let them know what I had found as I led Roux down the stairs and out the door. I looked both ways on Dauphine Street as I locked the front door. Spenser might be running an errand and making his way back to his new hiding place. It was more likely that my rummaging around the apartment on the second floor would spook him back into the open. All I knew for sure at that moment was that Spenser Duncan was running out of places to hide.

thirty-one

Tony gave instructions to the prep cooks before he and a young, fat porter nick-named Pie began handling the day's deliveries after lunch. They stood at the curb as a transit bus led a line of cars up Decatur Street. Pie began telling Tony about his audition with a brass band from the Seventh Ward to fill the time. Tony was privately glad to learn Pie's special skill was legal. I have always been amazed at how many instruments local kids learn to make a living with that are utterly esoteric anywhere else in the nation. Country music has no use for Pie's tuba, and rock and roll has never employed a cymbal player, but kids make a living in New Orleans playing both instruments. One does not have to be a great athlete to escape poverty here. It only takes having talent at something.

Tony checked his order against what the Sysco delivery driver handed Pie and was just about to head back inside when he noticed a vendor truck pulling to the curb in front of the bistro and watched as two men got out. They stacked three cases of frozen seafood on a hand truck and wheeled it through the front doors of the restaurant. The pair caught Tony's attention because they were delivering to the wrong door, and did not work for any vendor Tony used. His suspicions were raised further because the two men intended to deliver frozen seafood, which is something this chef would never allow to be served from his kitchen.

Tony said nothing to the men before he returned to the kitchen through the side door the regular delivery drivers know to use. The kitchen is designed in such a fashion that this side door opens from the sidewalk into a corridor which ends at the dry storage shelves along the back wall of the prep kitchen. The doors to the beer and produce coolers open into this hallway, and the bistro's freezer can only be accessed through a door in the produce cooler. The freezer is small, because Tony only uses it to store the ice blocks he keeps on hand to create ice sculptures for high-end catered events.

"What's going on?" Juaquin demanded. He was holding open one of the swinging doors between the dining room and kitchen and looking back and forth from the delivery men

Hannah had detained at the bar's service well and Tony standing in the middle of the kitchen.

"I need a minute before you let them in, and then keep everyone busy," Tony calmly instructed him. Juaquin started to repeat his question but thought better of it after considering Tony's instructions. He wasn't going to argue with an owner, and he felt confident the chef knew what he was doing.

None of the prep cooks paid any of this the least attention as they hustled about doing what they were expected to do. There was no time in their schedule for idle speculation or listening in on conversations between the chef and the general manager.

Tony stepped into the office for a moment before walking through the prep kitchen. He removed a heavy-bottomed three-quart brazier pan from the pot stand and carried it into the walk-in. He set the sauté skillet on the shelf just inside the freezer door, beside the electric chain saw he had mentioned to SAC Conroy.

"Is the chef here to sign for this?" one of the drivers inquired as the pair wheeled their boxes past Juaquin and entered the bustling kitchen.

"He's waiting for you in the cooler. It's the first door on your left in that hallway on the far side of the kitchen," Juaquin informed them and pointed towards the hallway. He closed the kitchen's double swinging doors and silently followed the pair. Juaquin positioned himself where he could watch the pair and while keeping an eye on the cooks. He wanted to be able to sound an alarm if anyone stepped out of the cooler before the chef. He also needed to be sure none of the cooks entered the coolers.

Tony opened the freezer door as soon as he entered the cooler so the suspicious delivery men could not squeeze him against it. He turned and studied the pair as they entered the produce cooler and instantly grasped that they were not going to settle for stripping the watch from his wrist. These were men in their late thirties, who likely had experience doing this sort of work. One of them carried a clipboard in his left hand, which hid his right hand. Tony assumed there was a weapon in the waistband of the man's purloined uniform. The second man used only one hand to steer the cart and did his best to limit Tony's ability to move in the confined space. Tony stepped to the left, dangerously close to the first assailant, in order to keep the second assailant from pinning him against the shelves. He was still left standing between the two men, but the second one needed to set the cart down and turn around to attack him and the first assailant would need to do something with his clipboard. Tony created distance between himself and the first man by following the partner towards the open freezer. The gap between them spanned four footsteps, but this was enough room for Tony to maneuver.

Tony's first defensive act was to grab the skillet with one hand and smash it against the back of the second assailant's skull the moment he stepped into the freezer. The man screeched as much in shock as in pain, but the noise was quickly muffled as Tony closed the freezer door and locked him inside. Tony turned off the light and spun around to deliver a solid uppercut blow to the second attacker's chin with the heavy skillet as the man hastily advanced on Tony in the narrow space between the wire racks.

This assailant fumbled to pull a snub-nosed revolver from inside his shirt and began to raise it just as Tony swung the skillet in a sharp sideways motion against his face. The stunned assailant's nose made an audible snap, and blood began pouring from his broken nose and split lower lip. Tony made sure the assailant dropped the revolver before tossing the pan aside and taking the bloodied face in his left hand.

Tony fast walked the flummoxed assailant backwards until the man's back was against the insulated wall separating the grocery and beer coolers. Tony pulled a narrow letter opener from his hip pocket. He had spent hours honing a razor-sharp edge on the normally blunt stiletto-shaped blade. The letter opener's hilt was ornamental, so Tony was careful not to let his hand slide onto the narrow blade as he drove it through the thin material of the man's shirt. The blade entered his chest at a sharply upwards angle until its full length was pressed flat against the back of the sternum. Tony only intended to take the fight out of his assailant, not to slice through his heart or lungs. He did want his victim to understand doing so was an immediate option. The would-be gunman grasped how precarious his situation was once he looked down and saw only

Tony's hand on the handle of what he understood was a blade wedged into his chest.

"Move and die," was all Tony needed to say to confirm that capitulation was the only option open to the now ashen-faced assailant. The slightest movement by either of them could be fatal.

"Got it," the man said and barely nodded to acknowledge defeat.

"You came for this?" Tony demanded and raised his left arm to expose Puglisi's watch under his jacket sleeve.

"That, too." There was no sense in lying about the purpose of their failed ruse. "We were supposed to rough you up some."

"So, someone sent you." It was a statement more than a question. They expected a much larger payday than what Puglisi was offering just for the watch. "Who?"

"I'm a dead man if I tell you." Tony gave him a chilling smile and then looked down to draw the man's attention to the blade in his chest. "Or if I don't."

"Dying here is your choice, not mine," Tony clarified those two options.

This was enough to make the hired thug reconsider his answer.

"Some lawyer wanted the watch," the man blurted out. He knew better than to tell Tony everything he knew at once. Surely someone would open the cooler door and save him from the chef if he talked long enough.

"His name?" Tony demanded. He did not try to hide his impatience. He was in no mood for lengthy interrogations, and never has been in my experience.

"Go ahead and kill me," the man refused to answer.

This was the moment when I walked into the cooler with Roux. Juaquin had filled me in when I entered the kitchen and we both came to the same conclusion about why Tony wanted privacy. The impaled assailant was not at all relieved to see Roux.

I took a moment to assess the situation. I could hear muffled pounding on the inside of the freezer door. I knew Tony kept the workspace at twenty degrees below zero, so that poor sap's life expectancy had dropped to an hour once he was locked inside.

132

My attention was then drawn to the blade lodged in the second man's chest. Tony was obviously questioning him; obvious to me because I had seen this technique employed before. This was the sort of enhanced interrogation I recruited Tony to handle in Iraq because it was a war crime for me to do the same thing. Stabbing someone like this is one the more pleasant things Tony can do with a sharp-edged weapon. I once watched him skin the flesh from a man's palm. The chef's comfort with such violence was what prompted me to insist that he not date my sister when he first emigrated to New Orleans. I had proved powerless to keep Tulip from pursuing him, however.

"He tells me a lawyer sent them," Tony filled me in.

"Lawyer got a name?" I had one or two in mind.

"Not one he wants to share," Tony informed me before the assailant could respond. I gave the prisoner a look that invited elaboration.

"He's from Brooklyn," the guy offered. I could tell this was as much as he planned to share. "We've done some work for him before."

"Here?" I pressed while he was being talkative. This time he shook his head. I took this as a negative response rather than a return to his code of silence.

"What are the odds of there being two attorneys from Brooklyn in New Orleans?" I rhetorically asked the pair. I was less than pleased to be having to deal with an out-of-town version of the Duncan brothers.

"He's got some other big shot lawyer as a client." The man would keep blabbing such fragments of information until Tony grew bored with hearing his voice and twisted the blade. I had not yet identified myself as a police officer to Tony's assailant and he certainly did not act like he knew I was one.

"That's enough, we know who you are talking about," I assured the unrelieved assailant. I pulled out my cellphone and hit a number in its speed dial. Chief Avery picked up on the second ring.

"What are you up to this afternoon?" my boss grumbled. It was barely two thirty, so he knew there was some major development I felt like sharing.

"Send an ambulance and prisoner transport to Strada. I've

got a pair of suspects who need transport. At least one of them will need to stop by the ER."

"I'm listening." This is Chief Avery's way of demanding a fuller explanation.

"Two guys made a run at Tony. It didn't go well for them. One is locked in our freezer and Tony's put a knife in the other guy's chest," I filled him in.

"Tony's stabbed a man?" Avery wondered aloud. We both knew that was an act even the Chief of Detectives could not sweep under a rug.

"You'll have to see it to understand it," I said and hung up. I turned to the only slightly relieved suspect and wagged my index finger at him. "You, sir, are under arrest."

"Thank God," the man caught himself as he began to slump in relief. I read him his rights and then went to unlock the freezer and handcuff his shivering partner.

Chief Avery and Detective Bassett arrived within moments of my phone calls to each of them. Avery's office is in the criminal court building on Tulane Avenue and he can park wherever he chooses at a crime scene, so he was in the kitchen within ten minutes. Bassett walked from the Eighth District on Royal Street. SAC Conroy and a pair of agents met them at the cooler door. The FBI's surveillance suspected the delivery drivers were bogus before Tony did, but they waited for SAC Conroy to arrive before they entered the restaurant. Conroy joined us in the cooler moments before Avery arrived but was so flummoxed by what he found that he had done nothing to control the scene.

"I can't let you handle this," Chief Avery made sure Conroy was within earshot when he informed me of my recusal. We were watching my prisoners being readied for transport from the walk-in cooler by a pair of uniformed NOPD officers. One of them placed their own handcuffs on the still shivering assailant and handed me mine with a broad grin on his face. The thug Tony stabbed was cuffed by one hand to a gurney while the EMTs sorted out how to secure the blade protruding from his chest during what would be a thankfully short trip to an emergency room. Hitting just one of the city's legendary potholes could shift his destination from an operating table to the morgue.

"I wouldn't expect to," I assured him, also making sure Conroy heard my response, and then shrugged for good measure. "The guy with the letter opener in his chest told Tony they were sent to dissuade him from pestering Matranga about his outstanding dinner tab. I am too close to the matter."

The truth was considerably more complicated, but it was going to be days before either of the men who attacked Tony gave a credible voluntary statement. The one I questioned refused to repeat his confession with anyone else present in the cooler and probably knew lawyers were already waiting to represent the two assailants at their arraignments. They would plead not guilty and then keep their mouths shut to protect the man who hired them. Their silence was all that might keep them alive.

"So, this was about the dinner tab and not the contract out on Puglisi's watch?" Avery asked. His question was his way of letting the two of us know the bounty on Puglisi's watch was common knowledge.

"We are telling you what he told me," Tony assured him. He couldn't be proved to be lying unless the assailant broke his silence.

"Where is the watch?" SAC Conroy inquired. He stopped watching the crime lab technicians document the crime scene long enough to check for blood on Tony's electric chainsaw. Apparently, Tony's offhand response at our last meeting had struck a nerve with the FBI agent.

"Here," Tony said and raised the sleeve of his chef jacket.

"That isn't the watch Puglisi wore when I interviewed him," Bassett spoke up. "His was an older one, with a metal band."

"This was a present. Mister Matranga gave it to him," Tony informed us all.

"Any reason you didn't think to mention that before now?" I grumbled.

"It is why I said I would hold the watch. I knew they would have to come back for it," Tony ignored my irritation and considered his response to be an adequate explanation for his decision to take it. He had a point, but this was an entirely new factor to consider.

"And you're okay?" Avery queried Tony. Avery's concern made me doubt whether he might revisit the tableau he found in the walk-in later and come to a different conclusion on who needed rescued.

"That was some quick thinking you did in there," Conroy complimented the chef. "I never would have thought to grab that frying pan as a weapon. And I sure would not have chosen a letter opener over a knife. That's a curious choice, don't you think?"

Conroy was addressing this last question to everybody in the cooler except Tony. It was such a precise choice of sharp objects that somebody was eventually bound to wonder why Tony chose to wield it rather than a readily available kitchen knife.

"I did not wish to get my knives dirty." I doubt Tony

thought anyone present was going to believe him, but he didn't much care and nobody could prove otherwise. "Anything else?"

"Why is there a floor drain in your freezer?" Conroy asked with a tone that implied he had a specific reason in mind. He wasn't prepared to accept that melting ice needs somewhere to go whenever Tony defrosts the freezer.

"I think that was addressed when we were discussing Matranga and his pals hanging out at the pizzeria," I responded with a straight face. The FBI agent seemed intent upon imagining the worst possible things about Tony, so I told him what he probably already believed. His expression and abrupt silence certainly indicated as much.

"I need to cook," Tony excused himself. I believe he hoped his absence would make Conroy's charged topic less interesting.

"Are you going to hand this over to Detective Bassett as well?" I asked Avery as we watched Tony and Juaquin head back to work.

"I don't know. He hasn't shown me very much on the last case I gave him," Avery lamented for Conroy's benefit. "I think the two of you are secretly hoping the Marshals find Spenser Duncan, so you don't have to look for him."

"Well, we haven't found him, either. I think he headed back to Mississippi. He has more resources to call upon to hide there than he does here," Conroy shared.

"We'll let you know as soon as we find him," Chief Avery assured SAC Conroy, with all the honesty and sincerity Conroy put behind his own theory. Conroy seemed satisfied enough that our investigation was floundering that he motioned for his agents to follow him out of the kitchen. They were undoubtedly anxious to begin interrogating the one assailant they could speak with.

"I think Spenser is hiding in Boudreaux's place on Dauphine. Someone is staying there and has been ripping out the remaining sinks," I informed Avery and Bassett as soon as we were alone. "They are climbing in and out of a rear window. If it really is Spenser, he must have lost his key."

"When did you discover that useful bit of information?" Avery nearly roared.

"About an hour ago. I was going to call you about it, but

then I walked in on this." I defended myself. I would never have mentioned it at all had Avery not needed some sort of good news to brighten his day. I planned to watch the house on my own to corner Spenser and question him at length before arresting him.

"This whole thing is giving me a headache," Avery sighed. "Neither of you are any closer to positively identifying who broke into the house, verifying the reason for the burglary, or delivering a prosecutable case than the day I assigned this to you. Bassett is spinning his wheels and you, and your partner there, have done little besides get yourself on the wrong side of some very nasty octogenarians. You also ruined my sleep by telling me some dying mobster might have diaries that would expose a lot of things that are best left in the past."

"You told me there shouldn't be anything to worry about," I reminded him. "I seriously doubt Puglisi recorded every free meal he saw beat cops eat over a thirty-year period. It's not like you helped anyone break the law or turned your back on something you should have arrested anyone for doing."

"You don't get it, do you?" Avery snapped at me. "There were crimes we never touched because we knew we couldn't make a case. We chose to leave it up to the Feds to pursue them, but nobody is likely to question the FBI about ignoring those same crimes. The reputations of a lot of good people, your father for one, will be shredded if those diaries prove to be real."

"Not to mention damage to the careers of anyone still on the force," I said to let him know I was paying attention. "The sort of things that could do that are what Puglisi absolutely did keep track of."

Avery sighed. "All I know is that Puglisi must have promised the Feds something worth the bad press they risked taking over paroling him. Why else would the FBI and Justice Department sign off on his release?"

"Someone needs to get hold of the diaries before they do, if they exist at all," I did not need him to be the one to state what he obviously wanted of me. "You can't count on Puglisi having scammed his way out of prison on a deal he cannot deliver on."

"Nobody can," Avery assured me. I escorted the pair out of the building before walking back to the service side of the

138

cook's line to stand next to the expediter.

Jacquie was arranging the garnishes she was charged with adding to the appropriate dishes. It seemed like a lot of mind-numbing nonsense to remember as far as I was concerned, but nonetheless I was fascinated by her ability to spend hours at a time repeatedly decorating each plate before sending orders to the right tables while they are still hot. She is the culinary equivalent of an air traffic controller.

"Tony," I half-shouted over the bustle on his side of the line.

"Yes?" he responded without looking up from his inspection of the cook stations.

"Let me have the watch." I made a 'come on' motion with my fingertips.

"Why?" Tony paused and glared at me through the low gap of the hot window.

"I'll bring it back. I just want someone to take a good look at it," I explained. "There must be something more than sentimental value to explain why they are going to this much trouble to get it from you."

"I am loaning this only," Tony stated as he removed the timepiece. He was not about to surrender his trophy to me any longer than necessary.

"I don't want the headache of having it," I assured him and reached a hand beneath the infrared lamps to accept the watch. It seemed unusually light for something that was so much trouble. I tucked it into a zippered pocket on the cargo pants I was wearing and headed to a jeweler I knew on Metarie Road.

thirty-three

There were other jewelers I could have asked to help me understand the watch. I was initially tempted to run it by the antique jewelry dealer on Royal Street who sold me a pair of earrings I had given Katie for Christmas. The store owner was a twice-convicted fence and could have given me a very full understanding of the watch and the significance it held as a gift between mobsters. Showing him the watch would also mean risking that anything we discussed would find its way back to Matranga and Puglisi. My best alternative was Alhambra Fine Jewelers in Old Metarie because they have been our family's jewelry store for two generations. Marcie Fleming greeted me at the door. She was the granddaughter of the owner who helped my father find an engagement ring he could afford which would also be worthy of Camille Deveraux's ring finger.

"Detective Holland!" Marcie hugged me with exaggerated enthusiasm. She was a willowy brunette in a pencil skirt and silk blouse, which was unbuttoned just enough to draw attention to the expensive necklace she wanted to display for the day. The store is her personal jewelry box. "Have you come to pick out a ring for your fiancée?"

"Katie would kill me in my sleep if she thought I had a fiancée on the side," I joked in an attempt to stop any further discussion of my personal life.

"Then what brings you here today?" she asked as she led me deeper into the store. She was being polite, but her intent was to sell me something before I made it out the door again. Her father coined the phrase she loved to repeat: "They came here to spend money and we would be fools to disappoint them."

I tugged Puglisi's watch from my pocket and laid it on the square of green felt beside the cash register.

"I need to know the value of this watch. We took it as collateral for an unpaid dinner tab and the owner has done everything but pay the bill to get it back." I saw no point in going into further detail.

Marcie lifted the watch and laid it across her delicate palm to examine it. She could probably judge the size of the man who wore the watch by which hole in the band the catch went through. She assessed the face before she studied the back, and then scrutinized the front again before she returned the time piece to where I set it.

"It's a Corso model made by Citizen. It's practically new. You can tell the age of a watch by the way the crystal ages. This one is still bright." This was what I expected to learn, but it was still painful to hear. Puglisi had barely received this one as a welcome home present before Tony took it as collateral.

"How much did this cost new?" It lacked any diamonds or other obvious signs of added value. To be honest, it looked like a basic dress watch.

"Less than two hundred dollars. Does that help you at all?"

"Not as much as we both hoped it might," I admitted. I didn't want to disappoint her efforts towards helping me understand the watch, but learning it was worth this much less than the Paget Philippe that Matranga gave Puglisi as consolation did nothing to lessen the mystery of why Puglisi was offering five times what it was worth to get it back. "Can you tell me anything else just by looking at the watch?"

"It's the sort of watch people usually give family members as a gift." Marcie was mining for anything that might help me. "There are far nicer dress watches in this price range most people buy for themselves if they want to impress people."

"Family is about right on this one," I chuckled to myself.

"People like Citizen watches because they don't need a battery," she continued. "The mechanism is unique. Let me show you."

Marcie picked up a tool and began unscrewing the back of the watch before I had a chance to express any interest in its Eco-Drive mechanism. She had the gleam in her eye experts get from an opportunity to share their arcane knowledge. She gave the metal back a twist and set it aside to expose the inner workings of the timepiece.

"See? It's powered by light rather than needing to be wound. Look how everything flows in perfect motion," Marcie picked up a magnifying loupe and held the watch in a fashion which made it possible for me to see what she was gushing about. The part of my brain that appreciates comic irony caught that Matranga celebrated Puglisi's release from prison by giving him a watch that runs on sunlight.

My attention turned to the back of the watch. Citizen's imprint was engraved on the back and left no room for any sort of personal inscription. I turned the cover over and an inscription inside the cover caught my eye. Engraved inside the back cover were letters and numbers grouped over two lines, much like a code might be.

I took my digital camera from my overstuffed messenger bag and took two photographs of the engraving before Marcie replaced the cover and handed me the watch.

"You've come too far to leave empty handed," the eternal saleslady prodded me.

"And I would not want to seem ungrateful for your help," I allowed as I led her towards her store's own selection of expensive watches.

thirty-four

"I need your professional expertise," I told my sister and showed her the better of the two photographs of the back to Puglisi's watch. "I believe this is a bank account number. Can you help me find out whose account this is and where the bank is located?"

"No," she immediately stated. "This is obviously not your own bank account, and you know I can't tell you anything about another person's bank account. I am just guessing here, but you don't have a court order, do you?"

"Not in hand, no," I admitted and sighed as I took a seat.

"What I can tell you, just from looking at the numbers is that this is a foreign bank account number. Domestic routing numbers don't use letters. Do I dare ask the reason you didn't bother to see a friendly judge on your way here?"

"I'm not entirely sure what I want to do with this information just yet. A foreign bank account will get a lot of law enforcement attention if it becomes part of the case I'm working on. The problem is that attention like that will cost me its value as a bargaining chip." I explained without explaining a thing. I stood up and started for the door.

"So, this ties to the mobsters hanging out at the pizzeria and that dinner tab they still owe you guys?" She just wanted to be sure we were discussing the same case.

"Yeah. This is off the watch Tony is holding for collateral. It turns out the watch is only worth about two hundred bucks," I didn't want to tell her much more than Tony had shared with her. "If this is a bank account number it would explain why Puglisi wants his watch back."

"That it would. How much do you think is in the account?" Tulip was becoming too interested in the matter. I had hoped to not catch her full attention.

"I assume it is where they deposited the millions they paid Puglisi to keep his mouth shut while he was in prison. Somebody could have had him killed in there for a lot less."

"Puglisi obviously knows something important and had an insurance policy on the outside. He may have been paying someone to do something for him,' Tulip specializes in civil

143

matters, but it didn't take a law degree to question what a man serving a life sentence might do with so much money.

"And this may be the key to finding out what that is." I studied the image on the camera screen just to keep it in her line of sight. She looked at it for a long moment and then turned her head away. I returned the camera to my bag as I stood up to leave. I wasn't sure what to do next, because asking Katie Reilly to help me is entirely out of the question when it comes to skirting laws or ethics.

"Hang on just a second, big brother. Try rephrasing your question," Tulip suggested. I was surprised to find semantics offered a way to get an answer.

I tried a new approach. "Can you identify a foreign bank just by its routing number?"

"Absolutely. Not a problem at all," Tulip declared and snatched the camera from me. She typed both lines of the account into her computer and had an answer barely a moment later. Tulip wrote what she found on a piece of notepaper, folded it over, and handed it to me as she explained what she had discovered. "The first line identifies this Swiss bank's Nassau branch. I am afraid the only way to find out who owns the account number on the second line would be to get that court order or have the FBI give you a hand. They'll be at your door the minute you get that court order, anyway."

"I think I may have to sit on this for now. The FBI and I don't have nearly the same relationship I have with you," I laughed.

"Don't get your hopes up that this leads to hidden treasure," Tulip advised me. "The Bahamas is no longer the Wild West of banking that they used to be. Their banks are taking a lot closer look at their account holders than they have in the past."

"Thanks for your help. I may only need to know the account exists to get what I need."

"I dare not ask what that might be. As always, I am glad to have been of service, Detective Holland." She opened her office door to politely encourage me to leave.

"Not a word to Katie," I both implored and directed her.

"I don't want her to know everything I do for you either," she assured me without much humor in her voice.

thirty-five

Lenny Bonetti is reliable in that he can always be found drinking at the street end of Jack's Lounge after lunch. The locals' bar is just five blocks from Strada Ammazzarre, on Chartres Street, and just a block from his apartment. He divides each day between three parts of the Quarter. He starts at Jack's in mid-morning and moves on about three o'clock, when the business transitions from his fellow day drinkers to servers and bartenders drinking away their lunch shift tips. He grifts his evenings away on Bourbon Street doing small hustles and steering tourists to the drug dealers and pimps willing to kick back a modest commission. He wraps up at The Alibi on Iberville, where he uses his dwindling charm to lure off-duty strippers or other working girls turning pro bono tricks back to his apartment sometime before dawn. It is an almost enviable way to live out a bachelor's final days.

I needed to pester Lenny with a range of questions I knew he would not want to answer. Being reluctant did not mean he could not be convinced that telling me what I wanted to know was the only way to get me to leave him alone. I arrived to find him espousing his opinion on the politics behind the way bands were assigned to their stage during the city's multiple music festivals. There was no percentage in correcting his deeply flawed assumptions and conspiracy theories, so I waited for him to take a breath before I interrupted the diatribe the bartender was actively ignoring.

I tapped Lenny on his right shoulder as I passed his bar stool and nodded my head to motion him to join me at one of the four-top tables set against the tall doors opened to Chartres Street. The bartender knew me well enough to pour an Abita Amber from the tap and set it in front of me, along with the first of however many Tanqueray and tonics it was going to take to loosen Lenny's tongue. The bartender silently palmed the twenty-dollar bill I laid on the table as a down payment on our bar tab.

"You here about that dinner?" he asked nervously. It made sense that he thought this was the case because I had not spoken with him since that night.

145

"We know you cannot afford to pay for it," I dismissed that concern. "Besides, you know it isn't the debt that gets you, it's the vig."

The interest on a Mob loan compounds faster than most people can raise the money to repay the principal. I honestly had no idea what interest Tony had in mind when he told Matranga he intended to collect more than the amount of the unpaid bill. It may have only been his way to make the point that it needed to be settled the next day.

"Well, I am not talking to you, Cooter," he declared, but remained seated, because he wanted everyone in the place to know he was no cop's informant. I appreciated his using my real name instead of Cadillac, which was coined by a sergeant in the Sixth District as an insult. My father named me Cooter after his hometown in Missouri. I am known as Cadillac because the first patrol car I was assigned was a CTS sedan NOPD appropriated from Sewell Cadillac in the aftermath of Hurricane Katrina.

"Lenny," I sighed and clinked my glass to the one he was nervously clutching. "You are already talking to me. I am not here to ask you what is going on right now. I just want to know what was going on right before Sunset got sent to prison."

"Like what?" he remained wary of any topic involving people by name.

"Sunset tried to blackmail my dad with some pictures of him and one of the girls in his brothel on Dauphine. I just want to know what you heard about all this back then." This topic was a convenient place to start, if only because a juicy rumor could usually loosen his tongue. Lenny's ability to hustle rests on his ability to convince his victims that he has inside information on everything that happens in the French Quarter.

Lenny tried to create a dramatic pause by taking off the raggedy pork pie hat he bought years ago at Meyer the Hatter's and combed what was left of his thinning black hair. "That girl he slept with, she called herself Vanity, after the singer. She wasn't Sunset's girl. She was Pete's girl! She wasn't supposed to pull tricks because she was underage. Pete has always had a taste for very young girls. Hammer told me Pete had to move to Miami Beach because the Italians wanted to question him about a couple of teenage girls he had sex with after he slipped

146

EVERYBODY PAYS

something in their drinks."

Lenny's facial expression betrayed his opinion of
Matranga's 'dating' habits before he could catch it. "Pete kept
Vanity parked at Puglisi's place so his wife would think he was
just sleeping with some whore and wouldn't suspect Vanity
was his mistress. The one thing is okay but the other will
always start a fight."

"So, my father was trying to provoke Matranga by sleeping
with her, not Sunset?" I pressed forward. Surely this had been
a topic of conversation among the rank-and-file hoods at the
time when the bosses involved were not around.

"I don't know whose girl your dad thought he was messing
with. All I do know for sure is that Sunset got sent up for
murder right after those pictures got out. Nothing against your
old man, Cooter, but the timing on that really stunk."

"So, you think there was a connection between the
blackmail and the cops finding a murder weapon on Puglisi?" I
repeated this back to him because I could count on Lenny
staying in the good graces of Matranga and Puglisi by
informing them about every question I asked. He would be less
forthcoming about anything he divulged.

"I ain't going to say a bad thing about your old man. I don't
think he was the kind of cop who would frame someone over a
personal beef like that. The guy Sunset killed wasn't keeping
up with the payments on what he owed Hammer. At least that
was the reason they gave Sunset for killing the guy," Lenny
recalled. He would have mentioned the man was an informant
had he known.

"Who put out the hit?" I asked this without expectation of a
useful answer.

"It had to be Pete, but I never told you that. He was the
capo for both Hammer and Sunset. If the shylock wanted it
done, then Pete had to approve the hit. Sunset was the guy
Pete always called to do them things. All of that is old news.
What did you really come here to find out?"

"I dunno, Lenny, why don't you tell me what I should want
to know?" I sensed that he was too deep into the day's gin to be
able to unravel what I had just said.

"You mean about what's going on right now?" He was not
fooled for a second by my transparency.

147

"Yeah, Lenny, I want to know about this little reunion they have going and why the Outfit in Chicago decided to send down a chaperone." I needed to avoid asking questions with one-word answers. I hoped Lenny's knowledge of the players would help me piece together some of the puzzle scrawled on my office whiteboards.

"Everything is still blown up after Katrina, and Pete wants a piece of whatever gets put back together. He says they owe it to him. The Outfit in Chicago and Los Angeles are worried about diaries Sunset supposedly kept. I hear he promised them to the Feds to get out of prison. Chicago expects Pete to get them from Sunset or to make sure nobody else does. I guess the guy they sent is here to take care of both of them if Sunset doesn't deliver the diaries."

"And who do you think killed Cammarato?"

"Beats me, but I know whoever did it would like Sunset to get the blame," Lenny said, choosing his words carefully. "It makes a nice story that he killed Hammer to scare Pete into getting the watch back for him."

"What's with the watch anyway? Why would Matranga give Puglisi a watch and then make him give it to us?" This question had been nagging at me since Tony mentioned the watch was a present. At least I finally knew the real value the watch had for Puglisi.

"To remind Sunset who the boss is," Lenny explained and looked at me like this was something everybody should understand. "I'm sure he plans to get it back."

It was a lot to process, but Lenny made sense. Six years after Katrina disrupted the existing order of things in the city's underworld, New Orleans remained little more than a meaty carcass waiting for the jackals to divide amongst themselves all over again. I had uncovered and blocked sloppy attempts by the Dixie Mafia and the El Camino cartel from Mexico to carve off pieces of New Orleans for themselves in the past few months. I had to wonder if the thugs from New Jersey who were sent to give Tony a beating were a sign that the New York crime families sensed the same weakness in the local criminal elements other enterprising criminals had tried to exploit. Of all the things New Orleans desperately needed to get back to 'normal,' a Mafia-style war was not among them.

thirty-six

"I hear you boys had an exciting afternoon," Katie greeted me when I arrived unannounced at the district attorney's office on Tulane Avenue. She had a large office with a commanding view of Central Lockup down the street.

"Tony did," I said and gave her a hug.

"He stabbed a man in self-defense?" she asked in a worried near-whisper.

"Stabbed is not entirely accurate, and self-defense is an exaggeration," I tried to calm her concern. "Two guys were hired to get Puglisi's watch. Tony locked one of them in the freezer and sent the other one to the hospital to get a letter opener pulled out of his chest. Neither of them came close to killing Tony, and he chose not to kill anyone."

"The letter opener Tulip bought him for Christmas?"

"Same one," I said and nodded my head. The opener fits inside a scabbard on a stand shaped like the Eiffel Tower. Tulip gave it to him to remind Tony where she wants to honeymoon someday. Tony likes it because the blade is nearly identical to a stiletto he wielded in Iraq. "It's not like he gutted the guy with a chef knife."

"Are you here to see if my boss is inclined to charge Tony?" she wondered.

"No." The possibility of Tony being indicted never crossed my mind, but her innocent sounding question made it a fresh concern. "I am wondering what you know about Bear Brovartey's defense counsel."

"Is this related to the attack on Tony?" she asked and frowned.

"It may be, but I am at a loss to understand how or why if it is," I admitted.

"Then what are you looking for?"

"I am pretty sure I need to add him to the puzzle I am trying to solve," I explained my interest without really answering her question. She is used to me doing this.

"Being an attorney doesn't mean you are above the law," she pointed out in her very best assistant state's attorney tone of voice.

"It seems to make some of them believe they know ways around them, though."

"Ask Bear Brovartey how that has worked out for him," Katie scoffed.

"Well, please see what you can find out about Brovartey's attorney," I repeated my request without offering any further reason to do so.

"No problem. This is what I like about my job," Katie grinned and sat down behind her desk. "My part in the messes you make does not start until you piece it together into something that makes enough sense I can prosecute someone. You get the headaches and I get all the glory. Do you think the guys who attacked Tony were paid by this lawyer?"

"Maybe you should ask Bear Brovartey whether attorneys might hire a pair of thugs to do something illegal," I said to distract her and get her to laugh. "The guys who went after Tony are pros and know they aren't likely to stand trial."

"I can ask around, but Brovartey is being tried in Federal court. My making inquiries about his attorney will almost certainly catch someone's attention," Katie warned me.

"That could be a problem," I sighed. There was no way I wanted SAC Conroy to be aware of my interest.

"I'll be as discreet as I can," Katie promised. She didn't need anyone wondering what her own interest was, either.

thirty-seven

I returned to the house on Dauphine. There was no reason to believe Spenser might have returned to the house during my brief absence. Granted, he was unlikely to have anyplace else to hide, but returning in broad daylight was too dangerous even for a desperate man. The Quarter was full of bars with dark corners where he could hide until the sun set.

Spenser had come back to rip the place apart because his patron remained convinced Sunset Puglisi's journals were still hidden inside the walls. The fact that they were not hidden in any of the bathrooms must not have been enough to discourage them from ordering Spenser to keep looking. Whoever was bankrolling the break-ins must have been convinced their source was reliable enough to risk continuing the search. I had no difficulty grasping the journals held some sort of value, but that value changed with each suspect I had in mind for being behind these burglaries.

The FBI wanted to pursue any crimes they could solve and prosecute. Puglisi needed them to satisfy whatever deal he made to get out of prison, and his gangster pals needed them to deny the FBI any evidence the journals contained of their past misdeeds. Junior Hauser, and perhaps crime families from Chicago and New York, might be planning to use them to wedge themselves into post-Katrina New Orleans' rebuilt rackets.

My objective in returning to the address was to find a place from which to watch the house that would not expose me to anyone else doing so. I needed to be able to watch the front door and the fire escape in the rear. There was no single spot to do both, but I could use Roux to watch one angle and to alert me when an attempt was made to gain access. I doubted that even one of Conroy's experienced surveillance teams would think to pay attention to a stray dog near the house. I could scale the patio wall, as Spenser likely was doing, and find a place to hide that would also allow me to watch Roux. I thought about asking Ritchie from the pizzeria to leave Roux in the doorway across the street from the house, because nobody would think twice about a young Black kid walking a pit bull in this neighborhood. This would be an ideal opportunity to test the short list of hand gestures Roger and I had been teaching Roux in order to silently maneuver him from a distance.

My plan went into the trash as I rounded the corner of St. Phillip and Dauphine. Roux caught the scent of something he recognized as a threat and stopped walking as he gave a low growl before I walked the two of us into a trap. I stopped and crouched beside him and raised my head enough to look ahead through the window of a parked car.

It took me a couple of minutes to see what Roux had located solely by scent. Matranga was standing in front of a shotgun house with a for sale sign out front on the opposite side of the street. Puglisi's former brothel was in the next block, so he must have believed he was far enough away not to be seen. Matranga was talking with someone, but his body initially blocked that individual from my view. I rubbed Roux behind the ear and whispered my praise for his actions. Matranga spoke with the other person for ten minutes before he moved and exposed Vincent Contaldo.

I was not happy to see the muscle from Chicago sitting on the stoop. Anyone passing by might mistake him as a client waiting for a realtor or a bum sunning himself. Matranga was as impeccably dressed as ever, but Contaldo wore jeans and a light jacket in an obvious effort to blend into the street scene. He wore a baseball cap and sunglasses, but his coiled stance gave him away. It was unlikely Spenser had ever met the man, so he would not see the danger if he were to approach the house. Dauphine is a one-way street, so Russo drove Matranga away from my position rather than past me once his boss climbed into the backseat of his Town Car. Contaldo briefly glanced in my direction before he turned to focus his attention on Puglisi's former brothel.

I paused to study the windows, doorways, and parked vehicles between myself and Contaldo. I then looked up the street from where I remained uncomfortably crouched, and then past where Contaldo stood guard. I saw no indication of any other surveillance on the house. Conroy either lacked the resources or the interest necessary to place the crime scene under constant surveillance in addition to tailing Puglisi and Matranga around the clock. I suspected that the SUV which turned the corner behind the Lincoln as it crossed Barracks Street was Matranga's FBI tail.

I led Roux behind a group of tourists as they crossed the street. I slowed down and fell further behind the unsuspecting sightseers in order to use them to block Contaldo's view in my direction. I did my best to stay behind the tallest members of the group, assuming I could not be seen if I could not see my target. Roux loped along at his practiced pace and distance, but his head was up and his nose was hard at work.

I closed the distance as we neared Contaldo, so that I was standing in front of him barely seconds after he assessed the risk the passing tourists posed. Having Roux in tow meant I did not need to worry about having to pull my Glock to defend myself. He was entirely capable of incapacitating Contaldo if the situation called for him to do so.

"Good afternoon, Vincent," I called out, which startled him. He spun to face me and began to react, and then stopped moving at all when he spotted Roux's paws on the bottom step of the four-step stoop. I made sure there was plenty of slack in the leash.

"And to you, Detective Holland," he sounded as casual as was possible under the circumstances. Small talk was apparently not one of his social skills. "What brings you to this side of the Quarter?"

"I'd say it is the same thing that brought you here." My broad grin was as fake as the conversation we were having. "I guess we both like looking at empty houses."

"Seems like. Do you still think that one is really empty?" he inquired. There was no need to point out the house in question.

"It's supposed to be," I shrugged. I wasn't going to share what I knew with him. "What do you think?"

"I think it might be worth keeping an eye on," he said. His expression had begun to harden now that he sensed there was only minimal danger of attack or arrest.

"Might be," I concurred in a neutral tone. "You'll want to avoid looking like you're loitering if you plan on being here for a while. NOPD doesn't like strangers lurking in this neighborhood."

"Thanks for the advice." He nodded to let me know he

understood the warning.

"Been here long? I saw your pal Matranga drive off," I said to let him know how long I had watched him before making my approach.

"Not long. We were talking and he suggested lightning might strike twice."

"You never know." I shrugged and gave a sharp snap to Roux's leash to let the pit bull know it was time to start walking again.

It's true that lightning strikes the same place twice with a frightening statistical frequency, but this instance didn't sit right with me. I felt it was unlikely that Contaldo, or anyone else in Matranga's circle, was watching the house until this very minute. I wondered whether Contaldo was there to watch the place or to be Spenser's lookout while he continued ransacking the house. I needed more support than Roux before I entered any house with experienced killers to either side of me.

What especially bothered me as I headed home was why Matranga and Contaldo developed a sudden interest in watching the house so soon after I informed Chief Avery and Detective Bassett about evidence I found of Spenser Duncan continuing his search. I trusted my boss more than I did my assigned partner, but Avery shared some history with Matranga and the local mobsters, while Bassett was only suspected of being a dirty cop.

thirty-eight

The day only got stranger.

I was standing at the end of the bar in Strada when one of our favorite dinner patrons sought me out. Doctor Jericho Fletcher is the emergency room surgeon who gets the call whenever a police officer is shot in the line of duty, and is the on-call trauma surgeon whenever the President comes to town. He also co-developed the combat trauma medicine protocols which saved my life in Iraq. The guy Tony stabbed was lucky to have Doc Fletcher be the one to pull the blade from his chest.

I assumed this was a business call when he arrived without a dinner date. Katie refers to Doctor Fletcher's female companions as his 'golf bag' of women. Fletcher is handsome enough in his sixties to attract enough younger women to be able to assign each a purpose: Julie accompanies him to the theatre, Debra dines with him weekdays and Katherine dines with him on the weekends, Sharon shares his enthusiasm for horse-back riding. We assume all of them share his bed.

"Your chef demonstrated an impressive knowledge of anatomy this morning. He avoided slicing into any internal organs and missed every major blood vessel," he said to compliment Tony's skills. The unsaid part of this praise was that Tony obviously knew how to do the exact opposite if he chose. Jason stepped up to serve Doc Fletcher the first of the three Scotches the surgeon allows himself when drinking alone in public.

"The guy was lucky he caught Tony in a good mood," I grinned. Doctor Fletcher does not discuss his work outside of the hospital, so I was waiting for his bad news.

"I thought you should know that the FBI has taken an interest."

"In the guy you operated on?" I felt this posed no issues for Tony or myself.

"No, in the knife he used," Fletcher said. I could tell he was studying my reaction.

"Really?" I was beginning to regret the flippancy Tony and I used to answer Conroy's earnest questions in the cooler, and Tony's comment about the chain saw.

"Two agents confiscated the letter opener before NOPD's forensic people could bag it as evidence. They claimed their orders were to arrest the man I operated upon and to retrieve the blade Tony used to defend himself. Their interest in the incident seemed strange." He paused to hear my own opinion.

"That it is."

Conroy would need something to deter my interest if Spenser Duncan claimed the FBI sent him into the house on Dauphine Street. We both knew I would trade my silence about any accusations Spenser might voice against the FBI for Tony's freedom.

thirty-nine

Katie and Tulip arrived at Strada together shortly after eight o'clock that evening. They were dressed considerably more casually than they were when had they left their respective offices because they were coming from a kickboxing class I had recommended to them. My sister and Katie also join me at the NOPD shooting range a few times each month as well, while I practice twice a week. They both accepted that their lives were at greater risk dating Tony and me than if they were romantically involved with almost anyone else in the city.

Neither of them was smiling as they came through the open double doors, but both plastered on passable looks of calm as they greeted the row of regulars along the bar while making their way to where I stood near the host stand.

"I was about to call to see where the two of you were," I lied as I pecked my sister on the cheek and brushed lips with Katie.

"Good thing you didn't," Tulip said rather curtly. Jason followed them the length of the bar with glasses and a bottle of Marquis de Perlade champagne. He hastily filled the glasses, and then needed to refill them almost immediately.

"We have been comparing notes," Tulip explained their mood.

"This cannot be good."

"There are a couple of things you are going to want to take into consideration going forward," Katie allowed. She held the thought as I led them through the dining room and into the kitchen to take our usual seats at the chef's table. Tony paused long enough to acknowledge Tulip's arrival before transferring the fish in the skillet he had just pulled from the range top to a plate.

"Okay, what did you find?" I asked once we were settled. Juaquin set the remainder of the bottle of sparkling wine in an ice bucket on the table and one of the servers laid silverware for each of us. Tony would determine our menu.

"The attorney representing both Marion Puglisi and Bear Brovartey is Marvin Alexander," Tulip spoke up. "Dan Logan personally recommended him to Brovartey when he was ordered to drop either Alex Boudreaux or Bear Brovartey as a client. Logan and Alexander are both from Brooklyn, and the pair's previous claim to fame is that they were both minor attorneys on the defense team that represented John Gotti in his last trial. Logan has been here since 2005 and Alexander has been representing Russian Mob figures out in Brighton Beach since the Gotti trial ended. Gotti was convicted, for what that is worth."

"Let me guess, you asked my sister to do your sleuthing rather than ask anyone on the courthouse grapevine," I suggested to Katie.

"I thought it was a better idea than asking the FBI," Katie confirmed.

"I tend to agree now that we know Marvin Alexander's background. So, why did a guy who likes defending Russian mobsters come all the way to New Orleans to represent an old-school mobster in a book deal and defend the former attorney to a guy who imagines himself to be the Dixie Mafia's version of Don Corleone?" I asked without any expectation of a response.

"I think he plans to move to New Orleans," Katie shared the hypothesis behind her own dark mood. "Brovartey's trial is going to expose how unsettled things are in New Orleans's underworld, and Dan Logan cannot represent all of the new players this will bring to town."

"Well, that is an ugly thing to consider," I sighed. I considered my plate to be quite full, and I was not eager to add unfamiliar names to the boards in my office.

"Puglisi might decide to make his own moves while everyone he knows is distracted by Brovartey's trial," Katie continued her theory.

"When did you become an expert on Mob attorneys?" I asked a little to pointedly. Organized crime cases had been an anomaly in the city for the past few years. Most of the major felony cases Katie and Conroy focused on were individuals who ran disaster relief scams in the wake of Hurricane Katrina. There were so many cases they created a backlog in both the state and Federal courts.

"I am no expert, but I can certainly tell when I am facing an attorney who has experience in defending especially criminal clients," Katie explained.

"The thugs who attacked Tony this morning said they were paid by an attorney from Brooklyn. There are only two in town that I know of. One of them has a link to Italian mobsters and the other to Russian ones." I offered for their consideration.

"What language did the guys who went after Tony speak?" Tulip asked.

"You would swear they were hired out of Chalmette by their accents, but their rap sheets are from all over the five boroughs in New York," I told them. "I cannot pin them to either attorney, but the fact they' came from there points to these two."

"They were probably hired because they could not be traced to either attorney," Tulip answered. "Why implicate yourself in what should have been a simple job?"

"Indeed." I had to admit her theory had considerable merit.

One of the back waiters cleared our empty salad plates and replenished the bread while I refilled my companions' champagne flutes. Yet another server delivered our entrees as I did so. I was served a fist-sized medium-rare beef filet draped with a green olive tapenade and a side of salted pommes frites, while Tulip received her favorite dish of sautéed shrimp beneath a thin veil of Chandeleur sauce on a twirled bed of al dente linguine. The cream sauce is flavored with a hint of Tabasco, cracked red pepper, and a generous amount of aged sherry. Katie's choice was sea bass topped with an artichoke caponata.

"What are you going to do about the attack on Tony?" Tulip demanded when I offered no indication of what my professional or personal response was going to be. I used my trick of stuffing my mouth with food to buy a moment to formulate an appropriate response.

"Something to make sure it is never repeated," I said. I was already thinking of ways to make New Orleans feel inhospitable for both Brooklyn lawyers.

"And this is where we change the subject," Katie decided.

forty

I decided to give the trespasser I assumed to be Spenser Duncan a free night and went to bed with Katie shortly after midnight, after we returned from a nightclub called d.b.a. where we had gone to see which other musicians might sit in with John Mooney playing his slide guitar. It meant giving Vincent Contaldo the first shot, perhaps literally, at the recidivist burglar.

My phone rang while I was in the shower the next morning. I was surprised to see Captain Williams' name on the phone's ID when Katie handed it to me. I stepped out of the shower and motioned to Katie and placed the phone on speaker so she could hear.

"What can I do for you?" I assumed he meant to cash one of his many markers.

"Stay where you are, how about that?" His tone was too serious for this to be a social call.

"I can do that. I absolutely would have had you not called and interested me in making another day trip to the coast."

"A couple of fishermen found Spenser Duncan this morning. Somebody didn't use enough chain to hold him on the bottom of the bayou out back of the airport and he bobbed up just after sunrise. The plastic kept the crabs off him, but he has been in the water the whole time you have been looking for him," Williams elaborated.

"But you are sure he stole the truck I asked about?" I needed this confirmed before I dropped Spenser as my favorite suspect on Dauphine Street.

"The photo we have of him fueling the truck matches the clothes on the body."

"Who killed him?" I asked even as I realized this was a stupid question. "I mean, how did he die?"

"A pair of shots to the head, fired from behind, small caliber. He was probably surprised to be dead," the experienced Mississippi detective shared. "It could also be that whoever shot him did not want us to have trouble identifying him, but the trajectory indicates he was still on his feet when they shot him."

"I can name a couple of Feds over here that are going to be more surprised when this hits the news than he was to be dead," I said.

"Yeah, maybe I should have called the Marshal's office or the FBI before we let the TV stations file their reports. I'll keep you in the loop, but I think you have what you need from me," Williams said as a means of discouraging me from any further contact. He clearly wanted to share his delight over the discomfort he brought to the agencies which were so rude to him.

"I do have one weird question for you," I said before he could hang up.

"Try me," he said.

"What shoes was he wearing?" I inquired.

"Yep, that is a weird one," Williams laughed. "Does it mean anything to you that he was barefoot? The shoes may have fallen off, but I don't know how they would have made it out of the plastic."

"I seem to have made my job harder once again," I sighed and let him be the first to hang up. I was still rolling the lack of shoes around in my head when I realized we were done talking.

"What's that all about?" Katie asked as she stepped past me to get into the still warm shower. She unwrapped herself from the plush Turkish towel and draped it over my shoulder.

"Someone has continued ransacking the place on Dauphine, but it can't be Spenser Duncan," I said and tossed both of our towels atop my phone on the counter.

"Too bad for him," she said with little pity. She was well aware of his criminal record and was not upset that he no longer shared our planet. "How does this affect you?"

"Well, I have no idea who hired him to break into Puglisi's house, and no idea if he found what he was sent there to find," I ticked off a short list of things I counted on Spenser to answer. "There were fresh tracks the last time I was in the house. They looked like the same size shoes as the ones that made the first set of tracks. That is interesting now that I find out the new tracks were made after our prime suspect died. It looks like I still need to identify at least one burglar."

"No, I meant how does this affect you today? You promised to take the day off and spend it with me," she clarified her question and pointedly reminded me of my promise. She had gone to considerable trouble clearing her own calendar.

"I guess eliminating Spenser as my suspect is enough work for one day," I said and joined her in the marble-tiled shower.

forty-one

I called downstairs to the kitchen and ordered a plated breakfast for the two of us after we finally stepped out of the shower. My water heater was insufficient to provide hot water for as long as we wanted to spend together.

"Does Spenser's death change anything?" Katie asked as I factored his death into the timeline before us. It was the last thing I had learned and only one of the incidents on the nearly six-foot long timeline. I write big, but this was still ridiculous.

"I can no longer say for sure who did the break-in. This doesn't narrow the list of who might have sent someone to get the journals, but it does suggest that whoever broke in is only working for one person and not angling for a better position among his many enemies as Spenser may have been trying to do."

I explained that I had come to believe whatever prompted the break-in on Dauphine Street might date back to something which occurred in the house twenty years earlier.

"Puglisi served his sentence in silence paid for by his former capo. A shot at an early release may be what prompted him to agree to publish detailed memoirs which would expose prosecutable acts by surviving members of his former crew as well as high-ranking members of NOPD and the FBI. Matranga learned about his parole, and perhaps about the book deal, and arranged a house for him to live in following his release. His choice of rental properties ties the pair to Alex Boudreaux, which may only be a coincidence. Puglisi's story about being paid to keep his silence seemed to have been confirmed by the inscription in the watch Matranga gave Puglisi during the dinner somebody still needs to pay for. The burglary on Dauphine Street blows my entire timeline apart because I cannot figure out where it fits into this convoluted drama."

"Okay, I think I get all of this," Katie sighed once I had explained everything I knew and what I only suspected. "There are some things I would like for you to tell me, though."

"Like?" I set the marker down on the chalk tray before I sat down beside her. She was sitting on the padded leather bench which fills the middle of the room and allows me to view the whiteboards as one does large pieces of art in a museum.

"When were you going to mention the inscription in Puglisi's watch to me?" she asked in an unamused tone.

"When I decided what to do about it. It is just a piece of the puzzle right now," I tried to gloss over my omission. "This is still an active investigation and things change."

"No," she said and wagged her finger. "You don't get to sit on a bank account that could hold twenty million dollars. This is evidence which needs to be secured and shared with Chief Avery and the FBI."

"Puglisi having money in a foreign bank is a Federal tax law issue, and I do not want to feed the Feds any more cases. I don't have anything I can hand you that will stand up in court against anyone on that board. Letting Puglisi believe we don't know about the inscription may be what is holding things together. What do you think he is going to do after we seize the money he was promised by the guy who told him to hand me the watch with the account info? What do you think Puglisi would do if we seized the millions he was promised for not making a deal with the Feds for a reduced sentence?" I had thought much of this through before deciding that doing nothing was the least disruptive course of action.

"I don't know, but I do know none of that is your concern," Katie still balked.

"I think Puglisi's release is an unexpected speed bump interfering with something larger. There is every reason to believe Junior Hauser is still looking for a way into New Orleans. Matranga has been out of town for years, but is almost certain to want to find a way to get back in business now that he is here. Chicago sent one of their own shooters to town, probably to either help Matranga or to stop Puglisi or to kill them both. There are also two attorneys from Brooklyn in this. Alexander has ties to the Russian Mob and Logan probably still has connections among the Italian families. I think they intend to help carve up the city, which means there are going to be gangsters fighting among themselves until there is only one figurative man left standing."

"What can you do about any of that?" Katie asked. "Legally, I mean."

"Less than I can illegally." She did not find this amusing or reassuring. "But the options are still limited even if I do things illegally. Taking Puglisi's money from him would probably spur him to scorch as much earth as he can before he dies, but letting anyone kill him increases the likelihood of the journals falling into the wrong hands. The smartest move is to pit the players against one another before they reach some sort of agreement about who gets what piece of the pie. I can make case against the last of them rather than try to arrest an entire busload."

"Divide and conquer. Tell me how you would do that," Katie said and waved towards the board with all the warring factions posted on it.

"I would spark two separate battles. The first would be between Junior and the New Yorkers," I said and circled the individuals on each side with a red marker.

"Why start there?" Katie wondered. She looked thoroughly perplexed.

"Because they are the two sides best prepared to fight, and they won't fight it out here," I explained my self-serving rationale. "Junior is not going to do battle in New York. He will draw the Italians into a long fight on his own turf that will keep both of their armies too busy in Biloxi to invade New Orleans."

"You are halfway through and your hands are clean," Katie nodded her head in agreement. She may have just been happy that the bloodiest of the gang wars would happen far from her jurisdiction.

"Conroy can call Puglisi's delay in handing over his diaries a parole violation, but I need to delay the FBI getting their hands on Puglisi's journals until he is too sick to do anything with them. I would still need to find a way to keep them from the FBI once Puglisi is out of the picture. Avery is certain Conroy plans to comb the diaries for anything he can use to put NOPD under a consent decree. Conroy probably plans to arrest some of NOPD's senior leadership to force the issue."

"What if Puglisi were allowed to go live out his last days spending his money on a beach? It might be enough to keep him quiet," Katie unexpectedly suggested.

"Are you suggesting we help Puglisi skip town and trust him to stay quiet?" I was surprised by her suggestion and disappointed in her level of trust.

"I just wanted to see if it was something you are considering. Aiding and abetting are not unfamiliar items in your toolbox, detective," Katie chided me.

"The shooter from Chicago is the wild card in any fight," I said and hovered the marker over Matranga and Puglisi's names. "I cannot tell if he is here as a referee or to kill off the old guard to make room for some new blood from Chicago. The Chicago and Los Angeles crime syndicates were quick to stake their claims after Marcello went to prison, but many of their operations and people they controlled were lost in the storm. According to Avery, they always preferred to take a cut from the locals and to not get their own hands dirty. Maybe times have changed since Katrina."

"So, what do you plan to do about the shooter?" Katie asked with some concern. She saw no reason to trust me not to wind up on the hitman's To Do list.

"Beats me. I doubt he would tell me the truth if I asked him. I am not inclined to interfere until I understand his mission a lot better. He can thin the herd all he wants as far as I am concerned," I admitted, with an indifferent shrug.

"So, you are okay with him killing more people?" Katie was aghast at this.

"Well, he is hardly a gang banger shooting the place up. He will only kill one or two more bad guys, and he will probably clean up after himself as well," I clarified.

"Yeah, that was a real clean hit he made on Cammarato," Katie scoffed.

"We don't know that was him," I pointed out. "It could have been almost anyone who wanted us to suspect Puglisi. It could have been Puglisi hoping we would waste our time chasing less obvious suspects. It's not my case and I don't care that Cammarato is dead."

"You are just Mister Sentimental this morning, aren't you?" Katie asked with a bit of a frown. "What if the war you want to start has already begun without you?"

"I don't think it has, but either way I intend to stay on the sidelines as long as I can." I sat down beside her and nibbled on the last piece of cold bacon from my plate.

forty-two

I apologized to Katie that I needed to run an errand before we headed to her house after lunch. Katie understood where I meant to go even if she was not entirely clear on what it was I intended to do. I led the way across Decatur Street as we began Roux's final patrol of the Quarter for the week. He would spend the next few days guarding her back yard like it was his own.

"Roux remains a good judge of character," Katie whispered as we approached the tableful of gangsters. The fur running along Roux's spine was raised in response to either seeing the men or catching their scent. "He probably has the good sense to avoid them as well."

"I guess I would make a terrible K-9," I admitted and continued towards the table.

Matranga spotted our approach and said something which paused their private conversation. The two men doing most of the talking on that day's topic were Puglisi and Contaldo. They both let Matranga handle our intrusion.

"You must be Katie Reilly." Matranga rose to his feet to address her. He chose to acknowledge her to diminish whatever authority I might be bringing his way. I barely got a nod from him before he motioned for additional wine glasses. "I cannot understand why such a beautiful and intelligent woman would waste her time on someone like this."

"He keeps things lively," she said with a straight face and waved away the offer of a glass of wine.

"I'll bet he does. How are things, Detective Holland?" Matranga finally deigned to address me. I noticed his offer of wine did not include a place to sit.

"Oh, you know, crime never sleeps but the dead do," I said a little too strongly.

"Are you telling us something?" Matranga chuckled. "Has someone else died?"

"I doubt any of you knew Spenser Duncan, but he popped up in Mississippi this morning with a couple of holes in his head. He was the guy who burglarized your place," I addressed this to Puglisi.

"I keep telling you I don't own that place on Dauphine," he snarled.

"And yet you knew exactly where I was talking about," I intentionally provoked him. "I guess someone else will have to find what he was looking for."

"I guess so," Puglisi mumbled in hopes I would drop the subject.

"And when did you get in town?" I asked this of Contaldo.

"I hope this is your way of changing subjects," the button man huffed.

"Let's all agree that nobody at this table brought harm to whoever this was you say has died," Matranga suggested.

"You're going to put my girlfriend out of a job if everyone is just going to agree on whether or not they did anything from now on," I mocked him. "You guys can't even agree to pay your dinner tab. I am hardly going to take your word about a homicide."

"Why would we want this man dead?" Contaldo asked.

"Spenser Duncan. At least use his name," I insisted. "From what I hear, you are not the sort of men who take disappointment well. Spenser was supposed to retrieve something from Mister Puglisi's place last weekend. I'd say he died because he either failed to do so or someone did not want him discussing what he found. He didn't have much trouble telling the FBI things, because he was ratting out his old boss when he disappeared last weekend."

"Then perhaps Junior Hauser is who you should be pestering," Matranga suggested.

"Oh, I plan to first thing Monday morning," I assured them without bringing up that I never mentioned who the FBI was questioning Spenser Duncan about. "The FBI is likely to be a bit distracted because losing Spenser Duncan means they have lost his testimony. That would free his previous client to pursue another run on New Orleans."

"That would..." Contaldo started to speak but fell silent when Matranga clamped one meaty hand on the man's wrist.

"We should be going," Katie declared and gave my own arm a light tug. I left without saying another word and Katie held her tongue until we were around the corner and out of earshot. "What was all of that supposed to accomplish?"

"I needed to throw some fresh meat in the shark tank. Now they know Puglisi's journals were not recovered, and they might begin to read some things into Spenser's involvement. They will waste the rest of the weekend deciding whether Spenser was working for the FBI or for Junior Hauser. Puglisi will start to worry that his old pals are reconsidering the validity of all those rumors about his journals. Puglisi might even start to think he needs to get those journals himself."

"And you'll be there to catch him when he does," Katie surmised.

"I have caught smarter thugs with less work," I neither confirmed nor denied her thoughts on the matter. She knew that taking Puglisi's journals directly from the mobster's own hands remained the surest way of authenticating them. Setting evil men upon one another would just be a bonus.

forty-three

Roux always enjoyed this walk more than our morning or late-night patrols. It was because we encountered more tourists and had more time to speak with the locals, which meant more people offered him treats. Roger discouraged allowing him to accept anything from anyone who would not have a normal reason to handle him, such as Tony or Katie. I broke the rule because allowing anyone to pet or feed him while on patrol served to conceal our identities. I never patrol with my badge or sidearm in sight, which means trusting NOPD's officers and mounted patrols to recognize us on sight. This initially risked one of them using this intentional confusion to justify beating or shooting me, but that concern has diminished with each passing year.

This afternoon I concealed my Glock and badge under the loose Henley I wore against the spring chill and Katie was wearing the hoodie I bought her a couple of months earlier. There were soft ballistic panels sewn into the material capable of stopping pistol rounds. It was perhaps the least romantic thing I could give her, but she understood the loving intent behind wanting her to be safe in my company. Half the reason I dress in loose clothes is to hide the fact I wear a light-weight ballistic vest even on my days off. My trust relies on a lot of preparation for that trust being broken.

"So, this is how you make your living," she mused as we walked towards Bourbon Street from the pizzeria by way of the riverfront.

"Pretty much." I saw no point in explaining I was scanning the French Market for the muggers and pickpockets whose faces I have committed to memory. Roux's size and toothy grin parted the crowds shopping amongst the stalls for trinkets and t-shirts.

"I can see why you like your job," she said and hooked her arm in mine. She made sure it was the arm which held Roux's leash rather than the hand I needed free to reach my Glock.

The riverbank was quiet as we made our way through the floodwall gate next to the shuttered restaurant building and continued walking towards the Moonwalk. The one red streetcar which passed us was packed as it headed towards Canal Street. Boomer and Darnell waved at us but were relieved that we walked past them without stopping to engage them in conversation as I would if Roux and I had been alone. They are happy that I have a love interest, but they remain wary of Katie due to her enforcement of the state's vagrancy laws. She was oblivious, or acted as though she were, to their disengagement.

The throng in Jackson Square seemed to be deciding what to do with the rest of their afternoon. The weather was nearly perfect and the Quarter offered a thousand reasons not to hurry home. I did not rush Katie as she paused to admire some of the paintings and other crafts for sale as we ambled towards the cathedral square to watch one of the acrobatic groups try to hustle enough money they wouldn't feel the need to break into these same tourists' cars later that night.

I steered Roux past St. Louis Cathedral by way of Pirate's Alley. Katie detoured us to window shop the jewelry stores and artist studios along Exchange Alley, which brought us out on Toulouse Street rather than Royal. The Pelican Club, at the corner of Toulouse and Exchange Alley, was still doing a good lunchtime business. This is one of Katie's favorite restaurants for our occasional dinner dates. She considers Strada to be home cooking because I live above the restaurant, and because I don't have to pay to wine and dine her in the style she deserves.

We stepped onto Bourbon Street at roughly the mid-point in the Quarter's best known entertainment district. The blocks from Canal to Saint Ann would be aglow in neon once the sun set. The last few blocks between Dumaine and Esplanade are residential and tend to be dark and considerably less safe to walk at night. We turned left, towards Canal, and walked down the middle of the tourist-congested street. The crowds here were far less observant and entertained us with their varied reactions to bumping into Roux, who could have taken their leg off were he so inclined. Katie noted that not one person tried to tell me not to walk my pit bull on Bourbon Street and laughingly suggested that I looked like the kind of guy who would let loose of the leash in mid-argument.

"Hey, man," a burly young Black man called out to me and

171

waved from the strip club doorway he was paid to fill.

"Friend of yours?" Katie sarcastically inquired.

"More like my eyes and ears," I replied. She took Roux's leash and then stepped away while I spoke with Big Mack. I only know him as this and am not even sure Mack is his real name. I suspect it is a name that came from a lifetime of eating take-out burgers.

"What's up?" I asked and pressed my back to the wall so I could watch the crowd passing by.

"Something nasty is going on at the Night Owl," he offered.

"You are going to have clarify nasty when you are talking about that place," I jested, but I was interested to hear what he wanted to share.

"Lenny told me every pimp in town is meeting there tomorrow night. He said some girl is auctioning off her virginity to settle some debt she owes."

Lenny was not going to be who I contacted about this, not just because he was an unreliable source, but because letting him know the auction had caught my attention might change the plan. I had a much better source for learning what was going on, and felt he was certain to be planning to attend.

Marquis Lewis is a nearly sixty-year-old old-school pimp I began rubbing shoulders with when the Black Knights started using his girls to staff the strip club they use to launder their drug money. The bike gang and I have a history of our own, but co-exist peacefully because I don't do drug or vice cases. They and Marquis are part of the informant network I began building after I figured out New Orleans East was the gateway for the Dixie Mafia to infiltrate the city. It serves everyone's self-interest, regardless of their side of the law, to keep that from happening.

"Thanks. I will look into it," I said as he stepped away to deal with the knot of drunken college-aged boys trying to get past him. The steep cover charge deterred them more than his size did.

"Did Lenny say when is this supposed to happen?" I prodded as patiently as I could. My mind was already spinning. I only knew one person who fit the bill for the auction.

"They are closing at midnight tomorrow night. Lenny told

172

me the place has a new partner. I guess this is his way of letting people know the sort of place he plans to run." he further informed me. "Tell me you ain't going to let that happen."

"It won't. Any word on who the new owner is?" I had only one name in mind.

"Lenny told me, but the name didn't stick. All I remember is that it is some Mob guy from Miami." Mack turned away just then to check out a better-behaved group seeking admission and I slipped away to take the leash from Katie.

"What's up? One of your old girlfriends passing you a note?" Katie poked at me.

"No," I said in a troubled enough voice that she stopped mocking me.

"What did he tell you?"

"I think Matranga has wormed his way back into the Quarter. He may have taken over the Night Owl on Iberville and plans to auction off a teenager's virginity," I told her. "I think I know who the girl is."

"How so?" Katie asked and stopped walking. She was back at work that fast.

"I saw a runaway from Colorado hanging out on the Moonwalk a few days ago that Boomer told me took a job waiting tables at the Night Owl," I began to explain.

"You knew the girl was a runaway and didn't turn her in to Family Services?"

"Boomer claimed she ran away rather than allow her stepfather to molest her. Family Services is obligated to send her home if they pick her up. Having my guys keep an eye on her seemed like the best option at the time."

"Well, you were wrong," Katie needlessly informed me. "You were wrong legally, and your decision itself was obviously flawed. What are you going to do now?"

"I have already tried to get Liquor Control to do a sweep and gather her up, but they won't get in the middle of what they consider to be a family matter," I declared without knowing this for certain. Katie still expected a fuller answer from me. "What I would like to do is to roll Matranga up for sex trafficking and find a way to keep her from winding up back in Colorado."

"Her problems are not your fight," Katie reminded me. "Someone other than you is going to deal with the girl's situation in Colorado. Your authority and responsibility both end at the state line."

"Does that rationalization ever make you feel better when a criminal skips town and commits a crime somewhere else?" I asked without meaning to start an argument.

"Never, but I also make a point not to pick fights I won't win. You need to stop taking up every noble cause that comes your way," she responded without meaning to argue, either. "I will see that anyone you arrest gets the biggest book I can find thrown at them, but you are going to have to let the girl go."

"Maybe," I said while nodding my head as though I were prepared to do so.

"You're impossible," she sighed and took my arm again as I urged Roux forward. We still had plenty of the Quarter ahead of us to patrol.

forty-four

Any hopes I may have harbored of nothing else happening to ruin our day sank when I saw movement in the house on Dauphine Street, a shadow cast against a window on the second floor as the intruder moved from one room to the next. It seemed unlikely anyone with a key might be searching the house on a Saturday afternoon. I had not spoken to Detective Bassett since he responded to the attack on Tony, but saw no reason for him to be searching the house unless he had a new lead he had not shared with me. I did not view my own failure to inform him of Katie's theory in the same light.

"Call it in," Katie insisted. She was already reaching for her own phone because she knew it would not be my plan of attack. I had Roux, my badge, my Glock, and plenty of poor judgement at my disposal to attempt a one-man raid on the house.

"Contact Bill. Do not call 911," I suggested and moved my messenger bag from my shoulder to hers. I did not want her to call NOPD's dispatchers because the call would be picked up on a scanner, if the burglar had one, long before any police units responded to the call.

"Fine," she sighed and pulled her phone from her purse. "Just be careful."

"Always." I grinned and started down the block. Katie immediately took refuge in a doorway just a couple of doors from the house. She would have a view of the front door but would be at a sharp angle to the windows. This placed her out of the most likely trajectory of any stray gunshots if things came to that.

I ducked to keep myself below the level of the glass in the front door. Roux was stuck between me and the door as I unclipped his leash and let it drop. I reached up for the doorknob with my left hand and adjusted my grip on the Glock in my right hand. I took a calming breath and twisted the doorknob. I was not at all reassured that the door was locked. This might be a break-in by someone using the fire escape. I pulled my keys from my pants pocket and reached up to unlock the door with my copy of the house key.

The distance from the entry to the top of the stairs was further than I wanted Roux to travel on his own. I would need at least ten seconds to safely close that distance myself, and that was too long to leave Roux without the sort of support he was there to give me. He sensed this as well and stood still, but impatiently glanced back at me.

"Volg mij," I whispered the Dutch words for 'Follow Me' and stepped past him to ascend the wide cypress staircase. I remembered the thick stair treads had not creaked any of the previous times I had climbed the staircase, and hoped it would remain silent as we approached the second floor. The gentle clicking of Roux's claws on the bare wood was soft but still loud enough to invite attention. I planned to allow Roux to do what he does best if anyone appeared at the top of the stairs. I made a better target if they decided to shoot, but shooting at me was the wrong decision with Roux charging them. They were not going to be able to thwart our double threat before one or the other of us was upon them.

Roux and I paused before our heads crested the second floor. I waited until I tracked the latest burglar's movements to the bedroom on the far rear left-hand side. There were two apartments between the staircase and that room, and the first of these had an open door.

I stepped to the left side of the staircase and hurried Roux up the last steps and into the bedroom. My intention was to use the sounds of our hurried movement to ambush the intruder from behind once the noise drew them to the staircase.

It took a long moment for my target to muster enough bravery to step into the hallway. Roux crouched and appeared anxious to spring through the open doorway. I pressed my back to the bedroom wall, prepared to step into the doorway in a shooting position. The last thing I wanted to do was to shoot someone only to spend the rest of the evening doing paperwork and the next two weeks going through yet another shooting review while on desk duty. I could not spare the time to do either of these things.

I heard soft footsteps pass the doorway. I was surprised whoever this was did not have the common sense to check each room they passed on their way to the staircase. Whoever was in the hallway seemed to be far more anxious about someone else being in the house than we were. I would have begun clearing rooms as I moved down the hallway rather than allow anyone to position himself behind me. I began a slow count to three before I gave Roux the command he loves to hear.

"Annval," I said in a voice loud enough to let the suspect know I was behind them. I like the linguistic irony of this command, as the Dutch word sounds like 'anvil,' which is what Roux feels like when he tackles you. The seconds the burglar spent adjusting to what I shouted were less time than Roux needed to propel his seventy pounds of muscle and teeth from the doorway and into the man's left side. I heard the pair crash to the floor before I moved into the hallway. Roux was blocking the man's face as I walked towards them with my pistol in a ready-to-fire position. I aimed the Glock's laser sight along Roux's right flank as I stepped forward and finally focused the beam from the laser sight on my Glock on the exasperated face looking up at me from the floor.

"I could have shot you!" Detective Bassett declared. He was not holding a pistol.

"Doubtful," I dissuaded his misplaced confidence. "What are you doing here?"

"My job," he hissed and stood up. "What are you doing here?"

"Your job as well," I said a bit too glibly. "We were walking past and saw your shadow in one of the windows. Katie has called for reinforcements, but I wanted to be sure whoever was in here didn't leave before NOPD arrived."

I texted Katie to let her know the house was secure. I could explain things better in person and did not want to shift my focus from the still immobile detective.

"Well call them off," Bassett insisted. "Start with your dog."

"Too late to stop the cavalry," I told him without a trace of an apology. I tapped Roux's left shoulder to let him know he could let Bassett stand up. "What were you looking for anyway?"

"I was just taking another look at the crime scene," he explained but with a very evasive expression.

"You could have done that in your usual clothes," I pointed

out. It was the first time I had ever seen him not wearing a suit and tie, but he wore jeans, a sweatshirt with NOPD's crescent emblem on the chest, and a pair of sneakers to do this odd search. His badge was dangling from a lanyard around his neck.

"Clear?" Katie called from the ground floor.

"Yeah, come on up and bring Roux's leash, if you please," I shouted back at her.

"Bill is on his way," she informed us as she climbed the stairs. She paused at the top of the stairs to assess the situation and did not like what she saw. For one thing, I had yet to holster my Glock. She turned to the NOPD detective. "Good afternoon. I hope we didn't disturb you."

"No," he sighed and shook his head for emphasis. "I came to refresh my memory of the crime scene. The photographs do not really capture the mess this made."

"Avery does not expect us to make an arrest over poor housekeeping," I said and made a point to laugh as though I were joking rather than mocking him. I was, in fact, openly mocking not just his language but his excuse for being there. This was far too long after the break-in to be trying a half-assed reenactment or refreshing any of our memories. Nothing about the individual holes in the walls was important. We needed to figure out what the burglar sought, and I was way ahead on finding that answer.

"Hey," Avery hailed from the bottom of the stairs.

"We're on the second floor," I shouted back and holstered my pistol.

"I am aware of that. Come on down, because I am in no mood for climbing stairs," our mutual boss beckoned. He did not sound like he was the mood for anything he was going to see or hear in the next hour.

Katie's presence seemed to surprise to Avery even though she had called him. There were four uniformed officers milling about the entryway and stoop to the house when we presented ourselves to Chief Avery. He was wearing far more casual clothes than he normally wore to a crime scene and I imagined he was enjoying a rare weekend at home when Katie called. Not changing clothes was an indication he anticipated finding something ridiculous when he arrived.

"You first," he said and pointed to Detective Bassett.

"I wanted to refamiliarize myself with the crime scene. I feel like Detective Holland and I are spinning our wheels and hoped revisiting the scene might shake a clue or two loose," Bassett offered what initially sounded like a reasonable explanation for his own presence.

"And you?" Avery demanded.

"We spotted his shadow as we were passing by and, not having been informed of his plans, I entered the property in hopes of catching whoever was searching the premises for whatever the burglar failed to locate," I defended my own presence without giving Bassett any clue that I knew what might remain hidden in the walls.

"So, this could have been avoided with a phone call between y'all?" Avery snarled in his least pleasant tone of voice. He directed the comment at both of us but it was Detective Bassett who would later catch the full brunt of the Chief's anger.

"On that note," I broke the abrupt silence which filled the space. Even Katie was reluctant to say a word with Chief Avery in this mood. "I may as well let you both know that I received a call from Captain Williams to inform us that he recovered the body of Spenser Duncan from Bayou Bernard early this morning. He said it looks like Spenser has been there for quite a while."

"Grand," he sighed. "Okay, both of you give me your keys to this place. You can go through me if you intend to play these games in the future."

"I cannot find mine," Bassett announced as he patted himself down. I handed my copy to Avery and joined him in watching Bassett's antics. "It must have fallen out while we were wrestling."

"We were never wrestling," I reminded him. "Roux kicked your ass and I pulled a gun on you. Maybe you left it somewhere upstairs while you practiced ransacking the place."

"I will go check," he said and ran up the stairs before Avery called his bluff.

I led Katie and Roux outside but stopped at the bottom of the stoop until Chief Avery came out and I held up a hand to delay his departure.

"What else?" he sighed.

"I don't suppose you noticed Bassett's shoes," I said. Avery gave me that look he gets when he wants me to tell him everything at once. "Their tread is identical to the ones the burglar wore the night of the break-in."

"Are you suggesting I assigned a detective to investigate a crime they committed?" he angrily asked.

"No, sir," I hastily clarified. "I am just wondering why Detective Bassett wanted anyone who came here after this private visit to believe Spenser Duncan had returned to the scene of the crime."

Avery gave me an especially displeased look and Katie's expression became one of even deeper concern.

"Great. Now I have that to worry about, as well," he groaned. Avery reached in his pocket and retrieved the key I had just given him. He dropped it in my hand. "Maybe you should take a walk through here after he is gone, just to be sure he did not find anything he isn't prepared to share with us."

The three of us fell silent as Detective Bassett came down the steps. The detective was carrying a nylon gym bag I had not seen him with when we were inside the house.

"I seem to have lost the key." Angering the Chief of Detectives must have been an acceptable price to pay to keep his copy of the key.

"Find it," Avery snarled before he allowed his rookie detective to get in his car and drive away. We waited for a few minutes to make sure Bassett did not double back, and then Avery left Katie and me alone to see what might have changed in the crime scene since my last visit.

The ground floor showed no signs of change. I was not convinced any of these lower apartments had been the focus of Bassett's attention that afternoon. I took the opportunity to show Katie the precise holes behind each of the sinks. She agreed that the burglar used an unnecessary amount of thoroughness in searching for whatever it was they came to find.

We made our way to the second floor and meticulously looked through each room. Katie spent an increasing amount of time inspecting each of the holes in the bathrooms as we made our rounds. I could tell she was seeing something more than a pattern, that something was tickling her brain.

We reached the bedroom I had come to assume was the one where my father had the ill-considered affair with the hooker named Vanity. It only made sense that room adorned with posters with the singer's name and image, and a royal purple bedspread, was hers. Katie followed me into the room's bathroom and came to a silent pause as she left the bathroom and looked around the bedroom one more time. A smile formed on her lips and then she broke into laughter.

"What's so funny?" I asked. I saw nothing worth this much amusement.

Katie pointed to the poster of Vanity hanging above the empty dresser at the foot of the bed as she brought her laughter under control.

"Men," was her initial response. "Someone was sent here to look behind Vanity and wasted hours ripping out every sink in the place."

I felt my head swivel from the cabinet in the bathroom to the poster on the wall, and then back and forth again before I realized she was smarter than at least a half dozen police officers who saw the exact same damage and came to an entirely different interpretation. Granted, five of us had looked at what the burglar misinterpreted and never considered any other explanation than that they failed to find what they sought. Not one of us considered what Katie seemed to instinctively grasp, which was why the burglar had failed.

"It cannot be that easy," I chuckled and moved to stand beside her. I set my messenger bag on the dresser and opened it to remove a civilian copy of a military K-bar knife, a heavy blade with a Bowie knife tip and protective powder-coat finish. I set the poster on the bed and unsheathed the knife.

"Whoa, cowboy," Katie said and grabbed my wrist. "What are you doing?"

"I'm going to check out your theory," I explained. It seemed like the obvious thing to do.

"Not without a search warrant, you aren't," she declared and tugged my arm.

"I just want to see if the journals are here or not," I insisted.

"You cannot use them in any legal matter if they are," Katie explained the importance of the search warrant she insisted I obtain to play this hunch.

"I do not plan on doing so," I pointed out. "The minute I apply for that search warrant Conroy will get one that supersedes mine and take them."

"And your plan is to do what?" she relented just slightly.

"My plan is to let Pete Matranga and his buddies hear that the journals are here and then stake this place out to catch whoever brings them out," I told her. "I do not need a search warrant to strip them from anyone who finds them and can delay processing them into evidence to aggravate the FBI."

"Why are you so set on tweaking the nose of the FBI?" Katie asked. She let go of my arm but her expression made it clear she was not going to be happy if I made a hole in the wall and crossed the legal boundary she was sworn to defend.

"Conroy and Avery have a long-standing feud over the gun Puglisi used to murder the man he went to prison for killing. They found the gun in his apartment upstairs and have spent the last twenty-something years suspecting the other one planted it. Conroy plans to use Puglisi's journals to expose a history of corruption in NOPD that will justify placing the department under a consent decree, which would place the FBI in charge and justify firing Avery and any other members of command they care to disgrace and terminate to make room for their own lackeys," I explained what I understood of Conroy's dreams and Avery's nightmares.

"What is Bill afraid the FBI will find?" she asked without trying to pick sides.

"It won't matter what the FBI finds. All they need is the name of anyone they want to target in Puglisi's journals to be able to claim they were cozy with mobsters. Can you imagine what they would have done to my father with what we know he did back then?"

Katie swallowed hard at that thought. She could imagine the headlines the FBI would generate, using smoke even when there was no real fire to impugn the integrity of ranking NOPD commanders, politicians, and powerful businessmen to boost the careers of people like Conroy and the FBI Director, and seize control of a police department barely able to get back on its feet after the resignations and expulsions following Katrina.

"I understand," she said and sighed, but still looked me in the eye when she made her decision. "But you are still going to need a search warrant to open that wall with me standing here."

I do love semantics.

"Alright," I surrendered. I sheathed the knife and replaced it in my bag. "I will get a search warrant before you watch me open this wall."

Katie studied my face, wanting to be sure we were on the same page. What she was saying was not what she meant for me to hear.

"Good. I just want to be clear that you cannot open that wall in my presence without a warrant," she repeated and watched as I replaced the poster. I took her hand and led her out of the house.

forty-five

Katie cooked French toast in the well-appointed kitchen of her Uptown home. Tulip and I sat on the stools at the marble-topped island while I tried to explain my current case's tangled web over brunch and mimosas. They were the two brightest legal minds at my disposal.

"Tell your sister about your runaway situation," Katie prodded me while she was still flipping pieces of the battered brioche appropriated from the bistro's kitchen.

"Maybe later," I stalled. "It isn't really breakfast table conversation."

"It is now," Tulip declared and turned to face me. "What have you done this time?"

"I didn't report a runaway from Colorado to Family Services that I probably should have," I owned up. "Boomer told me she was avoiding a stepfather that was looking for love in all the wrong places after her mother moved out. He was supposed to keep an eye on her until I figured out what to do."

"Tell her what happened," Katie dug my grave a little deeper. She pulled the pan from the stove to focus on the conversation. This is never a good sign. I had the full attention of both women.

"She is working at the Night Owl." I was ready for every reaction possible except my sister slapping me so hard it caught Roux's interest.

"Did that hurt? Good," she snapped. "How could you let this happen?"

"Like I said, I should have turned her in and let Family Services send her back to Colorado to be raped by her stepfather. My bad," I fought back with what little I had at my disposal, which was nothing but the fact that there was no good solution.

"Lord knows what is happening to her at the Night Owl," Tulip persisted.

"That's not true. We know what's happening to her, don't we?" Katie said and gave me a look that demanded full disclosure.

"She is allegedly having her virginity auctioned off this

evening. I do not know for sure that the girl I was told about is her, but she is the only one I know who matches the description of the girl being sold off by Pete Matranga," I said, adding everything I thought Katie wanted me to share.

"And you think having an eighty-year-old mobster sell her virginity is somehow an improvement over her stepfather's advances?" Tulip ground me down a bit more.

"I think having whatever bad thing is going to happen to her to happen here is better than in some state out of my jurisdiction. I can deal with Matranga. Her stepfather is beyond my reach," I lamely argued. It was, in fact, my one saving grace.

"Okay, how are you going to fix this?" Katie wanted to know. "Legally, I mean."

"I wasn't entirely concerned about that aspect," I confessed. I was struggling against the temptation to storm the proceedings with guns blazing.

"Well, you need to be," Katie reminded me as she refilled empty mimosa glasses for herself and Tulip.

"Fine," I sighed and proposed a response so complicated it would need both of their assistance to accomplish on a short timetable. "I can send someone to be the high bidder and deliver her to me, to us, safely. I will need them to also gather enough evidence of the transaction to build a case against Matranga for sex trafficking. His arrest should neutralize the threat he poses on other fronts."

"That sounds reasonable," Tulip relented.

"Except for the parts where you need to find a buyer that won't raise anyone's suspicions and you manage to come up with the money to outbid Matranga," Katie began poking every hole she could find in the barely formed plan.

"I know a guy I can use, and I have the money," I assured her a little too confidently.

"You have buy money in hand?" Katie asked incredulously. "How is that?"

"I have a stash with the serial numbers recorded in my safe. I do not want to count on being able to convince NOPD or the State Police to give me money. I try not to let it change hands, but this time I am going to have to," I calmly explained.

"How do you expect to testify to the source of the money in

185

court?" Katie hammered me. "Much less how do you expect to get it back?"

"Like I said, I have never lost control of the money in the past. It has always been a prop. I think I have only done this a couple of times," I explained for a second time. I was hard pressed to think of the last time I had used it in a case and hoped she didn't ask.

"How much are we talking about?" Katie's focus was now entirely on me.

"A hundred grand, but only half of it has the serial numbers written down."

"Why would you keep that much money here?" Tulip asked and then allowed her eyebrows to shoot up when she answered her own question. "It's your bug-out money."

"His what?" Katie asked.

"Tony has a stash of gold bars, and you keep a stack of cash ready in case either of you have to leave town in a hurry, right?" Tulip correctly assumed. "This all ties back to that thing you two did in Iraq."

"I can neither confirm nor deny the reason," I said in my own best lawyerly wording. I turned my attention to Katie as I explained the matter a little further. "There was a point in time that it seemed like a reasonable thing to have. This was way before you."

"It would still seem to be a good idea the way you two operate," Katie sighed but also smiled. "Okay, let's say there is a way to recover the money before it becomes evidence and still make a case against Matranga. That leaves the matter of what to do with the girl."

"I'll take care of that," Tulip volunteered. "I can put a roof over her head as my client and keep Family Services out of this until we can deal with her father."

"Stepfather," I unnecessarily corrected her.

"What can I do to help this along?" Katie offered.

"You mean now that you brought everything to this point?" I asked. My companions did not find the comment to be as funny as I hoped they might. I covered their unamused response by answering the question before either of them bit my head off. "I need a warrant authorizing the money and one allowing us to record the transaction inside the Night Owl. I will also need whatever it takes to put the girl into Tulip's custody. She is not yet your client, and she is unlikely going to hire you in the middle of me arresting everyone around her."

"What about an arrest warrant for Matranga?" Katie suggested.

"I can worry about that later," I shrugged off the obvious thing to do. "The possibility of his being arrested will weigh heavier on him than his being arrested would. He has attorneys to make his legal problems go away, but he will be left to stew if he is only a person of interest in a crime. Who knows what other crimes he might commit trying to clean up this one?"

"Like killing people?" Katie suggested.

"Like any number of things," I shrugged, but did mean exactly that.

"Okay, I will write up the warrants and help you find a way to make having your own buy money seem reasonable and legal in case it winds up in evidence against Matranga. His lawyers could have a field day if you testify about why you keep that much money on hand." Katie said and leaned over to give me a hug. "You say you know a criminal who can act as your buyer and I know a judge or two who will not ask very many hard questions about the warrants."

"See why I set you two up?" Tulip said. "You are the perfect match for one another."

"And you and Tony..." Katie began.

"Don't say it," I shouted and pointed a finger at Katie. "It is bad enough as it is."

"You'll have to come around eventually, big brother," Tulip laughed and kissed my furrowed brow.

"Maybe so." But not today I mumbled to myself.

I waited until Katie and I finished the request for a warrant for the electronic recordings in the Night Owl and emailed it to her choice of judges before ruining Chief Avery's Sunday.

"I need a favor from you. Can you put out a BOLO for Marquis Lewis?" I requested. I intentionally do not have Marquis' phone number or that of anyone in the Black Knights Motorcycle Club in my phone contacts. It would be far too difficult to explain how I could be in frequent contact and not also be in league with them. This is why we only speak face to face.

"Not without knowing why you want to roust that nasty assed pimp," Avery less than patiently refused. Phillip 'Marquis' Lewis still recruits his prospects off the streets by making them feel comfortable under his wing while he gets them hooked on a reliable narcotic like heroin before renting them out to strip clubs or arranging dates at cheap motels over the internet. His primary market became New Orleans East because he was the first pimp to re-establish business after Katrina and the strip clubs on Downman Road were the first ones to reopen, to an enthusiastic audience of National Guard soldiers, paid-in-cash construction workers, and out-of-state electrical linemen who were earning multiples of their normal salaries far, far from home. Marquis is my first stop when Avery asks me to track down runaways and otherwise missing young women for NOPD when parents need reassurance that something is being done to find their child. I have found a lot of individuals of all ages with good reasons to have left home, including the girl from Colorado who I feared Matranga had groomed to be the evening's offering on the Night Owl auction block.

"I'll tell you if you really want to know," I offered, but only because I knew he wouldn't. "I promise that it ties to the case you gave me and I will be happy to explain everything when I know more."

"Just be sure to have a good explanation at breakfast tomorrow morning. I will see if we can find him," Avery relented.

"Your best bet is either the bus station or the Camelot Club on Downman Road." The first location is his most fertile hunting ground for new talent, and the Camelot Club is the Black Knight's gentleman's club, a place clearly marketed towards those who wish to be less than gentlemen.

"How is your case coming? Anything new on the burglary?" Tulip asked to kill the time. Finding Marquis could take hours unless he was in either of his usual haunts.

"My prime suspect is dead," I informed her. "I got a call yesterday that they found Spenser Duncan with two bullets in his head. I need the coroner's report to pinpoint his time of death, but based on what the state police over there told me I see no reason to believe he survived forty-eight hours from the point he eluded the marshals until he died."

"And he found his new partner rummaging around the crime scene yesterday," Katie tossed in for good measure.

"Uh huh," I mumbled and hoped Tulip would ignore the comment.

The ringing of my iPhone saved me from the headache this conversation promised to create.

"Good news I hope," I said by way of greeting when I saw the call was from Avery.

"Marquis Lewis is in the Quarter," Avery reported. "His car is being towed as we speak. You can catch up to him at the tow lot."

"What did he do?" I inquired. Marquis is not the sort of miscreant to get his car towed. He strives to avoid such petty run-ins with the law.

"He parked in the loading zone out front of the House of Blues. He told them he just needed to run an errand and would be back in five minutes. They gave him an hour before they called it in," Avery said with a touch of humor in his voice.

"Thanks. I promise to give you that full explanation at breakfast."

"It will be lunchtime before I see you. Someone else has already promised to muck up my morning," Avery disconnected the call without offering a fuller explanation.

I hung up and called the dispatcher at NOPD's tow lot. It cost me dinner for two at Strada to bribe the dispatcher to order the tow truck bearing Marquis Lewis' car to park somewhere for an hour before dropping off its load.

My next phone call was to my supervisor at the State Police. Captain Hammond has done his best to keep me at arm's length since I joined the ranks of the state's investigators five years earlier. I received an 'indefinite assignment' to NOPD the same day I received my gold badge, and I have been under the direction of Chief Avery ever since. I am, though, still able to call upon the state police for assistance or direction. Captain Hammond has occasionally called upon me to resolve an awkward situation with the level of discretion Chief Avery has come to expect and appreciate.

"I need to borrow four officers for an hour or so tonight," I told Hammond rather than requested.

"To do what?" he was prepared to listen to my full explanation before telling me no, which is his standard position on anything I request.

"I need a show of force, and maybe a little crowd control," I said. "I am raiding the Night Owl to break up a private party Pete Matranga is throwing."

This abbreviated explanation was meant to spare both of us a long argument over the limits of my legal authority, keeping my own buy money, and not going through his office for my search warrants.

"Why can't you use local officers for this?" he argued.

"I hate to say it, but I could not be certain they wouldn't tip off the target." I was playing to his low opinion of NOPD. I did not believe any uniformed officers Avery would have sent were on Matranga's payroll. My real purpose in using a phalanx of state police officers was that they look more intimidating than members of NOPD.

"Fine," Hammond unexpectedly conceded. "When and where?"

"On the patio at the House of Blues at eleven forty-five tonight. And thank you." This would put us close to the Night Owl without anyone suspecting us of staking out the strip club. Anyone who saw the state police standing outside the House of Blues would believe something was going on inside the famous music club.

"Just don't let me see you on the front-page tomorrow morning," Hammond demanded. Keeping a low profile was the first condition of my being assigned to New Orleans.

"I will do my best to stay below the fold of the Metro section," I assured him.

forty-six

"Marquis. Long time no see," I greeted the pimp as I stepped into the dingy trailer that houses the tow-lot office under the I-10 overpass on Claiborne. Katie excused herself from joining me to meet with him, as she had expressed how low her opinion of the pimp was during one of his rare court appearances.

My quarry was waiting impatiently for his automobile in the trailer's cramped confines rather than near the electronic gate to the holding lot. The city has always meant for retrieving an impounded automobile to be a terrible experience. It makes drivers pay better attention to where they park in the future. The condition of the trailer we were standing in was not a result of the flooding this part of the city suffered during Hurricane Katrina. This trailer replaced an even worse one lost in the storm's aftermath.

Marquis was wearing a suit cut from some sort of plush green velvet-like fabric, with a too-wide tie and a pocket square handkerchief that did the opposite of making him look stylish. His long curls of black hair were slick with gel, and his pungent cologne was enough to drive everyone else waiting for their cars out of the building. He took one look at me and the shiny gold badge I purposefully displayed on my belt as I entered the office, and immediately understood why his car was not yet at the lot despite the short distance it needed to travel.

"What is it today, detective?" he got to the point.

"You are going to do me a favor," I informed him. Negotiations took more time than was available, and I did not want Marquis to believe he had a choice in the matter.

"Do tell," he resisted for our small audience standing behind the thick plexiglass.

"I need you to be the winning bid at the Night Owl tonight." I paused to give him a chance to lie to me.

"I have no idea what is going on in that dump. I never let my girls work there, and you know that," he convincingly protested.

"What I also know is that you spent over an hour running a five-minute errand just around the corner from there this morning. I think you went by to check out the merchandise ahead of the sale," I cornered him. The geography and timing were both right. The purpose of his errand was my only real guesswork.

"No crime in looking, is there?" He finally grasped that I knew about the auction.

I gave Marquis a glare that suggested my reaction to any further such comments would make his car being towed the best part of his day.

"Contributing to the delinquency of a minor has always been a crime," I informed him. "Tell me you didn't touch her."

He sensed that having done so was likely a separate felony and shook his head. I did not imagine Matranga allowed Marquis to touch the merchandise considering the value of an unsullied product on the auction block. It seemed likely prospective bidders accepted an offer to meet the virgin and estimate their financial returns after her deflowering, not unlike horse traders checking the teeth on a filly.

"She is an emancipated minor." Marquis weakly protested. "I saw the papers."

"She is still a minor when it comes to this. Her consent is not going to save any adult that has sex with her from a world of trouble in court."

"I am not going to bid, so it does not matter. She is a tough one and only doing this because of some deal she made with Matranga," he began to distance himself.

"What sort of deal?" I asked without expecting an honest answer.

"Pete said she wanted to get custody of her kid brother and to get him away from her stepfather. He claims she ran away from home because the stepfather tried to molest her. Matranga promised to take care of all that for ten grand that he would loan her. He waited until he took care of everything to tell her how she would be paying the money back. The whole thing was a setup."

"Oldest trick in the book," I said and shook my head that this well-known deal with the devil still works. I was curious how Matranga convinced the girl's stepfather to surrender custody of both of his stepchildren. They were valuable dependents on his taxes if nothing else. I was disappointed at how naïve the child was to believe she could get legal custody of her even younger brother when she was supporting herself by selling her body.

"Don't mess with what works," Marquis tried to joke. This may have been a funny thing to say in his own circle, but it fell very flat when told to a state police detective with a younger sister. He was especially lucky he did not say it directly to Tulip.

"All the same, I need you to go back tonight and bring me the girl," I instructed him.

"I am not going to buy a contract on my life," he immediately balked. "They are only selling her virginity, not the girl."

"How's that?"

"Matranga is looking for someone to pay to break her in, but he is never going to let her go. The opening bid is twenty-five thousand dollars. Pete just wants to turn a nice profit on what he has already invested in her before he puts her to work."

"What's he paid for?" I was at a loss despite his trying to tell me a moment earlier.

"Well, he had to deal with her old man and pay a lawyer to do the paperwork on that emancipated minor thing. It starts to add up."

"I'll give you fifty grand," I suggested. "But make it for the girl as well."

"That might get the job done. I do not have that kind of cash lying around, though." Marquis looked hopeful that he had found a good excuse not to participate in what even he saw as a bad idea.

"I don't expect you to spend your own money." This was not the response he wanted.

"He's still going to kill me if I try to take the girl and he doesn't want to give her up," Marquis pointed out what he saw as being the fly in the ointment.

"He will not be the one who shoots you. Guys like Matranga always have someone else get their hands dirty. Did you meet a guy named Vincent Contaldo? About my height and build, strong silent type in a nice suit? That is his shooter."

"Yeah, he was there. Are you trying to get me killed?" he

demanded. "We can step out back and you can shoot me now. That is quicker than what they will do to me."

"You'll be fine," I patted him on the shoulder. "It is good for my case if they try to kill you, but I won't let them do it. I promise."

"What's any of this to you, anyway?" Marquis finally demanded. "All you're going to do is waste a lot of money and make some really bad people angry."

"I want them to get angry," I explained the part he would understand. Rescuing a teenage runaway exceeded his own sense of humanity. "Anger makes people like Matranga lose their focus on the bigger picture. He did not come back to New Orleans to solve a runaway's family problems."

"I can tell you why he's here." Marquis seemed relieved see a way out of this suicide mission. "Puglisi was paid to keep his mouth shut when he went to prison and now that he is outta prison they think is going to double cross them."

"I heard there was a deal to pay him to keep quiet," I shared without going into details. "Something else is going on, but none of that is why the two of us are talking. I just need you to be my man at the auction."

"What's in it for me?" Marquis tried to open a new escape route.

"I could say you would be doing right by the girl," I offered, knowing full well that morality would never be a factor in his decision. His entire business model was based on doing the exact opposite of what I expected him to do. "But, instead, I will pay you five grand."

"Five grand cash money?" he said with open disbelief. "You are going to hand me five thousand dollars and walk away with the girl? No strings attached?"

"The girl is the string," I pointed out. "You do not get paid unless you deliver her to me. Come by Strada at ten for the buy money. I think fifty grand should be enough to at least make the girl the most expensive mistake Matranga has ever made."

We both turned as the tow truck carrying his five-year old Jaguar sedan arrived on the lot. It was nowhere near as flashy as the Cadillacs and Lincolns driven by the pimps my father used to roust.

"Hey, aren't you going to get my car released?" he shouted

as I began to walk away.

"You can afford to get it out," I reminded him. He gave me an angry look and then remembered his coming payday.

forty-seven

Tony raised an eyebrow but voiced no objection when I told him I was going to tie up half our ready cash in an NOPD investigation. Our concerns about leaving town felt less pressing, but Tony knew informing Chief Avery or Captain Hammond about the hundred thousand dollars in my gun safe, which was already full of Class 3 weapons, could start an unpleasant discussion. I counted on charging Matranga with a convictable felony to mitigate their irritation.

I loaded the banded cash into a satchel that looked like something Marquis Lewis might own. There was a miniature recording device hidden in its lining that would give me the video and audio evidence I needed to make a case against Matranga without having to rely upon Marquis or the girl to testify.

Marquis arrived at nine-thirty. He looked nervous for a man who was about to make the sort of transaction he makes on a too frequent basis. Jason began pouring Courvoisier and Coke cocktails to calm the pimp's nerves while I talked him through what I expected him to do for his five thousand dollars.

"Keep the bag on the table, this side up." I demonstrated what I meant on the bar top. I opened the satchel and showed him the bundles of cash before I showed him the hidden switch for the electronics sewn into the lining. He would survive the sort of quick-glance inspection meant to confirm he carried money and not a weapon that we both expected would happen at the club's door. He was going to have do a lot of fast talking if anyone ran their hands or a metal detector over the bag. The state police officers and I would need a full minute to rescue him. "Flip this before you go inside and point the bag at whatever you want to record. It shoots a nice wide angle, so you do not have to keep moving it around to catch everything. I'd say point it at the girl and leave it alone."

"I still don't feel good about this," he wavered.

I pulled a bundle of hundred-dollar bills from my jacket pocket and laid it on the bar in front of him. It received a lot of attention from everyone at our end of the bar. I kept one hand on it.

"I'll have this for you when you leave there," I reminded him. The part of his brain that was shouting he was going to die was drowned out by the part telling him he was going to make at least a day's illicit earnings for an hour's worth of work and there might be a favor he could call in down the line. I placed my left hand on his shoulder and felt the tension in his body. I lightly squeezed and looked him in the eye. "You've literally got this in the bag, Marquis."

"More like a body bag," he gamely quipped. I could only hope that whatever bravery the liquor provided lasted until this was over.

forty-eight

As it turned out the officers and I never had to set foot in the club. The auction started promptly at midnight and was over in barely half an hour. My objective had never been to arrest Matranga on the spot. I only meant to set the hook should making an arrest be worth the paperwork and explanations. The film record Marquis would provide had everything I needed to make Matranga worry about a prison sentence so long he could expect to die there. The second objective, getting the girl loose from Matranga, proved to be surprisingly simple to accomplish.

Marquis was exiting the Night Owl with Matranga, Contaldo, and a third man I had not yet encountered. Matranga kept a firm hold of the young girl's right arm as the officers and I rounded the corner from Decatur Street. Storming the Night Owl was thankfully no longer necessary. Matranga's party was traveling in his Lincoln Town Car. Russo was standing beside the open rear passenger door as we approached. Marquis spotted the knot of state police headed his way and stepped aside but had the presence of mind to leave the camera and audio running to record Matranga's arrest. I glanced back over my shoulder to make sure Tulip was keeping her distance until the state police officers and I secured the crime scene.

"Pietro Matranga," I said in a voice loud enough to catch his attention without waking the neighborhood. "We need a word with the young lady."

"Excuse me?" he asked. He knew what he had done wrong inside the building, and the massed police presence headed his way gave him reason to believe that I did, as well.

"She is a runaway juvenile from Denver. I am here to send her home," I lied with all the conviction I felt necessary to befuddle everyone, including the girl.

We closed the distance and one of the uniformed officers went so far as to slam the passenger door closed while I finished my business. Russo wisely returned to his seat behind the wheel. Tulip remained by the front bumper, within earshot but out of range of any physical altercation that might occur.

"Detective Holland, is it? There seems to be a considerable misunderstanding," the unknown member of the party spoke up. "She is not a runaway. She is an emancipated minor and free to travel as she sees fit, with whomever she sees fit."

"Not tonight," I dug in. "I take it you are Matranga's new mouthpiece?"

"Attorney is the preferred term," the man calmly suggested, but also failed to answer the question. He was in his late fifties, bald, a head shorter than me and not nearly as muscled. He did not need a lot of strength to beat weak cases. He wore a nicely tailored suit and a pair of shoes I was certain someone had made by hand just for his own two feet. He oozed the sort of charm and wealth that comes from protesting allegations against his egregiously guilty clients. "Allow me to show you the paperwork."

I caught myself before I commented on his having the young woman's emancipation paperwork in hand. He had clearly anticipated someone challenging her legal status during the evening. I barely skimmed the paperwork. I studied the signatures and dates rather than the content. I finally had a name to put with the girl's face, Rebecca Conners. There was no reason to question the legality of the paperwork. The legality of what transpired to emancipate the blonde waif was what might not stand up to scrutiny.

"And you represent Miss Conners here as well?" I said as I looked up from reading the pages. I glanced at her and hoped my expression seemed reassuring because she looked like she might explode at any moment. She was clearly too young to be in this company, and her costume emphasized the fact. It came complete with freckles and her blonde hair pulled into school-girl braids. She was shivering in the cool night air because the rest of her costume for the auction was a gauze-thin white blouse which revealed her bare breasts and what looked to be a much-shortened plaid skirt from a private Catholic school. There was a toughness in the girl's jawline and eyes that told me she was not as innocent or helpless as she had led Boomer to believe. Her dilated pupils especially troubled me.

"I have assisted Miss Connors on some matters, but I am not on a retainer. I have only one client," the mysterious attorney casually distanced himself from the sort of connection he sensed I wanted to make.

"I need to question her, so I have arranged for an attorney to represent her during questioning. Rebecca is underage to be on the premises, emancipated or not. She is clearly under the influence of alcohol, and perhaps illegal narcotics, as well." I introduced Tulip and handed her Rebecca's paperwork rather than returning it to the attorney. Tulip presented him with her business card.

"I had no idea she was underage," Matranga declared without being prompted. This unsolicited denial was absurd after the girl's attorney had just declared she was a minor. "I am going home unless you plan to arrest me."

He rapped on the side window of the limo and Russo nervously came around to open the passenger door one more time.

"As a minor, she knows better than to be in there," I said to let him believe he was getting away clean. "It's not like you own the place and allowed her to drink, now, is it?"

I hoped, in the fleeting moment it occurred, that the camera captured the look which passed between the attorney and Matranga when I said this. I counted on his legal exposure on that matter to seriously bother the two of them.

"What are your plans for the young woman?" the attorney asked. His blustering had abruptly transformed into the voice of reason with concern for the young woman's well-being. My sister has developed a similar collection of voices for all occasions, so I did not fall for his apparent change of heart.

"That is not your concern. You have already made it clear that you do not represent her," I said to test his resolve.

"Call it professional curiosity. She may make some unfounded allegations against my client," he began defending Matranga. "Also, the young lady and I have business to discuss, but we can do that after her release."

He handed the confused girl his business card before joining Matranga in the limousine. Russo looked inquiringly at me through the windshield, making sure I was okay with his passengers leaving the scene. The two men left Rebecca Connors cowering between two brawny state troopers under the strip club's awning.

I turned my attention to Marquis Lewis. He remained

glued to the wall beneath the club's buzzing neon sign. His breathing was unusually rapid, and he was sweating.

"You okay?" I asked and eased him away from the wall.

"That was close," he said in two short breaths.

"How so?" I asked and removed my satchel from his hand.

"I won the auction, like you wanted. We were on our way to Matranga's house so I could close the deal, if you know what I mean. I was afraid you were not going to show up and I knew you would mess me up if I touched her. They would have killed me if I did not go through with it when we got there," Marquis explained his anxieties.

"Did you record everything?" I asked.

"I think so. I did what you told me to do," he tried to assure me.

"I'll watch it tonight," I told him. "I'll get you your money tomorrow if it checks out."

"That wasn't our deal." His anxiety dissipated rapidly when it came to money.

"Our deal was that you would record the auction and pass the money to Matranga. I assume he has the money because the bag here is empty. I just need to confirm you recorded everything so I can get my money back." I was not going to stiff him either way because I might be need his services again someday.

"Tomorrow," he demanded loud enough for everyone to hear and put some mojo back in his step as he strutted towards Bourbon Street.

"Thank you, officers. We can take it from here," I declared and grabbed Rebecca's trembling arm. I had my handcuffs out for all to see, but the state police officers did not wait for me to restrain her before they headed back to their duty posts.

"What do you want?" Rebecca spun around and demanded once the three of us were alone on the sidewalk. I could see the club's bouncer watching us through the grimy window in the heavy door. He had the good sense to stay inside until we left.

"Things I will never have," I sighed and grabbed her arm again to tug her towards Decatur Street. "From you, though, I just want a few answers before I go to bed."

"Hello, Rebecca, my name is Tulip Holland. I am going to be your attorney, and the detective is not going to question you until we have had a chance to talk to one another," Tulip introduced herself.

"What if I do not want an attorney? I never did anything wrong," she unwisely rebuffed my sister's generosity. Tulip has a five-hundred-dollar billable hour.

"According to Detective Holland you are at least guilty of drinking underage. The company we found you in indicates you are in far more need of an attorney that you can imagine," Tulip patiently explained. "Imagine how upset the owner of this place will be when he loses his liquor license for serving you. He might sue you for compensation."

This would have been an absurd thought to anyone older than Rebecca Connors. She was naïve, but she clearly understood the danger in crossing the men whose company she had just left.

"You two have the same last name," she said after taking a moment to consider her position. "What are the odds of that happening?"

"Better than you would think," I said and steered her toward Canal Place, where Tulip had parked her Porsche Cayenne. I was exhausted and had no problem with my sister interviewing her new client rather than allowing me to question her.

"Wasn't Marvin Alexander the name of the attorney who sent the men after Tony?" Tulip asked as we waited to cross North Peters. The street is four lanes wide as it passes the hotel and there was a surprising amount of traffic for such a late hour.

"Sounds right, you were the one who dug into his past," I reminded her.

"Well, we just put a face to the name," Tulip said and handed me the business card of the well-dressed attorney at Matranga's side. Marvin Alexander had his business card printed on heavy stock black paper with embossed script in a brilliant shade of white. I was certain the fine script on the card did not match his signature. Alexander's law office had an address in Brooklyn, New York. More specifically, it was located on Brighton Beach Boulevard.

"You're going to dig into him a lot further, aren't you?" I tried not to alarm Rebecca with the question.

"I already am," Tulip said with a fierce lack of concern for what her pro-bono client thought about her tone of voice, or whatever loyalty the young girl harbored towards the attorney who had freed her from the custody of her stepfather.

forty-nine

Katie spent Sunday night at her own place Uptown rather than risk our having a conversation on my return from the Night Owl that anyone's defense attorney might try to twist in court. This gave me the perfect opportunity to test my theory on the location of Puglisi's journals. My run-in with Matranga and his attorney made me even more aware of their value, and Bassett's recent foray indicated just how narrow my window of opportunity to secure them was.

I left Roux in his kennel before heading to Puglisi's former brothel on foot. I heard a whistle as I rounded the corner at Esplanade and looked across the street, to where a heavyset dark-haired man standing outside of Checkpoint Charlie's was signaling someone on Decatur Street. I initially took this to be his way of hailing a taxi or motioning to a friend headed his way from Molly's or Coops. I would have ignored him had he not immediately began walking in stride with me on his side of Esplanade. The thug blew his cover when he motioned to his companion only to begin walking away in the same instant. I know a bad tail when I see one, and these two were not particularly good at surveillance.

I stopped and crossed the street towards the first man, but then backtracked as soon as he stopped walking. I went so far as to stand still and stare at the man to let him know his cover was blown, but he simply stared back and waited for my next move. I noticed his partner was leaning against the high metal fence surrounding the Old Mint. They were both tall, stocky, Slavic looking guys wearing jeans and lightweight jackets. I assumed they were armed but I assume everybody is armed, including schoolchildren.

I continued backtracking and led them through the largely vacant French Market and past the line of shuttered shops along North Peters Street from the Market to Jackson Square. I calmly stepped into Café du Monde, at the end of the shops and directly across from the Square and took a seat near the street. I ordered a plate of beignets and a black coffee from the thin Vietnamese woman who came around to serve me and watched the pair split up. They each stood at a corner to the

Square, so one or the other could fall in behind me if I made my way past the Cathedral as I would do if I were on one of my usual patrols. Someone had either briefed them on my routine or I had managed to overlook the starkly obvious pair long enough for them to learn my routes. Either way I was seriously remiss in my counter-surveillance.

I dropped enough cash on the table for the food and a generous tip and stepped back onto the sidewalk. I headed towards Strada rather than across the street and timed my walk to take advantage of the passing of two transit busses. I dashed across the street ahead of a transit bus headed towards Elysian Fields and immediately crossed behind the bus headed towards Canal Street. I crouched between two cars and waited for the men to realize they had lost sight of me. I waited until they dashed into the middle of North Peters together to look for me before I sprinted onto Madison Street.

Madison runs only one block, but it connects North Peters to Chartres Street. Movie crews love to film on Madison because they can have French Quarter exteriors without blocking a lot of traffic. I like it because it is a path from the riverfront to the heart of the Quarter that almost nobody knows about. The far end of the narrow street would put me just two doorways from the corner of Chartres and Dumaine. I sprinted half-way down the street before ducking into a courtyard. The tenants of the apartment building are lax about keeping the ornamental gate to their patio locked and I counted on one of them to have left it unlocked as they staggered home from the bars hours earlier.

I hastily took a position behind the courtyard fountain and watched the entrance for what I hoped was only a two-man team. I believed I had made it onto Madison Street before the buses passed one another and exposed my disappearing act. Normal protocol now called for one of them to retrace our steps from Esplanade while the other combed the river side of the floodwall in case I had slipped over the Moonwalk. I did not give their unknown employer credit for bankrolling more than this pair to watch me this late at night. I was normally in bed by now and would not be on my usual routine until five o'clock in the morning. I began to wonder if they had begun following me outside of the Night Owl.

It took five minutes for one of them to walk past the gate. I imagined that the closest of the pair hurried down North Peters to catch up to me. His partner on the far side of the Square would have checked the Moonwalk and then hurried past the Cathedral before checking the side streets. This one would walk the length of Madison and then wait for a signal from his partner about what to do next. I was becoming more confident that my destination was not one they anticipated. They would give up the search and fall back to stake out Strada once they accepted that I had eluded them, so I only needed to avoid them for the three blocks between where I was and Puglisi's place.

I kept to the shadows as I made my way to the gate and then peered as far as I could in both directions before easing the creaking metal gate open a little at a time and extending my head far enough to scan both ends of the short street. I wasted no time before sprinting for the corner and then running even harder across Royal Street and Bourbon Street to reach Dauphine. I stepped into a doorway to catch my breath before I rounded the final corner. I spotted no sign of my unexpected tail before I made it to the relative safety of the empty house.

I used my key to enter Puglisi's former brothel and locked the door behind me before I ran up the steps in the dark. I took off my Merrell work boots and sat on the landing for a few minutes, making sure I was not visible through the windows or the glass in the front door, while I assessed the unexpected surveillance. Counter-surveillance is a habit left over from my intelligence training, which itself was an extension of the situational awareness I honed during my long career in Special Operations. I was at a loss for who these men were, but there were plenty of candidates.

SAC Conroy had made it clear that he had Puglisi and Matranga under close watch and were concerned Tony might fall in league with them. A pair of agents could have been detached from that operation to watch me after I left the Night Owl. I would not have been at all surprised had FBI agents sprung up to arrest Pete Matranga when I chose not to do so, and Conroy was certain to ask Chief Avery what transpired at the Night Owl once the sun came up. I discounted Matranga or

Puglisi paying anyone to follow me. I did not threaten either of them enough that they might make a preemptive strike. I also did not believe any of the possible employers of my new tail believed I had solved the mystery of where the journals were hidden.

This left Marvin Alexander as the most likely person behind the pair. He may have already paid for out-of-town talent to take on my partner, so having additional men tail me after Tulip and I bested him at the Night Owl was not out of the question.

I left my boots on the landing. I did not want to risk leaving a boot print in any dust or loose drywall I disturbed while probing the wall where I was convinced Puglisi had hidden his journals. I removed the poster of Vanity and set it on the bed before reaching into my messenger bag for the same knife I had intended to use previously. I chose to make my inspection from the bedroom because the poster would hide any damage I made to this wall, while even a small hole would be a neon sign in the patch made to the closet wall.

I moistened a handcloth with a bottle of water taken from my messenger bag before I used it to saturate the wallpaper behind the poster where I intended to cut into the wall. I needed to minimize the amount of dust created in carving an opening. I used the tip of the blade to pry the top corners of the roughly one-foot size hole I carved into the drywall. I was relieved that this was not lath and plaster after I removed the material in one piece. The damp edges of the wallpaper were smoother than I had any reason to hope for using such a big blade.

It did not take long to realize the cavity was empty of anything, in particular the hundred or so journals I anticipated finding. I had no way of knowing how much space Puglisi's journals would have taken, but even writing only one page each day over the course of thirty years would have created a sizeable library.

I returned the knife to my bag and turned my attention back to the hole in the wall. I damped the washcloth again and moistened the edges of the drywall on both the wall and the plug. I gently pressed the piece back in place and made sure the wallpaper pattern was lined up properly before I dampened the a few inches of wall to either side of the patch and rehung the poster. The average observer was unlikely to notice the faint scar-like lines of the patch once it dried.

I used my last few minutes in the room to be sure I had left nothing to link me to the scene. I used the moist handcloth to wipe away the dust on the dresser before I placed the cloth and water bottle in my bag and carried my boots to the entryway before putting them on.

I locked the house and walked towards Esplanade and then veered to the right as I approached Governor Nicholls Street. I glanced both ways as I made my way along the deserted street. I suspected my tail was re-positioned to watch Strada to note what time I returned. The hour or so between the time they lost me and when they saw me next was going to be hard to account for when they reported their lapse.

I walked two blocks out of my way so the two men watching my apartment would base their theories on where I had been on the street corner I rounded on my way home. I chose to step onto Decatur Street at St. Phillip because backtracking from there would lead to series of gay bars, and that would lead to some hilariously wrong conclusions.

fifty

Chief Avery called just after seven o'clock the next morning to remind me that we were having lunch together at Strada. He did not elaborate on what was causing him so much stress at such an early hour of the day. I promised to have something by then and allowed him to be the one to hang up. I have a bad habit of being the one who breaks our connection.

I elected to let Tulip reach out to me about Rebecca Collins. There was little I was going to be able to do for the girl. I counted on Tulip to convince Rebecca to testify against Matranga. That promised to be an especially difficult conversation because Rebecca apparently did not seem to grasp what she had taken part in the night before.

I needed to keep my promise to pay Marquis Lewis for his help, so I stuffed five thousand dollars into an envelope and drove my Cadillac XLR to New Orleans East to pay the man. The coupe is bright red, low slung, supercharged and stands out like a sore thumb. I could have taken my station wagon or the company truck, but I wanted to be sure I could outrun anyone who might try to tail me or to give chase. I remained a bit rattled by the pair that had followed me the night before. My concern had less to do with their potential menace than it did with not knowing who was paying them for their wasted time.

Meeting Marquis in the open might expose our connection to my new tail, so I chose to use the Black Knights to make the payment on my behalf. The bikers' clubhouse is in a cinder block strip mall on Downman Road. I did not see Marquis' Jaguar in the parking lot when I parked near the heavy double-door entrance to the former bar and grill the bikers occupied in the wake of Hurricane Katrina, but I also did not expect him to be up and about at such an early hour.

The probationary member of the gang working the door at nine in the morning failed to slow me down. I distracted the man by waving my badge in his fat bearded face with one hand while I opened the door with the other. I paused to let my eyes adjust to the darkness as I stepped into the place. The interior is illuminated only by the lights over the heavy billiard tables and the purloined neon signs behind the bar in the center of the room. I was glumly nodded at by the half dozen members I suspect live on the premises before I turned to my left and headed towards their chapter president's office. This door was guarded by much more capable members, ones who feared the Glock on my hip more than they did the badge beside it.

"Good morning gentlemen," I blithely greeted them. "I need to see Jimmy."

"He expecting you?" one of them demanded.

"Is he ever expecting me?" I asked in return. We had been through this before.

"I'll let him know you're here." The biker motioned for me to stay put while he went into the office to announce my arrival. It allowed Jimmy Hancock time to clear his office of anything which might invite my attention as a member of law enforcement.

Jimmy Hancock and the Black Knights Bike Club were a middling bunch of tough-guy bikers and almost comically wannabe hoodlums before Hurricane Katrina. New Orleans East was over-represented by far better organized criminals who tolerated the bike gang's petty crimes and drug dealing. The evacuation of nearly the city's entire population reset the board, and Jimmy had made sure the Black Knights were the ones to return from Houston ahead of those who had owned the community prior to the storm. The Knights evicted or disappeared their opposition with an enthusiasm that dissuaded anyone from challenging their newfound ruthlessness. I was never tasked with battling street gangs or investigating gang-related crimes in general, so Jimmy and I were able to develop a comfortable détente.

The burly security guard came out of the office and held the door open without saying another word. The reinforced door closed with its usual heavy thud.

"What is it today, Detective?" Jimmy asked and flashed a bright white smile. He was alone in the office, which was somewhat unusual. His second-in-command is seldom absent from his side.

"I have business with Marquis." I couldn't help noticing the 1911 Colt .45 on his desk.

"He said you would probably be dropping by," Jimmy said

and gave me a faintly amused look. "You really dropped him in the pot last night, didn't you?"

"I didn't think it was going to boil over in quite that way," I responded. I honestly saw it as a straightforward transaction. My failure was in not knowing the guest list.

"Marquis thinks you're going to get him killed," Jimmy shared.

"I hope not." It was the best I could offer. "Might I prevail upon you to watch his back until I clean this up?"

"It will cost you, you know," Jimmy taunted me.

"I am sure you owe me at least one more favor than I do you," I countered. Neither of us was counting such things, and neither of us was in the habit of creating situations which generate favors. Asking Jimmy to back Marquis was little more than asking him to protect his own interests. Marquis supplied most of the girls in the strip club just down the street. It is the Knights' only legitimate business, but they use it to launder the proceeds from everything else they have going. Recruiting hookers was not one of the bike gang's many criminal interests. "As it is, I owe Marquis for his help. Perhaps you could pass this along to him."

I set the thick envelope on the desk and pushed it towards him.

"Next time I see him," Jimmy said more than promised as he slid the sealed envelope into a desk drawer. Jimmy not counting the cash was a good sign that Marquis was never getting paid. "What you gonna do about them mobsters?"

"Are they nosing around your business, too?" I asked. "They seem ambitious."

"Ambitious. I like that word," Jimmy grinned again. "Curiosity killed the cat, but ambition may kill a few of these cats before this all blows over."

"Did Matranga come to you in person, or did he send someone?" I figured tossing a name or two into the conversation might keep his tongue flowing. He was never going to articulate a specific crime or enterprise that might help me do my job, but he had come to appreciate the value of someone on my side of the badge seeing his side of the law.

"Two guys, a couple of weeks apart. One was a tough guy type from Chicago who said there was plenty of business for both of us if we stayed in our own lanes. The other was a slick attorney with a Yat accent. He told me he represented parties who would approve our managing the businesses of ours they intended to acquire."

"That's a very lawyerly way to threaten someone. Also, we share that Yats accent with Brooklyn," I mused. "I assume you took the second guy a lot more seriously than the first."

"I don't take anyone's threats very serious," Jimmy wanted me to understand. "But the lawyer guy came at me like that bald lawyer dude in The Usual Suspects, only he is a lot shorter than that guy. He thought we would roll over when he said we didn't have a choice."

"Do you?" I wondered just how widespread and bloody this could get. "We're talking about the Russian Mob in case he didn't mention that part of his deal."

"Home field advantage," Jimmy said and dropped a hand on the Colt.

"Home field, indeed," I smiled and stood up to leave but then found one more question to ask. "Have you seen anyone snooping around your business since then?"

"No, why? Do you know something?" Jimmy answered and pressed me for more information. I was the one who brought it up so there must be a reason.

"I had a couple of nasty looking guys try to tail me last night. Tall, short hair, not friendly looking at all. You might keep an eye out," I suggested. The Knights were unlikely to send the thugs away with a polite warning. Jimmy nodded in a way that let me know he understood why I mentioned them.

Marvin Alexander walked through the doors of Strada Ammazarre moments after the bistro opened for business. Hannah, our Goth-loving daytime bartender, dialed my cellphone number to reach me even though I was in the building. She does this on those rare occasions she is unnerved by someone. Alexander and the brutish-looking duo from the night before were enough to make anyone quiver. The attorney was well dressed, with his hair and manicured fingernails as tailored as his suit. The presence of his goons was meant to say that Alexander never gets his own hands dirty because men who enjoy doing so are at his disposal.

"Three for lunch?" I asked and calmly grabbed menus from the stack beside the hostess stand. I wanted something handy to smack anyone who moved aggressively.

"Oh, we won't be staying that long," the attorney calmly shook his head. He set his briefcase on the bar, opened it, and removed the five banded bundles of cash I had given Marquis Lewis the night before. He calmly set them on the bar for all to see and then closed his briefcase before he spoke another word. Hannah could not take her eyes off the mound of cash. "I believe all of this is yours, Detective Holland."

"You need lessons on how to bribe a policeman, Mister Alexander," I tried to refrain from showing any emotional reaction to the money.

"You amuse me," he said with a razor-thin smile. "I am returning the money your informant used to frame Mister Matranga last night. Marquis Lewis misunderstood what was clearly a joke."

"It can't have been that unclear if your client accepted fifty thousand dollars from him," I countered before realizing I made a mistake by telling Alexander I knew exactly how much money was piled on the bar. I made a second one in not protesting knowledge of Marquis Lewis or his actions. The attorney raised one eyebrow and smiled to let me know he caught both mistakes.

"It became obvious that Mister Lewis did not lose his own money because he has not yet contacted Mister Matranga

213

about restitution. I cannot imagine he is able to absorb that sort of financial setback. It was a very short line to draw between the two of you after your interdiction. I assure you it was never anyone's intent to traffic a minor for sex," Alexander explained the series of minor errors which led him to my doorstep and continued to make his argument against my charging Matranga.

"There is evidence to the contrary," I persisted. His eyes narrowed just a bit and the seconds-long delay in his response suggested he was deciding whether I was bluffing or had anything beyond my criminal's word against another criminal.

"Evidence has a way of playing both ways in a courtroom," he finally dismissed the threat. "I came here in hopes of sparing both of you that exercise. The young girl is in the care of your sister, your money has been returned, and I personally promise you that Mister Matranga will not make the same mistake again."

"Your client doesn't strike me as the sort who learns lessons," I replied.

"Your own reputation is much the same, Detective Holland," Alexander said and flashed another grin. I saw no humor in his expression and worried it came from his remembering the sort of terrible things that had happened to anyone at whom he had flashed this grin in the past. Neither of his goons said a word or changed their stony expressions once during our conversation.

"I have a reputation for many things," I offered my own oblique warning.

"Well earned ones, I might add," Alexander unexpectedly concurred. "Isn't that right, fellows?"

The two men I had bested the night before gave me glum nods to acknowledge their failure to perform the man's assignment. I doubt their debriefing was this calm or polite. The backhand compliment was Alexander's way of promising they would do better in the future.

"Enough with all that," the attorney abruptly declared. "I encourage you to give serious consideration before proceeding. Mister Matranga is embarrassed that things got out of hand, but he bears no ill will over your attempt to frame him for such a heinous act. There would be no cause for a defamation suit were you to decide against filing criminal charges."

"Defamation. That is certainly a novel defense angle," I laughed in his face. "Does that sort of threat work well in New York?"

"It works everywhere because defamation cases involve depositions. Trust me, you would not enjoy us probing your past cases or certain work you have done for your government," Alexander explained the hidden dangers his defense strategy posed to a plaintiff. "Perhaps there are incidents in your past which were outside the boundaries of the law you swore to uphold. How much light can your past stand having shone upon it, Detective?"

"More than you can possibly shine," I heard myself lie. I abruptly realized I had lost this fight from the beginning.

"I have delivered your money and Mister Matranga's apology and assurances. Do what you feel you must, and his attorney will do what he must," Alexander sighed and stepped away from the bar.

"Wait. You are not his attorney?" I asked.

"I agreed to represent him solely in the matter of returning your money. As I told you last night, I have only one client and neither Mister Matranga nor Mister Puglisi are that client," Alexander informed me. He was the one who slipped up now, by adding Puglisi to his list of non-clients in this discussion rather than Rebecca Collins.

"That's right, you are here to defend Bear Brovartey," I recalled.

Alexander's grin returned as he spoke. "Mister Brovartey will not need anyone to represent him shortly. But, for the record, my client did ask me to advise and assist Mister Brovartey with his defense."

"Did that assistance include killing Spenser Duncan?"

"You will have a difficult time pinning that on Mister Brovartey or his defense team. There were plenty of people who wished that man harm," Alexander neither confirmed nor denied the underlying accusation before he turned to leave. I had a dozen fresh questions but knew he would answer none of them, so I stood mutely while he swaggered out the door with his men flanking him.

fifty-two

I was not Marvin Alexander's only stop that morning. Tulip was waiting for the trio before they arrived at her office located above a row of shops on Magazine Street. Her response when I called to warn her to expect their visit was delivered in the familiar voice of an attorney already spoiling for a good fight.

"You're late," she brusquely informed Alexander as he stepped confidently into her office. She barely glanced at the men flanking him, despite the pair blocking the only doorway if she needed to escape. "You'll need to leave your guard dogs outside."

"Well, I am here now," Alexander said with a bit of confusion as he waved his hands to send his men into her outer office. He had meant this visit to take her by surprise.

"I am not entirely sure why," Tulip casually suggested. "I assume you want me to believe you came by to relay a message to Rebecca. I think this is more likely to be some old-school way to intimidate my brother. You know, letting him know you can get to me and all that nonsense."

"We both know my ability to reach out to you is not really nonsense at all," Alexander validated the perceived threat as he moved to sit on the long sofa in the corner where Tulip prefers to interview her clients.

"It's quaint that you believe this will work," Tulip said and laughed. The sound of the electronic lock on the office's steel-reinforced solid-core door engaging caught the smug attorney's attention. He had also arrived too late to see her position the high-capacity Ruger handgun she and I spent hours training with beneath an open file on her desktop. "Marv, I assume I can call you what everyone else does, far more intimidating people than you have made a run at me. I used to get scared, but now I just get angry. How are your skills with angry women?"

"I see all of the stories of your take-no-nonsense attitude are true," he said as he adjusted his position. It allowed his suit jacket to open enough to show he was armed as well.

"Nonsense is my polite term for the sort of empty posturing men like to do before they get to know me," Tulip set him straight. "You are wasting both of our time if this is all you came here to do."

"Indeed," he nodded and then smiled almost genuinely. Her attitude confirmed whatever his sources had told him about my sister's refusal to be easily intimidated, and he turned to more mundane matters to see if she might drop her guard. "I merely wanted to let you know that Miss Connors is no longer welcome at the Night Owl and that any calls she makes to Mister Matranga will go unanswered. To put it even more bluntly, the girl is now entirely your problem, as you will discover if you have not already done so. I also wanted to let you know that I spoke with your brother this morning and want to repeat to you personally that neither of you have reason to fear any repercussions for your actions last evening. I think the three of us can agree it is in all our best interests if things are allowed to end as they presently stand."

"I do not agree to anything," she strode across her office to sit in one of the two upholstered chairs across from Alexander. She had changed clothes after our phone call and very deliberately crossed her left leg over her right. Alexander watched as she flashed a distracting amount of thigh in her shorter than usual skirt in the process. His lapse allowed her to casually rest her right hand on the seat cushion. The small Beretta handgun she normally carries in her purse was cocked and pressed beside her hip under the cushion. Alexander's visit was unfolding precisely as she envisioned it would, and not at all as he expected. "The State Police were informed of a female minor being exploited and refused to act, which forced my brother to remove her from the situation, so the State Police will certainly need to answer for that. Your client very clearly did not have Rebecca's best interests in mind when he arranged to auction her virginity and, as the presumptive owner of the Night Owl, he is responsible for alcohol being served to a minor. Your own presence during the Night Owl incident carries ethical issues for yourself as well."

"You are an aggressive one, aren't you?" Alexander's use of a condescending tone was his first truly serious mistake.

"The laws are there for a reason, Marvin," she icily reminded him. "I merely use all of the tools the system provides."

"Don't misunderstand me. I am all in favor of your admonishing the State Police for their lackadaisical attitude towards human trafficking," Alexander sought to regain control of anything happening in the office, starting with their conversation. "I only ask that you reconsider any accusations you intend to lodge against Mister Matranga. He could hardly auction something he did not own. He humored Miss Connors' own sordid fantasy, but he was never going to allow Marquis Lewis to touch the girl. Your brother confirmed for me that Marquis Lewis never intended to touch her either, as Marquis is an informant for the State Police."

"I cannot imagine my brother identifying an informant," Tulip laughed.

"Not in so many words, no, but he did confirm it all the same. I returned the money Marquis Lewis gave Mister Matranga last evening in hopes your brother would desist from filing charges. What good is it to go to court to hear two criminals debate their misdeeds?" Alexander continued to eat up my sister's time and patience.

"I don't spend much time in criminal courtrooms. My work involves civil matters such as emotional distress and workplace exploitation. There could be a case to make for the latter if Pietro Matranga owns any share of the Night Owl," Tulip persisted. Alexander considered her unanticipated threats and paused before continuing.

"Such difficult things to prove." He said as though unconcerned about the unexpected legal jeopardy in which she meant to present to himself as well as Matranga.

"True," Tulip initially seemed to relent. "But juries worry more about the parties involved than they do over the merits of evidence or testimony. Who would they side with, a sixteen-year-old runaway lost in the big city or a former Mafia capo? He is a former capo, unless my brother is incorrect."

"Yes, former. I am surprised you would dredge up a man's past like that considering your own brother's history. I am sure a jury would love to hear his life story," Alexander asked with feigned injury and then attempted another threat. "Your own family should be careful about throwing rocks at glass houses."

"I wouldn't drag any of that into this if I were you," Tulip firmly recommended.

"I can see why you would prefer not. Has Mister al-Majid, did I say his name right, told you the millions of dollars he has in an account in Dominican Republic in order to obtain citizenship were stolen from the government in Iraq? The State Department is still protecting Mister al-Majid from Interpol's inquiries into the money and a series of unsolved homicides, but political winds change all the time, don't they? You handled the chef's EB-5 visa application. Did you personally certify his finances were legal?"

Tulip's expression did not register the surprise or alarm he anticipated as he told her things she already knew and brought up others she always suspected Tony and I were keeping from her. Alexander decided to scrape closer to the bone. "I am especially interested to meet your Uncle Felix. I should put a fixer able to arrange your brother's police commission and assignment to NOPD on retainer, don't you think? I also hope you are not having your mother and that dog handler babysit Miss Connors. Dealing with the whims of a teenager would surely tax both their health, and you know how bad Roger Kline's asthma can be."

Tulip barely managed to keep her composure. She needed to find a way to convince Alexander this verbal duel was a waste of time. "None of that would find its way into court so your plan would be to leak it to the press in tidbits like chum in a shark tank."

"The press has not shown much interest before now. They have had ample time to investigate all of this, but their interest seems to be considerably less than your brother's interest is in locating your father."

That finally caused her to flinch. "Our father died helping people after Katrina."

"We both know an FBI informant claimed your father was shot and killed by one of their own agents," Alexander insisted. Tulip realized baiting her about our father's death was meant to show the depth and breadth of Alexander's sources of information. The informant's statement was captured on a wiretap which was never released to the public. Tulip and I never tell anyone precisely how our father died following the storm.

"You're saying the man lied?" Her tone of voice encouraged

him to keep attacking.

"I see no reason to doubt the dead man's version of events, but did it ever occur to you that your brother had already decided to stop looking? I mean, he spent four years looking for the answer but was quick to use this man's story as a reason to stop. Perhaps the FBI agent who shot your father verified the story before dying in his staged auto accident. The FBI still considers your brother to be a suspect in their investigation."

"Perhaps we were all ready to move on," Tulip calmly retorted. She was anything but calm about the man's arguments and accusations. It was time to begin pushing back. "Did you come here just to try and drive a wedge into my family? You made a point of declaring that Matranga is not your client when you left the club last night. You certainly don't strike me as the sort of attorney who would take him on after you witnessed him commit a felony."

"I assure you, I am just a simple city lawyer," he chuckled at his paraphrase of the popular lawyer joke. She allowed him a moment to continue believing his life remained a sealed book before she proceeded to rip the cover off.

"I suppose that is easiest when you only have one client," she suggested as she calmly returned to her desk. She leaned her knuckles beside the open file on her desk, placing the heavier pistol within easy reach before she weaponized what her initial search into Marvin Alexander's own life revealed. "And how is Uncle Dudiyn? Does he call you Marvin or Malek?"

Her adversary tried to stare her down as he stood up unsteadily and silently crossed the room. Tulip made sure not to be the one to blink. The crimson-faced attorney paused as though he was going to say something but chose to leave instead. Tulip smiled as she unlocked the heavy door for him but didn't wait for the door to close before she held the heavy pistol in both hands, as she was trained.

She confirmed all three men had left her building before she released the breath she was holding and called me to invite herself to lunch.

fifty-three

Chief Avery had just finished explaining what had upset his morning when Tulip stormed through the kitchen doors. She would have been even more irate to learn Michael Conroy had taken it upon himself to forward photos of the bloody letter opener and his own version of the assault on Tony to Interpol. SAC Conroy informed Chief Avery that he was concerned enough about Tony's checkered past that he wanted to know if the chef had displayed his unique knife skills anywhere else before he emigrated. He had to know the Chief of Detectives would relay the news to me. Avery was as unhappy about the FBI agent's actions as he was being used as a messenger between the two of us on matter that had nothing to do with him or NOPD business.

Tulip's arrival allowed us to focus on things we could do something about. She was still running on the adrenaline left from her brief encounter with Marvin Alexander. She had dissected every comment he made during the drive from her office to Strada, and had already deduced where he had learned the most damaging things he mentioned. Tulip was well versed on the declassified version of an after-action report for Operation Stoplight. The anti-terrorism mission brought Anthony Venzo Hussein al-Majid, since shortened to Tony Venzo, and I together in Baghdad in 2002. She assumed the attorney found the same file in some dark corner of the internet the government had not yet scoured. She was far more concerned to learn Tony's personal finances were less secure than we all believed and that there might be a mole in the FBI.

"I see your encounter with Marvin was as refreshing as my own," I tried to jest. Tulip can usually be distracted enough by such comments that she calms down.

"The three of us will be having a refreshing conversation, as well," she barked and pointed an index finger at Tony and me. Chief Avery did not bother to hide the relief he found in not being included in whatever Tulip came to discuss.

"Then I'll need my strength. Let's eat." I made a second attempt at distraction.

Tulip sat on the opposite side of Avery. It wasn't until she did so that I realized the entire kitchen had ground to a standstill during her outburst. Hannah broke the stillness by delivering a glass of Tulip's favorite Italian pinot grigio from the bar. The daytime bartender must have seen the look on Tulip's face when she arrived and took it upon herself to save the rest of us.

"Alright then, tell me what's going on," Avery demanded of me as he spread a linen napkin across his broad lap.

"I was tipped off that Matranga intended to auction off a sixteen-year-old runaway at the Night Owl last night. I provided Marquis Lewis with enough buy money to be the high bidder. I wanted to place money we could definitively identify into Matranga's hands so we could trace how he spent it," I began. I got farther into the story than I thought I might before Avery interrupted me.

"From the beginning," he demanded. "Who told you about the Night Owl, how do you know the girl, and where the heck did you get the money?"

"Details," I sighed in mock frustration. "One of my contacts told me Lenny Bonetti was spreading the word about the auction. Lenny also let slip that Matranga has staked a claim to the Night Owl, which makes sense because he needs a place to operate out of while making his big comeback," I more fully informed NOPD's Chief of Detectives. "I encountered the girl when she lived with the homeless vets on the Moonwalk. I called Captain Hammond when I learned she was working at the Night Owl, but his position at the time was that the State Police needed a better reason to raid the place than gathering up runaways. I talked him into assigning four officers to accompany me to the club to investigate the matter."

"This is why you wanted Marquis, isn't it?" Avery wasn't about to comment on Captain Hammond's part in this, but he felt I had played him.

"Who better to send than a criminal Matranga already knew? How could I go in there undercover?" It was a lame justification for my actions. The arrival of small hearts of palm salads topped with shaved Parmesan gave Avery something to chew on besides my rear end while I continued debriefing him. "Tulip accompanied the officers and me to the Night Owl to act as the minor's attorney if need be. We encountered Matranga as he and another man were leaving the Night Owl with Marquis and the victim. Matranga was in possession of the buy money and tried to claim that he did nothing wrong and the girl is an emancipated minor. I may have claimed Tulip was appointed to be the girl's attorney rather than that she was simply available to her."

Tulip was unnecessarily quick to confirm I exaggerated the extent of her authority. Avery frowned and shook his head before I continued debriefing him.

"The attorney denied he was representing anyone present, but he still acted like he was for both Matranga and the young girl. I waited until Matranga and Alexander left before recovering the recording Marquis made of the auction."

"For which there is or is not a search warrant?" Avery asked between bites of the trout almondine a server had just set before him. His appetite was unaffected by our various disclosures.

"There are search warrants for the surveillance and for the money Matranga had in his possession until this morning." I strove to satisfy Avery's concerns, but knew he was going to leave Strada deeply unsettled by my full report.

"What happened to the money this morning?" Avery demanded. He was frustrated that getting specific details out of me seemed to require that he press me for them.

"The attorney who still insists he is not Matranga's attorney returned it to me. He insisted that nothing criminal occurred because the event was meant to satisfy a young girl's sick fantasy which nobody present took seriously. He outed Marquis as being my informant and then warned against filing any charges because doing so would be considered slanderous." I tried to leave Avery with few questions.

"And who is this guy who isn't anybody's attorney?" my boss wondered. I was relieved that he changed the topic rather than pursue the source of the money in question.

"He calls himself Marvin Alexander," Tulip chimed in, but left off the part Avery would find most distressing about his background. "He also dropped by my office to wash his hands of the girl and suggest my brother drop the matter. Dan Logan recommended Alexander to Bear Brovartey when he had to drop him as a client. There is a lot more to know, but you can think of Alexander as being one of those Russian dolls where there are things crammed into larger things."

"The company he keeps tells me a lot," Avery mumbled around his last bite of fish.

"The company he keeps here is better than his usual companions," my sister said, which caused Avery to take an unfortunate interest in the attorney.

"Hmm. You said he calls himself Marvin Alexander. What is his real name?" Avery asked, but clearly believed it was a much less loaded question that it was.

"His birth name was Malek Alekhin. His constant refrain is that he has only one client despite all the legal work he has been doing here. That client is Dudiyn Alekhin and Marvin's mother is Dudiyn's youngest sister. Dudiyn runs one of the largest Russian crime syndicates. He recruits Russian military veterans, mostly Spetsnaz, and they are into everything that makes life bad for everybody else: drugs, human trafficking, arms deals with cartels and terrorists. Malek anglicized his name to Marvin before he applied to college. Alekhin is Russian for Alexander. I think he and his uncle were trying to cover his tracks."

"Why do that?" Avery inquired. Alexander was now on his own radar.

"Because anyone looking into his past would not normally check back further than where he went to college. I called the college where he earned his undergraduate degree, hoping to trick someone into telling me where he went to high school. They gave me the name of the private school he attended, but they also let slip that there was also a notation that he changed his name when he turned eighteen. His application included a copy of the paperwork he filed to do just that. I think the plan all along was for him to keep anyone from knowing he is related to his uncle. He did everything right in high school to get into an Ivy League college. He was active in organizations and sports and got top grades and test scores, but he also made sure not to get his picture in the yearbook. He did the exact opposite in college. He was not active in anything. He was not part of the law review and he did not even clerk, probably because he never intended to work for anyone besides his uncle." My sister was willing to make broad suppositions about

Marvin's motives after meeting the man.

"Then how did he wind up on Gotti's defense team?" I asked. It was the one thing I knew about the attorney that stuck out like a sore thumb.

"Good question, but it might be where he met Daniel Logan. They both worked as junior attorneys on the case, basically doing the crap work for the big names that made the newspapers. Keep in mind that this was the only case John Gotti ever lost. Gotti's entire operation fell apart after he went to prison. Maybe Conroy can tell you if any of Gotti's operations have new Russian managers," Tulip said and made sure Avery understood she was giving him orders and not just talking.

"I wonder how much of this Conroy knows and isn't sharing." I knew for certain that the FBI was not going to share anything this volatile with me.

"My guess would be every damn thing you two just told me, and more." Avery tossed his napkin on the table before glaring at me and then at Tulip. "You two really know how to ruin a good meal."

"That's why the food is always free, boss."

Avery cracked a smile at my comment before he excused himself. I didn't ask to accompany him to confront SAC Conroy. My only reason for wanting to be in that meeting was to watch Chief Avery break everything he could find in the Special Agent in Charge's office.

fifty-four

Tony turned the restaurant over to Miss J and joined Tulip and me in my office. I considered letting Roux out of his kennel but thought better of adding distractions to what promised to be a heated conversation. Tony and I sat on the padded leather bench to allow my sister all the space she needed to walk off her agitation. She was clearly in her courtroom mode, and we knew from experience to let her do the talking.

"Marvin Alexander truly scares me," she was quick to admit. "I thought the Mexican cartel was bad, but the Russian mobster he is related to is even more dangerous."

"How so?" Tony asked so she knew we were listening.

"Violence is the only way they negotiate. They will track down and kill your second-grade teacher in front of you just to prove they don't care who they hurt to get what they want." I had no idea what additional information she may have learned about Marvin Alexander but accepted her hyperbole about the Russian mobsters was accurate.

"Okay," I spoke up. "What does Marvin Alexander's uncle want him to do? Defending Brovartey should be enough to keep him busy, but he made time to get Puglisi out of prison and to become Matranga's mouthpiece."

Tulip did not respond to my question. She turned to study the timeline and then focused on the whiteboard with my current theory of the case beneath it.

"You have this all wrong," she declared. I swallowed my instinctive reaction to defend my hard work only because I also disliked the theory, as well. "None of us have seen a large enough picture to understand what is really happening."

"How big is the picture?" Tony prompted her. We glanced at one another and smiled because we both felt like we were sitting in one of our mission briefings.

"That's the thing. I don't think any of us know. I came across some dates and a few facts that seem to show someone has been planning something for quite a while. There must be a good reason Alexander changed his name," Tulip said and picked up a red dry erase marker from the tray beneath the now empty white board. Surely the man had not spent nearly fifty years planning to defend Junior Hauser's attorney. Junior's father was still in charge of the Dixie Mafia when Alexander applied to college. "Everything he does is meant to distract us."

She wrote August 29, 2005, on the timeline and needlessly labeled it as Hurricane Katrina. That date was permanently etched into our memories. She stepped to her right and wrote the next date, June 1, 2006, before extending her arms to bracket the dates. "Orleans Parish did not have a formal courtroom for these ten months. It was obvious long before the courts reopened that most of the open cases would have to be plea bargained or dismissed, either because the evidence was lost in the storm or because the criminals and witnesses involved could not be located after they evacuated. The Orleans Parish Sheriff's office managed to lose track of five hundred of their prisoners after they evacuated the jail and prison after the floodwalls broke and the cells flooded. They also lost the paperwork on just about everyone they evacuated."

"What does that have to do with anything happening now?" I piped up. I had spent my first year as a detective tracking down dozens of these lost prisoners. Most had simply gone back to their usual routines and seemed surprised they were still suspects.

"An attorney from any of the other forty-nine states can pass the bar in most other states with little prep. Louisiana is the only state that bases its laws on the Napoleonic Code used in France, and that means even experienced lawyers need to take courses to pass the bar exam here," my sister patiently led us through her own investigation. She turned back to the whiteboard and wrote the date February 19, 2006, and then the date March 12, 2006. "Dan Logan passed the Louisiana Bar exam in February and the MPRE exam in March. It positioned him to represent clients before the courts even reopened. The only defendants he chose to represent were high level gang members and white-collar criminals."

"It gave him repeat business if nothing else," I suggested. I was still at a loss as to what she wanted us to understand about Dan Logan. I was also unclear why we were talking about him and not about Marvin Alexander.

"It was also the perfect way to test our district attorney's ability to convict organized crime figures and his interest in pursuing certain kinds of financial crimes," Tulip suggested. "I might add, Katie's office still has a lousy record for doing either of them."

"You're saying Dan Logan passed the bar exam just to see how bad our courts are?" I felt compelled to challenge the idea that the cherub-faced attorney was that conniving.

"Dan Logan is licensed to practice law in New York, New Jersey, Louisiana and Mississippi. He took the bar exam in Mississippi only after Bear Brovartey was arrested, even though Brovartey did not hire him until two months later. Would you like to guess when Marvin Alexander passed his exams to practice in Louisiana?"

She wrote dates within the last ninety days on the timeline. Both of the exam dates were less than a month before Dan Logan supposedly decided to drop Bear Brovartey as a client. I finally saw the connection she was trying to make.

I did not protest as Tulip printed Daniel Logan and Marvin Alexander's names in a box at the center of the board because the pair did seem to be tightly linked. Tulip began boxing other familiar names and drawing lines between each name we discussed to the box containing Logan and Alexander. What emerged was a gigantic wheel with the two Brooklyn attorneys at the very center, looking and acting very much like a hub.

"I believe Dan Logan came here as Marvin's advance man. Logan defended the local gang leaders while he looked for a way to become Biggie Charles' personal attorney. Logan and Alexander probably believed the same thing that the FBI did about Biggie using his record studio as a front for some sort of large-scale criminal enterprise."

"Do you think Logan knew the FBI had infiltrated Biggie's operation?" I wondered. Tulip was beginning to make far too much sense and that was making me nervous.

"I haven't a clue, but Logan undoubtedly learned something about how the local FBI operates by the time their investigation fell apart. Fell apart thanks to you, I might add," she reminded me. "I also don't know if he was aware Alex Boudreaux was working for Junior Hauser until after

Brovartey's arrest. Answer me this, why do you think Logan is licensed in both Louisiana and Mississippi, but Alexander is only licensed in Louisiana?"

"Brovartey is only facing charges in Louisiana. Mississippi dropped all their cases against him back when it looked like such a slam dunk to convict him here," I suggested. "At least it was going to be until Spenser Duncan died. I have never understood why Logan kept Spenser and Alex as clients instead of Brovartey. He claimed he had to avoid any conflicts of interest, but then he kept two small fish rather than the big one. He must have planned to persuade Brovartey to hire Alexander from the start. Maybe he told him Alexander defended John Gotti, but then left out the part about Gotti being convicted. You need to keep in mind that Marvin Alexander also represented Puglisi in his book deal and at his parole hearing. That work started after he was already in town."

"So, Alexander used Puglisi to learn how New Orleans crime families work," I said.

"Gavin told you that a condition of the book deal was that the FBI was to get the first look at Puglisi's journals. Alexander must have been aware of that stipulation," Tulip continued building her far-ranging theory, which was sounding less and less far-fetched.

I began adding my own pieces to her elaborate puzzle. "Okay, how about if Alexander found out Puglisi kept journals that could bring down the last of the Marcello crime family along with a few high-ranking cops and politicians. That should have cleared the decks for his uncle to step right in and fill the space. I will check with Gavin on whether Alexander began representing Puglisi before or after he offered Puglisi the book deal. I am going to bet Alexander talked Puglisi into hiring him after he heard about the book deal. It makes sense that Alexander shared what he knew with Logan and the two of them conspired to find the journals before Puglisi could retrieve them. Brovartey's arrest meant Junior Hauser needed a new attorney, and what better calling card for Logan than delivering Spenser Duncan and Puglisi's journals on a silver platter? Maybe Logan convinced his client that Junior would forgive him for ratting out Brovartey if he recovered the journals. I think Puglisi told Matranga where he stashed the journals, and that is how Spenser knew where to look. It was his bad luck they weren't they were supposed to be."

"He was dead whether he found the diaries or not," Tony pointed out.

"Absolutely, but Dan Logan only needed to deliver Spenser to Junior to show Junior he could do what Brovartey used to do for him" Tulip said. "All the charges against Brovartey that Mississippi dropped, and every charge related to trying to steal the election, magically vanished after Spenser Duncan's murder. Alexander can plea bargain what is left down to a slap on Brovartey's wrist."

"But Brovartey still gets disbarred," I reminded her this should be important.

"Dan Logan has positioned himself to replace Brovartey in Junior's operation," Tulip pressed her case. "I imagine the plan is for Logan to go to Mississippi and Alexander to take over here. They would be in perfect positions to steer the two rival operations."

"Explain what Alexander is doing with Matranga." I wanted to move things ahead because we were veering away from what we could prove beyond our own doubts.

"Probably everything he can to destroy him," Tulip surmised. "He didn't stop him from auctioning off Rebecca but had to know the authorities were going to find out after Lenny blabbed about it all over the Quarter. Maybe he hoped you would barge in and arrest Matranga in the act. Maybe he wanted Matranga to die in a shoot-out."

"Then why try to talk me out of arresting him?" I challenged her supposition.

"Was that ever going to work?" Tulip asked me and laughed. "Alexander could go back and tell Matranga he did everything he could to stop you, but it sounds to me like he only made a half-hearted effort. He made the rounds today to convince both of us that he is way smarter than we are. He tricked you into identifying your informant and admitting you tried to set up Matranga and then he sprang some surprises about the two of you on me to show he does his homework as well as I do mine. I still beat him."

"I should know better than to tangle with an attorney," I

admitted and grinned.

"Yes, you should," Tony consoled me and jokingly patted my shoulder. "I have."

"Okay, tell me this," I said as I focused my thoughts. "What did Alexander tell you that you didn't already know?"

"Are you aware Roger has asthma?" she said to open the topic she was secretly anxious to begin addressing.

"No. Are you?" I asked her. "I mean, do you know for sure?"

"Alexander claims Roger does. Now I am starting to think Alexander may have only said that to let me know he knows who is living with our mother," Tulip reconsidered Alexander's purpose in telling her such innocuous information.

"What else?" I asked.

"He is unusually well informed about both of your pasts. He says Interpol suspects you of killing some people in Europe," she said and looked towards Tony.

"I have told you that," he reminded her before I could speak up.

"They would have already come after him if they had any evidence," I mentioned. "On that note, however, the Chief let me know Conroy took it upon himself to send photos of the letter opener and his version of what transpired to Interpol to see if this might help with any of those unsolved homicides. I don't see where it can because the blade will not match any wounds they have, and people get stabbed to death a lot."

"But Tony did kill people for Saddam Hussein," she reminded both of us. "There may be something to find."

"Alexander just repackaged an old accusation, and Conroy is trying to distract Avery and me from our investigation. He is afraid something Spenser Duncan did or said is going to get out and embarrass him," I tried to calm her fears. "Alexander only mentioned it to show he has sources of his own in Interpol. The last I heard, the State Department asked the FBI Director to tell Conroy to stop poking around in our pasts, so getting Interpol to do his dirty work is all he has left."

"Well, Alexander has some very good sources," Tulip frowned as she focused on the person she came to discuss. "He knows what Bumper told you about how our father died."

"What can he do with that information?" I tried to

minimize her concerns about this. Our family and the FBI were the only ones interested in Bumper's confession. He told me he was present when a guy who later became an FBI agent gunned down our father when he tried to intervene in their slaughter of dozens of hardened criminals rounded up during the Katrina evacuation.

"He also insinuated you were involved in that FBI agent's car wreck."

"Conroy has said the same thing. Maybe the two of them are pals," I said but found it was becoming harder and harder to pop every balloon Alexander had set sail in her mind. It did concern me that they both mentioned Interpol and were both well informed on the unexpected revelations made during my investigation into Biggie Charles' murder.

"Can you explain how Alexander knows about your money?" she demanded of Tony.

"What does he say he knows?" Tony resisted sharing anything more than she already knew about his murky finances. Tulip makes a point to discuss Tony's apparent wealth less than he and I ever do. I go out of my way to avoid knowing any details so I can allow myself to spend the monthly checks he claims are restaurant profits.

"That you stole millions of dollars the Iraqi's want back. Was it part of what we sent to Iraq after Saddam Hussein was deposed?" she asked. The United States shipped tons of new one-hundred-dollar bills, totaling twelve billion dollars, to Iraq's interim government to pay out money frozen in American accounts under sanctions related to Iraq's invasion of Kuwait. The classified mission Tony and I spearheaded involved tracking down Iraqis using this money to finance attacks on American troops and contractors rebuilding Iraq.

"No," Tony insisted. It was an almost honest answer. The source of our fortune was the money siphoned from overseas accounts held by a family that ripped off millions of dollars from Saddam Hussein. Tony returned the amount of money the Iraqis accused him of stealing from their cash infusion, but this left a considerable fortune he covertly transferred to an account in the Dominican Republic while I lay in a coma in Italy. He gradually converted most of that traceable cash into less easily tracked gold bullion, which had unexpectedly exploded in value in the past five years.

"So how does he know where you have your offshore account?" Tulip pressed harder. I began to give Tony an inquisitive look as well. We were both in considerable trouble if the IRS or the State Department began asking similar questions.

"The diamonds," he muttered after a long moment of silence. I punched his shoulder to jog more information loose from his pursed lips. "I converted some of the gold into diamonds. Maybe the diamond broker knows some Russians."

"Ya think?" I all but mocked my otherwise brilliant partner. Selling the gold in small amounts was how he had heretofore stayed under the radar of the international bank examiners. "Guess who sells the most diamonds?"

"What were you thinking?" Tulip demanded before gently smacking Tony's forehead.

"I bought one and thought it would be good to buy more. They are lighter than gold," the man who was proving to be my partner in crime tried to reason with us.

"Great reason," I chided him further. "Why did you only start with one?"

"Wait here," he said and stood up to leave. Tulip started to protest but held her comments for his return. She waited until she heard my front door close before she resumed discussing the larger problem with me. Tony's apartment takes up the other half of the third floor of the building so he would be back in only a couple of minutes.

"Alexander is obviously paving the way for the Russian Mob to make a move." Tulip no longer need to convince me. "He and Dan Logan recognized the opportunities in New Orleans right after Katrina. It didn't matter who you were or what kind of criminal you were the day before the hurricane, everybody had to start over afterward. The old-style rackets waited for businesses to reopen and for people to start coming home, but a lot of businesses never reopened, and a lot of people stayed where they were, so the entire playing field changed. This was why Junior Hauser thought he could slip into town unnoticed. He gave Alex Boudreaux a blank check to gentrify the city because Alex was laundering Junior's money through his real estate flips. Brovartey tried to frame Alex to cover the mess his meddling caused in Junior's plan, but that was also how you linked Alex to Junior. Puglisi and his journals forced Matranga to come back so he could tell Puglisi to abandon his book deal. That deal seems to have fallen apart all on its own because nobody can find the journals. Matranga's plans to get back in business will create a very large obstacle for Alexander's uncle. The Chicago Outfit supports Matranga, so Alexander's uncle's plans risk starting a gang war. Having Logan inside Junior's camp means the Dixie Mafia might be the uncle's ally."

"Yes, it does," I sighed at the thought of just how violent such a battle over territory would be. This would dwarf the sort of daily gang violence the city had numbed itself to since the storm. "Everything you said makes sense. The pieces fit together better than they have so far, but it doesn't tell me anything I can legally do to intervene. Convicting Matranga for human trafficking would put an end to the Marcello family starting over. Removing him will invite everyone else to make their next move. The Chicago Outfit and Dixie Mafia are both a lot closer to here than Alexander's uncle is."

"I am curious where Puglisi stands in all of this." Tulip seemed genuinely stumped. "For one thing the two of you still have his watch."

Ah, the infamous watch.

"There is that," I had to admit. "Why do you think nobody has stepped forward to pay the bill?"

"It is about power," Tony offered his insight as he reclaimed his seat. "Matranga is responsible for the bill so not paying us keeps the watch from Puglisi. Puglisi cannot pay the bill without insulting his capo. Matranga must want something from Puglisi that he cannot give."

"The journals," I surmised.

"Probably, but Matranga never intended to pay the bill," Tony suggested. "He knew I was going to want something to make them pay the bill, and that I would take the watch from his guest to make sure they did. We did what he wanted."

"What if we just give the watch back to Puglisi?" I wondered.

"Then Matranga would find a different way to get what he wants," Tony replied. "But it will be a messier way."

"Any infighting helps Alexander get what he wants," Tulip realized.

"So, I just need to find Alexander's underbelly to make all of this go away, right?" I concluded.

"Maybe," Tulip offered her opinion, which for once sounded more like a guess. She turned her attention to Tony. "Okay, tell us about the diamond that has caused so much trouble."

"This was not how I wanted to give it to you," Tony apologized and pulled a ring box from his pocket. The box was from an Uptown custom jewelry maker I knew Tulip always wished she could afford. Tulip's expression clearly showed that this was not how she expected to receive her engagement ring from Tony.

"Then don't," she snapped at Tony and clutched her hand around his fingers to keep him from opening it. They studied one another's faces for a long moment that I should never have been part of before he placed it a pants pocket. "Other than this, how many more diamonds do you have?"

"Here?" he asked for clarification. This response was more problematic than the ring.

"Oh, no. Are you keeping them in your apartment?" Tulip went a shade or two paler.

"Some, yes," Tony admitted without seeing the issue. I bit my tongue about the gold coins I knew he kept under a floorboard in his living room. I hoped he had converted the coins into these diamonds, but I suspected the jewels only added to our problem.

"What am I to do with you?" Tulip moaned and cupped her boyfriend's face in her hands rather than beat him with her fists, as I sensed she very much wanted to do. "You cannot explain the source of the money you used to pay for them if someone searches your apartment. You can be arrested and deported for this."

"Who is going to arrest me?" Tony wondered. He glanced at me, and I shook my head because I understood I was in considerably more trouble than Tony. I would not be the one who only faced deportation to a tropical island because of his money laundering.

"Somebody is going to if you keep being this sloppy," Tulip

235

assured him.

"I won't buy any more diamonds," Tony lamely offered.

"That's a start," Tulip sighed and looked to me for any help I might offer.

"We'll take care of this," I tried to reassure her. I was not about to tell her how, and she did not want to know anything else beyond what she had just learned from her least favorite pro-bono clients.

"You do that," she demanded and moved closer to the whiteboards. She turned to face them and then turned back to me as she headed towards the office door. She pointed her index finger at the boards as she spoke. "And then you figure out a way to make all of this go away."

This time I held my tongue. I had only a glimmer of an idea about how to handle Tony's obviously willful ignorance of his host country's financial laws. The deadly circus Dan Logan and Marvin Alexander had brought to town was well beyond my comprehension at the moment.

fifty-five

The first thing I did after Tulip left was to ask about the ring. Tony went into detail about the diamond's level of quality and what the platinum setting cost, which itself was not a small sum. All I heard was the that the diamond was just over two carats in size. It was a lot of engagement ring to match when the time came for me to propose to Katie.

Tony headed back to the kitchen while I continued staring glumly at Tulip's precise handwriting on the whiteboard and began making phone calls. I wished her logic was not as crisp as her handwriting. My first call was to Gavin Hendricks at his office in New York.

"I have a couple of quick questions for you about the Puglisi book deal," I said once we were through the obligatory Southern ritual of asking about each others' families.

"I thought you might. I have kept his file handy since the last time we spoke," Gavin informed me with humor in his voice. "Fire away."

"I am less interested in Puglisi than I am in his attorney, Marvin Alexander," I began.

"You should be," Gavin interrupted me. "The sort of people he chooses to represent are generally the worst of the worst."

"That's my first question," I continued. "When did he enter the picture in the book deal?"

"Marvin Alexander approached me in May of 2006. He claimed to represent a mobster interested in publishing the diaries he began keeping in 1958. I found a publishing house willing to guarantee one million dollars for the rights to the gangster's journals, but I only spoke directly with Marion Puglisi on two occasions. Everything was always conveyed through Mister Alexander, and the first thing he told me to do after the deal was signed was to sit on it until I heard back from him. Everything on my end ground to a halt at that point. That was a little over a year after Katrina," Gavin explained the origins of the book deal. I did some mental math and realized the book deal fell in his lap almost on the heels of Dan Logan arriving in New Orleans. Perhaps Logan had heard a rumor about Puglisi keeping journals and suggested Alexander ask the man in person. It may have been a mere coincidence that the rumors about Puglisi were true. Tossing Puglisi into the mix was guaranteed to stir things up when he came home. So far it was consuming the attention of the FBI and had drawn Matranga, Cammarato, and the Chicago Outfit within striking range of Dudiyn Alekhin's henchmen.

"So Marvin Alexander approached you about the journals, but put a hold on everything after you lined up the book deal," I needed him to confirm.

"That's right. I always found Marvin Alexander to be considerably less interested in publishing the journals than in seeing his client back on the street. He likely always planned to leverage any book deal into a pardon for his client. He is a bit of a dark horse, that one. There is no telling what his real motives are about anything," Gavin unnecessarily informed me.

"You know his uncle runs a Mob family in Russia, don't you?" I asked.

"That I did not know."

"Why did you seem to be so happy after Puglisi dropped the book deal?"

"Not having to deal with Alexander was a big part of it. I was also getting worried about how long Mister Puglisi was taking to hand the journals over to the FBI. The publisher is threatening to cancel the contract because they are worried Mister Puglisi might die before his book comes out. He is a major part of their publicity campaign because those journals are less valuable if he is not alive to corroborate what is in them."

"That's equally true for the FBI. You said the New Orleans office was supposed to get first crack at reading them, not D.C., right?" I moved on to the next topic.

"That is correct. Mister Alexander claims the New Orleans office will be better informed about any names that appear in the journals. I guess their guy in charge down there handled organized crime cases when he was a field agent," Gavin explained. I chose not to detour into Michael Conroy's past career.

"Do you know who made that part of the deal?" There was really no reason to believe Gavin would know what transpired between Conroy and Alexander.

"Mister Puglisi told me his attorney pitched it to the FBI. The way he described it to me was that Mister Alexander offered the journals to your local FBI office in exchange for their advocating for Puglisi's conditional pardon. Puglisi must turn over the journals or he goes back to prison. At least that is my understanding. Anything else I can tell you?"

"My head is already too full of things, but thanks for adding all of this," I sighed. "I have one last question. Are you still interested in making a deal with Puglisi?"

"With him directly? Sure. I know I could sell his story," Gavin assured me.

Marvin Alexander's involvement, and especially the very specific agreement between Marion Puglisi and SAC Michael Conroy, must play a major part in Alexander's own plans for controlling New Orleans. I realized that the attorney had artfully tied the futures of two sworn enemies, Marion Puglisi and Michael Conroy, to one another.

Conroy had put his career at risk trading Puglisi's freedom for Puglisi's journals. I did not trust Conroy to ignore the temptation to 'discover' the journals on his own and send Puglisi back to prison. Spenser Duncan's role in the break-in left unanswered questions about the FBI's possible involvement in that burglary. The indictments Conroy must anticipate filing based on the journals' disclosures could force the city council into allowing the DOJ to run the city's police department indefinitely. Conroy's plans were going to collapse on him like a ton of bricks if the journals were never recovered, as he was the one who sought the Mafia hit-man's release based on what would surely appear to have been a lie.

I felt certain Sunset Puglisi was headed back to prison in everyone's plans but his own. The FBI could renege on their deal if they recovered the journals before Puglisi surrendered them. Spenser Duncan's connection to the FBI and indirectly to Marvin Alexander made me wonder but what the attorney planned to eliminate Puglisi and cause problems for Conroy by arranging for Spenser Duncan to retrieve them. Puglisi certainly didn't arrange their theft, because he needed to deliver them to the FBI to keep his parole.

The one with the most to gain certainly appeared to be

Marvin Alexander. Having the journals would allow him to weaponize the misdeeds of public figures, cops, or other criminals they disclosed. Keeping them hidden would end Puglisi's bid for freedom, but also humiliate the head of the local FBI office. Conroy's failure in the eyes of the FBI Director might result in a change of command in our local office. That should distract the local FBI office long enough for Dudiyn Alekhin's lieutenants to embed in New Orleans' underworld. This chilling scenario was the one which made the most sense as I continued to fit each new piece of information into the puzzle on my office wall.

I saw only two pathways leading forward. I could keep looking for the edges of the larger picture Marvin Alexander was painting, or I could punch a hole in the middle of his canvas and see what happened next. One took too long, and the other was fraught with multiple unknown consequences. My compromise was to see how much of the larger picture Tulip spoke of was occupied by the elusive journals.

fifty-six

Marion Puglisi seemed even less pleased to see me when I knocked on his door a second time than the FBI agents staked out across the street were as they watched me park my bright red Cadillac XLR convertible in Puglisi's empty driveway. I half expected the men Marvin Alexander had sent after me to be protecting Puglisi rather than the local talent Matranga must have arranged prior to my first visit, but I was greeted by the same two sour faces.

It was only a matter of time before Marvin Alexander began tightening his control of things. I accepted that the attorney did not fear me or anyone else in law enforcement, but he seemed to feel my part in the break-in investigation was forcing him out of the shadows where he preferred to work. I also assumed the two men he had tailing me were there to give me something else to worry about than the house on Dauphine Street or his client's diaries.

"What is it this time, detective?" Puglisi demanded as I stepped through the wide doorway.

"I'd like to talk to you about your book deal," I said and glanced at the men standing to either side of me. They seemed to breathe a little easier when they understood I was not there to arrest the man in their care.

"I got nothing to say to you about that," Puglisi dismissed the topic.

"There are other things we can talk about," I countered and stepped face to face with him before I whispered a topic meant strictly for his own ears. "Let's discuss the bank account number inside your watch."

"Yeah, okay," Puglisi reversed himself and motioned for me to follow him. Neither of us said another word until we reached the flagstone patio. His bodyguards watched us through the patio's sliding glass doors.

Marion Puglisi seemed to be making himself at home in Alex Boudreaux's former residence. He wore a muted Guayabera style shirt with light linen slacks and tan leather loafers. He had a cigar in one hand and a cocktail of some sort in the other. Standing in the heat and tropical foliage on the

241

patio must have reminded him of being in Havana during his early years.

"You think your place is bugged?" I wondered. We did not step outside the first time we spoke and nothing we said was repeated back to me by Avery or Conroy.

"You wanna take the chance?" he challenged me. I saw his point.

"Let's start with how Marvin Alexander came to be your attorney," I returned to the only topic I came there to discuss. I knew he would answer anything I asked in order to learn what I discovered about his watch. My coming to see him alone was his only assurance I had not yet informed anyone else about his offshore bank account.

"I never heard of him until he showed up and offered to represent me for free," Puglisi began. I saw no reason to doubt this.

"For free?"

"He said a 'little birdie' told him about me maybe having some diaries. He said they were my ticket outta prison, and he had a client who was willing to trade my journals for my freedom," Puglisi shared a bit more.

"You ever figure out who that client was?"

"I didn't really care right then. The guy said he was getting me outta prison. Like I said," Puglisi repeated himself. Apparently knowing how Marvin Alexander showed up on his doorstep never mattered to him as much as why he showed up.

"So, you never wondered why a strange attorney was interested in getting you out of prison?" I pressed more gently than I normally would.

"Marvin told me this client of his was interested in moving into New Orleans and thought my journals were his key to the city," Puglisi continued to provide details. He had yet to admit to a specific crime, but was getting closer to doing so with each disclosure. "I figured their plan was going to take out the same people I wanted to take out."

"What was your original plan?" I asked with genuine curiosity.

"I was gonna leave a letter to the Feds where to find them diaries after I died. I could reach out from the grave and settle a bunch of old scores," Puglisi gave an angry smile.

"Tell me what Alexander promised to get you to go along."

"He promised me that parole. I figured giving him the journals would mean everyone I wanted to see dead was going to die because of his client without me doing a thing of my own," Puglisi replied. I would have taken the same deal if I were him.

"And did your attorney tell you how he planned to get that parole?" I asked without expecting an answer. He was, though, being unusually talkative.

"Marvin told me he heard about some agent looking for anyone with diaries like mine and he told me we could use the guy's book deal to get the Feds to let me loose. The FBI was willing to trade what I knew for my last years in prison. Marvin said he could get me out, but it was up to me to figure out a way to skip town while the Feds was busy reading," Puglisi explained even further. I realized he only shared this story because he knew I was never going to convince him to repeat it to anyone else in law enforcement.

"He wasn't going to arrange a magic carpet ride for you?" I pressed him.

"No, getting outta town is my problem. He dealt with the guy who left the gun I used in that murder where the cops could find it to prove he means to keep our deal."

"And who was that?" I wondered, again without expecting an honest answer. I might have kissed him had he said Michael Conroy's name.

"Hammer Cammarato," Puglisi spoke ill of the dead instead.

"How do you know it wasn't a cop who planted the gun?" I was interested in what he had to say, but I also wanted him to know I was familiar with his trial.

"I thought that for a long time. Then I remembered that I let Hammer use my apartment right before the cops showed up. He borrowed my place sometimes to be with some girl he had on the side. He must have planted the gun then."

"How did he have the murder weapon?" I wondered.

"One of Hammer's guys drove me across the bridge to Harvey to do the job. Hammer either wanted the money he was owed or the guy's life, and he got Pete's blessing to off the guy if it came to that," Puglisi elaborated. "That driver was supposed to ditch the gun, but I bet he gave it to Hammer to set me up."

"Why would Hammer do that to you?" I didn't believe this was a good time to tell the hitman that he could not be framed for a murder he actually commited.

"Pete was pissed about Vanity making trouble with the cops, but he couldn't be mad at her so he held me responsible for not stopping her," Puglisi patiently explained. "I had no idea she was running a blackmail scam on the side. She was Pete's side piece and all I was supposed to do was give her a room where them two could meet. He musta used Hammer to set me up."

"Why did the girl try to blackmail my father, anyway?" I interrupted him.

"Vanity told me Pete knew she heard him and Hammer talking about whacking some informant. She was looking for a way to get away from him, but then she decided getting him killed would be even better."

"That still doesn't explain what she did." I complained.

"She needed a shooter of her own, so she told your dad Pete was going to blackmail him because she knew your dad wasn't going to let that happen," Puglisi explained her twisted motive. "Vanity said conning your dad into taking Pete out was the only way she could get away clean. She figured the Feds would take Pete down if things worked out the other way around and he killed your father."

"That all makes a twisted sort of sense," I had to admit.

"Like I said, Pete blamed me for what she done with your dad. Getting Hammer to plant that gun on me was the first part of what he planned to do about his problem with what the girl heard." Puglisi's version of things made more sense, and was easier to accomplish, than being framed by Chief Avery and SAC Conroy.

"What was the rest of his plan to silence her?"

"Pete planned to use all that confusion the Feds caused when they threw the girls outta my place after I was convicted to shut her up for good, but she got away clean." It was an almost perfect plan on Matranga's part.

"What did happen to Vanity?" I asked on the off chance he knew.

Puglisi's face broke into a big smile. "I put her on a plane. Pete never found her and nobody else was even looking for her. Your dad was glad she was gone and never went looking for her, either."

"I imagine he was," I had to agree. "Where is she now?"

"Nah, we are done talking about that," Puglisi waved his hands at me.

"Then let's back up a bit. Why did Marvin try to make it look like you were the one who took out Cammarato? Hammer's body was found in the trunk of a car somebody stole from right over there," I said and pointed next door.

"Because Pete got the message that I knew he set me up, and the FBI is my best witness that I didn't have nothing to do with settling the score. Their agents was watching me the whole time. They watched me so close they never saw that car they found him in get stolen," Puglisi was still having a good laugh about that.

"So, Marvin Alexander arranged Cammarato's homicide to scare Matranga, and to make sure you honor your end of the deal the two of you made?" I casually asked and prayed he would slip up and confirm the attorney made good on his promise.

"I never said he did no such thing." Puglisi wanted that made clear. "Marvin only told me that he would take care of Hammer and the FBI would have to say I had nothing to do with it when it happened. That thing happened to Hammer but I don't know nothing about no hit. I am just glad the guy got his."

"When did Marvin Alexander tell you who his real client is?" I backed up on him.

"I figured that out for myself, after it was too late to say no," Puglisi gave a rare expression of personal embarrassment. He was played like a fiddle and knew it. "Do you know who the guy is?"

"Yeah, it's Dudiyn Alekhin. He is Alexander's uncle," I told him. I tried to make it sound like everyone else on the planet knew about the family connection.

"I don't want Russian Mob guys running around this place," Puglisi assured me, as though he was expressing his disdain for the palmetto bugs scurrying across the patio. "New

Orleans has always been run by Italians. It needs to stay that way."

"I would just as soon that neither of you are in charge," I said and grinned.

"All I wanted to do was get out of town to spend my money," Puglisi lamented.

"Matranga and Alexander seem pretty chummy," I let him know. "I stopped them coming out of the Night Owl together the other night."

"I heard about that," Puglisi laughed. "Caught them with both their little brains stuck between that young kid's thighs like bears in a honey jar."

"It was a dumb thing to do," I concurred. I didn't much appreciate his ruining Winne the Pooh for me with his choice of imagery. "It also suggests Matranga has made a move to take over the Night Owl."

"Nah, that has always been his," Puglisi said. He may have shared more than he meant to, or he may have acted like he did just to add one more thing I could use against the capo who turned on him. He also might have been goading me into doing something like Vanity did when she tried to trigger my father with her failed blackmail attempt.

"Where do you stand with the FBI right now?" I began wrapping up what I was there to learn. His caretakers would eventually tell someone we spoke, and it would be easier for Puglisi to explain a short chat than an interrogation.

"I still need to give the journals to the FBI, or I go back to prison. Marvin wants me to tell him where they are for real so he can get them and turn them in. He thinks I lied about where they were the first time I told him. I know it was him that sent someone looking for them before I got outta prison. I think he is gonna tell the FBI I lied about keeping any diaries at all as soon as I give them to him so they throw me back in prison," Puglisi astutely ascertained. He was running out of people he could trust. "I'm working on the diaries thing."

"How so?" I asked without expecting much in the way of an an answer.

"I got this magic memory thing. I don't need them journals because I remember everything I ever done or said even that far back. I figure if I write a couple of juicy ones it will buy me some time." Puglisi elaborated.

"How do you propose to do that?"

"I never said the ones I am writing was real," he grinned. "I might even toss in the story about the first time you and me met."

"You're telling me that we have met before now?" I challenged his memory. I had no comments about his plan. Forgery seemed the only viable way to stay alive.

"Oh yeah, we met," Puglisi said and roared with laughter. "You was drinking in one of Pete's clubs on Bourbon Street and some of the girls I was sitting with was talking to you and your high-school pals when your old man came storming in the door. He never told you what you done wrong to get sent away?"

"He was more preoccupied with packing me off than justifying his reasons," I said with more wit than I felt about that situation. I finally had an answer to why my life took such an abrupt turn when I was only sixteen.

"I'll bet," Puglisi continued to laugh. "Anyway, Matranga convinced Marcello that it was better to pay me off than kill me. My journals could make a lot of trouble if I was dead, but they aren't any use if I am alive and refuse to say they are real."

"So, they agreed to pay you a million dollars a year to bite your tongue," I tossed into the conversation to see if he would verify the amount of the payoff. "And your capo still expects you to keep your mouth shut now that you have the book deal."

"That's right," he saw no trouble in confirming what he thought I already knew.

"Then why didn't you know the account number until you got out of jail? I cannot see you taking Matranga at his word about paying you all that money after he put you in prison in the first place." I would have demanded proof the money was being paid long before now.

"The judge gave me a sentence so long I knew I was never going to get to spend a dime of that money, so I decided to let someone else spend it. I told Pete to give the account number to the attorney I sent to him. He must have thought the guy was mine, but he wasn't," Puglisi explained his odd largesse. It took me only a moment to guess who he handed the money over to as a final joke or final bit of revenge.

"Vanity has been cashing your paychecks," I surmised. Puglisi paused before he gave me a broad grin and punched my shoulder.

"But now you are out and want to enjoy some of that money yourself," I suggested.

"On a big white beach in the Bahamas. She already has a place for the two of us," he sighed. He was already dressing the part.

"Matranga and Alexander are comparing notes. You don't think your attorney has told your old boss about the deal he made to get you paroled?" I challenged him.

"Nah, he is letting them think I got out for my good behavior. Matranga would kill me if he found out I made a deal with the FBI for them journals, but he would want to get the journals before he had me whacked." He seemed to know what kept him alive.

"Ok then, can you please explain the watch to me?" He understood I still needed an explanation for why their nearly four-thousand-dollar dinner tab remained unpaid.

"Pete set up two accounts. He kept half in case I double crossed him while I was in prison. Now he wants the journals before he gives me the other half my money. He had already agreed to give me the watch so he needed to find a way not to let me have it that wouldn't cause problems between us. Pete ran the bill up as much as he could because he knew your chef would want to hold something until a bill that big gets paid. He gave me that watch like he promised but then he caused a scene so your chef would take it. That way Pete can say he didn't double cross me," he finally provided a plausible explanation for the size of the dinner tab and the intentional delay in paying it.

"Well, it has caused us nothing but grief," I assured him.

"Can I get it back from you?" he asked abruptly. "What if I give you the journals and you work it out with everyone else?"

"No deal to be made there, Sunset," I shook my head and left what I hoped was an excruciating pause. "You have as much admitted that they do not even exist."

"You think I am lying about them," he challenged me. He sounded crushed.

"The guy who broke in and ripped out the bathroom

vanities didn't find them. I thought you hid them behind that poster of Vanity, but I didn't find them either," I said to illustrate my point. "You must have told Marvin they were behind a vanity, or we all would have looked somewhere else. So, you either lied to your attorney about where they were or lied to the entire world about them even existing."

"Those are the only two possibilities you came up with, detective?" Puglisi asked and chuckled.

"The third one is that the whole story of the journals is part of some scheme you came up with to get out of prison. Alexander came to you to verify a wild rumor and made the mistake of dangling a way out of prison to get you to give him first crack at your diaries. You used his own plan against him to get paroled so you could take out Hammer and Pete. Then you found out what Marvin's real plan is and figured out you are dead man if you don't give him the journals," I calmly explained the scenario I was beginning to suspect was the real one. "I think your attorney has boxed you into a corner where the diaries are putting your life in danger whether they are real or just a story you told."

"And what would you do with my diaries?" Puglisi wondered. He had no reason to believe I was not going to stand by and let him die, if for no other reason than the turmoil he brought to my family and myself personally over the years.

"I don't want them, and I am honest when I say I hope they do not exist. Everyone else wants to mess with your life all over again. How about you and I figure out a way to twist your situation to our own benefit instead?"

"Why would you do that?" He was understandably wary that I might still hold a grudge over what happened when I was sixteen.

"Keep in mind I will want you to leave town," I clarified my offer. "You are only alive because everyone thinks the journals exist, and the FBI needs you to verify that the ones they get are real. Imagine the mess if your diaries turn up, but you go missing."

"Keep talking," Puglisi encouraged me. I didn't sound like I was setting him up to take another bad fall, but I kept talking until I admitted my plan involved doing so.

"You are going to have to bait a trap," I warned him.

"I am already the fox in everyone else's hunt," he pointed out. "What a dumb sport."

"You are going to have to send your attorney on another wild goose chase. It might prove to be one too many times to cross him," I said and waited for a heated objection.

"Then why would I do that?" he demanded.

"Because you need to convince him the journals are still out there. I think we agree that Alexander is clearly only representing you to advance his uncle's agenda. Dudiyn has no intentions of having of a bunch of eighty-year-old gangsters who used to run the Quarter as partners. He is going to be patient while you guys kill one another off."

"I think you are right about that," Puglisi was quick to agree.

"So, let's give him another taste of what he is hungry for," I suggested. "Give me one of the journals you just wrote and I will plant it in your place. Tell Marvin the journals are behind the poster of Vanity."

"Why there?" he wondered far less innocently than he tried to sound.

"Because that was where I looked for them. Whoever looks behind the poster is going to assume they are too late. Leaving just one behind will convince everyone the journals are real," I explained and ignored his expression.

"We do this as partners, right?" Puglisi wanted to confirm. He was no fool and understood the possible price for sending Alexander on a final wild goose chase.

"Not so much," I countered. "We just have mutual interests. Call your attorney and tell him I told you the journals have been found. Let's see who he sends to check."

"What's that going to tell you?"

"I have two different ideas for who he will send," I said. "We can figure out a next step once I know who he calls to check out your story."

"I'll call him right now," Puglisi said and pulled out his cellphone.

"Don't be so hasty and do not use your own phone. The FBI likely does have it tapped and we don't want them going after the journals before anyone else can. Ask one of the goons watching you if you can borrow their phone," I warned him. I also needed to slow him down long enough to have time to plant his fake diary in the house on Dauphine Street. "Call him after you eat supper, and we will see what happens."

"Fine," Puglisi finally conceded. "Anything else I can do for you?"

"Yeah, give me a journal to plant," I said.

"Wait here," he said and walked back inside. He said something to his keepers that made them look my direction and laugh, which was fine if it made them think I was not about to get one over on their boss. Puglisi was back in just a short moment and handed me a scuffed fake leather covered journal about the size of a small paperback. He had worn down the edges and probably used tea or coffee to age the pages. He probably did not worry about anyone testing the age of the ink, but he was savvy enough to use multiple pens so the entries seemed properly disjointed. "This do the trick?"

"I don't know who taught you forgery, but this is pretty good work. We want word to get out that the cops caught whoever Marvin sends to check out your story with evidence that the journals are real," I outlined the still nebulous plan I had in mind.

"You're a tricky bastard, just like your old man," he said and laughed.

"Confirm something for me." Puglisi was unlikely to confirm my suspicions if I asked him a direct question. "Detective Bassett gave you his business card after he interviewed you the day you got back in town. What did you do with it?"

"What do you mean?" Puglisi stalled. It was not a vague question.

"Did you throw it away? Is it still in your wallet? Did you pass it on to someone else?" I pressed harder and laid out the only three possibilities I ever considered.

Puglisi's unwillingness to discuss what should have been an insignificant matter with the same candor with which he had already discussed his book deal, being framed by Cammarato, and distrusting his attorney enough to forge his own diaries made me even more determined to leave with an answer to the question. Puglisi stewed in silence for a couple of minutes before he gave me an answer.

"I gave it to my attorney."

"That was what I was worried about," I sighed but did not explain any further.

"I guess some things stay the same no matter how long you leave town," Puglisi laughed to let me know he understood my real purpose in staging the charade of hiding his fake journal.

fifty-seven

"Why would you tell Puglisi to give his attorney bad information about where to find his journals?" Avery was quick to find fault in my asking Puglisi to lie to Marvin Alexander despite the Chief's tactic of lying to suspects during his own interrogations. Maybe his issue was that Puglisi was a criminal and not a cop.

"Sunset agreed to lie to Marvin Alexander because he doesn't trust his attorney not to screw him any more than he trusts Michael Conroy not to do so. I told him doing this would answer the question of who he can trust," I explained to shore up my fabrication. Chief Avery glared at me across his desk while he decided how to proceed.

I continued, "Pete Matranga and Marvin Alexander are obviously working together against Puglisi. Sunset knows breaking into his old place to get the journals himself and giving them to Alexander or personally handing them over to the FBI is a sure-fire way to die."

"That it is," Avery agreed. "We already have one dead gangster on our hands, there is no need to wish for more. What is your plan?"

"I do not have one. This needs to be your show," I passed the buck. My tall tale about Puglisi reaching out to me about his concerns over someone else recovering his diaries did not add up to my boss, but the chance to be the one who recovered the mobster's journals was a strong incentive to set aside his suspicions that this was a trap.

"Why is that?" he said and leaned back in his chair so whatever terrible thing I was about to ask of him would take a few milliseconds longer to reach his ears.

"Because NOPD needs to be the face on whatever happens. You will also get to put your hands on the journals before anyone else if they turn up. It becomes a State Police matter if I make any arrests, and an FBI matter if they do. Puglisi is going to call Marvin Alexander this evening to say he heard someone found the journals," I began. Avery began to slowly lean forward. "Alexander will not bother to check out Puglisi's story if Spenser Duncan found the journals during the first break in, but he is going to need to send someone to check the story if he does not have them. That means there will either be a second break-in or someone with a key to the house is going to check out Puglisi's story."

"I don't like what you are suggesting, Cooter," Avery's anger began to boil. "You think Puglisi's attorney is going to ask Detective Bassett to check this out."

"It would be hard for Detective Bassett to explain his presence if he shows up at the house tonight, but that does not mean we are setting a trap for him. Alexander probably has people of his own who can burglarize the place," I carefully phrased my response. The commanders who promoted Bassett from patrolman to detective under a cloud of suspicion would take the embarrassment of Bassett working for a Russian mobster quite poorly. "I would think you might prefer to catch whoever gets sent. If it is Detective Bassett, then you can keep the matter in house. It would be better for NOPD to fire Bassett for some other transgression than to let the Feds or internal affairs drag your whole department through the mud."

"What sort of transgression do you have in mind?" Avery wondered. He may have felt I had spent the weeks I should have been investigating the case secretly planning an elaborate way to destroy Detective Bassett's career. My plan was not all that elaborate. I had stopped by the house on Dauphine before I approached Avery with my story. I needed to make it look as though someone had made off with all of Puglisi's journals, so I had tossed the poster of Vanity on the floor and reopened the hole I had made earlier. I changed my mind about leaving the journal Puglisi forged because I doubted it would stand up to the level of analysis a piece of evidence that important would face from the NOPD or FBI crime labs. I decided to keep it in reserve for an easier patsy.

"That will not matter. He should swallow whatever poison you offer that spares him an indictment for selling his badge to the Russian Mob," I suggested. Bassett struck me as the sort of corrupt police officer who was going ask his union rep to embarrass NOPD into a generous cash settlement or to get his badge back.

"So, you are not going to lend a hand?" Avery asked to confirm my position.

"No," I said and surprised him. I pulled my own copy of the house key from my pocket and slid it across the desk to him. "In fact, here is my own key to the place. I do not think there is anything left to find there except whether Detective Bassett is dirty. It will only get messy if the State Patrol busts him, and messier still if the FBI does."

"I cannot tell you how bad the second of those would be," Avery seemed to plead for me to not spread my accusations against Bassett any farther than his office.

"I know exactly how bad it would be if the FBI arrests Bassett," I reassured him. "There was one other thing Puglisi felt like sharing. He claims Cammarato's murder was in retaliation for Hammer planting the murder weapon you and Conroy found in his place. Puglisi did not kill Hammer, but he knows who arranged the hit."

Avery fell silent and his expression changed a couple of times as he processed this surprising testimony in the problematic homicide case which initiated SAC Conroy's distrust of NOPD. That distrust led to the distaste NOPD's detectives had for working with the local FBI office.

"Would he be willing to tell the FBI the same thing?" Avery eventually asked.

"Not if it means they think he had anything to do with killing Cammarato," I spoke on behalf of Puglisi.

"The FBI does not believe Puglisi killed Cammarato," Avery offered a glimmer of what he and Conroy discussed behind closed doors. "But knowing who did is just as bad."

"Perhaps having Cammarato killed was a value-added service Alexander handled for his client," I suggested without implying I knew this was true.

"I am beginning to not like that attorney very much," Avery let me know. It was not the right moment to share everything Tulip told me about Marvin Alexander because my boss had more than enough things to worry about just then.

fifty-eight

Chief Avery missed breakfast Monday morning. He did not even call to let me know he was not coming. I saw this as a bad sign. Not for me, but certainly for both my Chief and Detective Bassett. I called the detective's number at the Eighth District and the call went straight to voicemail. I called back to speak with the desk sergeant, and he informed me that Detective Bassett had not yet arrived at work. His tone let me know his opinion of a rookie detective not being at his desk before ten in the morning.

I tried to fill the time until Avery called as constructively as possible, but I felt distracted by the variables in play if Bassett was the one Avery had stopped coming out of the former brothel. I had my doubts that Bassett was inclined to save himself by saying he received a call from Puglisi's Russian Mob attorney. Bassett may have believed silence was all he had to negotiate with. He could try to make a deal based on what he could say, but I knew Avery well enough to believe that was not a wise bargaining move. The Chief would slap an obstruction of justice charge on top of everything else if he suspected Bassett was intentionally withholding relevant information. I was concerned about how tight of a lid Avery could keep on Bassett's arrest. Michael Conroy would dearly love to add the detective as another example of the poor job NOPD does when vetting its own detectives to his argument for a consent decree.

Avery finally phoned me just after eleven o'clock. He sounded exhausted and I imagined he had been up all night.

"Bassett is dirty," he shared. "Do not even begin to say you told me so."

"I would never say that out loud," I assured him. I heard Avery's unamused grunt and immediately moved on. "What did he have to say for himself?"

"He tried to spin a story about Puglisi's attorney not trusting the FBI to honor his client's agreement with them and asked him to go by the house to verify whether the journals were where Sunset Puglisi said he hid them," Avery said. I had clearly underestimated Bassett's willingness to drag Marvin Alexander down the drain with him.

"It could have happened that way," I suggested but knew better.

"Except Bassett could not explain how Marvin Alexander had his personal phone number or why he was carrying a second cellphone we found on him. It was bad enough he used the key he told us he lost to get into the place. He was carrying a burner phone with about twenty calls back and forth between a phone number we traced to another burner phone in New Jersey. We have not been able to identify who owns that number, but there is only one name that comes to my mind. Who comes to yours?"

"Marvin Alexander," I answered his rhetorical question.

"Bassett will not tell us what he discussed in the other conversations. He claims we cannot prove they were anything that compromised the investigation. By the way, one of the calls came right after he responded to the attack on your chef. According to Bassett's daily reports, he and Marvin Alexander have never met face to face. The only one of the men sitting at that table across the street from you that he ever did speak to was Puglisi, and they supposedly only spoke that time Bassett interviewed him," Avery said to explain what destroyed Bassett's alibi. "I know your love for burner phones. Tell me you are not in touch with Alexander as well."

"Of course not," I had no problem assuring him. "Bassett wrote the number to his burner phone on the back of the card he gave Puglisi when he interviewed him."

"How long have you known that?" Avery demanded in exasperation.

"I don't know it for sure," I lied and offered a plausible explanation for what I ought not to have said. "I just remember the way Puglisi looked at what should have been the blank side on Bassett's card when Bassett passed it to him. I write my cellphone number on the back of my cards sometimes, so maybe he did, too."

"I guess I didn't catch that," Avery allowed. He sounded angry I had not shared my suspicion about Bassett doing so at the time.

"I wasn't sure he did until now," I decided to push things forward and away from anything else he might want to know about my own actions or inactions. "What are you going to do with him?"

"Bassett has been suspended pending a review by Internal Affairs," Avery sighed. "I have a week or so to find anything else to stack on top of his doing a defense attorney's legwork, which is all last night really amounted to."

"At least this closes Alexander's eyes and ears into NOPD," I attempted to assuage my boss's lingering concerns. I could tell he was already accepting Detective Bassett's eventual return to his command. I could not see how the transgression which got Bassett suspended would be enough to get him demoted to patrolman. The department's ranks remained so shorthanded five years after Hurricane Katrina that it took more than running after hours errands for a defense attorney to get fired.

"I hope so," Avery sounded unconvinced. "I have no idea who else Alexander may have put on his payroll by now."

"Did Bassett shed any light on the journals?"

"None at all. We found a hole in the wall large enough to have been used to remove anything hidden in there. I think the diaries have been gone for a while, which means someone is out there making a deal for them that does not involve honoring any deal Puglisi made with the FBI," Avery was unknowingly detailing the precise conclusion I wanted everyone to reach when I told Puglisi to call Alexander. We needed to keep the idea of the journals alive for as long as possible.

"So, now we know the journals are a real thing and that they are in the wind," I said in false commiseration meant to reinforce the illusion.

"And that is not a good thing for anyone. I am going to have to let some people above me know what is going on. This is the worst possible situation the department could be in. There are a lot of careers riding on our recovering those journals before they fall into the wrong hands for good," Avery did not need to remind me what NOPD faced if the FBI or Marvin Alexander recovered them.

"I'll bump a few trees and see what I can shake loose about them," I promised.

"I am counting on you for this," Avery pointedly reminded me. His tone approached that of a plea. "I would just as soon not be put out to pasture."

"Well, I am not looking forward to the day you retire on anyone's terms, including your own," I let him know. There was no reason to believe his successor and I would enjoy the same relationship. They might want me to do real police work.

fifty-nine

I did my best to ignore Marvin Alexander's comments about Rebecca Collins in the few minutes we discussed her when he returned the buy money. I simply noted she seemed to be far more than he was prepared to deal with and how relieved he seemed to be now that he was rid of her. I saw no reason to believe Rebecca Collins came from a family with the sort of social status or wealth which typically creates entitled brats. I was beginning to suspect she discovered she could use stories about an evil stepfather to exploit the concern others have for any girl in the situation she described.

I did not want to start my interview with Rebecca until I satisfied my curiosity about her actual home life in Colorado. Taking any sixteen-year-old runaway at their word for why they do anything is never a good idea.

It took a half dozen calls to two different agencies to find anyone familiar with her family's history. A helpful bureaucrat named Estelle Langley at the Division of Family Services informed me she could not disclose or confirm anything without a court order, but then she stayed on the line rather than hang up like everyone else had.

"Well, Estelle, I am about to interview the young girl and I could really use anything that might fall between the legal cracks," I began working my magic. "She is in considerable trouble here and it would be helpful to know what sort of trouble she left behind there. She is facing criminal charges for solicitation and for underage drinking. She was in the company of members of organized crime when we detained her, which raises the possibility she is a victim of some sort of human trafficking. I cannot imagine her life in Colorado was this colorful."

"I don't think any teenager's life in Colorado is that colorful," Estelle loosened up. She sounded like she was just at about the right level of curiosity and indignation it would take to learn things I ought to have a court order to hear. Her heart was in the exact right place for what I needed her to do for me.

"I would appreciate anything you can tell me about her becoming an emancipated minor. I have no idea what became of her mother, but I cannot understand why her stepfather agreed to let her begin making her own decisions when she made such a bad one in leaving home." I tried to plant opportunities for Estelle to divulge more than she should. I wanted her to feel wrong about obstructing a state police detective who was concerned enough about Rebecca's well-being to ask for more information.

"I cannot agree that her leaving home was an unwise decision. Rebecca's brother is in foster care now, and he has been telling stories about his stepfather's behavior towards Rebecca which paint a pretty horrible picture," Estelle let me know, without going into specifics I did not need to hear to imagine. Estelle's tone of voice and careful phrasing were meant to verify any claims Rebecca may have made to me. It occurred to me that Estelle Langley had played this game with other callers in the past.

"I don't suppose you can share what became of Rebecca's birth parents?"

"Only that her real father died in an accident at work. Her mother remarried within a year, and she abandoned the kids after she left the hospital after the last incident," Estelle shared. I could not ask about the couple's history of domestic abuse because Estelle was unlikely to answer such a direct question. Estelle's careful wording suggested but never stated that Rebecca's stepfather had hospitalized her mother more than once. "She signed custody over to the children's stepfather and left town with little more than her divorce decree and a black eye."

Rebecca's mother was never going to be nominated for sainthood. The woman had recognized any further fight she put up would involve progressively more painful fashions of losing and chose to save herself over her kids. It is likely that she figured the two kids would survive long enough to move out at eighteen.

"Any idea why Rebecca's stepfather signed the emancipation paperwork? He could have insisted she move home. If nothing else, he lost a dependent on his taxes," I eased into what I was really calling about.

"I cannot answer that question, but you might find your answer by talking to the sheriff's department about the matter.

I will just say karma was involved," Estelle politely steered me in the right direction. She sounded almost giddy about the story awaiting me with my next phone call.

"Well, thank you," I said with sincere gratitude. She had not given me much, but I felt better about the validity of the story Rebecca had spun to Boomer about why she left home and did not want to go back.

"Ask for Detective Briscoe," she offered and hung up.

Detective Jeremy Briscoe of the Denver Police Department turned out to be a guy about my age whose cases involve what he termed 'interpersonal violence.' His cases involved every imaginable type of physical altercation which did not end fatally. His open investigation involving Rebecca's stepfather had him stumped until I called.

"Two patrol officers in Lakewood found him in a public park with multiple broken bones and his genitals cut up. We got the case because he claimed two men abducted him at gunpoint from his home here in Denver," Detective Briscoe filled me in. "They broke every finger in his left hand before they slammed his car door shut on it. Then the same guys broke both his kneecaps and both big toes before they hacked up his crotch. That was the position he was in when the Lakewood officers found him."

"Either he was a slow learner or whoever did it enjoyed their work," I surmised. The detective did not share my sense of humor.

"What's your interest in this guy?" he asked rather stiffly.

"His daughter took off a couple of months ago and wound up in bad company here," I decided to start with the basics. "Did he say why he got worked over?"

"All he told us was that they told him he should know why he deserved such a beating. Some big city attorney showed up in his hospital room and told him to sign some sort of paperwork or expect another visit from the guys who worked him over," the detective elaborated a bit on the details of the stepfather's decision-making process.

"Did he say what that document was?"

"He did not bother reading it. He says he would have signed his soul over to the devil to get them to stop busting him up."

"Well, I believe his stepdaughter may well have sold her own soul to the devil," I mused, mostly to myself.

"Anyway, Family Services had his stepson out of the house by the time he got out of the hospital. He is back in the hospital right now getting more reconstructive surgery done. He is understandably afraid the two men who did this might decide to double back," Detective Briscoe rounded out what he had to share.

"I think he is safe from that happening," I informed the detective. "His signature was all they wanted. The beating was a special present from his stepdaughter."

"Who does a sixteen-year-old girl know who can deliver that kind of beating? He was not assaulted by a pair of high school kids," the detective was certain of his assessment.

"Type the name Dudiyn Alekhin into your computer," I instructed the distant detective. I had to spell both names for him, but the detective's choice of search engines produced results almost immediately.

I heard a low whistle and then what sounded like choking. "You're saying this guy's stepdaughter sent the Russian Mob to rough him up?"

"I am saying one of their attorneys' names is on the paperwork he wisely chose to sign. The attorney did not have to go all the way to Russia for the muscle that did this. I have a pair of them watching my place from across the street right now. They must like to work in pairs," I let the astounded detective know.

"That sounds insane. What the heck has that girl pulled you into, Detective Holland?" he asked in both awe and concern for my own safety.

"Rebecca has no idea what she has let herself be lured into," I assured him.

"I guess I can go tell my boss the case is solved but he should not expect any arrests," Detective Briscoe wisely deduced from our conversation. "We are not going to find the guys who beat him up anytime soon. I do not know that I would want to try to arrest them if we did."

"You truly wouldn't," I gave my experienced opinion. I had no intention of ever arresting the muscle Marvin Alexander assigned to constantly watch me. The only choices I would have in a confrontation with that sort of men would be to kill them both or die trying.

I hung up and called Tulip to arrange a time to interview Rebecca Collins. I felt better informed about Rebecca's actual homelife, which is to say it was as bad as she told Boomer, and how she managed to become a legally emancipated minor four states from home. I was concerned that she was now in debt to Pete Matranga and Marvin Alexander. I was also curious how much she knew, or at least how much she would admit knowing, about the thrashing her stepfather took. I was entirely prepared to believe the debt Matranga claimed her auction was meant to retire involved both the paperwork and the beating.

"When can I speak with Rebecca?" I asked my sister.

"As soon as you find her," she said with more than a little agitation in her voice. "I had her set up at Covenant House, but she signed herself out yesterday and they have not seen her since. I see no reason to believe the girl is ever going back."

"Why is that?" I wondered. I cannot say I was all that surprised that Rebecca did not stay in a shelter designed for society's stray minors. I had formed the distinct impression in the brief time I shared the girl's company that she did not think of herself as being a lost child, and she now had paperwork in hand which established she was a legal adult were anyone to challenge her.

"She kept asking me when she could call Matranga. He promised her the moon and she must still believe he plans to take her there. I explained the criminal aspects of everything which has transpired between the two of them. I even brought up the Mann Act when she claimed he wanted to take her traveling. Anyway, she has my business card with your number written on the back if she decides to ask for help before anything truly bad happens." Tulip's anger grew the longer she spoke. It was beginning to sound a lot like her tone of voice after she loses a court case on a technicality. Losing an abused runaway to a pedophile mobster was a major defeat on both of our scoresheets.

"I can try to track her down, but there isn't much we can do when I find her," I let Tulip know. She was the lawyer of the two of us, so she knew this better than I did.

"That's what has me so upset," Tulip ranted. "We did everything we could to get her out of that situation and she couldn't wait to go back."

"It's not unusual behavior, but it is still unfortunate," I mistakenly tried to console her rather than share her outrage.

"So, this is something else you are going to drop, is that it?" she turned on me.

"How so?"

"You stopped looking for our father when someone handed you a good excuse to do so. You have never verified if that man's story is true. Now you are going to let loose of Rebecca just because the law says you cannot do anything. I have never known you to worry this much about the letter of the law," Tulip raged.

"Two things, sis," I fought back. "I did not just give up on looking for our father. I spent four years asking everyone he knew what became of him, checking morgue records and speaking with people he rescued to reach the conclusion we were never going to know what became of him. In all that time the one thing that kept coming to mind was that you and I both considered him dead to us long before Katrina. I had not spoken to him in two years, and you once told me you never even bothered to check to see if he planned to evacuate. As for little Miss Colorado, she is damaged goods and going to make bad decisions one after the other until she finally gets hurt badly enough to get smart. We cannot push a mule that stubborn to safety."

"Being right doesn't mean you don't have to act like you care," Tulip smacked me with the sort of spontaneous profundity our father used to spew like ancient wisdom.

"Okay, I will start acting like I care," I sighed into the phone. "Meanwhile there are things I can do about other situations that need my attention. The bar here is always open and I will listen to your rants anytime you need to unload. How's that?"

"You're the best, big brother," Tulip snorted and hung up on me.

I was no less unhappy about the situation with Rebecca Collins than my little sister, but Rebecca being both an emancipated minor and above the age of consent in the eyes of

Louisiana meant whatever she and Matranga had going did not break any laws I had sworn to uphold.

The first thing I was taught about rescuing a drowning person is to let them sink if trying to save them meant both of us might drown. That advice has proven just as sound on dry land over the years.

sixty

My day, week, and future hit another unexpected bump when Special Agent in Charge Michael Conroy walked into Strada Ammazarre just after six o'clock that same afternoon. I changed duties at five o'clock, and Tony and I were standing at the bar being the bistro's convivial co-owners when I spotted Conroy standing in the doorway. He did not seem unsure of where he was or where he wanted to go. He knew exactly who he intended to speak with as well. The posturing in the doorway was his doing his best to make the sort of entrance gunslingers made by pushing open an Old West saloon's swinging door. He did not carry it off very well. The regulars barely paid him any mind.

"Michael," I further diminished his presence with my informal greeting from half-way down the bar. "Glad you could join us."

Tony was standing beside me. He leaned back to look down the bar at the FBI agent approaching us before he glanced at me with a vaguely nervous expression. I winked to let Tony know I saw nothing to be concerned about in Conroy's unexpected presence.

"Detective Holland," Conroy greeted me in a flat tone which expressed his displeasure with being addressed so casually.

"May we buy you a drink? It is the end of your workday, isn't it?" I asked.

"I have one last thing to handle, but no thanks all the same," Conroy shook his head and then confronted Tony.

"Anthony Venzo Hussein al-Majid, I need you to be in my office at ten o'clock next Monday morning to speak with representatives from Interpol. Bring an attorney if you wish, but be on time or I will send agents to bring you to speak with them," Conroy said loud enough for everyone who was the least interested in his presence to hear.

"And what do they wish to discuss with Mister Venzo?" I countered and spoke the name everyone around us knew Tony by to do my best to cover the one Conroy all but shouted. Nobody in the place knew the chef's real last name.

"I am sure you both know the answer to that question," Conroy smugly informed us and turned to leave. The regulars did their best to appear to ignore him.

"I will leave tonight," Tony said as soon as Conroy was out of earshot and the rest of the bar patrons had resumed their own conversations.

"No, you will not," I insisted and placed my hand on his wrist. "This is a fishing expedition at best and is probably just a way for him to save face. Conroy is as much on the line as Puglisi about the journals. One of the conditions of Puglisi's parole is that he must turn over his journals and he hasn't done that yet. Conroy needs something, or someone, just as flashy to show his bosses if the journals do not show up in his office very soon. We know the letter opener will not link to anything you did in Europe. I will talk to Ralph at the State Department in the morning and let him know what is going on. The FBI Director told Conroy to keep his nose out of our business in Iraq once before, so Conroy found a proxy to do his dirty work this time. Tulip can find a good defense attorney if I cannot make this go away by Monday."

"Okay," Tony sighed. Interpol does not send its agents on any wild goose chases. Someone besides Conroy must have seen Tony as being a fat goose.

sixty-one

Katie and Tulip agreed with my assessment that Michael Conroy's pursuit of Tony was a way to look aggressive to his own boss if Puglisi failed to produce the journals. Uncovering and extraditing a foreign government's assassin would be a nice shiny thing to distract from his failure to deliver a larger target. This would not get Conroy his consent decree, but it would buy breathing room from the FBI Director. I let Tulip and Tony worry about lining up his defense counsel.

"In other news, Detective Bassett has been suspended," I announced over dinner with the two women. Tony came by to drop off courses and to drink from Tulip's glass of wine. We were drinking one of the pricey bottles from Tony's personal cellar, and I was worried my friend's generosity betrayed his intention to empty his wine cellar because he would not be able to take it with him if he were deported. "I set a trap for Bassett, and he jumped in with both feet. I asked Puglisi to call his attorney and say someone found his journals. Avery caught Bassett coming out of the place on Dauphine with a burner phone full of calls to and from a number in New Jersey. NOPD is assuming he is in Marvin Alexander's pocket."

"Did Avery recover any of the journals?" Katie asked and gave me a particularly hard stare. She instinctively knew I had revisited the house after our last conversation.

"No. Apparently they are still in the wind." I ignored her suspicious look. I could not tell her I was conspiring with Puglisi to hide the truth about the journals lest she expect me to come clean to Avery and the FBI about what I knew. That my doing so would be a death sentence for Puglisi was more like a bonus than a reason not to in her view. "It has both Conroy and Avery on the ropes. Avery is worried about NOPD's twenty-year-old dirty laundry being hung out for all to see, and Conroy lobbied for Puglisi's parole based on getting to have the first look at the journals. It breaks the chain of evidence if anyone besides Puglisi turns them over to him or if we find them in anyone else's possession. Conroy would need Puglisi to testify that the journals are real and unedited in the time they were in someone else's control to be able to use them in any case he derived from their contents. The DOJ would still have to convince a jury to accept Puglisi's word over whomever they prosecuted, and we are talking about politically connected private citizens and high-ranking brass in NOPD."

"Juries are not trusting the testimony of anyone from NOPD any more than they do a criminal's, so those cases would not work out for them," Katie let me know. She could no longer take a case to court if the case were based on the judgement of an NOPD officer or detective. It took confessions in open court, irrefutable evidence that did not require a paid expert to explain, or the testimony of a co-conspirator to get convictions because of misbehavior by too many NOPD officers following Hurricane Katrina. Fully a third of the force had abandoned their posts or faced discipline for misconduct in the wake of the storm. Bassett's betrayal of his badge was certain to increase the public's distrust.

"I would think catching Bassett red-handed would make you happier than this. You look like there are still some big problems to tackle. Anything I can do?" Tulip observed. She has investigators and online researchers at her disposal. I might never have learned everything she told me about Marvin Alexander were it not for them.

"Michael Conroy has also chosen to take another swipe at Tony and me over the Iraq stuff. Using Interpol as his beard for this new thing is going to backfire on him unless Interpol chooses to pursue Tony as a suspect," I informed her, and tried to temper this news by assuring her that Conroy's gambit put both men in jeopardy.

"What are the odds of them doing that?" Tulip wanted to know. She sounded overly concerned. She only lets her usual façade drop if she cannot fake enough bravado.

"I like to think they aren't very good, but it was recently pointed out to me that the State Department's protection is subject to shifts in the political winds," I told her. I chose not to give her the source of this insight because it would only worry her even more. "I can tell you for certain that no cases can be tied to the best piece of evidence Conroy provided them."

"The letter opener," Tulip sighed.

"The letter opener," I repeated. "Next time you buy Tony a

present make it a stuffed animal or something else that doesn't have a point, okay?"

"No problem," Tulip finally managed to smile. She fell silent through the remainder of the meal, but Katie and I could tell she was mentally working as hard on Tony's problem as she was on mine. Anyone who failed to take Tulip into account was going to get a lesson in why they ought not mess with my sister's love life.

sixty-two

I am not at all convinced that Ralph Easter's real name is either Ralph or Easter. I wonder if he chose to identify himself to me as Ralph because it is also my father's name. Only someone unfamiliar with my family dynamic would believe a contact with that name was going to earn my trust.

Ralph has an innocuous office on the third floor of the State Department's building behind the Post Office on Loyola Avenue. Ralph is noticeably unremarkable; he is a forty-something guy of average build without a single distinguishing feature. Ralph keeps his brown hair cut short and his face shaved smooth. He wears off-the-rack suits from the sort of men's clothing stores one finds in upscale suburban malls. His hands bear no rings and his Tag Hauer watch looks brand new. You could speak with Ralph for an hour and not recognize him on the street a day later.

Tony and I only know Ralph as the person we must contact if anyone asks questions about a State Department interdiction operation the chef and I were part of until the night it became a political liability. Ralph's job title has something to do with immigration vetting, but I have always assumed he works for their Bureau of Intelligence and Research. The State Department's INR began as the Research Department within the OSS in the 1940s, and their mission of discreetly gathering political, economic, and social intelligence for the government continued unabated before and after the CIA received its charter.

Ralph knew all the right buttons to push and all the right palms to grease to transform a former Mukhabarat operative and assassin from Iraq named Anthony Venzo Hussein al-Majid into a wealthy Sicilian-born chef named Tony Venzo so he could emigrate to New Orleans on the EB-5 Immigrant Investor Visa which Tulip arranged. Ralph made it clear to both of us that the approval for this visa came from high up the chain of command and that it was based on keeping the two of us together rather than having to monitor our compliance with our NDAs separately.

"I cannot tell you how upset my stomach gets anytime you

272

call me with a Tony problem," Ralph complained and gestured towards the industrial sized bottle of antacid tablets on his desk as I took a seat. I admired his view of the nearby Superdome and what the locals were calling the Minidome next door which houses the Hornets basketball team.

"I can't begin to tell you how upset I am when I make these visits," I assured him. "I think it is safe to safe to say that our mutual ambition is to never speak to one another."

"Yet here we are, again. What mess are the two of you involved in this time?" Ralph went straight to business.

"Two men assaulted Tony at the restaurant, and he put a letter opener in the chest of one assailant. His unique technique gave Michael Conroy the bright idea of contacting Interpol to see if they had any cold cases that involved a similar knife wound. The blade will not trace to anything he may have done in the past, but something caught Interpol's attention and now they plan to sit down with Tony and Conroy on Monday." I explained as succinctly as possible.

"I hate that guy." Ralph remained displeased that Conroy had declassified the after-action report on Operation Stoplight to interfere with my recent investigation into domestic criminality by the defense contractor which had secretly bankrolled Stoplight. I imagined NSA minions were still frantically scrubbing the declassified report from the internet. "Director Mueller has personally told Conroy to ignore all things Tony Venzo."

"Interpol didn't get the same message, so Conroy is using them to do his dirty work," I gave my opinion.

"Well, we aren't in the habit of interfering with Interpol investigations," Ralph informed me with little apology in his tone. "We need their assistance on our own cases too much to tell them to bugger off when something involves people from this country. The goes double if they are not American citizens, people like Tony."

"So, are you telling me State cannot or will not do anything?" I demanded.

"I am telling you that Tony is going to have to sit down with them. I will make some calls to see what they are looking into and try to dissuade them all I can," Ralph offered at least some promise of assistance. "Anything else besides dusting off

273

his knife skills I need to be aware of?"

I paused while I tried to find a clever way to word the second issue that might arise. Ralph could tell I was stalling and began tapping his pen on his desk.

"Tony converted some of his gold into diamonds," I began. I rushed through the rest as Ralph began to suck the air out of the room. "He caught the attention of the Russian Mob and I am working a case that indicates they may be trying to move into New Orleans."

"Oh, Christ," Ralph sighed. He leaned back in his swivel chair and tossed his pen on his desk. "Do you know which bunch of Russians it is?"

"Dudiyn Alekhin. His nephew is a guy named Marvin Alexander, and it is the nephew I am working uphill against, not Dudiyn. Marvin is an attorney and his client list in New Orleans includes Junior Hauser's former attorney and two former members of Carlos Marcello's operation. I think he may be brokering a three-way deal on organized crime in New Orleans."

"Well, you would be wrong about that," Ralph immediately popped my balloon. "There is no way Alekhin would take only a third of any pie on the table. He will take the pie and the table along with it. The nephew is looking for a way to eliminate the other players for his uncle."

"Do you think Interpol might want to redirect their attention?" I suggested.

"From clearing a bunch of old cases to actively fighting Dudiyn Alekhin? I would not even know how to propose something so absurd. Bring them a case against the nephew or Alekhin personally and they might consider making the trade, otherwise they will stay focused on something easier," Ralph said. The room fell silent for a moment as we each considered the news the other shared. Ralph broke the silence. "I cannot believe Tony screwed up and started buying diamonds. I thought moving the cash he stole from Colonel Habib's family into gold was problematic enough. Buying diamonds from the Russians was straight up stupid."

"Tony started with just one diamond," I informed him. "He wanted to make an engagement ring for Tulip."

"Oh, you have got to be really happy about that," Ralph

finally found a reason to laugh.

"You can only imagine," I said with a bit of self-deprecation. He would have been surprised how prepared I was to accept what I finally saw was inevitable.

"Getting your pal's finances back under the rug is a problem for the two of you to solve. State is not going to get involved in that any further. The Iraqis stopped harping on the money he took from General Habib and his brothers after he gave the Treasury back what they wanted out of it. State considers anything in his account now to be his retirement fund from the time he spent in the Mukhabarat. The two of you need to start worrying about how Tony will explain his finances to the IRS when he applies to be an American citizen," Ralph patiently reiterated the State Department's position, and the limits to their assistance. I did not imagine for a second that Ralph could not tell me to the penny how much was in Tony's offshore accounts.

"We are working on it," I assured him. "I would appreciate anything you can do to pour sand into Conroy's gears, but I understand you may need to do some tough politicking."

"Tell Tony congratulations for me," Ralph jabbed at me one last time as I started out the door. I could still hear him laughing as I walked down the hallway.

sixty-three

Tulip surprised me during my afternoon patrol of the Quarter with Roux. She stepped in beside us as we passed Faulkner House Books. It was a workday for her, but she wore jeans and a loose blouse. She made a point of showing me the two books she had just purchased, a history of rum and the latest book in a local detective series she enjoys, so she could take stock of my stalking goons. The pair could not find a convincing way to stand thirty feet away without looking obvious. Tulip also discreetly lifted her blouse enough for me to see the holstered pistol inside her waistband. It was not something she would carry unless she was prepared to use it.

"They look serious," she commented. "You sure you are okay with them tailing you?"

"No," I readily admitted and patted her pistol. "But they have been little more than an annoyance so far."

"And you have a plan to eliminate them when that changes," she spoke aloud what I did not say. I shrugged and began walking. Roux fell a full step behind us and looked back over his own shoulder so I did not need to look over mine.

"You aren't here to check up on me, or to buy books," I surmised.

"I did want these," she defended her subterfuge. "But I also wanted to check out those two and to tell you about a very strange phone call I received this morning."

"Who called you?"

"Rebecca Collins," Tulip said and waited for some sort of pithy comment or guttural response. I held my tongue because I anticipated something more worthy of such commentary would be forthcoming. I managed to put the girl out of my thoughts after she jumped back into the hot frying pan with Matranga. "Rebecca says she wants to take out Matranga."

"I am not going to help a sixteen-year-old girl kill a mobster." I did not care how Tulip worded my refusal to be drug into any such scheme when she returned the call.

"She did not give me the impression she plans to kill him. She wants to run him onto larger legal rocks than his stunt with the auction proved to be and is looking for our advice or help," Tulip translated teenager-to-English for me. "She claims she went back to him because she knows he is dangerous, and he still expects payment for whatever he did for her in Colorado."

"What he did for her in Colorado was cripple her stepfather and send her kid brother into foster care. I can see why she thinks it best to pay the man," I informed my sister of what I knew of their transaction. "I imagine she owes Alexander for his legal services as well, though Matranga may have fronted that expense."

"So, will you help her take him down?" Tulip asked hopefully. I could not believe she expected me to assist the young girl's unreal proposition.

"No," I repeated. "However, if she sees a vulnerability I can exploit to arrest him then you can relay it to me. There is no way I am putting her life in any more danger than just being with him already is. Ideally, she would find a way to get him to take her across any state line to spend the night."

"What are the odds of him being that stupid?" Tulip sounded relieved I was not going to totally ignore the girl's offer, but disappointed in my admittedly unlikely scenario happening. We were both relieved to know Rebecca was not under immediate duress, nor was she the mindless blond-haired bimbo her decrepit benefactor believed her to be. I could not imagine Matranga was looking for a repeat of the Vanity fiasco. I was only worried that my sister did not see how manipulative the young girl could be. Honestly, I have no problem using a sixteen-year-old as an informant. My reluctance in this instance came because I simply did not trust Rebecca Collins not to turn on me, as well.

"While I have you with me, have you had any luck finding Tony a defense attorney for Monday?" I decided to use this rare opportunity to discuss the matter without anyone but the two of us present. I did not want Tony to see me worried about his situation. My being confident he would prevail was the only thing keeping Tony's fight-or-flight instincts in check.

"No, and I am not qualified to defend him. They could be talking about murder charges in multiple countries." I could tell my sister was intending to begin studying international criminal law.

"Well keep looking," I pleaded as much as encouraged her. "The State Department may be getting tired of covering for him."

Tulip's face reddened and I sensed tears were about start flowing so I hugged her until she felt strong enough to break the embrace. I did not care that we had an audience. We went our separate ways, which created a problem for the two men who preferred to tail their target as a pair. They chose to ignore Tulip and remain focused on me, which was fine by me as I did not want them to know where my sister lives.

sixty-four

I took Katie to Etienne for supper that night. It is a casual bistro in her neighborhood that serves magnificent food. Then again, it is nearly impossible to get a bad meal in anywhere in New Orleans. The quality of table service is what you need to be wary of, but the wait staff at Etienne always matches the quality of the pricey menu. I am spoiled by never seeing a bill for my meals at Strada, so dinner tabs often come as a shock when I take Katie to eat anywhere else.

We began with cocktails at the bar while we waited for our table. I always request the table beside the plate glass window facing Webster Street. Katie used to believe it was so we could watch the passersby, but she gradually realized my reason was rooted in the psychology of my past. I need to monitor my surroundings to feel safe, and that table allows me to monitor the traffic on the one-way street and the front door so I know who is entering and leaving the restaurant. It sucks most of the romance out of the notion of having 'our' table, but she has come to realize how much safer she is when I feel safe.

"Tulip showed up in the Quarter after lunch today," I opened the conversation as our waiter delivered an order of pommes frites with a smoked tomato aioli. Katie munched on one of the crisped fried potatoes while she waited for me to continue my story. "She said Rebecca Collins is offering her assistance to take down Matranga from the inside."

"You aren't considering using her are you?" Katie asked, clearly aghast at the idea.

"No," I hastily assured her, but without sharing my only reason for not doing so. "I told Tulip I would appreciate knowing anything that might be of help, but I do not want to put her in any danger. I doubt she understands Alexander is even more dangerous. He will have her killed if he has the slightest reason to believe she is anything but Matranga's arm candy. She was sitting at the pizzeria with some of them yesterday afternoon."

"With some of whom?" Katie asked, challenging my use of pronouns.

"Marvin Alexander was there with Matranga and Vincent

Contaldo, the shooter from Chicago," I clarified. Katie pulled another fancy-named French fry off the plate but left it dangling in her hand while she considered the lineup I had given her.

"Why does A group like that decide to meet in public? They have to know the FBI has the table under surveillance." Katie nibbled at the appetizer between thoughts on the subject. "They must want someone to know all three sides are cooperating, or at least that they are conversing. They may want word of the meeting to reach someone they cannot reach on their own. Did you consider they may just be pulling your chain? You know, reminding you of how outnumbered you are. You are interfering with the plans of all three crime families right now and sometimes I wonder how it is that you are still walking around."

"You know who wasn't represented in that meeting?" I asked her to stop any further discussion regarding the balancing act between my work habits and my life expectancy, at least until we were at her house.

"Junior Hauser," she knew the answer before I finished asking the question.

"Why do you suppose that is?" I wondered. "If these were negotiations, they should want the guy closest to New Orleans at the meeting. Unless the three of them were plotting to attack him in unison."

"Unlikely," Katie shook her head. She paused to allow the server to place a salad with hearts of palm, blue cheese, and walnuts on a bed of Boston lettuce in front of her. I received romaine leaves topped with crisp bacon crumbles and cherry tomatoes drizzled with a Parmesan dressing. I placed my hand over the unfinished appetizer to keep the server from taking it. I also gave him what I meant to be a polite expression to encourage him to slow our pace of service. Katie saw the look I gave him and worried he might not come back. "As I was saying, I do not see a scenario where three syndicates vying for control of New Orleans band together to wipe out a fourth competitor. There would be a Shakespearian number of crooked side deals and double crosses. We can both agree they staged the meeting for a reason. Perhaps their objective was to draw attention towards themselves in order to pull it away from someone or something else."

"What would that be?" I asked before I placed a bite of salad in my mouth. "Nobody turned up dead or went missing in the last two days that I know of."

I caught the furtive but unsettled look the woman seated to our left gave me.

"You're the detective, not me," she replied and lifted a forkful of her own salad. "My job is to prosecute them for whatever you can prove they were up to."

"Slacker," I laughed and stopped talking to allow her to enjoy her salad.

Katie ordered grilled pompano and I asked that my lamb chops be served medium rare. The waiter opened a bottle of Merlot from a Russian River vintner to allow it to breathe before he brought our entrees. The medium-bodied red wine would be fine with both meals, but I ordered it to tease Katie with the word 'Russian.'

I let my mind relax while I listened to Katie's oral dissertation on the cases she was prosecuting. One had the advantage of compelling evidence and a hideous defendant. The other was a toss-up because the likable defendant was on trial for embezzling from an unpopular local car dealer. Katie tailored her case to use the defendant's likability against him rather than try to rehabilitate the victim of the crime in the jury's eyes.

My mind began to stray to what the guests at the other tables were discussing. I did not lack interest in what my girlfriend was saying, but I am an analytical person by nature and neither of the cases posed problems Katie needed me to solve. I listened to snippets of conversations at the other tables about lawns needing mowed, kids doing well in sports they were too young to learn anything but aggression and competition from playing, funny stories that made the teller appear smarter than the sap they were talking about, and similar things civilians discuss to appear interesting to others.

I felt guilty for tuning out Katie's attempt at table conversation but felt punished when Rebecca Collin's offer began tumbling through my mind like a square block. It would give me a headache until the sharp edges wore smooth or the block shaped itself into a cog I might fit into a plan. Rebecca sat well poised to let me know what Matranga was saying and doing. Her position also made her the first person her benefactor would suspect of the slightest leak. I needed to find someone else to cast suspicion upon before I could use her information. Lenny Bonetti was going to get the job whether he realized I had set him up or not. I had nothing against him, but I would lose much less sleep at night if Lenny's body wound up in the trunk of a car than Rebecca's.

"You're checking out on me," Katie declared in mid-sentence. I knew she was explaining the difficulty of educating a jury in finance and accounting in the embezzler case because this is a recurring issue in her white-collar cases. Katie's closing argument would focus on painting the defendant as a horrible human being rather than upon any injury his crime caused his victims. Juries are always looking for someone to hate. They can learn to hate the judge, an attorney from either side of a case, someone's best witness, or even the prosecutor instead of the defendant on trial. Too often justice gets determined on a jury's whims or on their collective decision to 'punish' someone other than the person on trial. A little power is, as they say, a dangerous thing.

"Guilty," I apologized.

"Hmm," Katie murmured as she stared at me over the rim of her wineglass. "I am going to bet you are reconsidering Rebecca Collins' offer. You have nothing else to work with. Puglisi's journals are a one-shot weapon and that is only if you are the one who has them."

This was not her way of drawing a confession about the diaries out of me. She was stating the obvious. I could only use the journals against one opponent before everyone else would realize I had them. I faced prosecution because I was technically withholding evidence from the FBI which Puglisi had promised to give them. Neither Chief Avery nor Captain Hammond at the state police would stop the Feds from filing charges against me for hiding Puglisi's secrets from the Justice Department.

"Playing spy is going to get her killed," I immediately conceded. "I need to find a way to make her a legal liability for Matranga, hopefully a large enough one that he can be taken out of the equation before he knows what happened, and maybe even take one or two others down with him."

"The girl is sixteen. She is no longer jailbait and being an emancipated minor only makes her easier to exploit. It does nothing to protect her," Katie offered her expert legal opinion. "What sort of trap can you set that won't get her hurt?"

"Beats me," I had no problem admitting, but then glanced at my watch. "But it is still early."

"It's going to be too late for you to save our little date here if you don't drop it for the rest of the evening," Katie playfully stated what was clearly a threat to end the date at her doorstep as she waved her fork in a circle above the table. We were both counting on my staying with her until after breakfast.

"Drop what?" I said to reconfirm our date took precedence over my dark and tangled thoughts.

sixty-five

I visited Tulip in her office the next morning to rehash our earlier discussion regarding my idea to encourage Alex Boudreaux to stake a claim to any journals hidden within the walls of Puglisi's former brothel. She repeated her argument that the flaw in my plan was that Daniel Logan could file this claim on behalf of Alex's estate. My idea was nothing more than a good reason to murder Alex. It did not matter whether Alex or Logan was the one to hand over the journals to Marvin Alexander.

I remained fixated on the difficulty the FBI would have getting the journals because any civil court would rule that Puglisi no longer owned any diaries he promised the FBI in exchange for his parole. She also believed the FBI might lack legal grounds for seizing his diaries as Puglisi was not accused of any crime, but reminded me her expertise is in civil and not criminal law.

I told Tulip what I knew of Puglisi's parole agreement, and how we came to the same conclusion that Marvin Alexander intended to double-cross him. The only thing keeping Puglisi alive was everyone's belief that the diaries were real and only he knew where they were. I was beginning to suspect the diaries were a story Puglisi told Alexander to get the parole which would allow him to settle old scores and skip the country. I showed Tulip the fake journal Puglisi entrusted to my care and she thumbed through it as she considered the ways it might be weaponized.

"Let me get this straight," she said and then paused to read what seemed to be a juicy entry by the facial expression she made before she continued. "Puglisi needs his attorney and the FBI to believe this is one of what should be over a hundred diaries. The FBI wants to use them to solve some cold cases, and need Puglisi alive to verify the authenticity of his diaries in court. Marvin only needs him alive until he knows where Puglisi stashed the journals and has no intention of the FBI getting them."

"Correct," I said and nodded. "Marvin will use the same information the FBI expects to find to blackmail people on

Dudiyn's behalf. The diaries are literally a king maker for whoever winds up with them. That is if they exist."

"The belief they exist makes them real." Tulip waved the fake journal in her hand. "This is the gold coin that sends people chasing after buried treasure and sunken galleons. It proves the diaries are real to anyone who wants to believe in them."

"And that is why I need to be careful how I use it." This was why I was sitting in her office in the first place.

"Give it to whoever is positioned to make the most of it," she advised. "Conroy will wait forever to get the rest of them. His having any one of them would be enough reason for everyone else to kill Puglisi. His attorney will probably torture him until says where the rest are or admits there never were any to begin with."

"Okay, those two go on the list of people not to give it to," I laughingly said and began forming a pair of mental lists. "His pals from Marcello's old crew have not killed him yet, either, because they do not think the journals are real, or because he promised the journals to them along with everyone else."

"They must think they are real or Matranga would not have come from Miami to set him up in a house and pay him off with that watch," Tulip pointed out, but also to subtly remind me she was acutely aware Tony still had the watch. "I think you had the right idea about using Alex, but you had the wrong approach in mind."

"How so?"

"Dan Logan is tied to Marvin Alexander, but he is also lobbying to be Junior's new attorney. Alex must not know his attorney is waiting for the right time to sell him out," she said and gave a small laugh about Alex's blissful ignorance. "Alex has no idea that he connects to every side in the fight for the journals: the Russians, the Dixie Mafia, and owning Puglisi's old place links him to Matranga and to then to Chicago."

"How do you suggest I play my hand?" I asked. My inclination was to create a fake auction, perhaps at the Night Owl again, and take down anyone who showed up to pry them from Alex's cold dead fingers. It was a messy and marginally legal way to eliminate every threat I saw in one move. This plan did not account for the multiple unintended

285

consequences of such a bloodbath, and there would be plenty of those in the aftermath.

"You are crazy if you think I am going to give you a blueprint for how to break the law," Tulip immediately distanced herself from the conversation. "I will discuss things on a hypothetical basis with you all day long, but do not ever use my name if something blows up in your face."

"Understood," I was quick to assure her. "Now answer the question."

She gave me a very displeased look and sighed deeply. "Hypothetically, you need to create a feeding frenzy over the journals at the exact same time Puglisi disappears. Anyone who wants to use them for criminal reasons will believe he ran off with them and might be cutting a deal with someone else. Everyone with a badge, like NOPD or the FBI, needs him to use the journals in court if they catch him with them."

"I am looking for a way to make sure that anything messy happens in Mississippi. It keeps my fingerprints off whatever happens and embarrasses Conroy because he would not be there to make any arrests," I confided. She silently nodded as she considered this idea.

"Sounds good to me. I have no plans to share this conversation with Katie, and I am pretty sure you don't either or you would be talking to her right now instead of me," Tulip said to encourage me to keep her name out of how I used what we discussed in our purely hypothetical conversation. "See if you can get Alex to lure this circus across the state line. It's your best shot at putting an end to all of this."

sixty-six

I had a plan in mind by the time I returned to Strada for lunch. The only problem was how to make Puglisi disappear without being charged as an accessory to his escape. I needed to find a way to honestly state Puglisi disappeared and be able to honestly state that I had no idea where he was.

I needed the assistance of someone I could trust to accomplish my magic act. The only person I knew with a devious enough mind to help with this conundrum was Uncle Felix. I already owed favors he would never collect, so asking for another did not seem like a very big ask.

"I need to pick your brain, uncle." I waited while he confirmed I was using a burner phone to call his burner phone. Calling this number was an indication I was treading in very murky water.

"Better my brain than my pocket," he joked. "What can I help you with today?"

"I need to make a parolee disappear for an entire weekend in some fashion that allows me to honestly say I have no idea where he is but still know he is safe," I laid out the problem as best as I could.

"If you were speaking of Marion Puglisi, I would suggest booking him into the nearest old folks' home," my uncle suggested as much to let me know who this pertained to as to make what might have been a viable solution.

"They will want medical records," I said to dismiss the idea.

"You're welcome to use my name to get a suite at the Monteleone," he offered, perhaps in the belief this was why I called him with the problem.

"I cannot guarantee his safety without putting armed guards with him, and I cannot trust him to stay put even with room service," I argued. I had considered this option first and immediately discerned its multiple flaws.

"Did they did teach you at the academy that any parish can hold a suspect for seventy-two hours?" Uncle Felix said and almost immediately solved the problem. "Most sheriffs in smaller parishes routinely house their prisoners in larger parishes. You could make Marion the ball in a human game of three card Monte. What are the odds of anyone calling every single parish looking for him? The terms of a parole usually state he must cooperate in any law enforcement investigation."

"Wouldn't they have to let the State Police and FBI know they have him if there is a warrant or APB put out?" I asked. This idea might simply be a silver platter on which to serve Puglisi to Conroy.

"Things like that get overlooked all the time the farther you get from the city." He was beginning to sound like he had a specific parish in mind.

"I don't suppose you know of a law enforcement investigation in some remote parish that might need to make use of his expertise this weekend, or that might decide to transfer its newest prisoner due to overcrowding?" I warmed to his idea.

"I can think of one or two now that you mention it." It sounded like he was laughing on the other end of the phone. "Can your parolee be placed somewhere that he can be arrested without the locals getting involved?"

"I think so," I said before I began racking my brain for one.

"The detectives will leave if NOPD or FBI agents decide to intervene. I can ask them to hold him until Monday, but that is all the time you get," Uncle Felix offered.

"I will make what I want to do work within that window," I assured both of us. My career was over and Puglisi was dead if I failed to do so. An idea of where to stage the arrest came to mind as I was making this assurance. "Bayou Boogaloo started today. Have your guys meet us behind the Abita Stage at six o'clock tonight. A good public arrest ought to be enough to shake things up for a few days."

"Six o'clock. Don't be late, detective," Uncle Felix confirmed. Using my job title was his way of saying I incurred a professional and not a personal debt with this request.

sixty-seven

It was just approaching two o'clock when Roux and I left Strada for our mid-day patrol. I caught Matranga's eye before we crossed the street and made a beeline for the table outside the pizzeria.

"Gentlemen," I broke my staring contest with Matranga to look each man in the eye as I greeted them to the pizzeria. "Lovely day, is it not?"

"It's too humid," Rebecca spoke up. Nobody else was going to engage in even this light conversation. She fidgeted with the spaghetti straps on the short sundress she wore. Matranga was making sure his peers were aware of the charms of his new girl.

"Well, you know what they say about New Orleans in the summer," I said. "It's not the heat, it's the stupidity."

She giggled, but her male companions barely acknowledged the comment. They may or may not have grappled with whether I meant to insult them.

"It should be island cool this evening," I used this as my opening to contact Puglisi. "You should all come out to Bayou Boogaloo by City Park. My favorite band is playing on the Abita Stage at six o'clock."

Puglisi understood I was trying to send him a message because I looked him in the eye when I mentioned a location and a specific time.

"What's the band?" he asked to show he was listening for additional clues.

"The Bahama Mommas," I said, adding to what I was trying to convey. The truth was I had no idea what band would be on stage at that hour. I counted on the disinterest of the others to keep them from verifying my information. "They do a reggae cover of All Along the Watchtower."

"The Dylan song?" Vincent Contaldo finally joined the conversation.

"That's the one. You know, the opening line goes 'There must be some way out of here said the joker to the thief.' You really won't want to miss this opportunity," I looked directly at Puglisi one last time. He barely nodded his head as he raised his wineglass to his lips.

"I'll pass," Matranga snorted. "Crowds are not my thing."

"True enough. Crowds do some weird things in this town," I said and tugged Roux's leash to let him know we were leaving.

sixty-eight

I waited until nearly five o'clock to approach Alex with the forged journal. Anyone he gave it to would judge its authenticity on the strength of Puglisi's offer and not on its contents or the age of the ink and paper. I needed to leave myself enough time to get to the Abita stage, barely a mile away, without allowing enough time for word of the journal's existence to reach anyone who might keep Puglisi from meeting me.

I drove past three of Alex's properties in the Seventh Ward before I located his Ram work truck. I scanned North Gayoso Street for the Mercedes coupe Dan Logan drives and the rear-view mirrors on my Cadillac CTS-V station wagon for signs Marvin Alexander's thugs were tailing me. The pair were suspiciously intermittent about following me so I drove a vehicle they were unfamiliar with and were unlikely to have marked with a tracking device. The wagon's supercharged engine made this innocuous vehicle nearly as fast as my usual convertible coupe if need be.

"I do not wish to speak with you, detective," Alex immediately declared as I stepped through the back door of the developer's latest project. Alex's carpenters were preparing to leave for the day. "I do not have to talk to you, and I will call my attorney if you do not leave here right now."

"You have every right not to speak with me and to complain that I am harassing you to either your attorney or to Internal Affairs," I assured him even as I continued to walk through the newly gutted kitchen. "But any review board is unlikely to challenge why I questioned you. You should also worry more about who is paying Dan Logan than about my questions."

"I am paying him, as you well know," Alex said. His tone of voice made this less a declaration than something closer to a complaint about what he got for his money.

"Okay, tell me Dan Logan's hourly rate." I challenged him.

"Three hundred dollars an hour," Alex said with commendable confidence.

"It's five," I immediately corrected him. I had no idea what

291

Dan Logan charges his clients, but I knew how to make Alex question what he believes. "If you are only paying Logan part of his fee, what is he telling whoever pays the rest about your case?"

"What's your point?" Alex demanded in a subdued voice. I could tell I had rattled his confidence in his attorney.

"It might not hurt to hear me out without your attorney present just this once." I leaned against the kitchen doorframe to let him know I was not going away. Plywood covered the plate glass window behind him in the empty living room and what light there was came from halogen work lights run by the gasoline powered generator on the front porch. The generator's noisy motor kept our conversation private from his Spanish-speaking laborers.

"Fine, ask me what you came here to find out," he relented after only a moment's hesitation.

"I am sure he tells you Junior appreciates how you have kept your mouth shut, unlike the recently deceased Spenser Duncan. What Logan has not told you is that he is only representing you to get close to Junior Hauser." I fed Alex short sentences so he had time to consider each thing I said. "Why do you suppose Logan kept representing you instead of Bear Brovartey when the judge made him choose one client? Bear sure looks like a higher profile client, and that means a bigger payday."

"No idea," Alex admitted. His expression showed he was beginning to wonder.

"Bear hired Marvin Alexander on Logan's personal recommendation and less than a month later the FBI's primary witness against his client turned up dead. Marvin makes his living representing Russian Mobsters in New York and New Jersey and a lot of witnesses against those clients have died before any trials started. Logan kept his own hands clean in getting rid of the only witness against Brovartey and Junior, but he can still take credit for recommending Marvin Alexander." I patiently explained. "The pair worked together to eliminate Spenser Duncan after his part in finding Puglisi's journals was through. It is a good thing you did not find them or you would probably be dead as well. They planned to use the journals to identify and eliminate their enemies so they can run the entire Gulf Coast by themselves."

Alex digested what I said. He caught himself before he said something he knew was wrong at least twice before he put together a response.

"You cannot prove I had anything to do with that break in," He chose to go with a denial he must surely know I would not buy.

"Come here," I said with a chuckle and a smile. I waved for him to follow me down the newly drywalled hallway to the home's shared bathroom. I placed my hands on the new double vanity. "What is this?"

Alex looked at me for a long moment. He sensed there was only one right answer, and that it was not the one which came to mind. He finally gave up. "It's a vanity."

I removed my hand and pointed. "That's right. It's just not the sort of vanity you should have been looking for."

"What do you mean?" Alex was too anxious to know where he went wrong to grasp that he was admitting to vandalizing his own property.

"Do you happen to remember a large poster on the wall in one of the bedrooms? It had a cute girl with curly hair in a leather outfit on it, remember? Guess what her stage name is," I offered a clue.

"Vanity," he sighed. He may or may not have spotted the poster, but he knew the right answer to my leading question.

"Care to guess what was behind that poster?" I could tell his brain was becoming overloaded.

"Nothing. At least that is what I heard they found after they busted a crooked cop for looking for the journals," he said. He was unwisely proud of the knowledge he had of details which were never released to the public about Detective Bassett's suspension.

I reached into my messenger bag while delivered his huffy retort. "There used to be a two-way mirror where that poster is hung. Marion Puglisi hid his diaries in the wall when he drywalled over the hole before he went to prison. I am pretty sure Junior would still like to have what he sent the two of you after."

Alex's eyes lit up at the sight of the journal in my left hand. I was not ready to allow him to touch it.

"You found them." He sounded almost relieved that he might yet redeem himself.

"They were never lost and, no, I do not have them," I dissuaded his assumption the journals were at my disposal. "Marion Puglisi paid someone to move them after Marvin Alexander traded them to the FBI for his parole because he doesn't trust either of them. The guy just wants to leave town and I want him gone. I am here on his behalf to trade Puglisi's journals for a ride out of the country."

"This is some sort of joke, right?" he asked. "How am I supposed to do that?"

"Puglisi wants to die in the Bahamas, and Junior owns a big boat. I will bet your boss will make the trade if you approach him with it. I came to you because I do not trust your attorney to make an honest deal." I tempted him further by handing him the fake journal. "Puglisi is offering this one as a sign of his good faith. He will deliver the rest of them after he reaches his destination."

"I smell a trap," Alex abruptly declared and crossed his arms across his broad chest.

"I have no intention of arresting Junior," I assured him. "Anything illegal Puglisi and Junior do will happen outside of my jurisdiction. I don't want Junior anywhere near New Orleans, but he poses less of a menace to the city than the Russians or the Italians. Junior can demand a seat at his enemies' table if he controls the journals."

"So, you swear this isn't a trap for him or me?" Alex asked me to confirm.

"You're questioning a sweet deal. You can be the guy who delivers this to Junior, not your two-faced attorney. Ask yourself, will the Russians or Italians have any use for you if they take over?" I nudged him without answering his question.

"Who do I call if Junior wants to make the trade?" he asked as he fidgeted with the journal in his hand. His lousy poker face showed he could not wait to make the call that promised to put him back in Junior's good graces.

"Call me and I will put you in touch with Puglisi. Be careful. Dan Logan might not take you cutting him out of the loop all that well."

I handed him a card from Strada Ammazarre with a burner

phone number on the back to reach me. I did not bother trying to shake Alex's hand before I turned and walked out the back door. My convertible was parked through the block and I had to jump a low fence to cross the rear neighbor's backyard to get to it. I looked up and down the deserted street to see whether Marvin Alexander's men had caught up to me.

I did not expect to hear back from Alex Boudreax for at least a day. I envisioned him sitting on the offer overnight while he decided who to call. Dan Logan was going to be upset if Alex was so stupid as to contact Junior Hauser directly about anything, even the weather forecast. Junior, on the other hand, very likely wanted him dead and was going to need an incredibly good reason to not only pull any contract he placed on Alex's head, but to restore his standing within his syndicate. Millions of dollars of Junior's ill-gotten gains were lost when the FBI seized control of Alex's business, but there were lessons learned and millions more to launder if Alex could avoid prison and get back to running his own company.

"Junior will take the deal," Alex informed me after I answered the burner phone.

"That was quick," I said. It was a reaction more than a way to start a conversation.

"I think he knows some of what is in them," Alex allowed. "Anyway, he wants them and the price is cheap according to him. Have your guy at the Palace Casino Marina at ten o'clock tomorrow night, with the journals in hand."

"Okay," I promised and began to plan ways to use the meeting that was never going to happen to solve the problems that were certain to arise in New Orleans.

sixty-nine

Marvin Alexander had never anticipated his client would leave prison, either because the FBI would renege on their deal after Puglisi delivered the journals, or because Dudiyn would arrange Puglisi's murder in his cell once they fell into Marvin's hands. Matranga's ploy with the watch failed to bring his former underling in line, but he could not pressure Puglisi further without the approval of the Chicago Outfit bosses.

Michael Conroy had expected Puglisi to keep his agreement by delivering the journals to the FBI as soon as the mobster arrived in New Orleans, but the aging mobster was paroled three weeks ago and had not yet honored their agreement. Conroy was probably getting daily calls from the FBI Director at this point, and he was certain to get a phone call from the D.C. office when Marion 'Sunset' Puglisi was reported missing.

I suspected Marvin Alexander's men had planted a tracking device on my XL coupe. I drove to Bayou St. John in my CTS-V station wagon, which was unfamiliar to the pair, and parked in the driveway of a vacant house on Bell Street. I placed a police placard on the dashboard to dissuade anyone from having it towed. I did my best to blend into the Bayou Boogaloo crowd gathered near the footbridge spanning the bayou's narrowing path near Cabrini High School.

Puglisi passed behind me wearing a loose fitting bright red shirt. The conspicuous wardrobe choice made him a beacon in the throng of festival goers. His unsmiling companions stood out because they were the only ones attending the packed festival who were clearly not enjoying themselves.

I kept an eye on Puglisi and his two keepers, but my targets were the FBI agents I expected to find following them. I spotted one of the agents detailed to watch Puglisi's house by the frantic expression on his face as he struggled to keep Puglisi in sight while staying in radio contact with his partner. They must not have been able to find a place to park and decided his partner should circle the perimeter and call for back-up. The two FBI agents likely had notified the larger surveillance team Puglisi was on his way to dinner with

Matranga when he left his house because that was his normal routine. I counted on this unexpected detour to confuse and delay the arrival of additional agents.

I waited until the Abita stage was within sight to neutralize the lone agent. He was in his fifties and did not look like he ought to be the one in his team walking in the simmering early summer air. I eased a taser from my messenger bag and made a point of pressing it just below the man's belt line. I wanted to avoid inducing a heart attack. He spasmed uncontrollably as I moved away and left others in the crowd to shout and wave for the EMTs to treat his apparent seizure.

Puglisi glanced over his shoulder when he heard the commotion behind him. I signaled where to meet me. He said something to the men flanking him and the three of them began moving towards the left-hand side of the currently unoccupied stage.

NOPD blocked traffic behind the stage and redirected drivers into the neighborhood to the river side of the bayou or back towards City Park on the lake side. There was an unmarked sedan parked in the outside lane and a pair of detectives stood beside it while they spoke with NOPD's officers. I skirted to the right of the stage and flashed my badge at the beefy guy in a SECURITY t-shirt who wanted to block my access. I leaned over the barricade behind the stage and waved my arms over my head to get the attention of the out-of-town detectives. They pointed at me and the NOPD patrolmen let them pass.

"Glad you could make it," I said with a slight chuckle and shook their hands but offered no introductions. The last thing I wanted to know was where these two were from. I might need to pass a polygraph and needed to be able to say I had no idea what parish had detained Puglisi. If I was convincing about that, then I might be believed about having no idea how they knew where to find him.

"What's the plan?" the taller of the two asked. They were both well-groomed men in their early forties wearing sport coats and slacks. I saw no badges on their belts.

"Marion Puglisi is standing on the other side of this stage. He is eighty-two years old and wearing a bright red shirt. He has two armed bodyguards, but they will not risk being arrested for obstruction to defend him. Make sure you flash your badges and identify yourselves and this should go smoothly," I said.

"Are you coming along?" one of them asked as they turned to leave and he realized I was not moving.

"I am not even here right now," I let him know. He nodded silently, no doubt understanding what I meant from past experiences with Uncle Felix.

I hid among the throng at the front of the stage to watch the arrest. Puglisi was taken by surprise and his handlers offered only brief resistance. Matranga's men stepped back after one of the detectives waved his badge and drew his sidearm. The crowd backed up as well but reclaimed the space as the detectives led Puglisi away in handcuffs. I was tempted to stay and listen as the Funky Meters took the stage.

Instead I followed the detectives to their vehicle and tugged Puglisi out of earshot. He was still trying to adjust his wrists to the fit of the handcuffs holding his arms behind his back.

"What the hell is this?" he snarled. "What are they arresting me for anyway?"

"Think of this as protective custody. You need to disappear for a few days, and this is the only way to do that without you violating your parole. You are going to have to trust me when I say I am working on something that will benefit both of us," I informed him as I grabbed his wrist and used my own key to loosen the handcuffs. "You will be released on Monday with the perfect alibi."

"Why do I need an alibi?" he demanded but stopped struggling with the cuffs.

"If everything goes right you may be the last man standing on Monday morning," I told him with no elaboration. It sounded good, but the truth was I had no idea what the outcome of the weekend was going to be.

"So, this is for my own good. Is that what you want me to believe?" he demanded. My telling him this was for his own good was not going to ring any truer than when a parent says it just before grounding their errant child.

"You can go to jail, or you can become a fugitive and lose your parole," I explained his options.

I opened the sedan's rear door and told him to sit down. The detectives watched as I removed a narrow band of rubber and my taser from my messenger bag. I raised Puglisi's pants leg and tugged his sock down before sliding the rubber between the ankle monitor he wore and his bony ankle. It was a tight fit, but a necessary precaution. I touched the monitor with the taser and fried its wiring without shocking Puglisi.

The monitor's abrupt malfunction would signal Puglisi may have slipped his electronic collar and would immediately betray his last known location. It was not going to be so precise that it showed he was surrounded by police officers, but marshals and even more FBI agents would soon be dispatched to scour the crowd.

Conroy and his agents might scan hours of video footage looking for Puglisi. He would have agents looking for my red coupe if he suspected I had aided in the escape after speaking with the agent I had disabled. Station wagons are such unlikely getaway vehicles that mine would be overlooked in the parade of vehicles leaving the venue. I dashed back to my car to do my best to be standing at the bar in Strada Ammazarre when Conroy stormed in to announce Puglisi was in the wind. I practiced surprised facial expressions as I sped towards the Quarter.

seventy

Special-Agent-in-Charge Conroy was not the first to approach me about Puglisi's vanishing act. It was Marvin Alexander.

"Good evening," I calmly greeted him at the door. His usual bespoke English suit and hand-made Italian loafers which spoke of wealth and power did nothing to conceal the level of distress and powerlessness in the man's expression.

"Where is Marion Puglisi?" he demanded.

I finished enjoying a long sip of the chilled Manhattan the bartender had just set before me before I replied.

"It is not my job to keep track of your clients. The last I knew, the FBI had him under surveillance. Why don't you ask them? I can give you the number," I said and reached into the pants pocket holding my phone.

"They have agents combing that music festival you told him about this afternoon. One of their agents was attacked and the men Pete paid to protect my client claim he was arrested by a pair of plainclothes detectives," Alexander informed me. I chose to hide behind an expression which was an equal mix of surprise and annoyance.

"Well, I was not one of them," I assured him. "Can I buy you a drink while you wait for news on his whereabouts?"

"It does not bother you that Marion Puglisi is missing?" he asked.

"Why should it? He is not a suspect in any crimes I know of and I have no questions he needs to answer. People go missing every day. Most mobsters that disappear turn up in the trunk of a stolen car, like Puglisi's pal Cammarato," I offered my explanation for my demeanor and response. These were the same things I would have said if I did not know the story behind Puglisi's disappearing act. "I appreciate that you are responsible for him until he honors his agreement with the FBI. I am sure Michael Conroy was not pleased to learn your client is missing."

"What do you know about Puglisi having a deal with the FBI?" Alexander's face turned red, and I was unclear whether my knowledge angered or embarrassed him. I was content to upset him.

"The agent who handled his book deal represented my father as well. Plus, Puglisi told me about them himself. He told me a story about my father having an affair with Pete Matranga's mistress that I was able to independently verify." I was not going to drag my mother into this mess by name.

"Do you believe he kept a written record of everything he did?" Alexander tested me.

"I have no idea, but plenty of other people do and that includes the FBI," I parried the question. "What I can tell you for sure is that Marion Puglisi has the memory of an elephant and does not need to give the FBI diaries to tell them what they want to know."

"I don't understand," Alexander said. He seemed to be at genuine loss.

"He remembers the dates, times, places, and people involved in every criminal act he ever committed. When they say a guy knows where the bodies are buried, they meant a guy like Puglisi who can lead the FBI to every victim he buried and finger the men who told him to kill them. Why do you think his own crew paid him to stay quiet in prison? They know he has a steel trap memory. They paid him to keep his mouth shut rather than kill him just in case he actually kept a journal that could be found after he died."

"You're serious," he realized.

"I do not want to ruin your weekend, but have you considered the possibility that the FBI is putting on a public show of force when they have already spirited him off to a safe house to debrief him? Marion Puglisi may be sharing his memories as we speak." I took a perverse delight in the look of panic that crossed Marvin Alexander's face in the seconds before he spun around and all but ran through the bistro's open doors.

seventy-one

I had a more difficult time feigning surprise when SAC Michael Conroy and three of his agents came through the same door ten minutes after Marvin Alexander's hasty departure.

"Table for four?" I asked just as glibly as I had when Puglisi's attorney approached me.

"Drop the act, Holland," Conroy snarled. His agents began looking around, though it seemed they appreciated the ambiance more than they believed their target was hiding on the premises. "I know you tased one of my agents and helped Marion Puglisi escape."

"Escape? I thought he was on parole," I argued the finer points of his accusation.

"Funny," Conroy said and furrowed his brow even deeper.

"Take me in if you can make that stick. Otherwise believe me when I say I have no knowledge of an escape attempt by Marion Puglisi," I challenged him. My semantics were aligned with the facts. Marion Puglisi made no attempt to escape and it was very unlikely the tased agent would recall anything that had happened two or three minutes either side of his being jolted. "Are you telling me you have lost Marion Puglisi?"

"It's a finite universe. We'll locate him, and it will make my day if we prove you are involved in this," Conrad hissed.

"To be honest," I said and began to smile. "It would make my day, too."

That was certainly not the response Conroy or his agents expected to hear.

"You will want to be careful dragging Puglisi back into court," I advised the SAC. "His attorney will dig into Puglisi's past with his discovery motions. I could see where Marvin Alexander would want to revisit the matter of the handgun found in his client's apartment that led to his conviction."

"What are you suggesting?" Conroy demanded, but in a far quieter tone than he had used to this point.

"I am suggesting that Marion Puglisi dying at the hands of his mobster buddies might be what saves your career rather than what ends it," I said. "All of his secrets go to the grave with him and maybe whoever kills him is sloppy enough with the gun that you can put them in prison."

"I do not know what that liar has been feeding you, but you would be a fool to let him play you," Conroy advised me. To date, the few things Puglisi had shared with me had proved to be true, and the dozens of things Conroy shared with me were either late in coming or useless to know.

"I am not the fool who made the deal with Puglisi that let him out of prison," I pointed out. Conroy wanted to say something snappy as a retort but simply sputtered for a few seconds before he gave up. "If this helps, the last thing I heard about Puglisi and his journals was that he was trying to trade them to anyone who would get him out of the country."

"Where did you hear that?" Conroy asked and tried to step closer to intimidate me. I made sure to keep a barstool between us.

"This town is full of little birdies," I shrugged unhelpfully.

Conroy glared at me for a few seconds. He was doing the calculus on whether I would ever give up the source of what I had just told him and whether he even needed to know the identity of my source to keep Puglisi from striking a deal.

Far too many of Conroy's agents were about to waste time checking airports, rental car agencies, train stations, and marinas for any sign of Marion Puglisi. The SAC's available agents were already stretched thin looking for the motive behind Cammarato's homicide, monitoring the activities of Matranga and Vincent Contaldo, and salvaging what they could of Spenser Duncan's testimony against Bear Brovartey and Junior Hauser.

seventy-two

Katie joined Avery and me at breakfast at the chef's table the next morning. She had worked so late the day before that she had missed the drama of Puglisi's disappearance. I had mentioned it in passing over dinner before I succeeded in distracting her with questions about her own day.

"Any word on Puglisi?" I asked the Chief of Detectives as servers began setting plates and bowls of food on the large round table to save us from making repeated trips to the buffet line in the dining room. I poured mimosas for Katie and myself while Avery filled his coffee cup from the carafe next to the ice bucket containing the champagne bottle.

"He's still in the wind," Avery sighed and then stared at me. "I don't suppose you have anything to share?"

"Me? I have no idea where he woke up this morning," I said with complete honesty and some deniability.

"But you know he is alive," Avery pointed out. He took a large bite of the chicken and andouille hash on his plate and began chewing rather than pursue the matter.

"It seems like a safe assumption. Everyone he knows would like to see him dead, just not until they know where he stashed his journals," I said to explain away what seemed like too much confidence in Puglisi's situation.

"I have been surprised nobody tortured him to find out where they are," Katie said pointedly.

"He would die before he told anyone," I suggested. "The man is over eighty years old. Just keeping him from a bathroom for much longer than an hour would be considered torture."

My companions joined me in laughter at this comment and we spent a few quiet moments enjoying the spread laid out before us. There were croissants, beignets, and freshly baked buttermilk biscuits on one tray, and bacon, grilled andouille, and large sausage patties on another. Bowls were filled with shredded hash browns, scrambled eggs, the chicken and andouille hash Avery quietly maneuvered to be closest to his own elbow, as well as hollandaise sauce and sausage gravy.

"Oh, while I am thinking about it," Avery abruptly said and

set his fork on his plate. He reached inside his sport coat and came out with the photograph I had given him. "The girl's name was Marie Chauvin. She was arrested for prostitution a half dozen times but the charges were always dropped or reduced. There is no record of her after Puglisi's place was shut down. No telling what became of her."

"Not even a rumor?" I pushed a bit.

"I think something bad happened to her," Avery told us. "She crossed at least two men she never should have made angry. Your father would never have hurt her, but I cannot say the same for Matranga. He made a lot of people disappear."

"Hopefully she is sunning herself on a beach somewhere," I sighed a little too dramatically. Katie shot me a look, but Avery was ready to change the subject.

"Has Tony found an attorney to represent him on Monday?" he asked.

"I don't believe so," I said. "He and Tulip have been handling that, and to be honest I have avoided knowing where they stand. I have been assuming she will step in if need be."

"That doesn't sound like the best plan," Avery said and frowned.

"It would not be," I agreed. "But we also believe they lack enough evidence to do anything but ask him some questions. He didn't even own the blade he used here when he lived in Italy."

"I hope you are right. I still wonder why they sent agents this far to just ask him some questions. It doesn't strike me as typical," Avery argued before we returned to eating breakfast again.

"Where do you stand on the break-in?" Avery asked to break the silence, having exhausted any topic not involving work related matters. He may have hoped Katie would excuse herself before we got this far, but she was enjoying listening to the two of us too much to leave. She was finally getting to see what our breakfast meetings looked like.

"There was no break in," I declared. "I will write it up later, but I figured out Alex Boudreaux was the burglar. He owns the place and is allowed to do anything to his property that doesn't upset his lender or the Vieux Carré Commission. The FBI or the State Patrol in Mississippi do not seem inclined to link

Spenser Duncan's death to whatever happened on Dauphine Street."

"Just walk away from it, huh?" Avery asked and narrowed his eyes slightly as he gauged how much of my attitude was meant purely to dissuade his further interest. "And what about Puglisi's journals?"

"There is no reason to believe they exist, or that they will be found if they do," I attempted to add more weight to the idea of closing the case. "The hunt for them is beginning to create drama and situations NOPD is not prepared to handle."

"Now that I understand," Avery said and laughed. "You want to wash your hands of the mess."

"Our hands," I corrected him. "There is likely to be fallout from the search for the journals, but it does not have to be our responsibility to tie what Alex did on Dauphine Street to anything else."

"Fair enough. Well done," Avery decided. "I look forward to your report."

I thought we were done, but he had one last thing to say.

"I do not look forward to that fallout." He frowned and set his napkin in his empty plate. He had not lost his appetite. He was simply finished with our briefing and excused himself from the table after taking a final sip of his coffee.

Katie waited until Avery was out of the kitchen before she spoke. "What did he mean by that?"

"He is not going to be able to rest until Puglisi's journals are located and not being the ones to find them may be giving him something to worry about that he is not telling us about," I explained as best I could. "He is afraid of what may come out if the contents of those journals becomes public. NOPD did not have a clean house when those entries were made and people far above Avery have been counting on him to keep their secrets as well as his own."

"What do you have planned for today?" she asked.

"A bit of skullduggery and a lot of maneuvering of pieces into place," I replied and took a bite of food to indicate I did not want to discuss any details.

"Will you be done in time for dinner?" she asked without pressing me further. I gave her a chance to stay at arm's length from something she knew I might answer for later and she was smart enough, after dating me this long, to take the off ramp. "This is our weekend at my place, if you remember."

"I remember," I assured her. "Roux is already packed."

Katie is only slightly less unhappy about the seventy-pound pit bull's effect on her usually pristine patio and back yard than I am about leaving the comfort and safety of my apartment.

"Do you want me to take him with me now or will the two of you be playing cowboy together this afternoon?" she asked, adding the sort of jab I have come to expect when my plans conflict with ones she neglects to share until after I ruin them.

"I should run solo," I said and stood up to pull her chair back. She stood and we shared a brief embrace before walking to the elevator holding hands in silence.

seventy-three

I sent Katie home in a taxicab with Roux before walking across Decatur Street to the pizzeria. Pete Matranga and Rebecca Collins were seated in the shade of the large umbrella, while Russo and Lenny sat in what promised to remain direct sunlight. Marvin Alexander and Vincent Contaldo waited patiently for the sun to move just a little more to the west and place them in shade as well. Darlene was opening the table's first bottle of wine and a generously portioned charcuterie board was already on the table.

"No doggie today?" Matranga asked as I approached.

"Getting his teeth cleaned," I said to remind him I had the sharper wit.

"What is it today then?" he asked with more impatience than hostility.

"I am curious what you are doing here when all the action is in Biloxi," I set about laying my trap. "Well, I guess that is tomorrow, not today."

"What are you talking about?" Marvin Alexander spoke up. "If you have something to say, just say it and be on your way."

"I heard your client made a deal with Junior for his diaries. He is supposedly trading them for a boat ride out of the country tomorrow night," I casually lied.

"How is he going to do that when he is locked up in jail?" Matranga dismissed my news by demonstrating he had sources of his own. "A couple of detectives picked him up yesterday."

"Detectives from where? It's not like every guy carrying handcuffs in a suit is a real detective," I pointed out. This was a kernel of concern that was growing in my own thoughts, so I decided to share it. "Maybe someone helped him disappear from the FBI's radar so he can slip off to wherever he is headed."

"Believe what you want," Matranga tried to dismiss my rumor.

"All I know is he sent a guy by with the money to buy his watch back yesterday and the next thing I hear is he disappeared in the company of two detectives nobody can identify," I said and let this lie soak in before I planted the final seed. "And now I hear Junior is lending Puglisi his yacht in exchange for the journals. Sounds to me like your old pal plans on burning his bridges and everyone standing on them."

This was met with an uncomfortable silence and a lot of glances around the table. Lenny was most likely Matranga's source for what the police knew, which meant the men at the table were all aware his information was at best second or third hand. NOPD is not good about keeping a lid on things, and the statements by the patrol officers who witnessed Puglisi's 'arrest' probably shared the stories they told the FBI. I wondered whether Marvin Alexander's response was good acting, practiced discipline, or shock.

"I figured you would want to intercept Puglisi before he left the country," I said and started away. "My source says Junior keeps his yacht at the Palace Casino."

"Why are you telling us any of this?" Alexander spoke up. "Why don't you just arrest him yourself?"

"Biloxi is out of my jurisdiction, and the FBI can go to hell," I pointed out and only mildly exaggerated my disdain for the one agency that would truly take an interest in the meeting. "And, frankly, as many of you who can get yourselves killed in Mississippi, the better it is for everyone in Louisiana."

I left the men to discuss my revelation among themselves and went into the pizzeria as though I meant to talk to Ritchie or someone else on the staff. My real purpose was to speak with Rebecca after Matranga suggested she powder her nose or whatever he told her do to keep her away from his business conversations. He was quick to dismiss her, and she made a beeline for the pizzeria's air-conditioned interior. I positioned myself behind the display case holding the meats and cheeses used in the appetizers and she casually made her way in my direction in case anyone outside was watching through the open French doors.

"You got them all riled up," she said from a safe distance. Neither of us wanted it to look like we were having a conversation.

"That was the plan," I assured her.

"Is there anything I can do to help you?" she offered and turned her head enough to look directly at me.

"Convince your new boyfriend to take you with him when he heads to Biloxi. Find a way to let me know when you leave New Orleans," I instructed her without explaining why before I turned away rather then be seen speaking with her for very long.

seventy-four

The FBI kept the pizzeria under surveillance, and agents parked outside of Puglisi's residence to make the octogenarian mobsters and their new friends uncomfortable about their return to New Orleans. I used my Quarter Rat contacts to track every person sitting at the pizzeria table until I knew where every one of them lay their head at night shortly after SAC Conroy revealed they had his attention.

Lenny's address has not changed since the 1970s. I am mildly curious how Lenny's landlord addresses rent increases for a tenant with his past Mob connections. Marion Puglisi had been sequestered in Alex Boudreaux's former house by the lake until his disappearance. Alex Boudreaux presently occupied one of his short-term rental units in the Bywater neighborhood he had done so much to gentrify. Pete Matranga rented a large condo near the Bucktown neighborhood in Metarie, which he now shared with Rebecca Collins. Dan Logan had bought a Spanish-style house in the Carrollton neighborhood between Tulane University and Riverbend shortly after moving from Brooklyn. Marvin Alexander and Vincent Contaldo were both making themselves comfortable on someone else's dime in hotel suites. Alexander was enjoying the Napoleon Suite at the Le Pavillion Hotel on Poydras in the Central Business District, and Contaldo was staying in one of the guest cottages at a new boutique hotel on Dauphine Street barely five blocks from Puglisi's former brothel. I say guest cottage; the two-story structures are former slave quarters.

I was sitting beside that very hotel's pool when the Chicago Outfit's emissary returned from the pizzeria just after five o'clock. I only had a few minutes to speak with him before Katie expected to see me at her house.

"You are not very good at sneaking up on people, Detective Holland. I was told you were here before I left the pizzeria," Contaldo said with a kind laugh.

"You strike me as the sort of guy I should tackle head on," I complimented him. "Besides, maybe I am here to invite you to dinner."

"I doubt that. I am still full from all that meat and cheese," he politely declined and patted his firm abs. He stopped walking and turned to confront me. I assumed he was armed and hoped he was not looking for a shoot-out. "I doubt you want to buy my dinner. Someone still owes you for my last meal at your place."

"Puglisi paid that off yesterday," I maintained my earlier story. I could not tell if he was testing me. He may have ignored most of what I told Matranga.

"So you say," he chuckled. "The last I knew Sunset was living off an allowance from Pete. I guess he saved his money. You can stop wasting both of our time. I have no problem sitting down with you, Detective, as long as we both get to ask questions. You probably have more answers than I have questions."

"And I only have a couple of questions," I said to agree to his trade.

"All of my answers involve the word 'No'," he warned me as he sat down on one of the other chaise lounges. "Still want to talk?"

"Sure," I surprised him. "What do you think I know that you don't? You are the one on the inside, not me."

"I am in the position of having to trust what I am told and the people who tell me those things," he said and frowned. "I could use some of your distrust."

"I distrust everyone but Lenny and Puglisi," I freely admitted. "Lenny cannot tell a lie that doesn't sound like one. Puglisi's explanation for why he is here rings true."

"Care to share what he told you about coming back?" Vincent asked and looked around the empty patio. We were alone but entirely exposed to anyone passing by.

"He took the parole to settle an old score and to find a way out of the country. I think Cammarato's death satisfied the first part of his plan. Pete Matranga double crossed Puglisi on a payoff they agreed to by tricking us into taking Puglisi's new watch at dinner that night. There is a bank account number engraved on it, and he cannot leave town without his money," I said. I was uncertain what Contaldo knew about Marcello's arrangement to pay for Puglisi's silence. Engaging in this conversation was my way to gauge what Matranga wanted his partners in Chicago to know and to discover the purpose behind Contaldo's presence. Causing damage and damage control were my limited weapons of choice in causing friction between the disparate factions of mobsters now that I was convinced there was no plan for dividing up the city.

"Do the police think Sunset killed Hammer?" Vincent asked a little too directly.

"I have no idea what the FBI thinks, and NOPD has already washed their hands of the homicide. Personally, I think someone else handled that so Puglisi would owe them a future favor, or they did so to pay off an existing debt. It also sent a message to Puglisi and Matranga that someone could get to them, as well, if neither of them had a hand in it."

"Which of those do you favor?" he asked with what sounded like genuine interest.

"You're the expert on Mob hits," I said without accusing him anything. "Which scenario is more likely to you?"

"Puglisi is a hard-headed guy who needs pushed to do anything he doesn't want to do. I think you are right that dumping Hammer Cammarato in the trunk of that car might have been someone's way to send him a message." This sounded more like his opinion than an answer.

"You know their history, right?" I asked and waited to see his reaction. He shook his head to suggest he was ignorant of any details. "Cammarato planted the gun that sent Puglisi to prison. He may have done so on Matranga's orders, but he certainly had someone's permission to frame Puglisi. Matranga was upset over something his mistress did while she was living under Puglisi's roof."

"What did she do?" he asked with genuine curiosity.

"That is unimportant to the overall story." I was not prepared to share my father's infidelity with everyone. Vincent frowned but waited silently for the next part. "My theory is Marvin Alexander had Cammarato killed as part of the agreement he made to get Puglisi's diaries. Getting Marvin to do his dirty work kept Puglisi's hands clean, but it still accomplished what he wanted."

"I cannot imagine a guy like Puglisi letting anyone else get the satisfaction," the experienced hitman across from me argued from his professional viewpoint.

"Then perhaps it was just a warning to Puglisi and the

killer never knew their history," I allowed and began to believe Vincent Contaldo was the prime suspect in Cammarato's homicide. "Which brings me to your purpose in being here. There are Outfit members in Chicago who did business with these guys years ago. Why send a thirty-year-old shooter instead of an old friend?"

I did not expect an answer so there was no reason to sugar coat the question.

"Thirty-three-year-old," he corrected me and paused before answering. "Chicago began to see New Orleans as an open city after Katrina. The hurricane leveled the playing field because nobody has a stake in the place anymore. Now it comes down to who can hold onto whatever they take."

"The Outfit used to be okay with a small taste of someone else's pie," I said, and did my best not to act surprised that Vincent was being this open.

"There is no percentage when there is no pie. Chicago has decided it is time to bake their own pie. Think of the situation as being winner takes all," he shrugged. "I got a call that Pete and Marion were coming back to town. These guys are so far over the hill they can't even turn around to look at the hill anymore, so I was dispatched to discourage them from starting over," he said, without admitting to anything illegal.

"You seem to be taking your time," I pointed out. "I would not think they were that hard to convince. Puglisi doesn't even want back in the game."

"Pete is another matter, but he is not the problem," Vincent said without offering the sort of in-depth details I hoped to learn. "The problem is discouraging everyone else who wants to set up shop without paying Chicago's tribute."

"That would be Junior and the Russians," I leapt ahead in his story. He gave me a very puzzled look in response.

"What Russians?"

I kept my best poker face as I felt the skies open above me and the angels begin to sing. I had stumbled upon an opening to do some serious damage.

"Marvin Alexander is Dudiyn Alekhin's nephew," I informed him and paused to let this soak in. The way Vincent's eyebrows twitched meant I did not need to explain who Dudiyn Alekhin was. "Dudiyn sent his sister's kid to this country with the express purpose of the boy becoming an attorney. Marvin changed his name to hide the family connection once he turned eighteen. You didn't know this?"

"No. No idea at all," Vincent all but stammered. He reached into his pocket for his cellphone.

"Marvin tried to con Puglisi out of his diaries with a book deal so Dudiyn could use them to blackmail anyone he needed to start taking over New Orleans," I further explained. "They will go after the Dixie Mafia after they get established here. I doubt there will be any pie crumbs headed to Chicago. Do Russians even bake pies?"

"How do I know you are not just saying this to mess things up?" he paused to challenge me. He did not want to look like an idiot to his bosses in Chicago if what I told him proved to be untrue.

"I am saying it to shake things up, but it is still true. Have someone check Marvin out. The only clients he has represented until now are Russian mobsters. That should tell you something." I waited in silence while his young mind digested each new fact. He had no further questions, but he also seemed at a loss about what to do beyond calling his contact in Chicago.

"The last thing I want is a bloodbath in New Orleans," I said and grabbed the arm he needed free to dial his phone. "I think the two of us can help one another with our respective problems."

"How so?" Vincent seemed far more cooperative than I had anticipated. He may have been looking forward to killing people. He may also have preferred working with me than handling the situation as Chicago would likely dictate.

"We can take everyone out without firing a shot," I wanted to dissuade him from the idea that I was going to sanction some sort of hit list. "Anyone we kill can be replaced. I want to poison the pond to keep everyone out."

"Including Chicago?" he asked.

"For now, at least," I shrugged. "I do not imagine we can keep organized crime out of here forever, but you guys should at least let us get back on our feet."

"What do you have in mind?" he said after nodding his head, which I was careful not take as any sort of agreement.

"We break this down into pieces," I suggested. "I have a plan to neutralize Matranga. I need your help to stop Dudiyn's plans and keep Junior Hauser on his side of the state line."

"We still need to find Puglisi and his journals," Vincent added.

"Why is that?" I asked. I did not want Vincent to see that his continued interest in the diaries made me curious about the real purpose for his being in New Orleans.

"If Sunset wrote damaging things about what he did for Marcello and Matranga in New Orleans in those journals, then there are things about what he did in Chicago as well." I had my answer for what Chicago expected of him. In their opinion, his need to know and mission was limited to retrieving the diaries.

"Perhaps it would be best if Marion Puglisi stayed disappeared," I suggested. This time he frowned and barely shook his head in an unconscious reaction.

"What else do you think I can do for you, I mean, besides handling Pete Matranga?" he asked to change topics. He obviously was no longer concerned I was intent on trapping him, but he also remained careful about being specific about his plans.

"Help me shift this whole mess to Mississippi," I told him. "Let's make the Russians become Junior's problem. That way we both save money on bullets. Chicago can take on the winner rather than get drawn into a three-way gunfight."

"How do you propose to do that?" he asked and broke into a grin.

"Puglisi is looking for a way out of the country," I reminded him. "I gave one of Junior's guys a diary Puglisi forged with an offer to trade the rest for a ride on Junior's yacht."

"Puglisi forged a diary?" Vincent interrupted me.

"Just one. He wasn't about to give up one his real ones," I lied. I could not afford to have him suspect Puglisi had no diaries. "Junior needed enough of a taste that he would swallow the bait. Helping Puglisi skip the country exposes him to a lot of Fed trouble if the intercept his boat."

"Did Hauser take the bait?" Vincent pressed me. I sensed I may have misjudged our partnership. I realized the damage he could do by tipping off Chicago about the Russians and asking for more troops to go to war instead of helping me.

"I did not hear one way or the other before Puglisi went missing," I said. "Maybe he is already on board that yacht."

This brought alarm to the hitman's face.

"I propose you tell Matranga and Alexander that I let it slip Puglisi and Junior agreed to make a trade and suggest they catch Puglisi and Junior together to take the diaries. Whatever happens in Biloxi is none of my business," I offered a bare bones plan for his consideration. I had a fuller plan but thought better of sharing it with Chicago's hired gun.

"How do we get the Russians there?" he wanted to know.

"There is only one Russian to worry about. Marvin Alexander must keep Puglisi from handing over the journals Marvin promised to deliver to Dudiyn. I doubt Dudiyn has a back-up nephew in place to start over if Marvin gets taken out of the picture," I said and ignored the sudden blood lust in the hitman's expression. "You take care of anyone who shows up at the yacht and I will handle Pete Matranga and Marion Puglisi for you."

"How do you propose to do that?" he asked. I was uncertain enough of the relationship between the two that I was not about to give him specific details.

"Without firing a shot, just like I said. You and I can go a round or two after this is over with if you think it's necessary. Sooner or later, we will be back on opposite sides."

"Glad you said it so I didn't have to," he said and stood up to walk away. "What about Sunset's diaries?"

"Like you said, it will be winner takes all," I said and stood up to walk in the opposite direction.

I was going to be a few minutes late to dinner, but at least I would have a good story to tell.

seventy-five

Chief Avery stood amid a half-dozen police cars when I arrived at Katie's house. Her home's front door was wide open but neither she nor Roux were anywhere to be seen. There was one ambulance on hand, with its lights flashing and doors closed. I saw an EMT inside working on somebody and instinctively headed in that direction.

"It's not Katie," Avery shouted and moved to intercept me. "She is safe and okay."

"What happened?" I demanded. I glanced at my phone to be sure I had not missed a phone call or text message that would have sent me here even sooner.

"A guy kicked in the front door," Avery began with the short version. "Roux took him down and Katie shot him twice when he reached for his gun. It scared her more than anything."

"I am sure it did. She is not cut out for this sort of thing," I said and relaxed a bit. "She is okay with me living this way, but she still believes in houses with white picket fences and nine-to-five dads cooking out back on Saturday."

"If you say so," Avery sort of laughed. "There were three steaks set out on the counter. I assume you were supposed to be grilling the steaks tonight?"

"Yes, I ran a few minutes late or I might have been here when it happened." It would be the next morning before I began to consider whether Vincent Contaldo's being so talkative was meant to delay my arrival.

"I don't know that you would have done any better. She put two rounds square in the bad guy's brisket. He wore body armor so he will get to answer a lot of questions as soon as someone stitches up Roux's handiwork. Your dog ripped off a bunch of muscle tissue from his calf," Avery further informed me.

"Who was it?" I finally thought to ask.

"A guy named Francis Patrick. He has a record for sexual assault, but I do not think that was his motive this time. He will lawyer up and it will be a while before we know who sent him," Avery told me and sighed. "He might start talking when he finds out the penalty for attacking a deputy state's attorney."

The description of Katie's assailant Avery provided was not what I expected, but the man I suspected being behind it used talent that was not immediately traceable to himself in the assault on Tony. I was going to be interested to learn who he called with his one call to an attorney, but I was not inclined to allow a jury to decide the appropriate justice for this attack.

"Do you have a theory for his motive?" I asked. I had too many.

"It looks like the guy intended to abduct her. He had a cloth bag to put over her head and a pair of good handcuffs in his pack," Avery offered. "He was not carrying any ID or cell phone."

"That means he was not alone," I stated the obvious.

"Probably not, but none of her neighbors saw anyone drive off after the shooting stopped," he said. We took a moment to look at the neighbors gathered at the curb now that they felt safe to leave their homes. "This weekend just gets better and better. Marion Puglisi and his journals are in the wind and some foreigner just tried to kidnap a deputy state's attorney in broad daylight. I am not doing a very good job of showing I have things under control."

"Somebody gunning for your job?" I asked. His situation sounded more dire than Katie's.

"Nobody is out for my job. The brass needs scapegoats should things get any worse," he explained his dilemma. "Things like those diaries turning up in the wrong hands."

I was tempted to let Chief Avery know the diaries turning up was highly unlikely but explaining why I felt so confident of this only promised to add to his anxiety rather than alleviate it.

"Well, I have your back Chief," I assured him for what it was worth. "Where are Katie and Roux?"

"Your sister picked them up and drove away. I figure they are at her place or out in the Rigolets. She said to tell you to call her." Avery informed me. "You will want to take it slow with Katie. Do you remember what it was like shooting your first man?"

"Vaguely," I lied. Nobody forgets that moment, and most

people cannot handle it. I trained Katie to shoot from instinct, and to see a threat and not a human being, but her reaction was still going to be to blame me for her unsettled state of mind. I made shooting someone a permissible reaction, rather than retreating or using non-lethal resistance. It would take her a while to accept that what she did was the only viable response to the situation, and what likely saved her life. I could live with her anger more easily than I could with the scenario where Roux was with me and she was home alone and unarmed when her front door crashed open.

I called Tulip and was relieved she had chosen to take Katie to our mother's house rather than her own. I was not so relieved that I did not notice Katie chose someplace other than my apartment as a safe place to gather her wits.

My sister let the phone ring twice before answering. "She does not want to speak with you right now."

"I get that," I told her without trying to start an argument. "Thank you for this."

"There will be a bill, don't worry," Tulip said with absolutely no humor in her voice.

"How is Katie?" I asked to get to the point.

"She is still in shock. Roux will not leave her side." Tulip informed me.

"I'll bet not," I said and caught myself before I laughed. Roux spent weeks training with me as a K-9 and attack dog but has always been instinctively protective towards Katie. "I ruined a bath towel wiping that guy's blood off him when we got here."

"I will hear about that as well, I am sure," I said. My mother's welcoming Katie with open arms was no sign she was alright with the situation I had placed her in, or the target her presence might be putting on my mother and Roger. Hopefully she would remember the small arsenal I keep in a gun safe in the apartment Tony and I used to share above the unused boathouse next to the main house.

Tulip finally laughed. "Count on it."

I was at a loss for what else to say to Tulip. I did not want to burden her with the things I wanted to say to Katie, and I did not want her to reinterpret those things as she repeated them. I was satisfied to know Katie and Roux were physically unharmed and in a safe location. I clung to the hope that my mother would offer Katie the rationalizations she had developed over my father's career to help the woman I love survive our own future.

"Has Katie said anything?" I asked. It was an open-ended question because I was as interested in her reaction as I was in any details about the assault she may have shared with Tulip. Whatever initial statement she gave the NOPD officers was taken while she was undoubtedly still in a state of shock.

"Just one thing that you need to find a way to talk to her about," Tulip told me. She understood the way I phrased the question and chose to not share everything, or had already decided to let Katie speak about things at her own pace. "She is not mad at you. She is not even mad at the guy who broke in. She is mad that she liked shooting him. I think she wishes she had emptied the clip. Is that normal?"

"There is no normal when it comes to this," I let her know. "She may have wanted to keep hurting the man, but she never intended for him to die. She should take some comfort in knowing she is no killer."

"What makes you so sure?" Tulip asked and found herself in the strange position of defending her former babysitter's capacity for taking a human life.

"I taught both of you to put two in the chest and one in the head. Katie never took that third shot," I pointed out. "She was satisfied that he was down."

"I doubt telling her that fine point will make her feel any better," Tulip warned.

"She's a smart woman. It will come to her on her own, eventually," I said. As bad as I am at relationships and talking my girlfriend through tough spots, even I knew not to drop what I just said into any conversation on the matter until she did. "Thank you again for being there. Let her know I love her and that I am going after the man who sent the guy."

"I will tell her the love part," Tulip promised. "The revenge you can explain."

seventy-six

Vengeance is dangerous. It is an emotional faucet that becomes difficult to turn off once it is opened. Where should I start or stop seeking revenge for the attack on Katie?

Targeting Marvin's other henchman for his assumed role as the getaway driver was an obvious place to start, followed by Marvin for sending them. Do I go after Dan Logan for recommending Marvin Alexander to Bear Brovartey in the first place? Should I pursue Dudiyn for having sent Marvin to this country? Was I prepared to kill every minion Dudiyn would send if I killed Marvin? How many other civilians in my circle of family and friends would suffer the blowback on my actions when Marvin and Dudiyn began to defend themselves and seek their own revenge upon me?

The Napoleon Suite at Le Pavillion where Marvin Alexander was sleeping featured a single king-sized bed and a bathtub Napoleon Bonaparte had gifted to a rich plantation owner. The novelty of bathing in a Carrera marble tub wears off quickly once one discovers how hard it is to keep the water hot.

I could not allow the brazen assault on Katie to go unpunished, but I chose not to repay Marvin's attack with an act of criminal assault by kicking in the door to his suite and thrashing him as my emotions encouraged me to consider. My doing so may have been his goal, as getting me arrested and suspended would theoretically remove a thorn in his side.

I was concerned that the reason he wanted to abduct Katie was to negotiate a trade for Marion Puglisi. My fear was that Marvin knew I had played a role in Puglisi's vanishing act and suspected I knew where he was. It gave Marion Puglisi zero credit for being able to stage his disappearing act on his own. It also gave me credit for having the answer to his whereabouts, which was something I had gone out my way not to know.

Marvin was either a strategist of the highest order or he had a source close enough to me to know exactly what I was doing. Somebody had tipped off Contaldo that I was at his hotel, which meant they probably also let Alexander know

Katie was alone. His men had simply neglected to account for Roux. The battle plan I had was going to become extremely difficult to execute if Marvin Alexander proved to be both a brilliant strategist and to have a superior intelligence network.

seventy-seven

I waited until nearly two in the morning before I entered the Le Pavillion hotel in a loose sweatsuit that bore no emblems or labels. I poured a bottle of water down my chest and back to simulate sweat before I entered the hotel's high-ceilinged marble lobby. I wanted the desk clerk to dismiss me as a guest returning from a nocturnal run through the vacant streets surrounding the city's downtown office towers. I wore a ballcap to hide my face and avoided as many cameras as I could as I made my way to the stairwell off the lobby. The lone desk clerk barely acknowledged me as I walked past.

I paused at the door to the stairwell before I pulled the fire alarm and began sprinting up the stairs towards the seventh floor, where Marvin Alexander and his security detail were awakened by the siren blaring in their hallway. Marvin had to know this was a ruse to get him out of his hotel room. Even so, it might be a fire, and he did not want his suspicions to get him killed. It took me barely three minutes to cover the distance from the lobby to the seventh floor in the stairwell. This was less time than Marvin wasted considering his options once he was awake and dressed.

I proceeded to the window overlooking the street below to position a tall plant stand and a hotel employee between me and the door to his suite. I waited for the door to open and for a lone bodyguard to step out to assess the situation. His attention was going to be drawn towards the stretch of hallway between the suite and the stairwell, not on the route they would not take to safely evacuate Alexander. I only needed for him to step far enough into the hallway to not be able to close the door when I made my move.

I kicked over the plant stand to distract the bodyguard and pushed the hotel employee into him before I jumped into the room and slammed the door shut behind me to lock him out. I wore a .45 caliber pistol in a shoulder holster under my sweatshirt, but wielded a can of pepper spray to bring Alexander's other two bodyguards to their knees in pain and tears. I was through the bedroom door before Alexander had time to retreat and lock the door. I allowed my target to drop to his knees and surrender rather than be sprayed as well. I

324

needed the attorney to be coherent anyway.

"This is me when I am only upset with you, Marvin," I told him. He had folded his arms over his head to protect himself from whatever I came to do, but his expression showed not the slightest fear of what that might be. "Imagine I came here really angry about what you did to Katie Reilly."

"Who?" he asked. I sprayed his chest and let the odor cause him some discomfort.

"No time for that," I snapped. "One of your guys tried to kidnap her this evening. I won't stand for bringing civilians into this. Do you understand?"

"Yes," he assured me in a very convincing tone of voice.

"Good," I said and backed away. "You do not have enough firepower to protect you if you try something like that again."

"I get it," he said and began to stand up. "But I swear I did not send anyone to harm your girlfriend."

"Then who did?" I challenged him.

"I will deal with them," he promised.

"Let me," I insisted. "Give me a name."

"There is more going on than what you see," he said and shook his head. "Just go. I promise this will not happen again."

"I promise to leave with that name and your head if I ever come back," I said and motioned for him to lead the way out of the room. I did not have time to force him to tell me. NOPD officers were likely on their way to the room as we spoke, thanks to the hotel employee I had shoved. Alexander's bodyguards were still incapable of defending him, but both of them were waving their pistols in our general direction. I ordered Alexander to verbally order the guy I left in the hallway to stand down before I left the hotel room.

I have no idea how long I sat in my darkened office combing the whiteboards for the elusive name Marvin Alexander refused to share, but I awoke only a few hours later in a sitting position with my handgun still clutched in my right hand with the safety off.

seventy-eight

I was freshly showered and planning to eat breakfast at the bar when my phone rang. I paused getting dressed to take Tulip's phone call.

"I just received a text from Rebecca Collins. Is there something you would like to tell me before I rip your head off? I thought we agreed to keep her out of things," Tulip said with increasing anger.

"No, we agreed to allow her to help take down Matranga if she saw a way to do so that did not place her at risk," I reminded my sister. She was the one who had approached me with Rebecca's offer and desire to take down her mobster benefactor. "What does the text say?"

"That she is looking forward to spending a night at the Palace Casino in Biloxi," she said and waited for me to decode or explain the young girl's meaning about spending a night at the most expensive casino hotel on the strip.

"That's good news," I assured my sister.

There was a brief pause as my sister recalled our previous conversation.

"Well, it looks like another one of your ridiculous schemes is about to work," she said. I could see her broad smile in my mind's eye. "I need to stop betting against you."

"How is Katie this morning?" I asked while I had her on the line.

"She's talking to mother on the patio. She plans to take next week off," Tulip informed me.

"Oh," I heard myself let my first reaction to the news slip before I could properly phrase what I meant to say. This was not a good time to sound inconvenienced by my girlfriend's trauma.

"What?" Tulip demanded.

"We wrote up a half dozen charges to file against Matranga after the Night Owl incident. I need them filed in the morning so I can brick the door closed behind Matranga before he gets out of jail on bond." I explained my dilemma but did my best to minimize the concern remaining in my voice.

"I will speak with her and make sure somebody walks them over the courthouse first thing in the morning. I will also tell her how concerned you are for her mental well-being and how relieved you are that she is unharmed," Tulip assured me, taking yet another opportunity to chastise me for my apparent disregard for what Katie had been through the night before. I was worried about Katie, but my background involved dealing with soldiers who found a way to shoot other men and move on. I did not, and could not, expect Katie to know how to do this. I did not want her to learn to do so, either.

"Thank you," I said. "And thank you for not letting me be a jerk."

"You aren't a jerk, big brother," Tulip reassured me. "You're just an ass, but we both know you are doing your best to become a human being again."

"That may be on hold for another day or two," I admitted.

"As it should be," Tulip harshly said. "Get them all, okay?"

"I will talk to you tomorrow," I replied. My sister hung up without saying anything else.

seventy-nine

I hung up and immediately called Captain Williams at home. There was not going to be a good time to disturb him on a Sunday. Calling him while he was on his way to church was possibly the worst, as much for the timing as because we spoke with his phone set to hands-free so his wife and children were entertained by our call.

"Not a good time, Detective Holland," he warned me. It was the broadcast sound of his voice and the time of morning that tipped me off to his destination and companions.

"I apologize for that, Captain," I said in hopes using his rank rather than his name might keep him from hanging up on me. "I have one item of business that may be time sensitive if your preacher runs long this morning."

"Make it quick," he said. I could hear his wife and kids laughing because, as I later learned, theirs was a fire and brimstone Baptist minister who loved the sound of his voice raised against the evil in men.

"Pietro Matranga will be bringing an underaged girl to the Palace Casino sometime today. They will arrive in a Lincoln Town Car, and you should assume the men with him are armed. The girl is named Rebecca Collins and she is prepared to state she is with him involuntarily and he brought her across the state line for sexual purposes," I hastily explained. The captain's teenaged daughter gave an audible 'Eww" in reaction to this. I very intentionally did not mention the meeting at the casino's marina Matranga intended to attend later that evening. I wanted to limit the captain's role to things that would make him look good.

"And you know this how?" he demanded to know before he committed to do anything.

"That is a long story for when we speak alone," I hedged. "Short version is she put herself in a position to let this happen. She knows what it will take to convict him of a Mann Act violation and will help the most ambitious prosecutor you know advance their career to get loose of Matranga herself.

"So, is she trying to frame the guy?" he properly interpreted what I told him.

"We cannot frame Matranga if he is doing what she is willing to testify to. She sees this as the only way to get out of a debt she owes Matranga for a favor he did for her and some money she cannot hope to repay. This is her easiest way out of repaying both those debts." I tried to assuage his misgivings.

"Okay, fine. We will be on the lookout. I don't suppose you have a license plate number," he finally agreed.

"Nope, but how many black Lincoln Town Cars with Louisiana plates show up at the casino on a Sunday, anyway?" I pointed out.

I felt almost awkward not having Roux by my side as I made my way across the French Quarter to Vincent Contaldo's hotel. It was later in the morning than I normally made my routine patrol, which I had allowed myself to sleep through. The light foot traffic I encountered seem to be made up almost entirely of people on their way to brunch.

I had questions for Contaldo about our last conversation I doubted he was going to want to answer without an attorney present. All signs pointed to everyone sitting at that table being aware of an imminent attack upon Katie Reilly. I knew he did not authorize it, and his comments in retrospect did not indicate he sanctioned the idea of kidnapping a deputy state's attorney as ransom for Marion Puglisi. It was a rash and foolish act, and it ought not to have surprised anyone when it had come to a far different ending than intended or even imagined.

"Could you please ring room two thirteen?" I asked the young woman on the hotel's reception desk. It seemed foolhardy to knock on the hitman's door unannounced after an incident like yesterday's. He might well misinterpret my presence.

"I'm so sorry, Mister Contaldo checked out last evening," she apologized.

"Oh, I'm sure it was not your fault," I jokingly reassured her. "Can you tell me how he left the hotel? Did you call a ride for him, or did he have his own car?"

"I do believe he had a car of his own," she said and began to leaf through a stack of papers after a moment's thought. She located the folio for Contaldo's room and scanned it for a moment. "Yes. He registered with a Mercedes with Illinois plates."

I pulled my badge from beneath the blue polo with the state police emblem in it to show the woman I had not purchased the shirt in one of the Quarter's T-shirt shops and she surrendered the paperwork without a quibble. I wrote the Mercedes' license plate number on the notepad I pulled from my messenger bag and thanked her for her assistance.

I walked back to my apartment with a head full of conjecture. It made sense for Contaldo to be gone before I returned, which was a certainty as far as the Chicago muscle was concerned. He likely knew I was not going to blame him for the assault, and maybe not even for not telling me about it, but he had to have been certain I would be an angry boyfriend looking for the person who was responsible. Avoiding me to escape having to divulge that name only made sense.

I was tempted to call Captain Williams and provide the license number on Contaldo's S550 Mercedes coupe. There was no reason to believe the man had abandoned his mission. He very likely checked into one of the finer hotels on the Redneck Riviera, and merely shifted his operation to Mississippi in his own quest for Puglisi's journals. I had not seen the last of the hitman. At least now I knew what he was driving.

eighty-one

My stomach rumbled as I returned to Strada Ammazarre to remind me I had not yet eaten a bite of food that morning. Something or someone had interrupted me every time I gave it a thought, but I was finally free to do as I pleased for at least a couple of hours.

"Mimosa?" Hannah asked as I took my usual seat at the street end of the long cypress bar and laid my bag on its zinc top.

"Iced tea," I sighed. "It is going to be a long work day."

"I heard about Katie. Is she okay?" Hannah inquired when she set the tall glass of sweet tea in front of me along with the napkin-wrapped silverware I did not need to ask her to bring.

"I think she will be," was all I could say. I was in no position to speak on her behalf about the matter.

I left the bag and tea where Hannah and the regulars could keep an eye on them and went for a plate of food from the buffet. I was seriously underdressed in the Sunday crowd, in my loose pants and state police polo. I pulled the lanyard with my badge from beneath the shirt and let it hang on my chest to alleviate the concern anyone present who did not know me might have about the large pistol strapped to my thigh.

I returned to the bar with a plate filled with scrambled eggs, a fistful of bacon, shredded hash brown potatoes, and a pair of fresh baked croissants. It was comfort food, and I left Tony's more imaginative offerings to the paying guests. I took a couple of bites of food before I reached into my bag for my iPad and Contaldo's license number. It came to me that I had no idea if he was driving his own car, not that it really mattered.

The photograph of my father and Vanity which Chief Avery had returned to me when he told me the girl's real name fell onto the bar top and I hastily swooped it up. I began to return it to my bag when something caught my eye that had eluded me until that very moment.

The large bed needed to be positioned perpendicular to the two-way mirror for the photographer to get the images Vanity needed for her purpose. The bed was at a right angle to that position when I entered the room twenty years later. This did not seem to be an important point, except the poster of Vanity I believed Puglisi hid his journals behind was not where he left it.

The poster hung above the bed's headboard in the photograph of my father, which placed it between the room's towering windows. The poster was still in this location when Puglisi had gone to prison. Nobody asked his permission to rearrange the rooms in his absence. I noticed the wallpaper was different as well. Puglisi may have had that done to hide the new drywall behind the bed.

I swallowed the bite of food I realized I had been chewing during this entire moment of discovery. Surely things were not this simple.

"It's Sunday," Chief Avery grumpily reminded me when I called him.

"It's also the best day of your week," I assured him. "Can you meet me at Puglisi's place on Dauphine Street? I think I may have found the journals."

"Don't play with me. Not about this," he said in nearly a pleading voice.

"Honestly, Bill, I think I solved this. Just meet me there," I said and hung up.

eighty-two

I paced the corner of Dauphine and Esplanade on the Marigny side of the intersection until I spotted Chief Avery's Ford Explorer as he crossed Rampart Street. I crossed the neutral ground and waved to let him know I was already at the scene. He parked in the first available spot on Esplanade, which turned out to be a block away because even the illegal spaces on each corner were already filled with people headed into the Quarter for the day. It was warm and sunny and promised to be a nearly perfect weather for being outdoors.

"What's the big breakthrough?" Avery demanded as he stepped beside me.

I handed him the photograph. He barely glanced at it.

"We assumed the diaries were behind the poster of Vanity, but we never took into account someone might have moved the poster," I explained and pointed to where the poster had hung in the 1980s.

Avery looked up from the picture with a thin smile. "Jackpot."

We tried not to seem too eager to reach the house around the corner in case anyone was watching the house or tailing either of us. It was unusual to be at any crime scene on a Sunday this late in an investigation. Acting casual about doing so was meant to avoid betraying this importance of this development.

Avery unlocked the front door, and we ascended the stairs in silence. I was anxious to have one of my theories pan out. He was desperate to have his hands on the journals that might save his job, and perhaps even enhance his standing with his superiors.

The door to Vanity's room was partially open. I could not remember how I had left the door when I was last there. Every other door on the floor was closed, as though each was its own crime scene. The hallway smelled a bit musty from the lack of sunlight. I pushed the door open and looked across the room to where the poster once hung.

The new hole in the wall was crudely made and undoubtedly larger than necessary to have removed the journals hidden within. Neither of us believed it proved to be another dry hole. The plastic sheeting taped inside the wall cavity was evidence enough that I was right and that the two of us were too late to secure the journals.

I gave Avery a moment to express himself in a string of sailor-worthy profanities and a hard punch to the plastered wall beside him. He left an impression in the wall and one on me. I had never seen him this angry, and I have a history of making him very angry.

"I have never wanted to be wrong so badly in my life," I said to break the silence we could not allow to continue.

"I'm screwed," he mumbled in defeat.

"You do not know that for certain. We have no idea who has the journals," I tried to console him. I did, however, concede his point.

"Well, it isn't either of us," Avery lashed out and stepped towards the gaping hole. "There must have been a couple of hundred journals in here."

The plastic in the wall cavity would have covered an area approximately four studs wide, which would be over five feet in width, and nearly six feet in height. Puglisi had stapled sheets of plastic drop-cloth into place and used waterproof tape to seal the edges before stuffing his diaries into the cavity and sealing them into place with more plastic and tape. The amount of each he used was impressive, and most of it lay bundled in a plaster covered mass beneath the hole.

"I don't think he has them," I sighed in my own defeat.

"Why not? He could have grabbed them before he disappeared," Avery argued.

"No, he couldn't. He would not have needed to disappear if he had them," I suggested rather than confess the role I had played in Puglisi's vanishing act. "Someone else figured this out and came looking for them since the last time we were here. What's that been, a couple of weeks?"

"Something like that," Avery sighed again. He clearly did not feel like talking.

"All is not lost," I tried one last time to cheer him, "The journals are worthless unless Puglisi says he wrote them. Tony still has the watch Pete Matranga gave him and Puglisi needs that watch more than he wants those journals."

"Why is that?" Avery asked. He was losing his despair and returning to his role as my supervisor the more I spoke.

"There is a foreign bank account number engraved inside the watch. The account should be worth about twelve million dollars," I told him weeks after I should have. His expression made that abundantly clear.

"Were you planning on sharing that information with the rest of the world, or to keep the money?" he growled. "You should have logged the watch as evidence the minute you realized its value."

"Right." I caught myself before I laughed out loud. "Leave a watch worth millions of dollars in NOPD's evidence locker. What could go wrong?"

"Watch yourself," he snapped and jabbed a finger at me. "You and your pal have a clearer history of diverting evidence like this to your own pockets than we do."

"Different circumstances," I tried to argue his entirely valid point. "I was holding it as leverage to get Puglisi's cooperation. He was my eyes and ears in what has been going on with Matranga's group at the pizzeria."

"Okay, what has been going on?" he asked and relaxed a bit.

"Marvin Alexander, the attorney Dan Logan recommended to replace him as Bear Brovartey's attorney, is the nephew of a Russian mobster named Dudiyn Alekhin. He and Logan make their livings representing the worst of the worst in organized crime. My theory is that Logan was Alexander's advance man after Hurricane Katrina. I believe the two of them have been greasing the wheels for Dudiyn to make a power grab in New Orleans. I managed to turn Junior Hauser away, but then Matranga came back to town with the backing of the old school Mob families and messed up their plan all over again. Puglisi and his journals changed everyone's plan a third time, and the Outfit in Chicago sent a shooter named Vincent Contaldo down to see what needed done to restore some sense of order and to protect their interests." I paused to take a breath and wait for what I believed might be an afternoon's worth of questions.

"Any reason none of this made it into any of your reports?" was all Avery asked.

"You wanted me to figure out who broke in here. You never

asked me to explain why," I tried to excuse my behavior. "Alex Boudreaux staged the break-in. I think Junior Hauser heard rumors about the journals from his old man and made sure Alex bought this place when it came up for sale after Katrina. The Vieux Carré Commission keeps rejecting Alex's plans to renovate the place, so he has never had a good excuse to start opening walls to look for the journals. Puglisi's parole was the reason he needed to do so anyway, so he staged the burglary and helped implicate Spenser Duncan for the crime. I think word of the parole reached Junior through Alex's conversations with Dan Logan, and Logan must have heard about it from Marvin Alexander. Alexander probably told Logan to find a way to get his client, Spenser Duncan, involved so he could be killed before he testified against Bear Brovartey. The government's case against Brovartey went poof when Duncan died and Alex continued to refuse to testify against Junior."

"And you told me none of this," he restated his disappointment.

"What was NOPD going to do? We both know the State Police would have told me to hand my evidence over the FBI rather than let me get involved." I defended myself a bit too harshly and caught an all-too familiar flash of anger in his eyes before he swallowed the first thing that came to his mind.

"What were you going to do?" he asked instead of firing me.

"What I am doing right now," I said in voice meant to calm him. "I am using what I know for sure against the lot of them. I conned Pete Matranga into taking a female juvenile across state lines and into the custody of the Mississippi State Police. I used Alex Boudreaux to lure whoever is doing Marvin Alexander's dirty work into a trap Junior Hauser will set in Biloxi because he thinks Puglisi is on his way with these journals. Junior agreed to give Puglisi a ride to the Bahamas in exchange for the journals, but I doubt he intends to honor the deal. He never keeps his end of a bargain if there is enough profit in not doing so."

"So, what you are telling me is that you have managed to move all of our problems across the state line," he said after a moment's consideration.

"There was plenty to share," I said and tried using a grin to counter his grim expression. "The laws and my Glock are not the only tools I know how to use. Sometimes I can get the bad guys to do the hard work for me. And this was not only about kicking their circus out of town. It also overextends their supply lines and lines of communication, which is a tactic I learned in the army. Marvin Alexander and Dan Logan are not about to set foot in Mississippi while this is going on. The two of them will lower their defenses because they think our attention is over there. They will have no idea what happened when they lose touch with whoever they sent to do their dirty work."

"What good does that do you?" he wondered. Avery's career was built upon developing prosecutable cases, which bore no resemblance to my own background.

"Not one bit. But it opens the door for anyone else who wants to cut the head off the snake," I explained. "Chicago sent a shooter to town to protect their interests. This would be his best opportunity to do something."

"Are you telling me you arranged all of this to make it easier for a Mob hitman to kill someone?" he asked in shock and dismay.

"I am not telling you that," I held up both of my hands to signal he should calm down. "All I am saying is these conditions exist when things play out in Mississippi. I am far happier investigating the homicide of one man with links to the Russian Mob than I ever will be investigating what happens once Russian gangsters run loose in the French Quarter. In fact, the FBI will no doubt take over any such homicide investigation, if it happens, and we can get back to normal."

"Your version of normal is nowhere close to mine," Avery lamented. "And without the journals you may not be able to count on me covering for you when you pull stunts like this in the future."

"You are not covering for me now," I tried to point out. "There is no evidence I had anything to do with anything that has happened, or will happen, to any of the mobsters. Your hands are entirely clean."

"You should be so lucky that real life ever becomes as

simple as you see it," Avery grumbled and shrugged his shoulders. "Do you really think there is any chance of you winding up with the journals?"

"Some," I said. I did not want to promise what seemed unlikely even to me just then.

"Some is better than none," he said and turned to leave the room. There seemed to be no point in making this a fresh crime scene and calling out the forensic techs to do more paperwork on a Sunday.

If I did not recover the journals very soon, none of this was going to be his problem to deal with, anyway.

eighty-three

"I thought I should return the favor from yesterday," Captain Williams laughed when he woke me from a sound sleep just after six o'clock the next morning. His chipper attitude meant he had been awake for hours.

"You have good news to report," I mumbled and sat up to begin focusing on what he had to say and thinking ahead to what my day entailed.

"There is news," he allowed. "But mostly I have questions I would like answered, just like every other time you get involved in something over here."

"Fine, shoot," I said. I had answers prepared for everything I thought he might ask.

"Well, we followed up on your lead about Pietro Matranga," he began. "I set up surveillance in the room next door and we arrested him in a sex act with a minor. She did not seem like she was new to what they were doing by the way."

"I never said she was as virgin," I pointed out. "I only told you she is a minor and he brought her there for immoral purposes."

"Fine," Williams conceded. "We certainly have him for that."

"Well, you're welcome," I said to remind him why he was able to make the arrest.

"Don't start with that," he snapped. "Now let's discuss the dead bodies strewn all over the harbor."

"What dead bodies?" I asked as innocently as I possibly could.

"There was a shoot-out on Junior Hauser's yacht last night. Are you trying to tell me you don't know anything about it?" Williams informed me and then challenged my alibi even before I offered it.

"That's right," I lied and waited for the details he seemed anxious to share.

"In broad strokes it looks like a pair of double crosses gone wrong," Williams told me. "As best as we can make out, one of the gophers who used to work for Junior's dad and now runs errands for Junior was making a grocery and liquor delivery to the yacht just after ten o'clock last night. I am assuming Junior is not another dead body somewhere else, but we have not located him yet this morning. Four shooters from New Orleans stormed the boat after about a dozen cardboard boxes were unloaded from the delivery van. They shot him and the two guys Junior keeps on the yacht to keep us from planting any surveillance devices."

"Well, that's just sad. The poor guy didn't deserve to go out that way," I said to let him know I was paying attention. I had no idea who the unfortunate gopher was, but he died for no other reason than showing up with what might have been the journals right when Marion Puglisi was supposed to arrive. "Have you identified the four shooters?"

"All four of them are former Russian Spetsnaz, their tier-one commandos, linked to a Russian mobster named Alekhin Dudiyn," William's informed me. "They have long lists of arrests in their records but no convictions."

"Marvin Alexander has likely defended some of them," I tipped him off without mentioning the family ties between Alexander and Dudiyn.

"What is crazy is that all four of those shooters were then gunned down by one man," Williams said and waited for my reaction. He pressed forward when I said nothing. "It would take a guy with considerable skill, maybe even special training, to pull that off."

"How do you know it was just one guy?" I asked. I realized asking this made me even more of a suspect than I already was in Captain's Williams' eyes.

"We have the whole shoot-out on the casino's surveillance cameras, start to finish," he informed me. "The casino spent a lot of money making sure we have excellent images to work from."

"Have you identified that shooter?" I asked.

"No, he was very good about not showing his face," Williams admitted. "All I do know is that it was not you. This guy is a little smaller, and he used a Siaga shotgun. Do you even own one of those?"

"No, and you're right. I am not a big shotgun fan," I told him. I do like Saiga's clip-fed shotgun. It holds fewer rounds than a semi-automatic carbine, but it can recycle and fire nearly as fast and is much more lethal at close range. It was a good choice here.

Our conversation fell silent while he considered what else to share or to ask. I felt confident I had not given him reason to suspect me any further in the shoot-out.

"Has Matranga asked for an attorney yet?" I finally broke the silence.

"Funny thing you should mention that," Williams faked a chuckle. He never chuckles. "Matranga had us call Marvin Alexander when he stopped answering our questions last night. The attorney said he did not represent Matranga, but then he agreed to sit in on our questioning this morning."

"He has played that game with me," I let him know.

"Well, Alexander is done playing games," the captain stated very firmly.

"How so?" I wondered.

"I think the four shooters may have arrived in a rental sedan we found parked beside Pete Matranga's Town Car. We found Alexander dead in the back seat of the Town Car. He took two rounds behind his left ear, just like your buddy Spenser Duncan. The autopsy will tell us if the bullets match, but this was no suicide."

"Because you didn't recover the gun?" I wondered what led him to his conclusion.

"Blood spray," he said. "Whoever shot him sat close enough to leave a clean spot on the seat where they sat. The shooter was maybe six foot two or three, with really wide shoulders. That's why I am not suggesting Michael Conroy add your name to his short list of suspects."

"Michael Conroy?" I asked and tried to hide how interested I was in the answer.

"One and the same," Captain Williams confirmed. "He is a real tight ass. Imagine my surprise when he asked whether the two of us had spoken recently."

"What did you tell him?" I asked. This time I did not bother to hide my alarm.

"I told him we no longer speak because you are not allowed to cross the state line," he said. "Am I understood?"

"Loud and clear, Captain Williams," I assured him and

hung up. I was momentarily at a loss to identify anyone Marvin Alexander and I both knew who was the size of the assassin that Captain Williams described. A name finally came to me, and a lot of things to reconsider came with it.

eighty-four

I doubted whether Alex Boudreaux had mentioned Puglisi's deal to Junior Hauser. The scenario I began to imagine was that Alex acted against my advice and presented the barter to Dan Logan instead. Doing so would have kept Alex out of Junior's immediate presence, which he may have considered to be Spenser Duncan's fatal mistake in trying to redeem himself with their mutual employer. Alex also placed too much trust in Dan Logan by putting him in the position to bring the offer to Junior. Dan Logan most certainly would make himself look good by claiming any credit. This assumes the offer was mentioned to Junior. The fact that Junior's valued employee wound up as Puglisi's stand-in seemed to indicate Junior had no idea there was any deal, much less an ambush.

Dan Logan's loyalties never did lie with Junior Hauser. Bestowing the journals on the head of the Dixie Mafia, a man who could not even pull off stealing an election, was not the best use of such information. Logan would have taken the opportunity to gain more favor with Dudiyn Alekhin by delivering the journals to Marvin Alexander.

Marvin very likely intended to curry favor with his uncle by adding Junior's head to the journals bound for Moscow. Marvin had his own muscle, but I believe he used his relationship with Pete Matranga to persuade the aging mobster to provide the firepower to storm Junior's yacht once Puglisi stepped aboard. If anyone saw the trap Matranga had stepped into by bringing Rebecca Collins across the state line, it was Marvin Alexander. Allowing Pete Matranga to cancel himself so easily was not a tough decision to make.

Marvin Alexander's mistake, and my own, was underestimating Daniel Logan. My personal contempt for the defense attorney allowed me to accept Tulip's assessment of the relationship between the two attorneys without question. It only made sense that Dan Logan would be subordinate to the nephew of one of Russia's most ruthless crime lords. It also seemed entirely logical that the Russians greased the wheels for Dudiyn Alekhin's operation by having someone as unconnected to them as Dan Logan be their scout. Anyone looking into Logan's past would find only his record of defending the sort of criminals Brooklyn and New Orleans have no shortage of to represent. The only intersection between himself and Alexander was the Gotti case, in which they both played minor background roles. Logan's experiences in New York and New Jersey courtrooms made him the perfect attorney to assess the capacity of New Orleans prosecutors to try and convict the criminal defendants Logan and Alexander planned to eventually represent.

Somewhere along the line, Dan Logan had come up with a different plan altogether. He may have gone rogue, but it is more likely he just went native after spending five years eating gumbo and listening to brass bands marching the streets. He saw an opportunity to use Marvin Alexander's resources to seize control for himself.

Learning about Puglisi's journals might well have been the tipping point. Logan was bright enough to understand the notebooks were king-maker material. Whoever held the journals had something to use against anyone who might try to move against them because everyone in town had a past with Carlos Marcello, except for the Russians.

Puglisi and Dudiyn Alekhin shared no connection prior to Puglisi going to prison, so the journals would contain nothing incriminating against the Russian. This meant something else needed to be done about Dudiyn's plan to take over New Orleans. Logan was meticulous in leaving clues that implicated Marvin Alexander in the break-in, Hammer Cammarato's gangland slaying, and the big finale aboard Junior's yacht. Logan may have preyed on Russian paranoia to encourage Alexander to have his two men follow me in an effort to make Alexander seem like a larger threat than he was. Dan Logan must have approached the table after I left to tell them about his plan to abduct Katie Reilly. Everyone else who might have planned such an audacious act was already at the table, and Vincent Contaldo and Marvin Alexander both claimed they opposed the idea. Vincent Contaldo's delaying me at the pool and stating his objection to the plan may have been Dan Logan's way of trying to convince me it was Contaldo who shot Marvin Alexander rather than himself. It might have worked if

Logan was a smaller man.

I credit Alexander with experiencing his own epiphany about his partner in the brief moment before Dan Logan pulled the trigger. Logan likely saw no reason to fear Michael Conroy linking him to the crime. Conroy was at least as contemptuous of the baby-faced Brooklyn-born attorney as everyone else in New Orleans. Perhaps his mannerisms and public habits were meant to build the shifty façade that allowed him to work so well in private.

I envisioned Dan Logan enjoying a leisurely breakfast before informing Dudiyn about the sad news of his nephew's murder at the hands of the Chicago Outfit. Logan would then humbly offer his services to the angry and grieving Russian.

Dudiyn Alekhin's criminal record meant he would never get a visa to set foot in the United States. Logan would have free rein to do as he pleased with the blessing of the criminal kingpin whose nephew he murdered in cold blood. Logan knew enough about Junior Hauser and his operation to wipe out the Dixie Mafia, at least along the I-10 corridor. Dudiyn would provide the muscle to go after the rest of the redneck criminals once New Orleans was secure. In the meantime, Dudiyn would distract himself with a gang war against the befuddled Chicago Outfit. They would defend themselves with their usual ruthlessness, but also wonder what sparked the feud in the first place.

It was the perfect crime. Well, nearly perfect crime. I knew what Logan did.

eighty-five

"Ready to fight the good fight?" I asked my sister when I called her just before nine o'clock.

"I have never been any less prepared to go to court for a client," she admitted. "I crammed international law all weekend, but I have no idea what I even need to know."

"You only need to know your client has committed no crimes in New Orleans that Interpol might be interested in, and no crimes they are likely to make a case against him for in Europe. This is a long-distance fishing expedition at best, and you just need to keep Tony from taking their bait," I suggested. "I will be there to help with that."

"Really? Why?" she immediately demanded.

"Relax," I said in response. "I trust you to do a good job. I have an interest in how this goes as well, you know."

"Fair enough," she relented. "I'll see you in an hour."

I drove Tony to the FBI headquarters on Poydras in my Cadillac XLR. I made a point of taking up a space reserved for official police vehicles rather than use one of the pay-lots across the street. I was wearing my State Police uniform for the first time in over a year. It only comes out of mothballs when there is a police funeral. Tony wore one of his Armani suits and I was reminded how handsome he could be outside of a kitchen.

The FBI office was busier than I ever recalled seeing it as we were escorted to a small conference room. Almost every agent was on a telephone and none of them even glanced in our direction. Tulip was already seated with her back to the window and practicing her opening comments when we arrived. She wore one of her blue power suits and had her hair gathered into a bun, like a miniature version of Katie's war bonnet. She looked ready for battle, on the outside at least.

Interpol had sent two agents from their New York field office, a slender woman in her forties and what looked to be a retired male cop in his fifties. The male agent had the build and stiff mannerisms that come from years of police work, police lunches, and police desk duty. He told me about his detective career in Turkey prior to joining Interpol, which was a sign that there was still some interest in the classified work Tony and I did in Iraq. The woman wore a nicely tailored suit by a noted Italian fashion designer. Her hair and nails were perfect. Her being here to represent Italy's interests meant Interpol gave very serious consideration to Conroy's implications against Tony's knife work. Tony and I exchanged hand gestures and agreed the male cop was the one to worry about. I shared none of this with Tulip, who was doing her best to befriend the Italian agent. The pair sat down across from the three of us after we exchanged introductions.

Michael Conroy was nowhere to be seen. I could not imagine he would miss this interview after having gone to so much trouble to arrange it, but it was a tall silver-haired FBI Deputy Director that came through the door a few minutes after the rest of us were seated. He walked to the head of the table and stood silently until we all turned to face him.

"I am Deputy Director Clinton Douglas, from the D.C. office," he introduced himself. "Special Agent Conroy is handling an unexpected development in Biloxi, Mississippi and will not be joining us this morning.

"Did you come here just for this meeting?" the male Interpol agent inquired. He sounded almost alarmed that the FBI had sent such a high-ranking agent this far for a meeting which promised to deliver so little.

"No, sir," he said and took his seat. "I flew down early this morning in response to the situation over there. Michael informed me about this meeting when I arrived, and I was curious enough to know more about Mister al-Majid that I decided to be the one to sit in on this meeting."

Not a good sign.

"From what I understand, you were attacked and defended yourself by stabbing one of your assailants with a letter opener without striking a single internal organ," Deputy Director Douglas turned on the tape recorder at his elbow before he addressed Tony to begin the interview. "That is an impressive display of knife skills, even for a chef as talented as I understand you to be."

"Is there a question anywhere in that comment?" Tulip immediately went on the defensive.

"Many, I am sure," the Deputy Director said and smiled at her a bit too smugly. "I am, though, here more as an observer. I prefer to allow our guests the opportunity to ask the questions. They have made quite a trip and I would not want it to be all for nothing."

"I'm sure," I said before I could stop myself. The FBI agent scowled at me, but the pair of Interpol agents calmly opened their files and looked across the table at Tony and Tulip.

"You are his attorney?" the female agent inquired for the record.

"Yes. My name is Tulip Holland," my sister confirmed.

"You normally handle civil cases. Why are you representing Mister al-Majid in this matter?" the FBI agent interjected. His purpose was clearly to expose Tulip's lack of depth to the opposing agents. His comment also let us know Michael Conroy had given Douglas a thorough briefing on each of us.

"He is a family friend," she initially offered before going on the offensive. "My client chose not to seek local counsel because he does not wish his past disclosed to anyone in New Orleans, even under the protection of an attorney-client privilege. What he may have done under the name you insist on using has no connection to the Anthony Venzo the customers and staff at his restaurant have come to know."

"You have taken your mother's name then?" the Italian agent immediately asked.

"People expect an Italian to run an Italian restaurant, not someone they might see as being Muslim. Perhaps he would have kept his father's name had he opened a falafel stand," I interjected. I was going to say everything neither of my companions could say without angering everyone else in the room. The Interpol officers and the Deputy Director clearly wanted to hate someone, and I preferred that it be me.

"You and Mister Venzo worked together in Iraq," the male agent mentioned to keep me in my place.

"That is correct. He knew the local politics and players, and then he saw to my evacuation for medical treatment after our mission terminated. My sister repaid his assistance and generosity by assisting with his EB-5 application to emigrate to this country to open his restaurant," I confirmed and did my best to gloss over as much of the negative aspects of all of this that I possibly could.

"The two of you were doing classified work for the American government," the agent persisted.

"As you said, that is classified information," I decided to try to make one last joke.

"Can Mister Venzo comment on the money he left Iraq with?" he pressed. We had reached the first clear point of interest in the pair's questioning.

"Reparations," Tony stated. "Saddam Hussein ordered my father's execution."

"Reparations awarded by what court?" the agent pressed for details. It was not hard to see his trap. Perjury was going to earn Tony a plane ticket to Rome.

"By the government," Tony lied to their face. "The records may be hard to find."

"I imagine they might well be," the agent mumbled and almost smiled. "Apparently the Iraqi government forgot this agreement and has continued to seek thirty million dollars from Mister Venzo. I assume this is how you financed your restaurant, sir?"

"You should check your records," I piped up. "The money the Iraqi government sought was money they claimed Tony stole from our government's multi-billion-dollar cash infusion after Saddam Hussein's death. Those funds were misappropriated by the man we had in custody when we were ambushed, and those millions were returned in full to the Iraqi treasury prior to our departure. The reparations Tony refers to were made prior to the fall of Saddam Hussein's reign, and those court records may no longer exist."

"That is true. I will double check that the money was returned," the agent backed off. He was not at all convinced by my argument, and what he was reading in his file was likely the latest attempt by corrupt former members of Hussein's government to recoup the millions Tony stole from their secret foreign bank accounts. This was why Tony converted as much cash as possible into gold rather than leave it in bank accounts of his own which might be seized or illegally hacked, as our own team had done.

"We seem to have lost track," the FBI agent interrupted. "I was led to believe you came here to discuss the knife work

350

Mister...Venzo, is it, displayed."

"About that," Tulip immediately spoke up to distract the Interpol agents. "Tony used a letter opener I gave him as a Christmas present to stab the man. Are you here to investigate a rash of letter opener killings in Europe?"

"Stiletto, to be more precise," the Italian agent informed her and began setting color photographs of fatal stab wounds on the table between us and them. There were sixteen in total. Each wound was roughly an inch and a half wide and began almost exactly where Tony stabbed his assailant. I could not understand why my partner chose to murder his victims face to face rather than from behind, but I managed to hide my confusion behind an expression of only mild interest. "Can you pick out the wound he made to the man who attacked him in New Orleans?"

It was a brilliant strategic move on her part. Our failure to discern the defensive wound from the clearly offensive ones would bolster any accusation they might make about Tony's being responsible for every incision in question.

"This one," Tony declared with surprising speed and certainty. He lifted one of the photos from the table and handed it to her. I focused on her face and not his.

"How can you tell?" she asked as she turned the photograph over and frowned.

"I made the wound. I can tell what I have done," Tony calmly informed her. I took a moment to look at the photograph one more time before she filed it away. I caught what Tony noticed, which was this was the only photograph of an incision in living tissue. The skin tone was still warm and not yet turning to a shade of grayish white as dead tissue does. "I do not recognize any of these other injuries."

"Not injuries," the male agent huffily corrected him. "Death wounds."

"Death wounds then," Tony retracted his comment. "I do not recognize any of these death wounds."

Tony calmly spread his arm across the table to encompass the remaining fifteen photographs of his handiwork. He would not recognize them, because he never saw the wounds he made before he left his victims to die from the injuries he caused. I was never witness to any of these murders, but I had seen multiple insurgents in Baghdad die at his hand in this fashion. I began to wonder whether this interview was forcing my sister to reconsider her willingness to marry a modern-day Mack the Knife.

"Again, if I may interrupt," I said to derail the questioning by the Interpol agents. The FBI agent was noticeably quiet, and that was beginning to worry both my sister and me. "My friend here clearly could have killed the man who attacked him and claimed self-defense, yet in the heat of the moment he spared the man's life by inserting the blade at a sharply upward angle. The tight quarters in which the altercation occurred may have played a role in this as well, which you will need to consider. What angle was used to murder these victims? I assume the killer had the choice of how and where to insert his blade and that none of these people offered any resistance."

"What are you suggesting?" Douglas finally rejoined the conversation.

"That Agent Conroy allowed bias against myself and my friend to influence his opinion of what transpired. I belong to a locally influential family and Tony changed his name from something Muslim sounding to Italian when he moved to town. A Special Agent in Charge looking for terrorists and influence peddlers under every bed would see us as obvious targets. Michael Conroy has been repeatedly chastised for trying to access my classified records. His irresponsible allegations even forced our government to release a redacted copy of the classified after-action report on our mission in Iraq. He then invited these two here on nothing more than a hunch that Tony did something bad in Europe. The worst anyone can probably prove Tony ever did was burn an occasional plate of food. He worked as a chef until he was blackmailed into joining his father in Saddam's secret police in Iraq."

It was a lot of bluster and smoke screen, but it gave everyone who was looking for a way out of the situation we were in a person to blame for our being here.

"So, this is a waste of time?" the Italian woman snapped at the Deputy Director and began gathering up the photographs. She clearly understood she was going to have no more luck getting Tony to implicate himself as an assassin than her partner had in trying to make him confess to stealing money from the Iraqi government. If anything happened here at all, it would be these two agents eliminating Tony as a homicide suspect and to ignore the Iraqis' dubious claim to the money.

"It does not have to be," I spoke up one last time. "Deputy Director Douglas can provide you with a parting gift."

"How so?" Douglas warily inquired. He understood what had just transpired and was not going to be easily distracted from his own curiosity about Tony or myself.

"Pietro Matranga is in custody in Biloxi on felony sex-trafficking charges," I began. "Multiple charges were filed this morning related to his misconduct with the same victim in Louisiana. I believe Mister Matranga would find extradition to Italy to face whatever charges he fled to be a welcome alternative to serving hard time in Parchman or Angola."

"I imagine he would," Douglas immediately concurred.

"Is there anything else you wish to discuss with my client?" Tulip hastily inquired of the two Interpol agents, who had leaned close to one another in discussion. They broke their huddle and sat upright to respond to her question.

"No, I do not believe so," the man spoke up and closed the file in front of him. Neither of the Interpol agents offered anything in the way of an apology for their accusations against Tony, and none was expected considering the bullet he had dodged.

"It is early still, but I would like to offer you lunch for your inconvenience," Tony said as he rose from his chair and looked towards Agent Douglas to include him in his offer. "I would like your last thought on my skills to be about my cooking."

There was polite laughter before Tulip nudged Tony out of the room. There were no takers for his offer. The trio we left behind were too preoccupied packaging Pietro Matranga for his extradition and arranging the afternoon press conference which would not include Special Agent in Charge Michael Conroy.

eighty-six

Chief Avery joined me for lunch to learn Tony's fate, and to grill me over the drama still unfolding in Biloxi. He did not think for a second that I had played no role in what was happening across the state line. However, what was happening across the state line was out of both our jurisdictions, which made it lunchtime gossip rather than my needing to account for myself. The situation cost Avery his appetite so we stood at the bar discussing what we each knew until his hunger returned.

"From what I understand, Pietro Matranga was arrested for sex with a minor, Marvin Alexander was murdered in the parking lot of the Palace Casino, and seven men were shot to death on Junior Hauser's yacht," Avery succinctly summarized the past fourteen hours.

"They had not yet identified Alexander's shooter or found a motive for the all the mayhem the last time Captain Williams and I spoke. He also made it pretty clear to me that it is the last time we will ever speak," I informed my boss. Avery frowned at this last part.

"Then he believes you sent the circus in his direction," Avery surmised.

"I only informed him about Pete Matranga transporting Rebecca Collins across the state line. She and my sister have been texting and I found out about it from Tulip," I said in honesty, if not complete honesty. He did not want the full truth anyway.

"And the shootout?" he inquired.

"Alex Boudreaux was supposedly brokering a deal between Junior and Puglisi for the journals. It appears the journals never made it, or someone snatched them up in the middle of Junior and Puglisi double-crossing one another. I did not hear whether Puglisi was among the dead," I said as conversationally as possible.

"Neither of them were anywhere near the yacht. The FBI has clamped a lid on things, but I did hear that much," Avery let me know.

"Have they spotted either of them since last night?" I asked to keep the conversation moving in a fashion that at least offered the pretext that I was less knowledgeable about the shoot-out than I was.

"Junior went to ground but checked in with his attorney, who let the FBI know his client had no idea what happened. Puglisi is still in the wind."

"Who is Junior's attorney?" I asked.

"It should not surprise you that Dan Logan claims to be," Avery said. "Everything you told me yesterday is beginning to sound a lot more plausible."

"You didn't believe me yesterday?" I asked in mock pain.

"Let's just say I was less prepared to believe Dan Logan had the capacity to fool us on a Moriarty level," Avery allowed, reminding me of his taste for Sherlock Holmes novels. I accepted that I failed to convince him I was as brilliant as his fictional role model. "I would almost have to, now."

"Would?" I immediately asked in response to the odd choice of words.

"I am retiring," he announced. Holding this news may have played a larger role in his appetite issue than the shootings in Mississippi.

"That isn't very funny," I protested, but sensed he was telling me the truth.

"It's time," he said and shook his head. "The politics are getting to be as bad as the crime rate. The brass are more interested in assigning blame than in doing anything to get the situation under control. The cost of everything has gone up so much that even normally good people are needing to rob their neighbor to stay afloat. It is only going to get worse until we have a mayor and city council willing to address wages and the costs of living here. Things have always seemed bad, but the city will explode once this becomes a place where its minority population can no longer afford to be poor. The only thing keeping things in check before Katrina was that dirty social contract between the haves and have-nots. We used to only make them be the have-lesses."

"You're making me think about quitting now," I said to lighten his mood. He clearly needed to unburden himself, and he needed a lot more venting that I was not very interested in listening to because I had made the same arguments five years earlier.

"Breakfast will still be on me anytime you want to stop by," I promised.

"Maybe," he shrugged. "We have been talking about moving after I retire."

"Where can you move to after living here your whole life?" I challenged him. New Orleans is more of a way of life than it is a place to live. He should know that.

"Katie's dad and a couple of your father's other pals seem to like Missouri. We may decide to check it out," he said and forced a slight laugh at the idea. I had spent three summers in the hometown my father named me after and thought that was enough.

"Come on. Maybe Tony's cooking will put some sense back in your head," I said and tugged his sleeve to get him to follow me into the kitchen. I was now the one who needed to eat before I lost my own appetite.

eighty-seven

Katie went home after filing the charges against Pietro Matranga. There was a difficult conversation in our future that I pushed off as long as I thought I could without adding my avoidance to the agenda. I headed Uptown as soon as Chief Avery and I parted company. I carried a square of tiramisu with me as a peace offering.

Three carpenters were completing the installation of her new front door when I arrived. She was standing on the porch and greeted me as I walked towards her from the driveway.

"It is wood covered steel with a steel doorframe, just like you always said I should have," she said and pointed to the very solid door. There was a second deadbolt attached as well.

"Single girl, living alone. You never know what is going to happen," I tried to make a joke. She smiled but changed the subject.

"For me?" she asked and turned her attention to the cardboard box in my hand.

"A token of my esteem," I said and handed it to her.

"Entirely unnecessary, and equally inadequate as a distraction," she said and finally gave a genuine laugh. We stepped past the workmen and made our way to the kitchen for a fork. Roux was sitting at the back door waiting to be allowed inside, but I chose to leave him out of our conversation for the moment. "I am going to need more than a thousand calorie dessert to get past what happened."

"I can only give you dessert and a shoulder to cry or pound upon. Time is what this takes and I cannot rush or slow it down," I lamented.

"At least you understand I still need to process what happened," she said and smiled as she took the first forkful of the classic Italian dish. Tony flavors his with a touch of Sambuca.

"What do you remember about what happened?" I asked.

"I am unlikely to ever forget anything that happened," she pointedly reminded me. "I was standing about where you are when the guy kicked my door in and came charging at me. Roux bit his leg and took him down. That bought me time to

357

get the gun out of my purse."

"But you got it out," I said and immediately regretted interrupting her.

"Thanks to all that time you made me practice. I put the laser on his chest and fired until he stopped moving. I think he lost interest in me when he saw what Roux did to his leg." This realization seemed to come to her as she repeated the statement she must have given a half dozen times by then.

"You didn't kill him," I added as a conclusion to her story.

She paused and then stared me in the eye. "I did not need to kill him. I know you did your best to make two in the chest and one in the head a muscle memory, but my conscience seems to be stronger than your training."

"You're just a good Catholic girl," I suggested. "I am not saying you should have finished him off. I am glad you didn't need to."

"What are you saying?" she demanded.

"I am saying I am relieved that you are physically unharmed, and that I know from experience it takes time to get over pulling that trigger the first time, and that it was a good thing Roux was here to slow him down," I tried to back away from anything which might add to the anger she had yet to find an outlet for after the nightmarish experience of a home invasion.

"Okay, yes, I am glad you did not have him euthanized," she said and seemed to be trying to lighten the mood as well. "I hope you never believed that I accepted your story that this is a different dog than the one that killed Biggie Charles."

"I stand by my story," I swore yet again.

"I heard something about a big shootout in Biloxi last night when I was in the office this morning. Anything you would care to share?' she asked to change the subject, or to delay the further conflicts hidden in our first topic. This topic had its own issues.

"There was a shoot-out aboard Junior Hauser's yacht last night. Four gunmen from New Orleans shot Junior's men and then someone went aboard and shot all four of them. Junior was nowhere near the yacht, and I heard he seemed genuinely surprised and pissed off when he heard about it. Marvin Alexander was double tapped behind his left ear, just like

Spenser Duncan, while all of that was happening. It looks like someone wants the Russians to go after Junior." I decided to share the juicy part of the story before I ventured into the small role she had played without knowing about it. "I tipped off Captain Williams about Pete Matranga bringing Rebecca Collins to the Palace Casino yesterday morning. Filing those charges this morning boxed him in so the extradition offer the FBI made after Tony's meeting with them this morning looked like his only escape route. Uncle Felix was right about the Interpol agents not wanting to leave empty handed. They just needed someone better than Tony to take back with them."

"So, all those charges I filed were never meant to go to court?" she asked in a quite unamused tone.

"No. I had no idea I would be able to weaponize them this way," I feebly defended myself. I should have explained my plan when we spoke about this the day before. "They were all valid charges. No court was going to throw them out, but I could not count on a jury convicting him."

"That I have to agree with you about," Katie sighed and took another bite.

"I did not mean to make you look or feel like a fool," I needed her to believe.

"I don't," she said. "I just feel like you use me as a tool when I should be your partner."

"You're always my partner," I insisted despite the clear evidence to the contrary.

"Nice of you to say that." Katie dropped the empty dessert container in the trash can next to her. She licked the fork clean and leaned against the kitchen island separating us. "Maybe you should start showing me and not just keep saying it."

"I can do that," I said and set my messenger bag on the counter before me. I had to dig deep to find the box from the jewelry store. The bow was askew, and the paper had a couple of small rips from having been in the bag for so long.

"What's this?" she asked when I walked around the island to hand her the gift I had been at a loss to give her until now.

"Open it and I will explain," I said and watched her eyes light up as she loosened the ribbon and used her nails to delicately pry apart the taped ends. She opened the box less like a present than a bomb needing defused.

359

"It's lovely, though a little large for my wrist," she cooed when she opened the box and laid eyes on the massive and masculine looking watch. The watch comes in only one size and the one I wear looks large even on my wrist. "Does this make us a couple?"

"Lord, I hope we already are one," I said and chanced a kiss on her cheek. "It is a Brietling Emergency. Tony and I bought a pair when he first arrived here. See this knob here? It becomes an antenna if you pull it out all the way. It will activate a satellite signal to let the company know you are in trouble and exactly where you are. They will call me, and I will come to your rescue anywhere on this planet."

"I can do that with my phone," she drily pointed out, but kept rolling the watch over in her hands to show she remained very happy with her present.

"This does not drop calls," I gently argued. "Just keep it in your purse."

"Oh, no, I am going to wear this beast. I can punch somebody in the face with it if they try anything," she said and wrapped the band around her fist to simulate throwing a punch in a gesture she may have used to signal she was capable of setting her recent trauma aside.

I took her face in my hands and moved slowly to kiss her lips. She offered no resistance and nearly brought me to tears when she pulled me closer. We continued kissing for a couple of moments longer, until she broke the last kiss and rested her chin on my shoulder. I could feel her breathing heavily and kept my silence as she gently sobbed on my shoulder. She needed only a moment to relieve the tension in that moment of reconciliation before she stepped back to wipe her eyes with the back of her hands. I reached for the paper towels, but she told me leave them be. I watched her wipe the thin stream of mascara from her cheeks and take a deep breath.

"What now?" she finally said in an uncharacteristically open-ended question.

"We get on without lives together," I suggested for lack of a better answer.

"Good plan," she laughed and shook her head. "I mean about Puglisi and the journals and all of that mess."

"I don't know," I admitted. "The journals are real, and

someone has them. I want to believe Puglisi knows where they are, but I do not see him handing them over to the FBI anytime soon."

"No, I imagine not," she concurred. "What is going to happen now that the last of Marcello's guys and the Russian mob have been eliminated from competition? That just leaves Junior and Chicago to deal with, right?"

"I don't count the Russians out," I hated to say. "I finally understand Dan Logan's long game. I believe he shot Alexander and plans to blame it on Junior. Chicago will distance themselves from New Orleans until either the Dixie Mafia or the Russian Mob prevail in the gang war Logan set in motion. He wins either way because Junior still doesn't know his new attorney is working both sides."

"Maybe someone should tell him," Katie suggested, meaning me.

"Maybe someone will," I agreed, meaning someone besides myself.

"And what do you do in the meantime?" she asked.

"I step back and hope this stays on Mississippi's side of the border. I plan to leave Dan Logan to the FBI and limit my focus to things I can do something about. It was how my father kept his sanity all those years."

"It's about time," she said and hugged me. "Also keep in mind you do not get a free pass to act like your father in all ways."

"Understood," I smirked. "I am going to have start behaving myself anyway. Bill told me he has decided to retire. I think Conroy is on his way out, as well, after the meeting we had with the Interpol agents today. The deputy director sees him in a much different light."

"How so?" she held me tight but leaned back to look me in the face.

"I suggested his interest in Tony was some sort of bias based on his real last name and that Conroy was chasing windmills rather than dealing with real criminals. Maybe the deputy director sees the situation in Mississippi as something Conroy should have had a better handle on," I shared my morning's moment of joy.

"That was quite a suggestion," she laughed and kissed me. I

could feel how much tension had left her body. Perhaps it was knowing we still had a chance together, or that I was not expecting her to be as quick about recovering from her trauma as I make it appear I bounce back from my own. Perhaps it was hearing me accept being a typical detective going forward. That was something which promised a much more normal life for the two of us.

eighty-eight

Uncle Felix was enjoying a gin and tonic at the bar and entertaining Hannah with stories about something he decided to stop sharing when he spotted me headed his way. He was alone, which I did not expect him to be at this hour.

"You were expecting someone else?" he asked when he saw the look on my face.

"Let's say I am surprised to find you here alone," I allowed.

"Marion has come and gone," he declared and turned back to his drink. Hannah crooked her head to silently ask if I was going to need a cocktail to have this conversation. She was already reaching for the Elijah Craig bourbon before I nodded my head.

"And why is that?" I demanded but kept my voice down in the mostly empty space.

"He has other plans," Uncle Felix said and then turned to face me as I took the first sip of the chilled Manhattan my too-bright bartender set on the bar before finding other customers to attend to at the farthest end of the bar. "I did as you asked and found him a place to spend the weekend. Sheriff Mazant sends his regards, by the way. Imagine the odds of his winding up alone in a holding cell with a former cocaine pilot being held on an expired warrant."

"Better than even odds, I imagine. I am going out a limb and saying the pilot still has his license and owns a plane capable of reaching the Bahamas from here?" I asked, holding my anger in check. I had barely registered that my uncle had stashed Puglisi in the jail of a sheriff who I was certain did not feel he owed me any favors. The sheriff's patron was a now-former state senator who must have still owed Uncle Felix a debt or two.

"Those would be long odds, indeed." My sly uncle neither confirmed nor denied Marion Puglisi was airborne as we spoke. "Something like that would have to involve an agreement on the part of everyone involved."

"I am going to skip ahead and eliminate the local sheriff as being who set that up," I said to hurry things along. I had no idea if I still time to alert the FAA, FBI, or the Coast Guard

363

about Puglisi's leaving the country.

"Oh, come on, Cooter. Give me my moment here," Uncle Felix complained. He finished his drink in one long gulp and held his glass over his head to get Hannah's attention.

"What agreement did the two of you come to?" I played along. I had little choice that didn't involve senseless violence.

"I paid Marion ten thousand dollars for his diaries. He, in turn, paid the outstanding debt to your chef and retrieved his wristwatch. Marion seemed particularly sentimental about that watch," my uncle informed me. I could not tell if he was toying with me or if Puglisi had played my uncle for a fool. "Miss Hannah, may I have that bag I handed you? I believe this should make a number of people very happy."

Hannah was smiling as though she thought this was all some elaborate joke. She reached under the bar and came up with a sizeable gift bag. It looked heavy. Uncle Felix removed the manila envelope on top of the bag's contents and handed me the bag. There were four sealed cardboard boxes, each approximately ten inches square, in the bag. They were not wrapped or labeled in any way.

"Okay, what am I holding?" I asked my uncle. He was absolutely beaming.

"Those are Marion Puglisi's personal diaries," he informed me. The bag felt lighter than I believed it should have been. "Every last one of them. I know the operator of a local crematorium and asked him to make the diaries easier to transport."

"You had Puglisi's journals cremated," I mumbled in stunned response. Too many things to say and ask crossed my mind at the same time to respond any differently.

"These," he said and dropped the envelope on the bar, "Are notarized affidavits from Marion Puglisi and the crematory operator attesting to the intentional destruction of every diary Marion Puglisi wrote and hid in the wall of his home."

"Why?" was all I could ask.

"I had my best legal minds scour the agreement between Marion and Special Agent in Charge Michael Conroy. They were especially intrigued by the wording which made the agreement for Marion to surrender his diaries strictly between those two men despite the repeated use of terms and stationery which made it appear to be an agreement between Marion and the Federal Bureau of Investigations and the Department of Justice. All I needed was confirmation that there was no stipulation in the agreement related to the condition in which the diaries get delivered. It turns out Marion's parole is not tied to surrendering the journals, but I think keeping that part of their bargain may be the most fun I have had in quite some time."

"I imagine so," I said, and was finally able to laugh along with Uncle Felix.

"Our conversations about the diaries, and mine with Marion after we read through them, made it clear that these were going to be mishandled by anyone who came to possess them. I convinced him it is best if their authenticity were to be established and their value eliminated," Uncle Felix informed me. This was why he had a successful career in backroom politics.

"What do you want me to do with this?" I wondered and touched the bag.

"Not a thing. I just wanted to show them to you before I have them delivered to Michael Conroy so you know what became of them," Uncle Felix said and returned the manila envelope to the gift bag. I had to smile at the word CONGRATULATIONS printed on the side of the bag. The SAC was not going to feel much like celebrating his pyrrhic victory.

"You are not delivering them yourself? I imagine you would enjoy the look on Michael Conroy's face," I inquired.

"Marion specifically requested that an attorney named Daniel Logan deliver them," my uncle said and gave me very curious look when I laughed so hard that I cried.

"A hitman to the end," I said but failed to fully explain my admiration for Puglisi's final shot. Logan was surely sitting on the edge of his seat in anticipation of having the diaries hand delivered to his office. "Thank you, Uncle Felix."

"No, thank you," he said and shook his head. "I had a chance to catch up with my old friend and to continue keeping what he wrote about me secret, as well as what he wrote down about the people you are concerned about."

"You think I wasn't concerned about you as well?" I asked. I actually felt hurt.

"Nobody weeps for the jackal," he said in a conspiratorial whisper. He raised his voice to deliver the last of his news. "I am sorry I will miss your mother's visit this evening. I made a reservation for a private table at seven, so do please be sure your chef, sister and that lovely prosecutor lady friend of yours are able to attend."

"I will," I promised without knowing what I was getting them into. "Despite my usual instinct to spare them such things."

Uncle Felix was laughing as he left me at my own bar and had waved to his driver parked down the street.

"You uncle is quite a character," Hannah said as she presented me with an unbidden second cocktail.

"Among many other things," I said and toasted him in his absence before taking a drink from the chilled glass. My work day seemed to be over and it was only three o'clock in the afternoon, so this qualified as day drinking.

eighty-nine

Having dinner with my mother is as close to dining with the Queen as any of us were likely to get, and I privately believe the Queen would sit to my mother's right were she in attendance. My mother prefers to visit New Orleans in the light of day, and Tony and I have picked up the tab for the innumerable luncheons for her PEO sisters she has hosted on Strada Ammazarre's patio. She also expects me to pay for the birthday party she insists on having for my father to remind her inner circle that she considers him to be missing rather than dead because his remains are unrecovered. This is a way to hold her live-in boyfriend, Roger Kline, at arm's length, as well.

The pair entered Strada arm in arm before Roger stepped back to allow my mother to accept each of our gracious tidings and thanks for her invitation. Tony reluctantly turned the kitchen over to a senior line cook to be present. This was fine as Mondays are notoriously slow nights in every restaurant. The suit he had worn earlier in the day was freshly pressed and my mother paused for a long moment to assess him now that he was out of his usual all-white chef garb and considerably less sweaty than usual. I wore her favorite Hugo Boss suit and the Jerry Garcia tie she had given me for Christmas a few years prior, which still drew an appreciative comment on her own good taste. Tulip and Katie wore their best evening wear and the results of last-minute appointments for their hair and make-up at Paris Parker. None of us knew the nature of the occasion, but each of us seemed certain this was not purely social.

Juaquin led our party to the elevator and escorted us to one of the smaller private dining rooms on the mezzanine level. My mother's favorite waitress stood ready to greet us. The two of them bumped cheeks before Ginger returned to her service status and began filling wine glasses with my mother's preferred French white burgundy. Ginger normally works the day shift and serves as den mother to Juaquin's new hires and our less experienced servers, but tonight she had agreed to work a double in anticipation of the generous tip my mother

367

would insist I pay her.

Ginger's back waiter brought a course of appetizers and helped Ginger arrange them on the table, making certain that the crab cakes my mother intended to enjoy by herself were placed closest to her fork. It was interesting to watch Tony be a guest in his own restaurant. He looked like the world's harshest food critic as he judged each plate when it arrived at the table. Tulip gave him a reproachful look, and also enjoyed his discomfort.

Caesar salads and champagne followed the appetizers before pre-selected entrees arrived at the proper interval, with glasses of appropriate wine for each of us. My mother hates making decisions and especially dislikes dealing with menus, so Tony has gradually developed a handful of meals he knows she will enjoy, and which will not cost us an arm and a leg to comp when she leaves. Tony and I dined on filet mignon with a trio of sauces, while my mother and Roger enjoyed plates of veal shank Osso Buco about which my sister wisely kept her mouth shut. My sister is definitely not vegan, but veal and lamb are the two things that always make her reconsider her taste for meat. Tulip and Katie felt no remorse for the creatures that had perished to provide their plates of shrimp in a creamy Chandeleur sauce.

Ginger and her back waiter did their silent dance behind our seats to keep glasses filled and whisk away any empty plate once the last bite was chewed. It was as precise a set of maneuvers as any I had performed while a Special Forces operator on the battlefield.

"Enough pleasantries. We have things to discuss," my mother said as she tapped her spoon against the coffee cup Ginger had just set before her. My mother insists on enjoying at least one cup of coffee before allowing dessert to be served. She will tell anyone who challenges this routine with her philosophy that a proper meal requires a grace period between the food our bodies need and the pleasure we take from dessert. Ginger and the back waiter hurriedly completed setting and filling the rest of the coffee cups before Ginger ushered him out of the room. "Your Uncle Felix approached me with a problem last week, and today he offered a solution which he asked me to consider."

This could be anything, but at least I knew it did not pertain to the diaries which undoubtedly mentioned my father and uncle. They may have included her, as well, if Puglisi's story about their exchange at La Louisiane had made its way to the written page.

"I understand you offered Tulip an engagement ring she did not accept," my mother unexpectedly brought up a subject none of us anticipated. "Felix said it had to do with the diamond and not her affections towards you."

"Mother," Tulip tried to dissuade the conversation.

"The diamond is fine, Tulip has concerns about my source for the diamond," Tony spoke up anyway. He may have believed he needed to defend himself against one of my mother's illogical arguments. He should have known nothing was to be gained in any such discussion.

"Whatever the reason, my daughter decided to decline your offer at the time," my mother persisted. "Tulip, would you like to marry this man?"

She has never used Tony's name without his job title attached in all the time the two have known one another, including the year he spent living in her boathouse. She has always made a point of reminding Tony that he ranked among her servants.

"Yes, mother, more than anything," Tulip immediately acknowledged and held up her left hand. The two-carat diamond solitaire glittered under the candlelight. "That is why I accepted the ring when we returned from the Federal building this morning."

"Anything entails more than you know, my dear," my mother cautioned her. This was Old Money talking and my sister tended to be tone deaf when she ought not to be. My mother unexpectedly focused her attention on me. "And you, what are your plans with Miss Reilly?'

"They do not involve getting engaged this evening if that is what you are suggesting. I dare not ask her until I am certain of the answer," I replied. She and I had been dating for less than a year and were both on the rebound from toxic relationships.

"Smart man," Katie whispered without moving her lips.

"I love her. I want to spend my life with her, but marriage

may not be necessary to do so." I quickly realized what a poor choice of words this was.

"Your father had much the same low opinion of marriage, I am afraid." My mother clearly meant to send the two of us a message about our attitude on the matter. This was not the time to say Katie shared this opinion.

My mother slipped the ring my father used to propose to her from her finger and set it on the table. She pressed her index finger to the center and slid the ring across the tablecloth towards me.

"Take this, for when the time is right," she said began to explain the purpose in her calling us together. "I am old, and I am proud of my family name. My brother has made me realize I have held the two of you to standards expected of members of the Deveraux family. That has been a curse for you and a burden on me that never needed to happen."

I had no idea where this was going, but found myself taking Katie's hand as we began the roller coaster ride on which my mother seemed set upon taking all of us.

"The two of you are Hollands. You have your father's last name, and you both have your father's traits. Some of them are good and some of them are bad, but they are yours to change and not mine to judge. Cooter, you have managed to follow your father's trail and become a detective. He was never able to be orthodox in his thinking or professional in his manner and you seem to lack the ability to do either of those things, as well. Hopefully you will avoid repeating the worst of his failings. Tulip, you pursued a career rather than motherhood until it was nearly too late to make a choice between the two. I hope the two of you will provide me with the grandchild I no longer anticipate coming from your brother."

"I am sitting right here," I playfully objected. I was of no mind to father children at what would be age forty-three or forty-four. Katie squeezed my hand to make me stop provoking my mother.

"Yes, you are," my mother noted and smiled. "I have something for all of you as well."

Katie squeezed my hand to keep me silent. My mother reached beside her and set her small clutch on the table. There was not much room in the small purse, but it was not like she

370

was carrying money or credit cards to pay the dinner tab. She removed a small white envelope and passed it to Roger to hand to me in turn. I held the envelope in my hand but made no effort to feel it or open it to reveal its meager contents. I only knew it was not more jewelry.

"Open it," my mother finally insisted.

It was a pair of identical house keys.

"I am giving the two of you your father's house in the country," she announced. Tulip and I sat a little more upright in our chairs at the entirely unexpected gesture. "If you are going to follow in his footsteps, you may as well sleep under the roof of the house he built."

"We are getting a bit long in the tooth to be living with our mother," I said to break the tension which had suddenly filled the room. "Please tell us you are not dying of cancer or something."

"I am moving to Audubon Place," she announced but then paused and took Roger's hand in hers. "We are moving into the family home in Audubon Place. It is time for me to take my place among my own family. I have nieces and nephews to spoil until one of you gives me a grandchild."

"Thank you," I nearly stammered as I continued to roll the key over in my fingers. I looked to Tulip, but she shrugged in as much confusion about what to do as I felt.

"To the Hollands," my mother said and raised the last of her wine in a toast.

"To the Deverauxs," I countered without considering whether this was an insult or a compliment. I also had no inkling which of these she meant by her own toast.

"Well, that was interesting," Katie summed things up once my mother and Roger were gone and the four of us were once again standing at the bar with cocktails in our hands.

"May you live in interesting times is one of the three Chinese curses," I reminded her.

"Hey, at least we got a free house out of the deal," Tulip said before she waved the impressive ring on her finger around the room again.

"And congratulations to you two. I cannot, well I do, believe your mother managed to upstage the two of you getting engaged, " Katie said and laughed before she grabbed Tulip's hand to get a better look at the engagement ring.

"Free drinks on the house!" Ryan Kennedy, one of our most audacious regulars shouted and shoved his own champagne glass forward on the bar. Jason looked our way and Tony and I both nodded that a few dozen drinks were not going to break the bank.

"What do you think really brought all this on?" Katie asked. It was a question all of us had been mulling since my mother opened her mouth. Camille Deveraux Holland is not a capricious woman and handing out engagement rings and houses was nothing anyone would have ever believed she was capable of doing until now.

"She cannot bury your father, so has buried the two of you," Tony hypothesized. It was as canny and credible of an explanation as any we were likely to find. She wanted to get on with her life, and whatever the future held for her and Roger, but was bound by her marriage to my father. State law required the passing of seven years before she could go to court to have our father declared legally dead. The statement by a dead FBI informant that his dead FBI handler murdered our father and dumped his body in a swamp was not enough to satisfy the exceptions to this rule. The only thing left for her to do was to symbolically sever her ties to everything that reminded her of my father, be it their engagement ring or the house she rebuilt after the storm in anger about his leaving her. "But I do not think she will not expect to eat for free here again."

"No, that perk Camille Holland will definitely hold onto," I agreed and we all shared one last laugh before Tulip took Tony's hand and led him towards the elevator and his apartment on the third floor.

"What do you want to do?" Katie asked and slid her arm seductively across my shoulder.

"Nothing we have not done twice today," I grinned and took her in my arms.

"No, sir," she protested. "You have only walked Roux once today."

I gave her a quizzical look. She knew what I meant the first time.

"They need their privacy," she decided. "I am going to step outside and take a taxi to my newly reinforced abode. You should change your clothes, walk your dog, and join me. With or without Roux doesn't matter to me. We are all family now."

"I can do that," I said and kissed her lightly on the lips before I made my way to the elevator.

ninety

Roux and I walked our usual route through the Quarter. We wandered through the empty stalls of the French Market and along the riverside tracks as always. Roux was the center of attention among the homeless already beginning to transition from the dark side of the Moonwalk to the bright lights of Jackson Square. I informed Boomer and Darnell of Rebecca's role in taking down one of the city's most notorious mobsters, and they beamed like proud fathers. It was impossible to know the young blonde's future, but I think the three of us each quietly prayed it did not involve any of us.

I tugged Roux to the right side of Saint Louis Cathedral for a change of pace. The shops along Pere Antoine Alley were shuttered for the evening. The small stand-up bar on Pirate's Alley across the way was filled with an unexpected bachelorette party the bartender's stance seemed to indicate he wished would leave. I wondered whether Tulip planned to have a bachelorette party because it would mean having a bachelor party for Tony that I did not feel either of us found necessary. I also realized I was his only real friend in New Orleans.

I distracted myself enough with this nonsense that I missed spotting the figure standing in the shadows in Exchange Alley, and I failed to notice when they fell in step half a block behind Roux and I as we turned onto Orleans en route to Bourbon Street. The Quarter's flagship party blocks were doing a respectable business for a Monday. Conventioneers and early summer tourists mingled with the kids from Treme hustling for change or tap dancing on bottle-capped sneakers for a buck. Roux slowed to watch one boy do his dance, likely drawn to the sound of the bottlecaps than the motions of the dancer.

I wanted to get to Katie's house, so I cut the patrol short and walked directly across Bourbon to Dauphine Street. I had begun to make a habit of passing Puglisi's old place despite its increasing insignificance in my investigation and larger mobster problems.

My shadow probably hid among the thin crowd on Bourbon until the two of us rounded the corner and headed towards Puglisi's, now Boudreaux's, rambling mansion. I had a lifetime of stories to share about this address going forward. It might have been a very short lifetime had the shooter done their homework.

I felt Roux turn to confront someone behind us. He stood to my left and my hand was, as it would turn out, tightly clamped to his leash. Perhaps that clutch was a muscle reflex. Whatever possessed me to hold the leash prevented Roux from engaging the man who stepped behind me, and that in turn may have spared Roux's life.

I recall beginning to turn towards the sound of someone saying my name. Who fired the two rounds behind my left ear at point blank range was not the most important thing in that instant, and why barely matters at all when you are about to die.

The pair of hollow point.22 caliber bullets which struck me were all that mattered for one long second. The small caliber handgun is the classic choice of assassin murder weapons. One tends to imagine shotgun blasts and large caliber bullets doing the most damage. A shotgun at anything except point blank range spreads its shrapnel too wide to predict its lethality. Something like the Beretta my sister and Katie carry, or even the unforgivingly heavy rounds from my own Glock, need to be precisely aimed to kill because they stay true to their trajectory. The human body has an amazing capacity to survive gunshot wounds, which is why small bullets like the ones used to murder Spenser Duncan and Marvin Alexander were so effective. Rounds from a .22 will shatter into multiple razor-edged fragments on impact with bone, causing extensive and usually fatal bleeding from the multitude of internal cuts the pieces make as they ricochet inside a body. Tiny fragments of skull preceded the metal, doing their own damage. Spenser Duncan and Marvin Alexander were already dying when they heard the loud popping in their ears. The shooter was even confident enough of his surroundings to forgo a silencer. The rounds they used were subsonic, which reduced the noise of their being fired while using heavier than usual projectiles. This added to the lacerations made deep into their brains.

My luck was that the shooter was unfamiliar with my medical record, or they would have shot me behind my right ear instead of my left. The hammering I suffered at the butt end of an angry Iraqi youth's AK-47 had shattered much of the left side of my skull. It remains an interesting quilt of bone and titanium plates. One plate runs from the base of my skull to about three inches above my left ear canal, and both of my would-be assassin's rounds pinged off this and sent metal fragments into my outer ear and under the skin on my head. Some simply flew into the night air as I dropped like a dead man to the sidewalk.

My shooter was satisfied with their handiwork, and unprepared to deal with a pit bull intent upon protecting its fallen master. The same rounds they fired had eliminated their two previous victims, and perhaps nameless others I had never considered. I would later hear about the difficulty the EMTs had in coaxing Roux off my crumpled body to triage my wounds. The NOPD officers who responded to an anonymous phone call had the sense not to shoot Roux. They dared not face my ungrateful wrath if I survived my injuries only to find my dog was dead.

Doctor Fletcher must have been surprised at what he saw on the x-rays when he arrived in the emergency room. The devastating trauma he expected to see was absent. He spent nearly a hour making small cuts to pop the pieces of copper from beneath my scalp and suturing my ear before the pressure from the impact of the rounds caused my brain to begin to swell. Cutting new holes in the remaining bone in my skull proved to be unnecessary, but the induced coma meant to minimize any use of my brain gave my body the sense it was dead or dying.

Despite my past experience with death, I cannot honestly say what happens in the moment you die. Scientists point to the continuation of brain activity after the heart has surrendered to its fate. Perhaps all the theories about one's life passing before your eyes in the moment before death fail to consider that 'a moment' is not enough time to reconsider the totality of one's life. Perhaps all those brain waves and the slow demise of our consciousness are a sign that we are allowed, perhaps destined, to reimagine our lives.

Perhaps the creative side of our brain takes over and allows us to project our lives into the future our death has shortened. What if my return to New Orleans was just a cruel joke my mind played on me rather than allow the skull-crushing blows of an angry fourteen-year-old Iraqi youth to be the last thing I remembered of my time amongst the living? This evening was a perfect culmination of so many story lines in my life: Bill Avery was set to retire, my mother had found a way to move her life forward from the disappointment of my father's failure as a husband and into the arms of a man she clearly adores and who adores her, my sister was engaged to a man we both knew was capable of defending far more than her honor, but also respected her own capacity to defend them both in her own way, and I was in love with a woman I had known for years but only recently came to know on a level that brought romance. And Roux? What story is any good without a faithful hound at the hero's side?

These my random thoughts on death and dying may only have been my brain's way to reboot itself before I awoke to a different life and future than the one I left.

ninety-one

"Welcome back." Doctor Fletcher was leaning over me with a stethoscope in his hand and a bank of electronic monitors behind him. Multiple lines were feeding who knows what all into my aching body. I did not feel near as well rested as the amount of time I was unconscious might lead one to believe.

"Been here the whole time," I hoarsely joked. He looked at me and laughed as he waved his penlight back and forth across my eyes. I tracked his index finger as he asked and wiggled toes and fingers to reassure everyone present the attack did not do serious damage. Egos never mend, and being shot at point blank range for a second time had wounded mine.

"Hey, big brother," Tulip gushed as she took my hand once Doctor Fletcher was satisfied I survived my wounds.

"Nice to see you, too," I reassured her. She looked as pale and worn out as she had when she watched me awaken from the induced coma after my first brush with death. I missed a hastily arranged late-night medical evacuation from Baghdad and weeks of Italian sunlight streaming through the windows of the private hospital in Rome where Tony arranged for my care and rehabilitation under an assumed name. "How are things?"

"Better now. Tony doesn't have a second pick for his best man," she leaned close and forced herself to joke instead of cry in relief. I forced myself far enough up on my left elbow to hug her with my right arm. It had the fewest lines in it. She broke the embrace with tears in her eyes and left the room with Doctor Fletcher.

Tony came into view as I dropped back onto the hard mattress. He used the controls to raise me to a more upright position, so I looked more like a tired dad in his recliner. I made a quick sweep of the room once the bed stopped moving. Tony was in jeans and T-shirt, so someone else was running the restaurant. It was nighttime but there was still plenty of activity in the hallways, so I guessed we were about at the end of normal visiting hours. The television was not on, so I could not estimate the day or date. I saw my vital signs were acceptable, but a little weak. I raised a hand to feel for the bandages I could tell were taped in place. My left ear was completely covered, along with most of the crown of my head. I realized my head had been shaved to remove the fragments of the bullets with had ricocheted off the metal plate in my skull and had become wedged between my skull and scalp. At least there was no itching under the bandages.

"Would you like to try to explain what is going on? Is everyone else alright?" I asked him. My brain was beginning to function, and I began to considering scenarios. The one I feared most was that other people I knew were attacked at the same time I was.

"Not at all," he frowned in that confounding way where I am unable to tell whether he is joking or not. He sat down on the edge of my mattress. "My best friend was shot."

"Fine," I sighed. "Now, tell me what is really going on."

"Your mother had a mild heart attack when she heard you were shot. She is already home and making everyone's life miserable until they find who shot you," he began. "I don't suppose you know who shot you, do you? NOPD found the gun you were shot with in Detective Bassett's apartment, along with a suicide note he wrote. He took credit for killing that Spenser Duncan guy and Marvin Alexander as well. A little too tidy, huh?"

"Quite." I wanted to smack whoever had done such a sloppy investigation. Alexander would never have been alone in a vehicle with Bassett in New Orleans, much less Biloxi. I could not calculate the odds of the rogue detective being involved early enough to have shot Spenser Duncan and then have been assigned to investigate the break-in. I felt satisfied that planting the gun on Bassett's body meant his was the last name on the shooter's list.

"Who is running the restaurant?" I asked him. The one thing I knew for sure was that it was no longer Monday, at least not the last Monday I remembered.

"Miss J," he said and paused. "I think we need more partners. Tulip expects as much attention as I give the kitchen."

"Wise man," I grinned. "Did she tell you that?"

"So, these new partners," Tony sidestepped answering my question but laughed as he did so. "Maybe we give Miss J and

Juaquin a piece? They work as hard as we do to make it a good restaurant."

"I haven't done squat, so yeah, bring them in," I agreed. This was not my decision to make anyway. The restaurant was always Tony's world. I merely enjoy some perks, just like my mother.

"We can talk later," he said and stood up to allow Katie to take his place. She waited until we were alone in the room to begin speaking.

"You scared me," she sighed and took my hand. She shifted slightly to face me a little more directly. I was sure I was a mess to look at.

"I am sorry for that. I am always scared I will lose you," I admitted. She looked surprised at this and squeezed my hand.

"I cannot live in this much fear," she said and paused. I had the sense that she was about to give me a speech she had practiced for a while but lacked the heart to deliver. "I love you, but a part of me has always been waiting for the call I got last night."

At least I knew how long I was unconscious. I was guessing that Doctor Fletcher kept me sedated to reduce the odds of my brain swelling. The concussion from the two bullets was not much less potentially damaging than had the bullets been inside my brain.

"I am going to need some time alone," she finally delivered the words she seemed to be avoiding. "I just can't stand the thought of being divorced and widowed by the time I am forty-five years old."

"We have time," I said because I needed to say something and understood her point. I was not looking like a good candidate for the relationship she wanted or deserved. "You even have a new watch to measure it by."

"Yes, I do," she finally found something to smile about. Katie was still wearing the watch I gave her, and the clothes she wore the last time I saw her. I realized she had been at the hospital the entire time I was being operated on and unconscious. "Tulip and Tony are buying my house, and they are taking care of Roux. I am going to take some vacation time and go see my father in Missouri. Maybe we can talk about finding a place together when I get back, if you still want to be with me."

"I waited forty something years for you the first time. I just didn't know that was what I was doing. I can wait for you again," I assured her despite the sensation of having my heart ripped out. "I do some stupid things, but loving you has never been one of them."

"I love you, too," she said and kissed me lightly on my chapped lips. I wanted to hug her and hold her close one last time, but she wanted to leave before I witnessed the breakdown she barely managed to contain long enough to say goodbye.

ninety-two

Chief Avery dropped by the next morning to check on me and to express his own frustration with the investigation into my shooting.

"I do not buy Bassett as the shooter in any of the shootings he took credit for," Avery was quick to assure me. "The FBI and the Superintendent both put their seal of approval on closing the case because we have no other suspects. Who do you think shot you?"

"I don't know," I admitted. "The two guys Marvin Alexander had doing his dirty work were both presumably killed on Junior's yacht. He would not have hired anyone else to shoot me, and he was already dead when I got shot. That shooter from Chicago had no reason to do it. I am no threat to the Outfit, and he doesn't strike me as the sort of guy who kills for pleasure."

"Maybe Marvin Alexander's uncle blamed you for his nephew's murder," Avery offered, but without much conviction. We were fast running out of names.

"I am sure he is looking for whoever did shoot Marvin, but I do not think he saw me as being that dirty of a cop," I nixed that idea. "Junior would not go after a cop, and Alex Boudreaux is no wannabe assassin."

"That would be too embarrassing anyway," Avery said and chuckled at the thought. I was still smarting from having been shot and nearly beaten to death by a fourteen-year-old kid in Iraq nearly six years earlier. Alex Boudreaux getting close enough to shoot me in the back of my head would have been even more humiliating. "Like I said, we ran out of suspects and letting Romulus be the guy who shot you buries the whole thing. You are going to chew on this until you figure out who was responsible, and I will not want to be your supervisor when that day comes."

"Maybe I will let Tony do one more," I said because Avery would take this as a joke and not as a pre-admission of guilt, or let himself believe it was a genuine plan.

"I am not going to miss that part of the two of you," he readily admitted. "Maybe you could make a little more effort at being a by-the-book detective with whoever replaces me. The Superintendent has already narrowed that down to two candidates from outside of NOPD, which means he was already planning to put me out before I retired."

"Nobody can ever replace you," I said and waved away the very notion. "Your shoes are too damn big to fill."

"My office is the same size no matter who sits behind that desk," he reminded me.

"Well then, maybe they won't share your appetite," I said and made him laugh one last time before he left me alone in the room.

I was going to need to get used to being alone again sooner or later, but first I needed to get out of the hospital bed and find out who shot me.

ninety-three

Gavin Hendricks once told my father that all great love stories fall into one of three categories. The choices are limited to Boy Gets Girl, Boy Loses Girl, and Boy Gets Dog. I still had my dog, but I also had vacation time available, and thought I should also leave New Orleans until I had a clearer perspective of my life.

An unexpected postcard, blank but with a very clear cancellation stamp from the post office at Freeport in the Bahamas, arrived at Strada a week after I left the hospital and gave me an idea and a sense of purpose.

Locating Marion Puglisi was not all that difficult. I knew the name and location of the bank where Pete Matranga had deposited Puglisi's annual payments. I flew to Miami and chartered a private plane to leave the country rather than have my name pop up in the FAA database if the FBI thought to use me to track down Puglisi for jumping his parole.

I paid the bank manager a hundred dollars to deliver a telephone message after he refused to give me Puglisi's contact number. I waited for two hours at the poolside bar in the Wyndham resort for Puglisi to either show up, return my call, or decide to remain invisible. He contacted me by phone, with a voice that showed as much surprise as it did pleasure at my presence.

"I am sorry I am not there," he immediately dashed my hopes. He did not reveal his location or why he unavailable, and I did not ask. "Will you still be in Freeport for a couple of days? I can meet you for dinner the day after tomorrow. I am with someone who is dying to meet you."

"People dying is why I am here." I reminded him. His silence let me know this was not nearly as funny at his end of the line. "Sorry, bad joke. Yes, I can hang around. I have a mutual friend who might like to get reacquainted with you as well."

"Interesting idea," he said and chuckled. "Let's meet at Cappuccino's. It's in the market at Lucaya. Say seven o'clock the day after tomorrow?"

"You sound happy," I told him before he disconnected the call.

"You sound lucky to be alive," he laughed and hung up.

"To what do I owe the pleasure of your call?" Gavin asked when I reached him at his office an hour later.

"I have a book deal for you," I said to surprise him. "Actually, it is a book deal you had but lost."

"So, you're going to follow in your father's footsteps?" he asked, obviously missing my point.

"Somebody's, but not his. These footsteps are on a nice sandy beach," I hinted a bit more suggestively.

"That does sound nice," Gavin said after a long moment. "Tell me more."

"You always told my father to show and not to tell. I am emailing you a flight reservation and the name of a hotel. We have dinner reservations the day after tomorrow. Can you get away that soon?" I had not yet made any of these reservations because I was not certain Gavin would agree to the trip, much less reconsider the book deal which had proved so disappointing the first time.

"I can be there," Gavin assured me. He sounded considerably more interested in making the trip than had I imagined he might.

I was nursing an unexpected sunburn when Gavin and I entered the small Italian restaurant Marion Puglisi recommended. My nose was going to begin peeling in another day or so and be hard to explain when I returned to work. We had barely touched our first daiquiris when the aging gangster and his companion arrived.

Marie Chauvin was a slim Black woman in her mid-forties. There was never a point in her youth that she looked anything like Vanity. She was light skinned with tight braids hanging well past her shoulders. She wore a colorful wrap-around skirt and a top which left her shoulders bare. Puglisi had not been in the Bahamas all that much longer than I had, but he already sported a healthy tan. He wore a tropical weight suit and linen shirt with an open collar. He looked even happier in person than he had sounded on the phone.

"You look like hell, Detective," Puglisi all but shouted when he stepped through the doors to the restaurant and laid eyes on me. The hair on my head was barely grown out far enough to be considered stubble.

"Are you here on official business?" he asked before he formally introduced Marie.

"I am on vacation in every sense of the word," I reassured him. "And I am miles away from my jurisdiction if I should decide otherwise. Let's just enjoy dinner, alright?"

Puglisi shrugged and smiled before he motioned to the hostess. The young woman led us to a patio table away from the other patrons and set menus and a wine list on the table, which she picked up after Puglisi whispered something in her ear. A server was at the table moments later with a bottle of Chianti and four glasses. It felt strange to be the guest instead of a regular at an Italian restaurant for a change.

"Here's my thought," I said to open the discussion in which I had not intended to participate. I looked from man to man as I spoke to other two men at the table. "Sunset never needed the journals to write any memoirs, because he remembers everything like it was yesterday. I thought Gavin might still be able to sell your story without involving the journals."

"I could," Gavin assured Puglisi. "People never get tired of stories about the bad guy."

"I ain't such a bad guy," Puglisi protested in jest.

"Yes, you are, boss man," Marie laughed. She had been living here long enough to pick up an accent and learn the local slang. Puglisi laughed as well, which made it okay for Gavin and me to smile at her comment.

"I haven't killed nobody in years," Puglisi declared, but seemed to still be joking.

"I can attest to that," I spoke up. "I would be dead if you had shot me."

"I never shoot cops," he insisted, as though it mitigated his comfort with murder.

"I wish I knew who didn't share your high ethics." I meant this as a joke, but there was a fleeting wrinkle across Puglisi's brow and the smile on his lips disappeared.

"You ain't figured that out yet?" he demanded. "I thought you was a smart one."

"Hey," I defended myself. "It was dark, and they caught me off guard from behind."

"Like a coward," Puglisi all but spat on the floor saying the word. "You kill a man, you do him the dignity of looking him in the eye."

"I think you're going to like his book," I cracked to Gavin.

"You know who shot you," Puglisi told me. He was no longer joking. "Do the math."

"Well, that would be subtraction. Everybody who wanted me dead was already dead or in jail when I got shot." I was not prepared to get this serious about the one shooting I was certain the man across from me did not commit. Puglisi was no longer smiling so I held up my left hand and dropped one finger with each name I gave. "Your old capo was on his way back to Italy, and you were his shooter of choice anyway. Marvin Alexander was already dead, and I am not a likely enough suspect for his uncle to target me. Junior shares your attitude about whacking police officers, so he had nothing to do with it. Alex Boudreaux is no shooter, and the same gun was used to shoot me, Spenser Duncan, and Marvin Alexander."

This left one finger.

Puglisi was smiling again and rephrased his statement as a question. "That means it was someone who knew all three people."

"You think Dan Logan pulled the trigger on all three of us?" I challenged him. The attorney was the only person whose name came to mind that fit this narrow category. "He strikes me as a guy who gets other people's hands dirty."

"Trust me on this," Puglisi insisted. "He only hires out jobs where the victim gets to live, like your chef. The man likes pulling a trigger. He bragged to me about killing his own client, that Duncan kid, so the case against the attorney Alexander came down to New Orleans to represent would go bust."

"That would have endeared him to Junior Hauser." I had already considered the possibility that Logan orchestrated the hit on Spenser, but it never occurred to me that he had the stomach to pull the trigger himself.

"Logan was the only guy who could of got close enough to Marvin to put two bullets in his head," Puglisi offered his expert opinion. "You know who that guy really was, huh?"

"Alekhin Dudiyn's nephew." I surprised him by knowing the correct answer. "Now guess who Dudiyn is likely to tap to replace Marvin."

"You figuring that out is why Logan wants you dead," Puglisi said and set his napkin in his lap. "I am just saying this as a friend. Do what you want about the guy, but you better never turn your back on him again."

"I will keep that in mind," I said and wanted to change the subject. My head still hurt from being shot. Realizing Dan Logan may have shot me made it hurt even more.

"Get the seafood. It's fresh," Puglisi suggested and acted as though we had never had this conversation.

He proved right about the seafood. I decided to trust his opinion about Logan as well.

ninety-four

Ronald Jackson waved me down as I enjoyed my mid-day patrol on the Saturday after I returned from the Bahamas. I led Roux into the vacant house on Dumaine Street where Jackson and one of the Vieux Carré Commission's building inspectors were delivering unwelcome news to the homeowner undertaking an expensive renovation of the circa 1835 residence. There was a four-inch discrepancy between the new roof and the two-story structure's original height. The VCC considered this minor difference to be an intentional design change and Jackson was there to support the inspector when he informed the owner his building contractor needed to remove a newly installed slate roof and rebuild everything to the approved height. The inspector also the mentioned fines this incurred and the cease-and-desist order that would be the VCC's immediate response to any argument either the owner or contractor might care to make against this arbitrary ruling.

I suspected Commissioner Jackson invited me into the home because he feared the homeowner's reaction to the threat of an injunction over a discrepancy even the most hawk-eyed of hawks would never notice might turn violent. The discrepancy came about when the roofing contractor adjusted the soffit height to facilitate the installation of the costly copper gutters. These would also need to be remounted. The owner took the news better than either of us anticipated, but it proved to be a matter of picking one's battles as he began to berate the contractor who made the change without consulting the VCC. The argument over who would pay for the remediation was not one either Ronald Jackson or I cared to be part of.

"I have great news," he declared after we stepped outside. "Mister Boudreaux is selling his property on Dauphine Street to a buyer planning to convert it into a single-family residence. It will remove the rental property exemption!"

"That is going to be an expensive undertaking," I said mostly to myself. It would, in fact, cost the new owner double what restoring the same home in any of New Orleans' other historic districts would run because of the VCC's exacting standards. "Do you know the name of the new owner?"

"No, but that is no longer unusual," Jackson assured me. "Trusts and shell companies are the owners on record of most properties for tax reasons these days. I do know the name of the attorney who handled the transfer. You might know him, as well. His name is Daniel Logan."

I swallowed so hard I had a brief coughing episode.

"Do you know him?" Jackson asked. He was clearly concerned about my cough.

"Our paths have crossed," I allowed without going into detail.

"I have to run, but I thought you would be interested to know about the sale." Jackson and I shook hands before he patted Roux on his square head and began walking in the direction of Canal Street. Roux and I continued walking in the opposite direction, towards the shaded neutral ground on Esplanade.

I was interested enough in Logan's purchase of Puglisi's former brothel to stack it atop the evidence the former pimp had rubbed my nose in over dinner.

There was no way Alekhin Dudiyn would move to New Orleans. I could not imagine Dudiyn even being allowed into the country except in wrist and angle chains under the armed escort of Federal Marshals.

I doubted that Junior offered Logan a sweetheart deal on the property his credit union held the note on. The leader of the Dixie Mafia had to know Logan was behind the attempt to draw him into a kill box aboard his own yacht. Junior would have put a contract out on Logan were it not for the risk of going to war with the baby-faced attorney's new client. Convincing Junior to play in his own sandbox was the only good thing I saw coming out of everything that had transpired in the last month.

ninety-five

I looked for Dan Logan at the Columns Hotel just before six o'clock on the following Monday afternoon. The landmark hotel's broad porch is Uptown's place to be for happy hour, and Logan wanted to be seen as a regular in such a respectable place. For whatever reason he chose to drink at the dimly lit bar inside the hotel rather than mingle with the crowd outside.

"Nice hat," Logan laughed as I approached where he stood at the bar. I was wearing a Panama hat I bought in Freeport. He stopped short of taunting me about the flesh peeling from my still red nose.

"I need to find a good barber," I said to keep things light for the moment. I was not going to need a haircut any time in the near future. "New suit?"

"It's my first seersucker suit. Like it?" he asked and rubbed the cotton fabric.

"I suppose you needed a new suit," I tossed into the conversation just to test the waters. The one he wore when he shot Marvin Alexander was surely ashes by now.

"I heard about your shooting. Are you alright?" he returned my volley.

"Probably better than you hoped," I said, and let that set the tone for our discussion.

"I always hope for the best," he assured me over the rim of his Sazerac. "What may I do for you? I no longer assume these encounters are social in nature."

"That is probably wise," I had to admit. "I just wanted to tell you that going after me and my family was your bridge too far."

"That sounds rather harsh. Are you threatening me, detective?" he asked. He may not have understood the historical reference in my comment, but he showed no fear of what I might do in public or in private. He seemed quite confident that we both understood his next attempt on my life would succeed.

"Yes, counselor, that is exactly what I am doing," I told him. He did blink at this. "You played this whole thing perfectly, but we need to start ignoring one another."

"Played what?" he asked with exaggerated innocence. He wanted to hear me praise his manipulations, and perhaps assess any threat I posed to Dudiyn's plans.

"Everything," I said before I turned to order a Manhattan from the bartender, who had wisely stepped away from what sounded like it should be a private conversation. I paid for my drink and pointed Logan in the direction of a small table so we could sit down to threaten one another in comfort. "You turned the tables on Marvin. He sent you to scout the situation for his uncle and then you lured him into a trap in Biloxi. His uncle has no choice but to trust you to be his eyes and ears with his nephew out of the way."

"I do so miss Marvin," Logan sighed but then allowed his lips to form a thin smile. "He was so...ambitious."

"Too ambitious for New Orleans, anyway," I suggested. "You cannot move very fast here before people take notice. You have spent five lonely years making yourself into a court jester who is unusually lucky in court. You are actually a damn good attorney who counts on prosecutors underestimating you. None of them will likely believe you are the point man for one of the largest crime syndicates in Russia. That accusation would sound absurd if I tried to sell it to the FBI, and we both know it will be some time before they figure it out for themselves. Dudiyn will be too well entrenched by the time anyone else sees your role in his takeover."

"This new guy downtown is supposed to be fairly bright," Logan allowed. He did not sound concerned. I had not yet met the Special Agent who replaced Michael Conroy. The former Special Agent in Charge had been transferred to Washington D.C. while I was in the Bahamas. He would work at nothing until he took the hint and decided to retire.

"He will be playing catch-up for at least a year," I said what we both knew. "Far be it from me to pitch him the idea that Dudiyn Alekhin is making a move on New Orleans right under his nose."

"Why not? You two could bond or something," he mocked us.

"NOPD, the state police, and the FBI are never going to stop Dudiyn," I told him and picked up my phone.

"Do you think Junior Hauser is going to do your dirty work

for you?" he asked. He was trying hard to discover the approach I intended to take towards our situation.

"Junior is done. He will lick his wounds and keep to his side of the state line now that he sees who he is up against here." I was sure of that. Junior's sources inside the police and Feds would have already let him know who the players were in the shoot-out aboard his yacht. He did not want to tangle with either of those crime syndicates.

"Then what makes you think you can tell me who to leave alone and what I can and cannot do?" he quietly threatened me again.

"You have me all wrong," I said and picked up my phone. I had what I was looking for already queued up on my iPhone. "I am not telling you I am going to stop you. I am here to tell you I won't protect you from yourself."

"How so?" he asked. His tone of voice was losing its overconfidence and invincibility.

"I had dinner with Marion Puglisi last week," I said to rattle him a little more before I told him what I came to make clear to him in person. Like Puglisi said, one needs to honor an opponent by looking them in the eye when you destroy them. "He gave me a phone number in Russia, and the man who answered the phone was kind enough to share an email address for Alekhin Dudiyn."

"So, what, you two are pen pals now?" Logan wanted very badly to belittle me because of how limited my authority was against Dudiyn's crime syndicate, but he was beginning to realize I was not a completely powerless pawn.

"Not so much," I shrugged and showed him the email attachment I had sent the Russian crime lord. It was a crime scene photo of the backseat of Marvin Alexander's sedan. A tape measure extended from edge to edge of the unsoiled spot on the vehicle's backseat where Alexander's assassin sat. "My tailor says this was left by a man wearing a roughly size fifty-two blazer. What size is yours?"

"That is hardly scientific," Logan dismissed my implication but didn't answer my question.

"Maybe you should have murdered a scientist's nephew and not a Russian mobster's," I said and stood up. "Be careful accepting any of Dudiyn's invitations to meet."

"Do you really think he believes that I killed Marvin?" Logan persisted in trying to convince at least one of us that he was safe from the Russian's wrath.

"Somebody killed Marvin," I pointed out and tucked my phone in my pocket. "And Dudiyn is going to consider every lead he gets about who killed his nephew."

"You set me up," Logan stood up and grabbed my arm. People turned to watch what promised to be a very short fight. Logan's clever disguise as an overweight man-child would not be in his favor against someone with my hand-to-hand combat experience.

"I cannot frame a guilty man," I retorted and left him sitting alone and the focus of a dozen curious looks while he adjusted to his newfound sense of vulnerability.

Everybody pays in the end, especially those who get everything they deserve.

EVERYBODY PAYS

THE CADILLAC HOLLAND MYSTERIES

Blowback

Blue Garou

Can't Stop the Funk

Ghosts and Shadows

Parish the Thought

Everybody Pays